NAKED under the lights

A Novel

For Irene —
what sheer pleasure
to meet you.
Judith Peck

Judith Peck

Black Rose Writing | Texas

ISBN: 978-1-68433-575-6
PUBLISHED BY BLACK ROSE WRITING
www.blackrosewriting.com

Printed in the United States of America
Suggested Retail Price (SRP) $20.95

Naked Under the Lights is printed in Garamond

Cover illustration: Original drawing by Judith Peck

*As a planet-friendly publisher, Black Rose Writing does its best to eliminate
unnecessary waste to reduce paper usage and energy costs, while never
compromising the reading experience. As a result, the final word count vs. page
count may not meet common expectations.

For the Art Students League of New York City, where grateful artists learned, taught and pursued, to the world's benefit, their noble professions.

OTHER BOOKS BY JUDITH PECK

Sculpture as Experience:
Working with Clay, Wire, Wax, Plaster and Found Objects

Sculpture as Experience:
2nd Edition, Expanded with New Chapters

Art Activities for Mind and Imagination

Artistic Crafts: Inventive Creations with Cast-offs

Leap to the Sun: Learning through Dynamic Play

Art and Interaction:
A fieldwork Program for Colleges
An Activities Program for Institutions

Art & Social Interaction:
An Interactive Program for Human Service Staff
and College Internship Experience.

Smart Starts in the Arts:
Fostering Intelligence, Creativity and Serenity in the Early Years

Runaway Piggy Bank (children's picture book)

The Bright Blue Button and the Button-hole (children's picture book)

Seeing in the Dark, Arielle's Story (novel)

NAKED under the lights

RETROSPECTIVE
October 1976

1

Sonata Kossoff in jeans and wind breaker sprints up the marble steps and through the wide doors of the Art Students League. Upstairs in the League gallery is her father's retrospective exhibition which she is eager to see. She feels again her childhood curiosity tinged with somber imaginings, passing the closed door of his studio and not allowed to enter.

"Pose please."

She hears the monitor's voice from an open studio as the door marked *STUDENTS ONLY BEYOND THIS POINT* swings to a stop behind her. Her shoes deposit small clumps of wet fall leaves, joining the abstraction beneath her of spilled paint drops and scabs of leaked coffee. No matter, the Art Students League is used to such mess—since 1875 according to the inscription on the building.

She hurries along the League corridors pungent with the smells of linseed oil and turpentine, lugging an oversized manila sketch pad under her arm. Would he be as grandiose in her mind as he once was? Or was that vision of her father hazy all along, he'd existed so little in her life? Had she, in fact, been imagining him?

His paintings may not hold answers to the hurt she feels—and must rid herself of—but seeing the exhibition alone before the opening tonight will help. To sense the brush in his hand touching every picture. At the reception, scores of chattering people will clutter everything and she'll know nothing.

She glances inside the open door of a drawing studio and there among the students seated in a wide circle with their cumbersome sketch pads balanced against stools and chairbacks, she sees her mother. Ruth's back is to the door. Her drawing pad propped open in front of her is smaller than most others around her. A model sits on a raised platform in the center, the bright fluorescents highlighting her breasts and thighs. She could be in her forties, but her body with its long supple curves looks younger than her face whose lines around the mouth and eyes seem engraved with undecipherable text.

In the room's stillness, the traffic on 57th Street seems a distant world away, the steady hum of a heating unit and the scratching of pen and pencil against paper the only sounds. Her mother's dark hair is combed loose, falling so long the chairback obscures its ends. Her hair had always been fastened in a chignon before. Is she trying to be attractive to a young artist now that she's on her own? It's been something like a year since he'd been out of the house. Her *husband*. In name only. And *my father*? A title.

"Let it loose," she'd demand as a kid, begging her mother to unfurl the hair from its clasp. Maybe even then she'd sensed her mother needed freeing. From the constraints of Forest Hills, was it, or from him?

"It isn't neat," Ruth would say, as if neat is priority.

She smiles seeing her mother with her hair down. It goes with her features—the aristocratic nose, the perfect curves of her lips, and her skin, a cameo against that flood of black hair. A beautiful woman, Sonata admits.

Ruth turns to say something to the man beside her. Is she being coy? That tilt of her head—this is new—and there go those bow lips in a smile that sweeps her cheek bones into twin arches.

She did not inherit Ruth's good looks. No such luck. Ruth is charismatic and invariably noticed while she is awkward, or feels that way, and no one notices her unless she says or does something awful. She bombs at parties, a holdover from her early teen disasters which she hasn't totally repaired even at nineteen. Where Ruth's eyes are blue with luminescent centers that hold her audience like a glimpse of summer sky, her own dark brown eyes are capped with heavy brows

2

that make her appear angry when she isn't. Well, she has her father's features and there used to be pride in that, idolizing him the way she did. His features are bony and sharp, fine for a man, but a woman needs a more subtle face, everything flowing together, a hint of mystery in the combinations. Like Ruth's.

Her figure is another contrast. Her mother is petite and graceful, walking barefoot through the house with her nylon nightgown shimmering against her breasts and belly, and there is she: tall and ungainly, walking with the grace of a mountain climber in boots. She possesses a too-generous ass, even though Ruth insisted this was not so, and walking behind her she had a better view. Not that she is gross. All things being equal, she is passable. But all things are not equal, and Ruth is a winner hands down.

The model now stands. She twists her long torso and thrusts her breasts and hips forward in a come-and-get-me invitation, her arms hanging loosely at her sides.

Winner? For what contest? Certainly not for his attention, which wasn't on either of them.

Her mother is making flick-like movements with her pencil on the paper, glancing up and down, recording the model's body in broken line notations. Others in the room take that same up-down-up excursion, but even to her unpracticed eye, there isn't much sensitivity in her mother's drawing.

Sonata turns away and continues down the corridor. Finding her locker, she dumps the sketch pad inside to pick up later when her class begins, ignoring a page that creeps out and tears. The clang of the locker door slamming shut startles her, echoing the clamor of her thoughts as she turns toward the stairway leading to the gallery. Her heart proclaims how excited she is to see a grand retrospective of her father's work, even as her mind reminds her how small she stands in contrast. Resentment builds with each rise of the steps, her thoughts taking ridiculous tangents. *Forever having to tote around the name he gave her. A piece of music, ridiculous. And why not Tintoretta or Michaelangela if they were going for a designer label?*

Ruth explained they both wanted something classical for their only child, and Bert's mother being a pianist of sorts, that was his choice.

Her choice had been Martina after a ballet dancer. Naming her might have been his singular contribution after conveying his seed; dubbing her Sonata, he had done his part.

Upstairs on the door of the gallery is a poster announcing the exhibition.

THE ART STUDENTS LEAGUE PRESENTS
A RETROSPECTIVE EXHIBITION OF PAINTINGS
BY BERTRAM KOSSOFF
Oct. 15 - December 18, 1976
A Preview for Forthcoming Traveling Exhibitions at
The Boston Museum of Modern Art
The Pennsylvania Museum of Fine Art

The gallery is unattended but open. She stops in the doorway and for a moment stands there, overtaken by the presence of her father in a fantasy forest of his paintings. She wants a memory of this to burn behind her eyes to retrieve when anger overwhelms her. He will be a star of the American art scene now, she's sure of it.

Inside, she moves among the paintings. The canvases in the central area of the gallery are oversized and heavily textured. She can make out fabric, coarse papers, tree bark, straw, a leftover bird's nest. Scraps of this detritus remain on the canvases in some places, and in others are only pressed on to make imprints elaborated upon with strokes of color. But it is those colors, rich and sultry, evoking some kind of blazing tribal rite, that compel you to keep searching the canvases for treasures.

As she circles the gallery, she tries to account for the approximate years in which each group of work emerged from his studio and onto the walls of their home. He created the smaller oils hung in a far corner of the gallery almost a decade ago. They held no interest for her as a child. Some large canvases in acrylic completed about three years ago had intrigued her, by their size, no doubt. The most recent ones, done in industrial paints, she'd never seen before this. Those pictures went crazy with color as though he couldn't get enough of it, like fireworks finales. The earthbound, physical nature of his passion and copious infidelities lived in these paintings; he and his work inseparable.

She sits down finally on a bench tucked under one of the recessed windowsills to take in the great hall with its high ceilings and twelve-foot windows and this exhibition. Her father's vision, his vitality and his passion to get what he wants pervades the room. Leaning back against the window frame, she rests her feet on the polished wooden bench beneath her.

But didn't he always get what he wanted? The canvases blaze not only with color but power: cruelty cut into the dark crevices, the contrasts in light and shadow like bloody knife blades in sunlight. She had only to read the magentas and vivid yellows or touch the rips and ragged textures to know what he felt about her—the absence of feeling— neglect, disdain, shutting her out.

But his achievement is what's important now, and this exhibition is her achievement too, despite how little she meant to him. She recognized the success on its way, had the perception to see it. Before Ruth, yes, that. Others would be here tonight to guzzle champagne and peer at the pictures and spew a critique on this painting or that. And whether they loved his work or hated it, he wouldn't care, already on to something else. This more than anything she admired, a freedom she craved for herself.

Sonata catches her breath as a man enters the gallery. She watches without moving, recognizing Vincent. He stands in the doorway, not blown-away as she had been, just giving the familiar room and the new exhibition a *once-over*. He takes a notebook and pen from the inner pocket of his jacket and makes notes, not seeing her in her secluded spot by the window.

She notices he has grown a neatly trimmed beard, square-cut. Before, his beard was a silly chin affair which he'd shaved off; she remembers being awakened to see him standing beside their bed, clean shaven and pale where the beard had been. He'd done it on impulse in a moment of self-discovery brought about by her. Modeling for him, she had served as muse for the creative explosion occurring in his work and he saw himself a man no longer needing such contrivance. It was satisfying to see him now with a more elaborate beard and sideburns too.

He walks around the room in the same pattern she had made, making notes, stepping back from some pictures, then closing in to observe a detail and compose another note. He does not notice her until almost passing her on the bench under the window ledge.

"Hello, Vincent." Sonata observes a slight rise in color across his cheeks as she smiles at him. The color is out of place in his tweed-jacketed composure.

"Sonata! I didn't see you."

She observes him move to shake her hand as he would a business acquaintance before settling it on his notepad.

"Ah, you're reviewing this show," she says, realizing his presence here before the opening; it is the first time she is encountering him in his role as critic.

"I am," he says.

She tries to get beyond the complacent smile, the dark eyes that look at her amused but critical as always before. "It's wrong," she declares, "you being in a superior position to him."

He shrugs. "Wrong?"

"How can you write the holy words on him? You were his student." She lifts her palm to offer him the absurdity of his position.

"Yeah, I was in his class. As monitor," he corrects. He sets his foot on the bench and rests an elbow on a knee. The foot is encased in a scuffed and dusty loafer, a relic of his shabby past. "Three years to be accurate."

A glance at his shoe resting beside her own sends a sudden rise in her belly, remembering her clenched toes in the passion of the mountain top he could bring her to. As if shoes could shield against such biting memories like they do against earth's abrasions.

She shakes her head to dislodge the memory. "Three years as his student, so how are you qualified to pass judgment on him now?" she demands.

He laughs, his cheeks blooming in the clearing. "I've been passing judgment on him for years, Sonny. I've also been teaching his class for him. Oh, don't look so righteously wounded." He pauses, then softens his tone. "Questions came up that needed answers. I was there and he wasn't. Simple scenario."

"Okay, look, my father was no saint, but he took his art seriously and everything connected with that, including his students."

Vincent nods like a teacher trying for patience. "You keep that sweet image, honey, and don't you let anybody take it away from you."

"Damn you, Vincent!"

"You know," he presses on, accepting the curse as another volley over the net, "I wonder how you can see him now the same as a year ago—before you knew better." His lips purse and he cushions the pen against them. The dip into the softness sends a twinge through her body, though she would be quicker to bite rather than kiss those lips after what he did to her. "What makes you think you can do that? Edit out the pages you don't like?"

"He's a brilliant artist," she answers, trying for the edge she had before.

"Not an answer to the question," he mocks. "Oh, hell, forget it." His tone is impatient as he steps away from the bench and looks around. "I'm not interested in his teaching. I don't care about any of the scuttlebutt of his womanizing either. I care about his paintings, that's it."

"So why did you stay there for three years?" she persists, wriggling down from the windowsill to stand nearly as tall as he. She is aware of this ridiculous defense of her father, attacking Vincent's slim composure.

He edges back, placing more space between them. "I liked the price. Free as monitor. You can't do better than free for studio and models."

"Convenient arrangement."

"You could call it that. Your dad found some convenience in it." He taps his pen against the notepad.

She decides to ignore the new Pandora's Box. "And now you're back as the critic."

"I go where they send me." He nods toward the surrounding walls.

"It's funny, the way things turn out, don't you think?" She drops her shoulders, aware how tense she has been throughout the unexpected encounter.

His eyes are not amused, and she can see by the set of his jaw that his mind is on other things. He has the guarded look she remembers so well, guarding himself from hurt while peeling her open, layer by layer. Searching to find the beauty his soul craved while his fingers in more agony than pleasure pushed oil pastels over tone paper.

"So," he mused, "you've changed, Sonny."

"Changed?" Her smile wants to leave, though she keeps it there. "How?"

"You used to be sweet-natured. The first time you came up to my place, I'm sure you remember. You wanted to model for me, urged yourself on me, and then you sat with that towel practically glued on to you until I—"

"I was never sweet, Vincent. Maybe that's what you expected, or what you wanted, or imagined."

"Oh, never mind. Forget it."

"And you know why I came to you. You saw yourself what happened that night in my own home. I couldn't live there anymore. Are you really using that against me?"

He shrugs and seems ready to answer, but she continues.

"Anyway, you're the one who's changed. Important man, writing clever things in that notebook—the more destructive, the wittier. I've read some of your by-lines in that self-conscious rag you write for, telling people what's worth it and what isn't. A critic of Bert Kossoff, imagine!"

He smiles and takes a step away. "Another show," he says, "that's what it is. You can believe what you want, but I don't see Kossoff's temperament out there, or his demons or angels or whatever. I only see his paintings. Sure, I know a few things: he trained here, taught here, had exhibitions, won prizes, is in some decent collections and been a serious painter all his life." He turns toward the newest paintings. "I know a lot more—more than I want to—but none of it is as critical as that painting over there, and that one, and the sum of them together in this show. That's what I'm writing about and what anybody interested in coming here wants to read." He taps the notebook against his wrist, then tucks it into his pocket. "Enjoy yourself tonight," he advises. "It's a gala reception. The Board voted champagne for this one."

"You're not coming?"

"No, I never go to openings, French champagne or California Gallo."

She waits, hoping he will say more about what Kossoff's paintings signify to him personally. If he would do that, talk about him without sarcasm or innuendo, the way she had daydreamed Vincent and her father would talk to each other, one artist to another as she stood beside them, listening, inspiring them. If he would do only that, she'd try to forget that terrible night in his apartment. The night that crawled into an eerie dawn when he discarded her and she found herself walking in the alley among the cats, not knowing why, or where she would go.

She waits, hoping this will happen despite the confused emotions that entered the room with him.

"You owe him a lot, don't you?" she asks quietly, no longer throwing him a line to catch so much as pleading for him to take it and give her something back.

"I owe him nothing," he scoffs. He scans the walls again and his voice emerges more softly, as if he'd heard the need in her tone.

"Look, it's okay, why should I try to change your mind? You think because I occupied space in his studio for three years, I got something. I guess the rest of us should assume that as his kid, you got something from him too. Except it doesn't work that way because spending time with a man like Kossoff is like spending money on the stock market. Your profits depend on the product which is only him; what he perceives, how he behaves, how he's affected by his world, how he is with the people close to him. So, with Kossoff, you don't get your money's worth if it's a relationship you're looking for. Come on, you came to understand this, Sonny, didn't you?"

The question hangs between them, as if waiting for her to respond with another defense of this man and the mass of paintings that hover over the room like a dust storm they must both muscle through.

He reaches over and touches her arm. "No, I don't owe him anything, and I'm sorry to say it because he had a lot to give if he knew how or ever wanted to." His eyes now on her, he regards her for a moment, his foot on the bench, his arm resting on a knee. But when he speaks again, his voice holds conclusions. "You don't owe him either. That's something you'll find out, eventually."

She wants to slap him. She has never slapped anyone in her life, but she could smack him. And yet he could be kind and loving and was once to her. The truth is, she has never been sure what Vincent would do. For all his self-possession, he had that darkness about him, a shadow that kept appearing like sudden black spots in a tunnel while you were driving full speed.

She watches him as he continues his tour of the gallery. When he reaches the door, she calls out to him. "What will you write, Vincent?" She waits for an answer. "I'll see it for myself in a day or two, so can't you tell me?"

"About Bert Kossoff or your father, which?"

"Oh, come on. What criticism?"

"Not too much criticism." He turns from the door toward where she has taken a few steps to hear him.

"What, Vincent?"

"More statement than criticism."

"What kind of statement? Please, stop analyzing my words!"

"Oh, a summary, I'd call it, describing this odd assortment of scraps and what-not, the colors. A few words. I don't know yet how the copy will read, but it will be an opinion. An educated opinion, which is all critics write."

"And what is your educated opinion?" she asks, spitting out the consonants.

He smiles and she watches the square new beard lift and spread, observing a certain dominating presence she'd never seen before.

"That Bert Kossoff—well, your father, if you like—is one of the best artists this country has produced in half a century."

2

Bert Kossoff sits at one end of his studio and faces the blank wall opposite him. He pours from a bottle of Tanqueray into a glass of ice, takes a sip and waits. Not for the euphoria, something else. *Waiting for Godot.* The play darts in and out of his mind, electrifying space like an August firefly. He feels the waiting, always at the start of a painting and is impatient to be rid of it, this burden of expectation—that something worthy will come from his hands. Who is the phantom who put such ransom on the product of his imagination? Paint and paint goddamn well or pay the price. Is that pursuit of perfection or chasing your tail? When can you be sure of the difference, if there is one? Forget it. Too late and too long gone to dredge that swamp.

He searches for images in the endless whiteness of the wall, as if something is there he can seize upon, a moisture stain, a broken bit of plaster, shadows cast from the lamp. He drinks the gin, but it is too bitter and needs something—tonic. Unusual for him to drink in the daytime, but he needs what the drink needs and smiles at the thought—a tonic: A woman, to drive and spend his energies. A certain kind of woman—soft and vulnerable—awakens the memory of soaring to somewhere he needs to be, forgetting the shivering plummet and the crushing fatigue and emptiness that follows. The expectation, like hope itself, trumping everything.

He hears a soft shuffling in the other rooms, but no, he is alone, and it is only the house settling. Settling, a calming word for potential disaster. This old Victorian which he still rents after Irene has left him and now his daughter as well, as unsettled as the house, though at nineteen Sonata could be married and almost was.

He misses the footsteps and voices, the stir beyond the walls from other rooms. But aloneness is what he demanded—his studio off-limits to everyone—the message written in stone back in Forest Hills when his family was more or less intact. Ruth in her flip flops, too flimsy for traipsing about a brick-solid house in brick-like Forest Hills, let alone walking out on him. And Sonata too, and why not? Adoring him for no godly reason, what did she expect? And little Billy—

He gets up at last, too quickly, and the chair falls backwards. Leaving it there, he crosses the studio and unrolls a large bolt of canvas standing upright in a corner. He cuts two lengths—the short one to experiment with—steps onto a ladder and tacks both on the wall. He will work the canvas unprimed.

His paintings are installed already at the Art Students League Gallery. He is aware, as if something relayed to him along a hollow corridor filled with strangers, that the reception tonight will open on a preview exhibition of his finest work. The show will travel afterwards to the Boston Museum of Modern Art and after that, the Pennsylvania Museum of Fine Art, then possibly on to others, arrangements still in the making.

Forty canvases from about two hundred chosen by the curator are hung. Are these the best of him? Is the opening tonight a finale celebrating the end of original images to flow from his vision—that perception commanding his unreliable servant of a hand? Is that why he's standing here looking at this white mask of a canvas, fearful that what it hides is nothing more than his mocking self? He must be sure of his worth, for how else can he stride across the polished floors of the gallery shaking hands, acknowledging praise, discerning the honest tongue from the tongue in cheek? Yesterday was his history. He will not go to the opening tonight to declare his own death.

He selects his colors and spaces the paint generously across his palette with ample room to mix these and add more. He steps back and looks again at the wall on which a six-by-four-foot grainy off-white emptiness stares back. Godot again, flirting with him, eluding him. He downs some gin, then tosses the rest into his work sink. He stirs a mix of two colors and brushes this in slashes onto an edge of the trial canvas. Unsatisfied with the result, he adds a third and experiments, pulling liquid trails. He mixes and maneuvers other colors from the center outward, playing with his shapes and the thickness of his strokes. He steps back again, looks for a long time, waits. Satisfied for the moment or at least sufficient to start on the large canvas, he spreads a plastic tarp under the wall where the white whale waits for his next moves.

Hesitantly, he approaches the pristine canvas. The material seems instinctively to protect itself from his attack upon its virginal state. The hostility hovering between them is a familiar presence, mediated because the anger *belongs* to him; it is an energy that will help him to succeed.

He dips his brush into black paint and makes his strokes. They are firm strokes, he knows already where they need to go. The paint glides on, he steps back, looks, then adds lines, shapes, contrasts that excite him.

Swiftly now, with large brushes, he applies the colors. They collide with one another like reckless cars in an amusement park—grazing, just missing, burning somewhere near the center. A small portion drips and he lets it, guiding it in its plunge, he and the slender stream at play together. He applies more paint—here in this corner and on top over there. Waiting, watching, adding paint in sudden spurts of action, then nothing more for seconds, minutes. Slowly his hands, his brush, his puddles of paints, his arms flying at the canvas and the soft, steady tracking of the flow leave him for that other world. The brushes, the colors, the canvas, the painting coalesce into a totality.

It is getting darker in the studio. He glances toward the window where he should see afternoon, but the daylight is gone. He switches on the overhead lights and adds his spotlights. The paint falling on the plastic is tacky and his shoes track the fresh paint. More acrylic is needed near the edge. He grips a thinner brush; swipes strokes of deep cavernous color onto the top left corner; carries it through the side to the center. A fantasy, the total business, not real; a play—tragedy or comedy—a finish that means something or nothing, he can't yet be sure.

Stepping back, looking . . . endless looking. More there, carry it down, the line must move. Slow it, hear the music in it, the line's tempo, rhythm, this song on deaf space, this wind through night trees, these river bends flowing. Yes, that's it…slow, slower. And now— stop. No more, no more.

Exhausted, he turns away. He lifts the chair that had fallen and drops onto it, his back to the canvas, afraid to see what in his loneliness and anxiousness and horniness and godlessness he has made. He is sweating, the moisture appearing on his skin like the creative juices drying within him. The completion for him is more death than birth; why this is he cannot fathom, nor does he want to.

Still, he hesitates to look, yet he must. The skylight above him emits faint light which means the opening reception will begin in a few hours: his retrospective, his major accomplishments of the past, that blind giant which he must carry on his back.

And so he looks.

It is okay. God damn it. It is okay.

"Okay." He says the word aloud. His voice is raspy from disuse and surprises him, but the gentle, accommodating word is good. Something he can settle for.

•   •   •

Bert smiles as he often does preparing his bachelor dinner of scrambled eggs with melted cheese and English muffins, remembering Irene on Sundays in the Riverdale kitchen,. Sunday breakfasts with the works, he'd converted to near nightly meals *without the works* because eggs were easy and usually on hand. Irene had been the driving force for the successful retrospective now well into its second month with the traveling museum exhibitions soon to follow. Without her push, he's aware it would never have happened: hiring photography of his work, letter writing, museum visiting, getting an upscale Connecticut gallery to handle his work. She was a one-woman PR company with a one-man client, when all she wanted to do was dance and teach little kids how to do the same.

His women—Ruth, Sonata, Irene—how had they tolerated him at all? He had set himself apart from each of them, yet he could produce nothing without their presence. Simply being aware they were there. The essence of selfishness.

The thought brings him again to Irene. The lover who gave more than he should expect, yet never expected she would leave him. The feel of her dancer's body under his hands, her narrow waist fanning out to hips smooth as a baby's skin to touch, the surprise of her muscular legs. He sees in his mind's eye her dancing in the studio he'd made for her, practicing routines to teach later to the children and then smiling at him through the mirror as she sees him watching.

He scoops his cheese eggs onto a plate and an idea grips him. But as the muffin pops in the toaster he discards the idea as swiftly as he would a paint-hardened brush—unworkable. Still, he muses, setting out his eating utensils, how could everything between them be dead when there had been so much life?

Abruptly, he dashes out of the kitchen and into the bedroom. Skirting his bed, he kicks his shin on the end table.

"Shit!" He scours the room searching for something. Over the desk in the corner, scotch taped to the wall above it, is the scrap of paper he wants. He reads it aloud, his voice sounding hoarse and strange to him alone in the room. "Irene Lewis, 652 Whitewater Road, Xenia, Ohio. Where in hell is Xenia?"

There is a phone number. His leg hurts, but the pain pleases him, pulling attention from Irene and the bittersweet memories. The bitter of his hurts to her more hurtful than her leaving him. He lifts the phone crammed onto the cluttered end table and hesitates, reviewing in his mind the conversation to come. She will receive the call, not expecting it; his words will be stiff, her responses unpleasant or worse, polite. So much time has passed. He replaces the phone and presses the paper more firmly against the wall. The tape is worn but it holds.

PART ONE
THE FAMILY
One Year Earlier
October 1975

I

The problem was getting the breeze without the glare of morning sun in her eyes. What time was it? Bert's wallet on the dresser in front of the clock blocked her view. Ruth heard the water running in the bathroom. Bert in the shower meant it must be seven-thirty. Drowsy, behind closed lids she imagined her husband standing under a cascade of water, handles turned full throttle. She pulled the covers higher, relishing her state of languishing in bed while he so vigorously sloshed.

The shower turned off with the squeak of a pipe handle needing oil. She looked up as he opened the door to let steam escape. He dried with gusto, charged up she supposed because Monday began a new week and a new painting, and possibly the brisk tempo of fall excited his mood. Through the open door she watched him toss the towel over the shower door and begin shaving. The mirror reflected a large-boned and ruddy face, lips obliquely following the razor's progress. His eyes would note the endangered chin under the blade but take in other things: flickering spots of sun on the glass, droplets of water in patterns on the faucet, forms, colors and textures. Yet those eyes would keep an inner focus, one that blocked her way to him, no matter their twenty years of marriage. Their son Billy had that same expression when he was deep in thought. What could a little boy of eleven have on his mind to make him so thoughtful? Foreboding? She wondered if that were possible.

Bert washed off shaving cream and splinters of beard, then with a comb and two hands tamed the wild brown hair. He nodded in her direction as he left the bathroom. She propped herself up to watch him stand naked in front of the dresser, his hands on the open drawer, apparently studying underwear.

"Good morning," she mumbled. "What time is it?"

He glanced at her over his shoulder and then the clock, "Early."

"But what time? I can't see it."

"Seven-twenty," he said, squinting, "Or forty or sixty. Early."

His athletic build seemed wasted on a painter, she thought, following the landscape of his back which tapered to narrow buttocks, hips supporting long sturdy legs, the baggage of his testicles visible between his thighs. He slipped on jockey shorts and an undershirt in a kind of get-it-over-with rhythm. He should have been a long-distance runner, a professional tennis player, in something more active than abstract art. His hair was a mess again after donning the undershirt and would be worse later in the day after hours of absent-mindedly stalking through it with his fingers.

He opened the shirt drawer and she imagined his thoughts as seconds passed, smiling at this odd way in which she could enter his world. The red shirt placed over the yellow and sitting under the brown made a nice grouping, warm and hearty colors, but the colors to the right and left of the pile fought. His obsession with bright colors dominated his paintings of late.

Bert turned. "Say, Sonny's sleeping. Doesn't she have to get up?"

"She's not due in the library till afternoon," Ruth responded, adjusting the pillows behind her.

"Still has that part-time job from the summer?"

"Right and not a plan in the world." Ruth slumped down in the bed, her daughter's lack of action prompting a collapse of her own.

"Well, no plans are okay sometimes."

"Not when you have no interest in anything. Bert, I don't sense she's very happy. But nothing I say helps," she added.

"Maybe leave her alone," he said, closing the drawer with finality.

The winning color was brown. Bert tossed the shirt on a chair and put his socks on instead. He dressed in such a haphazard way, no sequence could be predicted.

"That boy she hangs out with," Ruth complained. "She doesn't much like him. Only sees him with the lack of purpose she does everything else." She wrinkled her nose. "His feet smell, did you notice? Every time he walks into the house, I smell feet."

Bert smiled. "I hadn't noticed."

"I could get used to the stringy hair and baggy pants and flea market jacket—haute couture in his set—but I can't stand the smell of feet. Bert, I can't remember her so unenthusiastic about things, so lethargic."

"Hey, when she's ready to put her nose to the grindstone and smell feet, she will. She's eighteen, has time, doesn't have your sense of urgency." He sat on the edge of the bed and worked on a knot in his shoelace, though he had not yet put on his pants. The bed bounced with his movements.

Ruth propped herself against the pillows. "What's wrong with having a sense of urgency? It's what accomplishes things."

"Is that your sister Ethel talking or you?"

"Me," she declared, irritated, but of course they would be her sister's words invading the space between them. Ethel, retired nurse married to a doctor, had strong opinions about work and getting things done and no flattering opinions toward Bert in that regard: zero effort to get himself into top galleries, uninspired teaching to meet expenses, and shutting himself forever in his studio. References to his social behavior was a subject tacitly agreed not to talk about with her sister.

"Sonny looks to you. You have a responsibility to be involved in her future," Ruth admonished. He didn't answer but she could see the girl was infatuated with her father. She remembered Bert saying casually to her after her graduation on the rare occasion of a meal together, "*You don't have to do anything that doesn't feel right, Sonny.*" It had made an instant impression like a boot in untrod snow.

Ruth sank back under the covers. "I think in her peculiar way she may want us to make the move, force her to apply to college." He shrugged, completing his task with the shoelace. "What kind of day is it out there?" she said, giving up. "Have you noticed?"

"Autumn—brown, orange and red—the usual." He reached over and gently pulled back the covers to look at her. "A big black angora cat is sitting on your head, did you know?" He reached over and brought long strands of her hair forward on her shoulder.

"Is it raining or anything?" Ruth asked, glancing at the window.

"No, just autumn and Monday. No imagination." He smiled at her and moved his hand over the nylon nightdress. "You want some company under those covers?"

"Bert, you've got a class to teach."

"They work with or without me. I can make time."

"Would you do me a favor and pull down the shade? The light bothers me."

He nodded reluctantly and scuffed to the window in his underwear and socks. The mission finished, he returned to crawl in beside her. She made room for him. He was cool and she curled up in the crook of his arm. He slipped out of his underwear.

"Come on, stay awake now, I can't do it by myself."

"You could."

He laughed.

For a moment, she could have dropped back to sleep, his hands caressing her as if smoothing away the wrinkles of morning, the smell of soap on his skin lingering. But when he lifted her over him, she helped him remove her nightgown.

"I have socks on," she said, "I'm sorry."

"Ummn. I do too, it's okay."

"Think of me from the ankles up."

"I'll try."

"Think lofty thoughts."

"There's a hole in the toe, and you have a very cold nose, Ruthie."

"That's the way my feet would be without socks. Be grateful."

"I am grateful," he said, looking into her eyes.

When his eyes held her in this way, when the restlessness inside him which she could never reach was on her, she could love him.

He buried his head in her hair as it fell across his shoulders. Then, he was inside her and she caught her breath and gripped his arms and tightened her knees around his flanks. He knew her so well. Knew how much she needed him. And didn't want to.

2

Sonata stood by the dining-room window looking out. Each gust of wind sent a cascade of leaves to the pavements in front of the brick houses lining the street. The dry leaves flitted across the narrow driveway, settling on a square of lawn and skittering off again like the restless ideas scattering about in her mind.

They owned only one of the trees showering leaves, which they spoiled ridiculously with mulch and vitamins and TLC. The tree was planted the year she was born, her mother told her, eighteen years ago, the house nearly new then too, bought from a doctor trading up from Forest Hills in Queens to Eastside Manhattan. His office became her father's studio and the family and tree grew up together, each of them reaching for their own sun. Except Billy.

It was seven years ago on an autumn morning like this. None of them talked about it, just stored it away in some forever-locked place, but she could never forget waking up on that Saturday to the horrifying news. He'd slept over at his friend Mike's house and something happened to him during the night—a ruptured spleen, the doctor said though he couldn't ascertain the cause nor could they. Billy was cute, small for the age of eleven, with dark curly hair and compelling brown eyes that seemed to shift between mischief and responsibility. Sometimes she'd wake in a sweat remembering.

Sonata heard the light scraping of her mother's sandals in the next room. It bothered her that Ruth wore sandals all year round not just summer, if she wasn't barefoot or in flip flops. In bed this morning, she'd listened to her mother's busy footsteps as they moved about the house, full of purpose. But what would she do today but put up laundry, prepare dinner for later and trot off to her job at that fancy boutique on Queens Boulevard to dress up some mannequins? So much for the artist she studied to be. Her father was the only one who'd accomplish anything worth getting up for today. She'd rushed out of bed to see him before he left to teach but he was gone. She was like him in many ways. The fierce energy he devoted to his painting, she had as well but with no idea where to put it. It got her out of bed and tossed her back into it with an empty agenda. No, she had his push, but going the wrong way like an internal combustion.

Ruth sailed into the room carrying a laundry basket and wearing a cotton button-down-the-front house dress. She deposited herself and her basket at the dining room table. Extracting a few clothes, she glanced at Sonata as she began folding.

Sonata turned her gaze back to the window, sighed and watched a circle of mist cloud the windowpane and fade. "I wish I could go down there and rake those leaves," she volunteered.

"Why? Do the leaves disturb you?" Ruth asked. She folded bras and underwear on her lap and laid them out in piles on the table.

"Not particularly."

"Well, Adrian takes care of it—leaves, lawn and snow shoveling too. He depends on the work."

"I'd like to rake them is all." Sonata pressed her forehead against the cool glass. "Do you remember Jocko, Mom?"

Ruth looked up. "Who?"

"Jocko. That kid when I was in junior high who came around trying to teach Billy how to play softball. After school we'd play in the street. I was catcher."

"I vaguely remember. Why?"

"Oh, just thinking. Once, Jocko got so disgusted when Billy dropped a pop fly that fell right into his mitt, he screamed at him and Billy ran crying into the house. 'He'll never learn how to play the game!' Jocko complained. And he was right." Sonata turned to look at her mother. "He never did learn."

When her mother shifted attention from the clothes basket to read her face Sonata knew their minds held the same trajectory. Why did autumn summon him back? It was not only the season of his death but the sense of death there in the leaves outside, leaves tumbling in the wisps of wind like playful children. And rotting.

"Autumn is the start of school semesters, Sonata, a time for plans," Ruth said, returning to her folding. "Those leaves out there were not dropped off here by United Parcel. We've been expecting them."

"Semesters, fall terms, secretarial schools, yuck! More compost piles." She heard the controlled exasperation curling under her name when Ruth called her Sonata and not the usual Sonny. Teased in second grade and coming home in tears, Ruth had patiently explained the source of her name related to the musical Grandma she never knew, her father's mother. Still, there didn't seem a sentimental bone in the man's body, so go figure.

She pressed her lips to the window enjoying the cool wet sensation, like a kiss which in a way it was. "God, how crisp they look flapping around out there. Don't they know they're finished? They've had it!"

Ruth shrugged and sliding her hands over the cotton percale sheets to smooth them, applied a further litany of suggestions. "You could still find something worthwhile if you made the effort. Some business schools would take you and there are certificate programs and adult-ed classes that start late. Honestly, Sonata," she said, "I don't understand this lassitude of yours."

"I'd like to clear them away. Organize them into piles and cart off the miserable things. Make the street tidy the way it's supposed to be."

"It's someone else's job, dear."

"I know. It's foolish doing things you're not expected to." She sighed resignedly and opened the window, letting in a cool waft of autumn air.

"Sonny! Shut that! The handkerchiefs are blowing off the table!"

Sonata watched her mother defend the handkerchiefs with arms and full body and laughed as she dropped the window sash. Ruth straightened up and laughed too. In that moment, her mother looked very pretty, and young. With her dark hair pinned up, she appeared not forty-six but like a child trying to act grown-up.

"Really, darling," Ruth began, leaning toward her, as if invited with the sudden softening of her daughter's expression. "You can't keep putting it off. Are you going to find a good job, go to secretarial school, college, take some courses? What? There's no future organizing leaves. Or books part-time at the library. That was fine for a summer job."

Her mother was beginning to sound like a schoolteacher. Her voice, there used to be a lilt to it, almost musical. *She* was the sonata presence in the house. Pulling out a chair, Sonata dropped into it as if it were the last movement she would consider for the day.

"I detest Mondays," she moaned. "Full of promises that never materialize by Friday. Such a damned energetic day, everybody perked up ready to race off somewhere." She roused herself, twisted the chair toward the table and began folding her father's undershirts, adding them to Ruth's collection on the table.

Sonata held up a sport shirt. "I like this. It's different."

"That? It's awful. I hate it."

"You hate it?"

"I do. It's gaudy, not at all suitable for him. I'm surprised you like it."

"Why did you buy it for him?"

"I wouldn't buy such a thing."

"Dad never shops for clothes! Brushes and paints and food for survival, that's it."

"Well, I'm not sure where it came from. His colors are like that lately. Perhaps it provides inspiration."

"Say, Mom, Dad's fiftieth birthday is coming up soon, did you remember?"

"Yes. What about it?"

"Well, I have an idea. I've been giving some thought to it."

"Really? I'd love to know *what* you've been giving thought to."

Sonata had to smile at the humor in her mother's tone. "Okay, don't get your hopes up. See, Dad will actually be half a century old with this birthday. He deserves some kind of — well, sort of, tribute as an artist."

"What did you have in mind? I have to iron the blouses so separate them," Ruth interrupted. "Here, put them in this pile."

"A party, one great big smash!" Sonata moved to the edge of the chair as her ideas followed in rapid succession. "We could invite other teachers at the League and his friends, and we'd tell his students to come. He's been teaching for about twenty years, that's a long time."

"Sonny, your elbow—watch what you're doing!"

"Hey, I can ask one of his students to make an abstract design on a cake, like in Dad's own style." She picked up the gaudy shirt. "With these colors! And we could have music, a little combo—I know a guy who has a group. We could move the furniture and roll the rug back . . . oh, Mom, it would be the greatest thing. An all-out splash and Dad deserves it, he does!"

"It's a lovely idea, darling, but impossible. Still, your father would be happy that you wanted to do this for him." She gave Sonata a bundle of socks to match.

"What! Mom look at me," Sonata demanded, standing up. "Why is it impossible? And for God's sake, don't tell Dad! It has to be a surprise, that's the whole idea. He can't suspect anything until the moment he sees all those people who respect him here in our house to honor him. Can't you picture it?" She plunked down again and pushed the clothes away so that Ruth would not be distracted. "Think about it!" she demanded.

Ruth sighed indulgently and folded her hands in her lap. "All right, I'm thinking about it." She closed her eyes, and in a moment, opened them. "I thought about it. No."

Sonata shook her head and tightened her lips.

"Look, darling, it's an expense to have a party like that, with music and all the things you want. But we should do something, you're right; make a lovely evening together, go out to dinner at an especially nice place." She pushed the basket of clothes away and stood. "I have to get dressed to go to work."

"Okay, forget the combo," Sonata blurted. "We'll use records."

"Oh, Sonny," she said resolutely, "think about the planning, especially if you want it to be a surprise. All the people we'd have to locate addresses for. People we don't even know?"

"I'll do that," Sonata insisted. "I can go to the Art Students League one night when he's not teaching and take care of most of the list right there. Hey, I'll buy the food and cook and bake and mix the drinks and

I'll clean the house and move the furniture too. You won't have to do a darn thing but wash your face and look pretty."

"My gosh, Sonny! What's gotten into you?"

Sonata stood with a bounce and scooped up the unfolded clothes. "And to show good faith, I will execute alone the remainder of Operation Socks Shorts and Unmentionables."

Over the mound of clothing in her arms and before she spun around to discharge her load in the living room, Sonata observed with satisfaction a surrender of sorts hidden in her mother's exasperated sigh.

•   •   •

No one was in the house when Ruth returned from work at the boutique. Designing the windows and the aisles was tedious preparing for the forthcoming fall sales. On her way to the kitchen she passed Sonata's stacked piles of folded clothes on the living room couch. Sonata had looked tired when she'd seen her this morning, despite having slept late, her head pressed against the window wanting to be out there but not knowing where she wanted to be.

Ruth was used to reading her daughter's face. She delighted in witnessing the expressions that appeared and disappeared, the emotional states they reflected. Her cherubic face had retained its child-like openness, displaying her vexations and delights. Her thick wavy hair, still uncombed this morning, was another readable sign, fastened with a hair tie one minute and ripped off the next to flare around her like uncontainable thoughts.

Sonata's vapid expression this morning made Ruth wonder how long she'd been there, staring out the window before she'd come in. Suggestions about her future had gone nowhere, that was clear. But just as disturbing were her passionate ideas about celebrating Bert. Truth be told, her father had barely been a part of her life, home but not engaged, rarely even speaking to her. Though perhaps that was it. She was lonely for him. Or did she hunger for someone strong like him to pull her out of the pit she was in?

What did Sonata want? And how could a tribute for Bert satisfy whatever it was? Clearly, she should be sending in applications to colleges. She'd gotten good grades in math, stood out in those classes where girls fell behind the boys, so that was something to pursue. And what about boys? She'd gone on some dates and to group parties but Ruth's impression from her demeanor coming home was they hadn't gone well.

She crossed to the sofa and picked up the pile of clothes. She smiled with the bundle in her arms remembering how warmed she'd been by her daughter's close presence as they performed the folding ritual together. Sharing the womanly work. A centuries-old picture: mother and daughter spreading their hands over creases in the father's jockey shorts—or loin cloths wrung out from the river and warm from the sun; a funny image to picture in Twentieth Century mid-seventies Forest Hills.

Bert's colorful shirt tucked away at the bottom lay against her palm. That was the way a model might perceive him, she supposed—hot, a little flashy, different—and buying it to please him. It crossed her mind that she could enlighten her daughter about the shirt, but what was the point? Climbing the stairs to the bedroom Ruth felt a rising flush and a dull ache that settled in her belly. It was an oddly familiar uneasiness she wanted to be rid of.

3

The next day, Sonata made it a point not to bring up the tribute matter with her mother, but that evening, she left the library early complaining to her supervisor of a headache. She was off to the Art Students League to do some scouting.

The League building was a graceful white structure in French Renaissance style with words carved into the face of the concrete: PAINTING ARCHITECTURE SCULPTURE. On either side of the entranceway, glass cases displayed selected paintings and lithographs of work by instructors. It disappointed Sonata not to find her father's work among them; his name, however, appeared in the alphabetical listing of teachers in a smaller case by the door.

In the lobby a seated life-size bronze figure of a boy caught her attention. The plate on the base informed her she was looking at Mercury the Messenger. The toes on the outstretched foot which had wings on its heel appeared like polished gold by what must have been countless bodies leaning against it through the years.

Several students in paint-smeared jeans sat on benches lining the hall or milled about near the bulletin boards, smoking, talking or staring into space. Lined up along one wall stood pedestals supporting bronze busts of past teachers, their names inscribed on plaques.

Sonata searched for some roster showing teachers with their room locations. She stopped a young Asian woman emerging from the art supply store off the corridor. Long black hair as straight as twin walls framed her face. "Excuse me, would you know where Bert Kossoff's painting class is?"

"Sure. Second floor," she said, adjusting the mammoth sketch book she was balancing against a canvas bag of art supplies. "He's in a studio on the left. My class is opposite."

Sonata thanked her and followed the girl's directions, at the same time considering it odd she hadn't visited the class before. But why would she have? The realm of art he occupied had nothing to do with her before this. She and Billy were never even allowed into his studio at home. Now she had a purpose.

Climbing the stairs to the second floor and finding the room, she was surprised to find no one there. A gray wooden platform with peeling paint stood in the center surrounded by about a dozen paint-encrusted easels. Elongated windows flanked one side of the room and rows of institutional lights shone down, but still the room with its dusty gray cast looked somber.

Hearing sounds in another space she sat down on the edge of the platform to wait. Noticing the dry paint splotches, she hoped they would not come off on her skirt. She was upset at herself for dressing like such an outsider in skirt, sweater and pea coat. Preppy to the hilt. Still, no chairs were around, only stools that looked smeared and dingier still.

"Looking for somebody?" a man asked emerging from a storage alcove. He was wearing jeans and a sweatshirt and carried a cumbersome canvas which he set on an easel. He returned to the alcove before she could answer.

She stood to peek at the canvas, a realistic picture of a shirtless man in jeans, the face a blur. She quickly stepped back when he returned.

"Who d'you want to see?" he asked, holding a coffee can from which tall brushes sprouted like vegetation and a flat box filled with paint tubes and rags. "Session starts in fifteen–twenty minutes."

"Well, I'm not sure," she said, getting out of his way as he pulled a stool over to the side of the easel and arranged his brushes and paints on top. "I need some assistance."

"What kind?" he asked, but instead of waiting for her answer he again disappeared into the alcove, returning this time with heavy-looking red material, a box of nails and a hammer. He nailed a section of the fabric to the wall behind the platform then turned toward her with a questioning look. He had a short, messy beard that made his age hard to guess, though she judged mid-twenties. His hair, dark brown and overgrown, was only slightly more tended to than the beard.

"You see, my father is Bert Kossoff," she began, hoping he would continue working instead of just looking at her. She noticed dark rings under his lower lids. He seemed mildly amused at the credentials she offered, a sparkle in his deep-set eyes.

"I didn't know Kossoff had a kid. What's your name?"

"Sonata," she said, laughing for no reason. "What's yours?"

"Vince." He still did not turn back to his work. "So, you're Kossoff's daughter?" For a few seconds he merely sized her up like a photograph he might be choosing a frame for. "Kossoff doesn't come in tonight," he said finally, returning to his drapery. He spread one end of the drape over a chair and arranged the folds as they cascaded down.

"Oh, I know. That's why I came. See, we're planning a kind of tribute to him on his milestone birthday and I need some help. Names of other teachers and friends to send invitations to. I figured we could invite the students in this class too, but of course he mustn't know anything about all this." She had followed him to the base of the platform and it crossed her mind to help him hold the material or something.

"A tribute?" he said and laughed, a short quick sound that had no amusement in it. "Why?"

Sonata was taken aback by the response and slow in answering. "Well, it's a special birthday." She hoped it was enough.

He regarded her quizzically, then shrugged. "Well, I can pull together some names, I guess. I know some, not all. When is this thing?"

"I figured Friday, December 12th. Saturday's his birthday, but it would be easier for people to come to our house together right after classes Friday than trying to find us themselves on a Saturday night.

What do you think? We live out in Forest Hills." She waited for a response but he continued draping his cloth.

He finished and stepped down from the platform. "You want me to tell the students about it or you want to invite them yourself when they get here?"

"Oh, no, you can do that, if you don't mind, I mean."

Suddenly the idea had become transformed into an event. Vince's questions had pushed the idea forward like a snowplow carving a path from here straight to Forest Hills. What would her mother say? It didn't matter. She'd take care of everything herself like she'd promised.

"I was wondering," Sonata began, forcing her voice to be matter of fact and efficient, "There will be a cake of course and a clever idea would be to decorate it in my father's style of painting, a sort of abstract picture in his blazing colors."

Vince raised his brow.

"I mean painted in acrylics on a round canvas made to fit on top of the cake. How does that sound?"

"Sounds weird."

"But could you do it, I mean, would you?" She'd come so far. Now she couldn't stop. "You're familiar with his colors and you're a good artist, judging from this." She waved his oversized canvas into their discussion. "It'd be great, can't you see it?"

"Frankly, no—a cake mixed up with a painting?"

"Oh, no, a painting on top of the cake," she mumbled tremulously, excitement draining from her face.

He looked at his watch. "It's ten of. The model should be getting here." He faced her directly, "So, what did you want—names of other teachers he knows?"

"Yes. Please."

He searched for a clear page in his sketchbook and scrawled several names. Sonata tried to see some of his drawings but he flipped by them too quickly.

"You can get the studio numbers and their teaching schedule from the office. I'll write the names."

"How about acquaintances?" she asked, knowing she was pushing her luck with him, but she had to—her only chance. "I mean, colleagues. It's a tribute, so they'd *want* to come."

Again, he looked at her in that peculiar way, head tilted, brow creased. "Well, I don't know about *acquaintances*." The word on his lips sounded itself quaint. "You want the names of models he—hangs out with sometimes?"

Sonata detected a smile flitting across his face. She was glad he was getting into it. "Sure," she said, "I want all his friends to come."

"I have no clue where they're booked and I know only first names. You can ask in the office." He shrugged then added a few more. "There are guys in the city, some painters I'm told he drinks with occasionally. I don't know them but somebody on the list might." Finished, he ripped out the page and handed it to her.

"Thanks so much, you've really been a help."

He moved two floor lights to focus on the platform. By the door he turned a switch on the heating unit and Sonata heard the fan begin to blow. He peeled off his sweatshirt revealing dark chest hair peeking over the open collar of his shirt, and rolling up his sleeves, hairy arms, smooth, not bushy. The resemblance to the painting she'd quickly glanced at was unmistakable.

Two students entered the studio, younger than Vince. They nodded to him as they crossed over to the supply corner.

"I guess I better go," Sonata announced without moving.

More students straggled in, similar in age to Vince and younger, and several older men and women. No one paid any attention to her as they moved their easels to specific places and brought out canvases and materials. The voices around her were friendly but subdued, as if they didn't know one another well or didn't care to.

A tall young black woman wearing a silk-looking bathrobe greeted Vince then scuffed over to the platform where she sat cross-legged, her arms with dangling bracelets on her wrists hanging beside her. Some unfinished canvases around the room had a clear likeness of her face; others were too abstract to show anything but the form of a figure. One painting near the door was so rudimentary that even

Sonata could tell it was a beginner's. The student, about her own age, stood far back from it, scrutinizing the picture with a sour expression.

Sonata would have liked to become friends with some of these people, to hang around, peer over everyone's shoulder, quiz them about their instructor. They looked interesting, even the beginner.

"Pose, please," Vince called out.

The model leisurely stood and loosened her robe. She folded it and placed it at the end of the platform. When she straightened to take her pose on the chair, the effect of her nudity under the lights and against the red drape stunned Sonata. She had never seen a nude female other than herself at such close range.

The woman's skin was deep brown, purple/black in the shadows and almost copper in the high curved areas of shoulders, belly and breasts, wherever the lights touched her skin and reflected color. Her nipples were erect, the areolas wide and Sonata felt a blush of heat on her face despite trying to observe her as casually as the students seemed to.

The model made several broad circles with her arms then arched her back and twisted her elegant torso from side to side before taking her pose on the red-draped chair, body facing to the side, eyes toward the students. Her face, in contrast to the complexities of her body, was open and friendly, holding no apparent secrets.

All the students in the room had a different view of her. Sonata wondered which view she might have chosen herself. Vince, working in the back of the room, squeezed small mountains of pigment onto a board, blended some together with a brush and applied them to his canvas. He worked shirtless, a mirror in front of him. Catching his glance, she headed toward the door. There she turned to take a last lingering look. The mood was charged, an intensity of concentration on each person's face, yet there was restraint, as if by unspoken consent, no person's inner thoughts or moods would be allowed to escape into the room. Sonata hated being so much an outsider.

Vince's eyes were on her. *He must think I'm a voyeur as well as a pest.* Hastily, she opened the door. But he was smiling and coming towards her, a brush still in his hand.

"Listen," he whispered, the voice friendly but the eyes retaining their cool detachment. "I haven't given you much time, I'm sorry." He took her arm and conducted her outside the door. "Stop back later in the week. I'm painting here most nights, might have more time end of the week. Sorry I can't help much now."

"Oh, don't worry. I understand, and you've been very helpful."

"Well, you're Kossoff's daughter. I should give you the royal treatment or something. Anyway, if you want to, come by at around four on Friday, go upstairs to the third-floor cafeteria; you'll find me there. I have an early dinner there in the cafeteria most nights before the five o'clock sketch class."

"Friday is great. It's my day off."

"Okay, I'll look for you around 4:00 in the cafeteria."

He returned to his easel and she was left standing alone in the hall. He was an efficient monitor; he had managed to get rid of her.

She decided to make a tour. Casually, as if looking for someone, she peered through the open doorways. The classrooms, their white walls gone gray and overhead pipes exposed here and there, were bare of decor and void of furnishings other than stools and standing easels caked with years of dried pigment. Even the students were dully clad in worn jeans and scrappy shirts, some wearing smeared gray smocks. Some pictures seemed taller than the students working on them and covered a quarter of a wall. A spray gun was used on one large canvas; on another, the painting lay on the floor, the student walking around it dripping paint from buckets. The paintings stood out from the bleak surroundings with gaudy brilliance, drawing your eyes to the vitality suffusing the rooms. An instructor's voice would bellow a message, but the sounds otherwise were low to silent, no radios, only the scraping of easels or stools across the floor.

The models frightened her a bit, standing on the platforms with only their eyes moving, darting about. Most were not very pretty. One pale woman with rounded shoulders and sagging breasts wore a blue ribbon in her hair. All the paintings in that room had that touch of blue.

She took the elevator down to the main floor and walked across the lobby to find the office Vince referred her to. Several young men and women idled on benches along the wall, smoking and talking. She passed them trying to appear like one of them and hoping to find the office on her own. Sensing their eyes on her, she was about to push through a door with a sign overhead reading STUDENTS ONLY BEYOND THIS POINT. Her hand hesitated—of course, nudes all over the place—but it was too late to turn back. She was not a tourist, not a voyeur. She was Kossoff's daughter.

She found herself in a corridor flanked by classes in progress on either side with students painting or drawing or busy doing things that looked important. In one room, crowded with students, a fat woman of about fifty posed sedately on a chair, nude but for a flowered hat perched at a rakish angle. It seemed funny, but no one was laughing and the pictures were actually beautiful.

Sonata arrived at the end of the corridor without finding the office. Spotting a janitor on a ladder changing a light bulb, she entrusted her problem to him. He very kindly led her back, through the marked swinging doors she'd trespassed, past the people on the bench where the squatters observed her return, through the open doorway into a vestibule leading back out into the street.

Tears came to her eyes at this unceremonious rejection—for passing beyond the "Students Only" sign? But the janitor pointed to a little door on the left before the door to the outside. Through glazed eyes she observed a counter behind which two secretaries sat busy at their desks. She turned to wave a thank you, but with the wide doors of the building directly in front of her, Sonata chose that route instead. She'd accomplished enough for one night.

Emerging into the cool autumn air and wide pavements of West 57th Street, Sonata punched her fist in the air. *Friday, I'll accomplish everything, I'll come in jeans like everybody else, find some paint in the garage to spatter them up…I'll push open the right doors, find the cafeteria, find Vince, ask the right questions. It'll all be right.*

She belonged here in the Art Students League. She was Kossoff's daughter.

4

The upstairs felt warm. Earlier they had turned up the steam heat after several days of frigid weather following a mild spell and today was mild again. Ruth opened a window in the guest room where her sister Ethel would sleep on her bi-monthly weekend ritual of Manhattan shopping.

She crossed the hall and raised the window in Sonata's room. Outside, Sonata's spirited leaves remained, their lawn man late in picking them up. A sudden breeze blew papers off the desk. Replacing them, Ruth noticed an open sketch book she recognized as Bert's, one of several stored away in his studio. The book was open to a page of nudes drawn in quick succession, several on the page.

Surprised to see the book in her daughter's room, she closed the window and sat down at the desk, switching on the lamp to see more clearly. The light illuminated the bold pencil lines of female models in standing, seated and reclining poses, figures captured in motion and at rest. The sketches were over twenty years old, the pages slightly yellowed.

Immersed now in the drawings, she turned several pages. Bert had caught the essence of each gesture pose, its sweep and thrust, eliminating anatomical detail where it thwarted the action and shading only where it crystallized the form. She smiled recalling him mentioning such things to her when they drew together at the League, he the advanced artist, she the neophyte.

Each page showed his distinctive style: curves rendered with such sensuality one could almost feel the rounded contour of flesh. The female nude, she sighed, sitting back in the chair, the house specialty.

She closed the sketch book and again wondered what it was doing on her daughter's desk when she noticed a pile of papers under the pad. Sonata had filled the papers with clumsy attempts at copying the sketches in the book. Ruth had an urge to laugh—the drawings were so crude, so far from the poetry of Bert's gifted hand—but she stopped herself; the efforts were painstaking and serious. Sonata had obviously taken the drawings from Bert's studio without his knowledge. Otherwise, he surely would have informed Ruth about this sudden interest in art, hearing all her worried concerns about their daughter's future.

So, here was Sonata reaching out to her father through the black and white pages of his drawings, as she was doing by wanting to celebrate him. The drawings on the desk displayed a meaningful father/daughter interaction, teaching and learning one from the other: one happy to give, the other eager to take. But that was a relationship that had never been. Bert in his circumscribed world had little to do with Sonata while she was growing up. Instead, Ruth had fashioned the man for her daughter to see: a man dedicated to his art. To protect her she explained his absence at every event that mattered to her and his neglect, even at home, as an unfortunate result of that dedication. It appeared she'd done a good job of it, she thought now, shifting through her daughter's ponderous copies.

How long had Sonata secretly been poring over and copying her father's drawings—days, weeks? Had this been the germ of her idea to plan a surprise tribute for him—it had been weeks since she'd mentioned that notion—or did the drawing come later? She'd expressed no earthly interest in art before. Still, finding something to be passionate about could possibly lift the girl from her doldrums.

Standing, she arranged Sonata's papers as they had been and replaced Bert's sketch book as their shield. She turned at the door, her eyes passing from the desk full of drawings to the still girlish posters on the wall and an orphaned stuffed animal on the bed, its ragged parents given to the Salvation Army. She doubted that her daughter would succeed as an artist and foresaw dismay on the horizon for all her eagerness now. Reluctantly, Ruth allowed the fear to surface that had been creeping inside her all the while she'd been skimming through the drawings. It wasn't about art.

After all these years of guiding and cherishing and protecting her daughter, she might now be the one to be left out of her life.

.　　.　　.

In the kitchen Ruth put up a large pot of water for pasta and took out seasonings for ground beef. Ethel, still out shopping, would be here for dinner. Sonata, socializing with her friend, would be back to eat with them; and Bert was—wherever Bert was.

Seeing Bert's drawings in Sonata's room the day before stirred memories of when she'd first met him, both of them studying at the League. So generous he was in helping her render the nude on the platform; so invested he became in helping her become the nude in his bed. She poured herself a glass of wine and sipped it as she mixed seasonings into the beef.

Nineteen and enrolled as a drawing student, her interest in fruits and flowers shifted to figure drawing. Working one late afternoon in her usual bewilderment on the last sketch of the day she felt someone's eyes on her. Bert had stopped drawing the model and was sketching her. Self-conscious and annoyed, she accomplished nothing for the rest of the pose. Only when the session ended did she look directly at him. Shocks of dark hair fell on his brow as he bent to his drawing. His eyes, as she haplessly observed when he glanced up at her, were deep-set and serious. But he smiled—a friendly smile—then someone called her and when she turned back, he had gone.

A week later in the open sketch class, she found him sitting beside her when she returned after a break. His drawings, even his renderings of the quick one-minute gestures which she barely had time to get on the paper, were exquisite. She began their conversation, comparing his drawings to her own overworked efforts. Sympathetic, he showed her how to control the proportions, what to look for in the model, what to minimize or avoid—elbows, collarbones, unnecessary details that confused the drawing.

After class they would often sit upstairs and go over her drawings in the League gallery surrounded by work of advanced students hanging on the walls. Seated close beside him made her conscious of the hair on his arms as he handled her pitiful sketches to make suggestions, the amusement in his eyes when he looked at her, his playful grin. Her concentration evaporated if his arm touched her as he turned a page of her sketchpad. He would take long looks at her body even while talking, his eyes lingering on her breasts though he never touched her. Sometimes she could feel his breath against her cheek, invading her bubble of personal space.

Soon the critiques included invitations to his rented studio to see the rest of his work. She tossed these entreaties aside with a casual joke, but as he talked about line and shadow and mass and proportion, the flush rising to her head obscured the words. She was not used to such feelings. At home she strived for the intellectual standards set by Ethel who planned to become a doctor, and at work to become more efficient in Gregg's shorthand. Her boss called her Lady Ruth for the ladylike refinement of her demeanor.

Bert began counseling her on her own body during those heady sessions, in the same patient way he urged her to think of contour and eliminate collarbones. She must learn to know her own body and enjoy it before she can represent the figure with sensitivity. "The figure is too alive to simply copy," he told her. "When I look at the nude model, I look with the tips of my fingers, feeling every line I make with the memory of touch. A woman's breasts," he explained, "are the most perfect forms ever created." He described how it felt to him when the nipples touched his chest as he lay on his back. If he were not so explicit an advocate of women's anatomy, she might have visited his rented studio sooner. His experience in the area seemed too formidable for a Lady Ruth who had no experience at all.

But she forgot all this when finally, she relented and spent her first night in his fourth-floor sublet studio. It was after a sketch class in late spring, shortly before their classes ended for the summer. But instead of going up to the gallery to talk as they usually did, he took her across the street to the Topside Bar for a drink, a joint suited to League sculpture students in plaster-soaked shoes. It had a jukebox that played songs with lyrics like *"You won't be satisfied until you break my heart"* and *"The girl that I marry will have to be, as soft and as pink as a nur-ser-y,"* revolting her, as much for what a man wanted, as for how she fit the bill.

His sublet was in a building next to Carnegie Hall rented from a theater producer temporarily living in Europe. Heavy oak and rosewood furnishings in the living room imparted an ambiance of shabby old world elegance. The maroon carpeting had worn through in several places and Oriental scatter rugs covered the bruises. A mammoth coffee table strewn with magazines, books and brochures occupied too much space in the crowded studio apartment while several oversized pillows covered in a flowery weave lay on the floor near the table. A single window shielded by thick maroon drapes completed the overstuffed ambiance. Adjacent to this room was an alcove holding a double bed. A kitchenette and bathroom, each large enough for only one adult at a time, completed the apartment.

"Where do you work?" Ruth asked, searching for a missing space.

"Every apartment comes with a basement storeroom. No windows but a good overhead light—all I need for painting. I'll show it to you later."

But he never did. Nor did she ask.

Bert stacked records to change automatically on a console player near the bookcase: *Full moon and empty arms* and *If I loved you,* and later, much later, *Oh, what it seemed to be.* She remembered these songs of the forties. They became her favorites until in time they were played only on late Saturday night nostalgia radio.

He led her into the bedroom alcove. Because it was warm, she wore only a skirt and peasant blouse over her panties and bra. He wore thin chino pants and a short-sleeved shirt which he pulled off. Slowly, he began to undress her. He kissed and caressed her as he exposed her body, taking his time. But before he removed her undergarments he stopped. He poured red wine into glasses, and as if they were at the Topside rather than half-dressed on a bed, they sipped their drinks. Embarrassed by her exposure, she could think of nothing to say. Still, he seemed content to do nothing but sip his wine and look at her for what seemed like endless minutes. When the music stopped, he left the alcove to arrange another stack of records. Sitting alone and nearly nude she became intimately conscious of her body. The familiar flush when he was near her rose but with it came a yearning for more of him. When he returned, he must have sensed this because, removing the rest of his own clothes, he then eased her back onto the bed. He slipped off her panties and then her bra. With the last remaining distance removed between them, his hands began stroking her slowly, exploring, his kisses gentle. When finally he entered her it was with husbandly care for her fragile state, an impediment that seemed as far away to her as childhood. He guided their movements and she accepted his pace as he led her in those lessons of the body he had so diligently explained. Willingly making the transition from the virginal to the no longer she followed, leaving her convoluted feelings behind like the hoarded crumbs that fairy tale children scattered to try to find their way home.

Later, as he lay beside her in the whirlwind room among the pillows on the floor—and she had dim recollection of how she got there—he said, "Now, we can begin to know each other. Look at the superficiality of that pile over there," he instructed, signaling to her clothes abandoned on the floor. "Compare that to the truth here under my hands as I touch you. Things will be different between us now, not only here but walking on the street, everywhere. You'll see." And he kissed her, not with passion but with a kind of closure signifying the end of superficiality.

After that night she found herself walking up those four flights often, perhaps less for the sex than for his cries of pleasure, her name whispered in the dark. He needed what she gave him and she would have given him anything. People were to say for years afterwards— Ethel, her uncompromising mother Vera, and even her taciturn father whose attentions lay buried in his morning and evening papers—that she was a fool and he gave her nothing, but they were wrong.

Bert's boldness in accepting the impressions of his senses as truth marked him an artist. He tuned into his inner world, listened to every sound that came from it. Women helped to make those voices sing.

She understood this though she believed that it was in her power to make him need only her.

But she discovered herself that night. She felt herself to be a beautiful woman and it had nothing to do with the style of her hair, her choice of makeup, her clothes, as she had been taught to believe. Naked, she was adorned with swellings and cavities, her flesh polished with the smoothness of marble.

Why Bert wanted *her* may have had something to do with the vision that owned every other aspect of his life. She was pliable, like clay in his hands. Whatever he imagined her she was. Reason enough for him to find her unique.

5

"Sorry I won't be joining you girls for cake," Sonata said, nodding toward the living room where Ethel sat on the couch. She rinsed off an apple. "I'm getting to the library early so my supervisor will let me out on time for a change. Dad's taking me to the late movie at Loews when I finish."

Ruth, running water into the electric coffee maker, shut the tap and looked up. "Did he say he'd be home in time?"

Sonata spoke with apple in her mouth. "Be here right after he takes care of something at the League."

"Oh?" Ruth leaned against the sink. "He didn't tell me he was taking you out tonight. I think—well, it's great," she said warily. "What show?"

"A James Bond." Sonata sliced a piece of peach cake while still finishing off the apple.

"Good." Ruth plugged in the coffeemaker and pulled cups and plates from the cupboard. Bert acting the good father to impress Ethel? No, her sister's opinions never mattered to him. Could he finally be setting up an opportunity to talk to Sonata about future plans? She didn't think so. "Let her alone," he'd said, "She'll be fine." She discounted both the advice and prognosis, still, their going out together pleased her. "Good," she said again, brightly. She'd not said anything to either of them about finding his drawings in her room.

"I'm off," Sonata announced, munching the last bite of cake and dumping the dish in the sink with a clatter. Through the doorway to the hall Ruth watched her run a comb through her hair. She lifted her skirt and pulled her jersey tight front and back. Standing sideways, a derisive squint at her reflection completed the ritual.

"Go inside and say goodnight to Aunt Ethel. She'll probably be asleep when you get home."

"Orders! Orders!" she mocked with a sashay into the living room.

Ruth followed her, carrying the peach cake.

"Goodnight, Aunt Ethel, see you in the morning," she mumbled, kissing her lightly on the cheek.

"I'll see you later, won't I, when the library closes?"

"Uh-uh, I'm going to the movies with Dad."

"Oh, really? Well, have fun then."

A few minutes later they heard the motor of the Ford station wagon.

"She's growing right away from you, isn't she?" Ethel said, "Becoming attractive too." Ethel's legs stretched out along the sofa; her feet, wrapped in alligator, skirted the upholstery. "Has she decided what she's going to do, now that she's finished high school?"

"No, it's still up in the air."

Ethel could zoom in on trouble spots, no one better at it. She had that talent, like a wild duck finding thin spots in a foot of ice and coming up with a fish. Ruth reached over for her cigarettes and without disturbing her position, Ethel pushed forward an ashtray.

"I want her to go to college," Ruth said, "She should probably major in some area of business. She's good at math and has terrific organizational skills—they prize her work at the library—but I'd settle for a two-year community college. Anything as a start."

"And where does her father stand on the issue? Or is he sitting this one out?"

Her sister caught another fish. Ruth had to give her credit. "Sonny doesn't want college and Bert says whatever she does should be her decision, not ours."

"Bert is an ass, as usual." She slipped off her shoes and curled her legs under her, a girlish gesture that did not fit the stocky matronly body mounted above.

Ruth winced at Ethel's freedom to express her view of her kid sister's husband. In fairness, Ruth gave her reason to do so with confessions about her marriage over the years. But Ethel and their mother had a similar problem. Every thought that came into their heads was uttered. They seemed to keep the same impeccable order in their heads as in their houses. If ideas began accumulating, they disposed of them either by use or discard. It wasn't that Ethel and Vera were narrow-minded, they were just compulsive housekeepers.

Ethel began expounding on the benefits of a college education. Despite the ring of truth to what she said it hurt to listen, like someone tapping a crystal glass with a steel chisel. Ethel had a take charge attitude with everything, which had included Ruth's life, something Ruth was used to if not happy about. They'd been close as children, shared a room and when they got older, double dated, one sometimes supplying the other. People called them Mutt and Jeff. Ethel, the big one—older, louder, more insistent—and she, Mutt, the little guy.

Ruth needed Ethel in that first year of confusion as Bert's wife. Feelings would sweep in on her in gusts, her emotions a baffle, opening to admit love for Bert and pride in herself for marrying him; shutting to trap resentment for Ethel's sharp opinions, which she was coming to sense were valid.

Ruth remembered one sultry afternoon in Shraffts waiting for the waitress to bring their lunch, chicken salad on wheat toast—they both always ordered chicken salad on wheat toast with a black and white soda for desert—and Ruth said, "Ethel, I have to talk to you. I have to talk to someone!"

And Ethel tried not to appear shocked as she listened to Ruth. "You poor dear," she uttered, "How can you stand his doing this?" Then: "How can you allow it?"

"His needs are different from the ordinary person's, Ethel. He loves women as objects of beauty, as inspiration and just can't keep his hands off them."

"He had better keep his hands off. Bert is a married man now, for God's sake! You don't have scenes? You let him run around looking and touching? What's the matter with you?"

"You don't understand, Ethel. He's an excitement—his attitude, his approach to life. You and I have led such sheltered lives, but he's so different. A passionate, amazing man. It's not that he can't keep his hands off other women, it's me too. It's mostly me." And somehow, she expected Ethel to find credible this dogged analysis.

It made things easier to talk to her sister, first because she was used to it, but also because she perceived her life showed off well against the mediocrity of Ethel's own marriage to Lou. Dr. Louis Abel was an ear, nose and throat specialist whom Ethel had met as a nurse at Connecticut Memorial Hospital. Ethel had taken up nursing after heroic attempts to get into medical school where female admittance in the forties and fifties was next to impossible. She was well qualified but all-male door-keepers viewed pregnancy down the line as a threat to recouping their investment, asserting that men as primary breadwinners required the limited spaces. Ethel moved up in the ranks of nursing, becoming head ENT nurse at the hospital, but the bitterness of being treated unfairly never left.

Ruth kicked off her shoes and rested her feet on the edge of the coffee table. She tried to follow Ethel's train of thought about Sonata's future.

"Have you considered the Peace Corps?" Ethel asked. Ruth shook her head. "It's becoming popular with bright kids who want to do something important. My neighbor's sister's daughter did that several years ago in Colombia. No, Chile, but she liked it. She came home with a South American husband, she liked it so much. Maybe Sonny should do that for a year or so until she gets her mind made up. Broaden her horizons."

Ruth thought again how helpful it would be if Bert took an interest in his daughter at this crucial point in her life. She lit a cigarette, inhaled then let out the smoke with a lengthy sigh. The cigarettes were stale and burned her throat but she smoked them anyway with the same weakness that she endured other things that satisfied some distant need.

Her own parents had taken little interest in *her* future, she reflected. Ethel was whom they set their hopes on. She was the scholar, the star with straight A's, while the younger sibling trailed with her head in the clouds and her hands in charcoal and paint. Ruth met the family's low expectations: marrying Bert, a starving artist with as little potential as herself. She had helped Bert make a go of it; wrote letters that secured him jobs teaching at the Art Students League and Pratt and she got herself hired to create window dressings at fancy stores. Sometimes she mused that her life *was* window dressing, the quality on the inside even she couldn't be sure of.

"Why don't you divorce him?" Ethel had asked her. Of course, she said it often. But only once had she come close to doing that. After Billy died. They sought comfort from each other during those terrible weeks but failed to find it, each of them emotionally alone to bear it. Yet even then she did not leave him. Why? The answer floundered under logic. That he made her feel needed was trite but true. Equally trite, facing her parents after a divorce. Vera's scorn was an edge that drew blood. Bert's indulgence was an ache she had found ways of soothing.

"Ruth, I would like a yes or a no or at least an answer."

"I'm sorry, what did you say? The Peace Corps?"

"I said the peach cake looks awfully good. How about serving it already?"

"Oh, I was waiting for the coffee, I'll get it now." She found her shoes under the chair and trudged into the kitchen, returning with the coffeepot and a tray with cups and a small pitcher of milk.

"Any plans for the winter?" Ruth asked as she poured.

Ethel, sitting upright, dropped a sweetener into her cup from a jeweled vial in her handbag. "Lou is covering another ENT man through December, plus his own practice, but I'm working on him to take two weeks in January. I've cut back my hours, taken on less responsibility. Actually, his practice has grown so, he's considering taking in another doctor."

"I guess you'd be encouraging that."

"I am. We can afford to earn a little less—well, with taxes, it hardly matters—and Lou's working too hard. He needs to take it easier, get away more. We missed two lovely dinner parties this month for emergencies. I was dressed and ready both times when he got called in."

"The pressures of a doctor's wife." She didn't mean to be flippant but knew as the words escaped Ethel would take them the wrong way. A threatening cloud hovered over even the most genial conversations between them, a potent mix of communication failure and kinship rivalry.

"As opposed, I infer, to the pleasures of an artist's wife?"

Ethel sipped her coffee and Ruth didn't answer. Counterthrust and forget, an unspoken pattern, oddly acceptable to both. They knew the other's weak spots and circled those areas like inflammation around infections, though there came with age, an increasing vulnerability to criticism—from every source, but particularly from each other. Here love was learned and each time it failed, they lost something of themselves, for they were sisters close in age, treasured children, the fulcrum around whom everything had turned. Who now but the other could remember the child, unspoiled and perfect?

"So, how is Bert doing these days? Is he selling?" Ethel asked.

"Not much, but an offer might come down to join the stable of a Madison Ave Gallery. It's not definite and he might not even take it, but it's something. And another break came, a good one. A colleague at the League, Willie Brockstein, entered Bert's *Study in Blue* into the Venice Biennial and it took a modest prize. But Bert doesn't put much emphasis on advancing his career."

"He should. He needs to mix some business sense onto his palette, hustle up exhibitions and commissions, go out and meet the deep pocket patrons. And why isn't he hanging his stuff in banks at least?" Ethel went on. "All of a sudden banks are showing fancy framed pictures on their walls. Money alone has become too crass." She sliced herself another sliver of cake and offered a piece to Ruth. "Ummn, this cake is good, Ruth."

It wasn't *that* good. Ethel's eloquence was cover for another piece. "More coffee?"

Ethel nodded and produced her saccharin as Ruth poured. When her cake was eaten, she stacked the plate on top of Ruth's and left it in front of her to clear.

"Bert has enormous discipline," Ruth volunteered. "Nothing stops him from painting, but he sees it as an end in itself."

"My take is he can't see the end of his nose, Ruth. He certainly doesn't see you, his family, the needs you have. He's irresponsible—selfish, actually." Her coffee cup missed the center of the saucer as she set it down and a few drops spilled onto the side.

Ruth lit another cigarette. What was this, her second, third? Anyway, it would be her last today.

"You're smoking a lot," Ethel said. "You're not nervous about anything, are you? Is it only Sonny or is it Bert?" Her expression as she leaned forward, pushing the ashtray near, offered confidence. "How are things going there, Ruth?"

Ruth smiled, trying not to need the question or its tone of sympathy. "Well, there's something. I'm not sure what to make of it." She shrugged. "Just that Sonny seems suddenly enamored of her father." Standing, she moved to take the dishes into the kitchen, to be busy and not take the familiar gift of solace.

"Wait, what do you mean?" Ethel asked, reaching over to grab her arm.

Ruth set the dishes back down on the table, wiped the small drips of coffee and faced her sister. "She's copying his drawings in secret. Don't tell her I told you, please. I found them in her room by accident. Not only that, she's talking about hosting a party for him. A tribute."

"A tribute? To Bert? What on earth for?"

"She feels he should be more appreciated and wants to use the fact of his turning fifty to…well, celebrate him. She wants something grand, wants important teachers at the League to come, students, friends, everyone who knows him."

"You're letting her do this? Waste energy on a bash for him at this crossroads in her own life? Have you lost your senses?"

"No, and I'm beginning to think it's not such a bad idea. Why shouldn't she get interested in what her father does? It's an interest, at least. Even tonight, going to the movies with him is a good thing. She's reaching for something, trying to help herself in some—intuitive way. Ethel, I'm not saying I understand, I don't. But if she's climbing out of some dark, dead-end place, and if her father at long last turns out to be the rescue that'll do it, let it be."

"Ruth, I must…"

The phone rang in the kitchen. Ruth picked it up. Bert's voice was on the other end. She heard some muted sounds, a faint clatter of dishes and recorded music in the background.

"Ruthie, I'm so sorry, but I'm not going to be able to take Sonny to the movies tonight. Something came up. Please explain to her will you? Call the library? I don't have that number. You can tell her we'll take a rain check."

He said more but she barely listened to his excuse. A rush of blistering anger flooded her knowing no way to stop her daughter's hurt.

"Will you do that? Tell her we'll take a rain check?" he repeated.

"She'll be...disappointed," she stammered, her lips pressed so tightly they hurt. "Here is the library number. You call."

Ruth replaced the receiver. Her little speech to Ethel in defense of daughterly love turned sour in her throat. She remained sitting at the kitchen table, staring through the window framed by flowery chintz curtains, at the dark uncluttered night.

Ethel came into the room and sat beside her. They talked for a long while, long after Sonata returned and went to bed, long after the coffeepot was empty and the peach cake was a residue of dry crumbs tossed into the trash.

6

Bert had no intention of going to the Topside Bar tonight. He had told Willie Brockstein, as they walked together out of the League building after attending an opening reception for the fall instructors exhibition, that he was heading home for a date with his daughter in Forest Hills. Actually, the date was as much to escape his visiting sister-in-law as to take Sonny to the movies, but once arranged he'd looked forward to it. They hadn't had a talk in a long time and Ruth was after him to give Sonny some direction, as she called it. He resisted Willie's invitation with conviction; he remembered that much, before getting sidetracked by seeing Juanita.

"Come on, a beer and a knockwurst," Willie had urged in his muscular German voice. "You will go later to the movies. Your daughter is young, she has time to wait."

"No, Willie, maybe Monday. She tells me it's the last day this flick is playing. And she's in the doldrums."

"Ah, I am sorry."

"Don't be. She'll get over it."

"So! Another time, yes?" Willie heaved his chubby arms and made himself taller.

"See you Monday, Willie."

Heading dutifully toward the subway, he caught sight of Juanita on the corner of 57th Street and Broadway, also heading home after modeling for the life drawing class. She appeared to be having a problem with her shoe. He walked toward where she stood, bent over sideways balancing on one spiked high-heeled shoe while attempting to extricate a foot from the other. Her coat open, the swell of her remarkable bosom rose above a pink ruffled blouse.

If Juanita needed assistance, it would be on some International crossroad. Arriving at her side he could see the depression of her navel through the clinging material of her jersey skirt. The purse gripped in her fingers was clear plastic, showing everything she carried.

"Hey, what's the trouble?" Bert asked, approaching beside her.

"The shoe broke on me. Now, the goddamn strap. Look at it."

"Yeah, looks like it snapped." He watched her examine the pinkish sandal now held in her hand.

"Uhhh, I don't know. What should I do?"

Bert looked at her, deciding what he wanted to do himself. Her breasts, so familiar to him in the studio, floated under the blouse. He'd done upwards of fifty drawings of her modeling in his class, but her body teased him here under the lamppost, maybe knowing what lay under the frou-frou.

She bent over again to replace the shoe, leaning on him for support. When his arm reached around her, he discovered she was wearing no bra.

"Come on, we'll hobble you across the street to the Topside. You need to get your strength up to totter on a broken shoe. Hang on, I'll ferry you across."

They waited for the light to change. He figured to stay at the bar just for a drink with her. Downing a knockwurst with Willie was not in the cards—no time, he was such a talker—but it was still early to meet Sonny. He had time.

The Topside interior was a dreary saloon that with only slight variation could become a luncheonette. Long and narrow it had a nondescript bar on one side and Formica-topped tables on the other. When they took their seats Juanita instructed him to order a double Scotch with a lemon twist and a single ice cube and excused herself to go to the bathroom. After a weary-eyed waitress took his order for a draft beer and her meticulous Scotch, Bert left for the men's room.

Juanita was at the table when he returned, hair higher on top, blouse lower in front, smile brighter. She had daubed herself with something that smelled like carnations. He had gotten a thick rubber band from the bar tender which managed to hold her shoe in place. Their drinks arrived and they talked for a while about the League, the administration that gave her a pain in the ass, the janitor who kept forgetting to clean the goddamn platform; and then her foot which she released from the good shoe began sliding under his pants leg under the table. It intrigued him how a lone foot could have such an effect. He took her hand and played with it, running his fingers along the inside of her palm, reflecting about his fingers being in some warmer, tighter place.

Maybe Willie was right. He'd have time to make it up to Sonny; take her to some place special—Radio City Music Hall or a Broadway show. He wanted to make it up to her.

"What do you say we finish up and have a second round at your place?" Bert suggested.

"Yeah, okay, but it's early. Maybe you'll take me to the Carnegie movie. You'd like it, I think."

"What's playing?" He couldn't believe he was asking this question.

"I forget the title."

"Who's in it?" His hand had been carried to her lap stroking over the thin jersey. The hollow between her thighs radiated the heat of her body.

"I don't know, but some court made a ruling so they could show it." She smiled showing a glimmer of gold tooth. Color everywhere: the flush of rouge over honey skin, deep crimson lipstick, dark blazing eyes.

"I'm hyperopic, did I ever tell you? I have to sit in the last row," he said with ornate apology.

"So am I." She drained her glass.

He was aware of the irony—going to a movie with Juanita—but he had no useful advice to offer Sonny and that's what Ruth wanted from him. Ruth was so much better at it. He might even do more harm than good. Before leaving the bar he telephoned Ruth explaining a meeting he'd forgotten about with some people at the League.

"I'll take a rain check, tell her. Radio City Music Hall or a Broadway show, her choice. I'm really sorry."

He was sorry. That was true. But Ruth seemed to make a big deal about it. He called the number she hissed at him and left Sonny a message.

At the movie theatre, leaving the ticket booth and pocketing his change, he observed Juanita waiting for him by the popcorn stand. A regal pose. She was used to standing still while people looked at her and several men did as they passed. Juanita was probably the most popular model at the League with her *cafe au lait* skin tones, high cheekbones and beautifully contoured body. A faint scar on the right side of her face, received at fifteen in a fight with her mother, created a lone imperfection. She had fled Cuba shortly after that incident and lived here in New York ever since. He had always wanted her but at the time she posed for him a Cuban boyfriend was in the picture. He crossed the lobby, feeling pretty good about claiming her.

The dialogue was in French and subtitles were half blocked by the heads of people in front. His arm around her, he watched the figures moving on the screen and wondered vaguely what they were talking about. Juanita's hand was stealthily stroking him. His fingers played inside her blouse circling a nipple, erect as the tip of a pinky. Juanita leaned into him and he kissed her, the kiss arousing some attention along their aisle. Finally, they decided it was prudent to leave, though the plot seemed to be just getting underway.

In the cab, with more privacy, Bert glided his hand under her skirt and after a few minutes of catching his fingers in the lace rim of her underpants, he asked her to slip them off.

"I'll be cold," she complained.

"I'll warm you," he told her, stuffing the panties in his jacket pocket afterwards, as he kissed her. He continued to caress her. If the cabbie, a newly arrived Russian immigrant, judging by the few words shared between them, noticed from sounds coming from Juanita's throat, he feigned oblivion. Juanita nibbled his ears, her long nails sliding along the back of his neck. She alternately pulled him to her and pushed him away with the cross-purpose of a rapid undertow.

Bert waited. He was used to restraining himself, something he lived with. He didn't know when it had begun, this white heat for women. Sure, in adolescence like every other guy, but the acuteness had never ebbed. He loved women—their skin tones and colors and smells, their sounds when excited.

Ruth excited him, from the start; it never ebbed. She was quiet, not flashy, never wore her sensuality like Juanita. She didn't even know she had it. A sense of discovery accompanied them in bed; she seemed surprised by what she did, the moves she'd make or her responses to what he did. He thought of her now, not with desire, not even with guilt, only an easy confidence that she was there.

The cab slowed, and his arm still around Juanita, he glanced out at the dark, deserted streets of her neighborhood. She lived downtown, south of Canal Street in an area they called Tribeca, a section of the city more used to daytime commerce and shipping activity than residential traffic. Tall buildings loomed overhead with unwelcoming entrances at their base and small evidence of warm human life.

"Aren't you afraid to live down here? It looks so deserted."

"That's only because it's late. Plenty of people—families too. They're inside sleeping. Shhhh." She laughed.

"If you say so." He paid the cab and took her arm.

"Are you hungry?" she asked him. "Maybe I should buy something. Cheese, roast beef? A 7-11 is around the corner."

"Really?" The towering concrete giants seemed unfriendly to such a slight neighbor.

"Sure, what do you think? Open late too. Come on, I don't have anything in the kitchen. We'll get hungry."

They walked together in step, arm in arm in the brisk evening air.

"So, how does your bottom feel?" he asked solicitously.

"Peculiar, you know, open to the elements?" She buttoned up her coat.

"Don't catch cold."

"A lot you care, Mister."

"My mother used to tell me you could catch a cold easiest through your feet. That's why you should always keep your socks on. Don't worry about the rest."

"My mother told me you could catch a lot of other things easy too. That's why you should keep your underpants on. Here, give them to me. I'll put 'em on now, nobody's around."

"Uh uh." He caught her hand as she reached into his pocket.

"Oh, all right. Anyway, I'm getting used to it. It's kind of nice, you know it? Breezy." They rounded the corner. "My mother is a pain in the ass, if you want to know," Juanita remarked. "How's yours?"

He nodded contemplatively. "The best," he said.

"Do you take after her?"

"I hope not."

"What?"

"She died when she was forty-eight. I'd like to hang around a little longer."

"Oh, I'm sorry," Juanita moaned. "How did she die?"

He took a moment to answer. "Cancer," he said softly.

Juanita let go of his arm. "Did she suffer a long time?"

"She did…three years, I guess it was."

"Three years? Oh, terrible!" Her hand pressed her cheek.

"Yeah. Not a pleasant time," he said, noticing she covered her scar as if instinctively sharing the pain.

"How old were you?" she asked.

"Eighteen when she died." They were walking more slowly. He'd been rushing forward to get where he wanted to be; now, in no hurry to go back to memories of his brave mother in her last years, still young, still beautiful.

"And the family? Your father? You have sisters, brothers?"

"Just me," he said, "and my father, but he wasn't home much."

"Why not?" The store, brightly lit, came into view across the street with sausages hanging in the window and yellow wheels of cheese leaning against the window sides.

"He traveled a lot selling greeting cards to stationery stores."

"Greeting cards, huh?"

He hadn't noticed the irony before. "He wasn't home much," he repeated.

"So you had to take care of her."

"After school, yeah. She held on alone till I came home. Tried to play the piano to take her mind from the pain—Debussy, her favorite." He paused, wondered why he was still talking. He tried to register the cheese wheels in the window, why they were heading toward them.

"She tried not to complain, but…" He grew silent as they crossed the street. Only a few cars passed by them sending tunnels of light along the wide avenue.

"But what?" she asked, as he held the door open for her.

Inside the store three men were being served in turn by a fast-moving man with eyes darting about between customers, their orders and the contents of his glass cases. Bert was glad so late at night to see other customers and to smell the aromas of sausage and roast chickens after the cold isolation of the street. The comfort warmed him, the brightly lit ordinariness of the place. Juanita stood in front of the case looking at the selection. She glanced up at Bert.

"But what?" she repeated. "Why'd you stop?"

"Nothing, never mind." He scanned with her the case full of smoked fish and salads and pickles and cheese and cold meats. He was sorry she'd picked up on his story.

"Go on please, there's time. We're not even next."

He didn't know what propelled him to go on, to keep talking. "It's not important, only my mother used to ask me this question. Asked it over and over."

"What question?" Juanita was staring at him, even as all three men in the store were staring at her.

"Can't you do something, Bert, dear?" The slender whitefish were lined up on ice, eyes glaring obscenely, declaring no dignity in death. "Can't you do something for me? Always the same question."

"What did she mean? Do something?"

He shrugged. "She didn't want to die."

"But what could you do?"

"Yes, lady? Help you?"

Bert stared at the glass case as Juanita turned to the clerk to order. He was dumbstruck to have said so much. Hadn't talked about his mother's death in decades, and never the last thing: what she asked of him. He'd been helpless to give her one year, one month of life or take away one day of pain. Newly a man at 18 and helpless. *Bert, dear, can't you do something?* The answer, never spoken, still welled in his throat.

"I'm set," Juanita said, gathering two bags from the counter.

"Good," Bert said, extracting his wallet, "How much?"

A hot barbeque chicken in one of the bags filled the cool air with a heady spice as they left the store.

•   •   •

Juanita's digs consisted of a parsimonious two rooms with bath and kitchenette neat and conservatively furnished for all her flamboyant ways. The couch and easy chair in what she called the "day" room were covered in a rust and green weave. A bright pink and lavender spread with pillows to match lay on the bed in the "night" room.

She put music on the record player, Spanish songs with a classical guitar and fast words. After eating and putting the food away, they left their dishes on the table and retired to the night room. Juanita's ritual included a lit candle, a change of tape to Streisand, and a rheostat bulb set to barely glowing. She took off her clothes in the bathroom, emerging in a fuchsia silk robe, the one she wore between poses on the stand. She could read his expression and they shared a smile.

He undressed without taking his eyes off her. How many times in his mind he'd taken her to bed. Once, he had asked her to take moving poses, something Rodin would have his model do, slow, lyrical changes. These the students were to draw in quick gestures. But the sensual flow of her bending and arching body was so provocative, he had to bring the exercise to a halt. The students' work was extraordinary that night but he couldn't take it, not there.

Her body, now shared with him alone, felt the ripe and heavy way he imagined. She rolled over onto him and set the palms of her hands, her fingernails, her tongue in motion like a spider, ensnaring.

"When you do something you do it all the way, don't you, my seductive Juanita?"

He held off to keep it going, to feel her smooth flesh in his hands and take each quiver of pleasure as far as it would go. She seemed to have the same unrestrained yielding to the throb of their bodies as he did, her thighs wrapped tightly around his hips, her own hips pulsing. The guttural sounds he'd heard earlier in the taxi arose and this excited him even more. Finally, he let his climax overtake him, submissive to it as he could never be in any other act.

For a while they lay beside each other. She spoke before he did. "I always had my eye on you, you know. Wondered why you never made your move."

He smiled. "You had a boyfriend, you don't remember?" He stroked her arm. "A big guy."

"You had a wife." She let this pass when he said nothing. "Well, never mind." She rose, grasped her robe to toss on a chair and stepped into the bathroom. She kept the door open to talk while she washed and he propped himself up to watch her. Even the way she cleaned herself was poetic—one foot on the tub, her long spine bending, a towel draping over her leg as she dried. A Degas pose.

"Let's get some sleep, okay?" she said, returning and climbing back into bed.

"Sure." But he didn't feel like sleeping and wouldn't anyway. It was time to go home. He lay still for some time then turned sideways to look at the woman beside him. Juanita's arm stretched out behind her back, her long legs bent toward him. A Rodin pose, dynamically opposing angles. He was tense, not relaxed as he should be after sex, fighting moves towards her and away, opposing dynamics of his own. Such unsettling feelings were familiar to him, they happened with others. Nothing about her turned him off, quite the opposite.

He made a move to get off the bed and go home when Juanita sighed and adjusted herself in sleep. She looked gentle asleep, in contrast to the wars she waged awake—calm, easy, gentle as Ruth. With Ruth he felt no tension, no *anger*.

Juanita opened her eyes and smiled. Her lips parted and a pink tongue appeared that waved at him.

He let her urge him back into her arms. Once again, without thought or memory, he lost himself in that eager mouth which fed his own hunger for her mother breasts and musky woman parts. And yet he sensed, even as he devoured her, he would never find enough in all those close but distant places to be satisfied and whole.

7

Ruth tied an apron over her blouse and skirt and crossed to the sink to put up coffee. She was setting margarine and cheese on the table when Ethel scuffed in, wearing Ruth's lounging robe. It was short in the sleeves and tight around the chest but managed to close with only small gaps over her nightgown. She packed nothing unnecessary on her trips to New York claiming she returned home with enough of that from the stores.

"Well, Sonny is up and away early this morning, isn't she?" she said, sitting down at the kitchen table. Her eyes were puffy and her cheek had a ridge mark from sleep. "That was her crashing around in the garage, I take it. Where is she off to?"

"Shopping," Ruth said as she popped wheat bread in the toaster. "She wants to get a special dress for the party."

"Ah, yes, the party. The tribute!" She spread the newspaper before her, moistening her finger with her tongue as she turned the pages. "If ever a man deserved a tribute...I'm afraid it isn't Bert."

"Ethel, try not to make fun of it, please. Sonny's excited and planning like crazy to organize this." Ruth poured coffee for Ethel and set the table for the two of them,

"Crazy is the operative word. But I'll say this. It makes a body wonder what she could accomplish if the cause was a worthy one."

"Oh, Ethel, you don't need to be so cynical. Isn't it a virtue for a girl to feel proud of her father?"

"This isn't Bible School, dear, and you don't have to tell me what virtue is. I'd like to see you get the tribute, that's what I'd like. That would be virtue. It breaks my heart to see Sonny make all this fuss for a man who treats you the way he does and if anybody should take credit for anything good about him it's you. Without you he'd be rotting in a garret somewhere and look how you've made a family life here with no help from him. You've raised that kid single handedly. It's you who deserves a tribute from her. Don't shush me, I'm not talking too loud and I won't wake him up. You're so darned mother-hennish over that man, honestly, Ruth. What would happen if he woke up at a normal hour on Sunday anyway and made eggs or took out the garbage? It wouldn't kill him. All right, all right! Here, let me butter the toast."

Ruth brought the coffee to the table with the toast and butter.

"I don't see Sonny worrying any over his sleep, judging from the way she banged things around getting the car out this morning for all the tribute she feels in her soul."

"Sonny's tribute is not for Bert the father and it's not for Bert the man either," Ruth countered, "with his…excesses, which, thank God, she's not aware of—"

"Thank Ruthie, never mind God."

"—it's for Bert the artist. She wants important people to come to this party, museum folks and art agents and collectors. I have no idea how she'll get them to accept, but I guess she does. Well, maybe they heard his name before or thought they must have. You know Sonny's enthusiasm can make it sound like the *in* party of the year. And it's all to be a surprise, by the way."

"Hummn." Ethel hesitated. "I don't like to drop any flies into this delicious soup that Sonny has cooked up but have you entertained the possibility that Daddy might not show up for his dandy little tribute?" Ethel smiled. "—that Daddy himself might not be *in*."

There was a pause in which both of them were silent.

"I seem to recall recently his not showing up for a movie date he *knew* about."

"You mean by that, he may not show up in time."

"Well, something like that." She continued to drink her coffee.

Ruth said after a pause, "I'll tell Sonny to arrange in advance for Willie to meet him here after class the night of the party."

"Who's Willie?"

"Willie is a painter too. He doesn't live far from here. He'll see Bert at the League and ask for help to select slides or something. That will be good—slides for a traveling art show."

"Well, that's settled. I'm glad you can be objective about these nasty little details. Now I'll have another cup of coffee, thank you."

Ruth smiled as she poured the coffee. "Sonny has a romantic notion of her father. I think that's at the root of this shindig: the great artist that the world doesn't appreciate."

"It comes from not having enough to do."

"Well, but—"

"No really. She hasn't got a single interest, thanks to Bert's great involvement with her future, so she picks up this thing that's been lying around the house all this time—to wit, Daddy, the all American unappreciated artist—and decides to do something with it out of sheer boredom."

"Well, maybe you're right about how she got involved in the first place, but it's growing into something else. She's becoming interested in being an artist herself. She'd kill me if I told you, but she's begun copying Bert's old figure drawings."

Ethel laughed. "Well, Bert's figure drawings must be something to see!"

"There are piles of sketches up there in her room every night and she works at it—ten, twenty attempts at the same figure. They're not good, which is a pity with all that effort put into it, but they might get good if she keeps on with it. I don't know, but it's exciting to see her motivated like this."

"Ruth, I wouldn't start building a career for her from a little flurry of effort. This could all be only an extension of that new idolatry of Daddy. A phase she's going through and when the tribute is over, it will be too. Want coffee?" She poured for herself and took another slice of toast.

Ruth stood abruptly. "Ethel, I want you to see the drawings and tell me if I'm seeing things or not." She lowered her voice. "I've been so worried about her. It's not normal for a girl of eighteen to be so bored, so aimless the way she's been since graduation. But now these drawings! And with such energy, such an attack! The drawings have made me accept this whole tribute business, which I thought was nonsense at first, well, like you, but I see it's all tied together."

Ethel hoisted herself up. "All right. I think you're a Pollyanna as usual but I'll look because I'd like to see Bert's drawings. In nineteen years that sonofabitch has never let me into his studio. I come here about twice a month and I still see only what everybody else sees hanging in the living room. That is no way to treat a sister-in-law as interested in him as I am."

Ruth laughed, then uttered "No. Stay here, I'll bring the pictures down. Bert is sleeping upstairs and anyway, I don't want both of us poking around in Sonny's room."

A short while later Ruth returned with some of her daughter's papers and Bert's sketch book. "Here, move the margarine."

Ethel made room as Ruth spread the work out across the table.

Sonny's drawings were worried over and messy. Figures were scratched out with angry strokes of a pencil and the same limbs were redrawn several times in repeated attempts to *get it right*.

"You see what I'm talking about? Okay, she might have started with an infatuation of sorts, but what's here is real work. Look at this." Ruth pointed to the finished sketch of a reclining figure. The pencil lines were awkward in places and the contours heavy and uncontrolled but the figure was grounded, not floating in space as most of the others were, and the legs and arms were fairly proportionate to the body. "Now that's beginning to show promise and look how she took pains to draw parts of it separately first."

Ethel was studying Bert's drawing of the reclining figure. She laughed. "Really, Ruth, how do you know she was copying this one? It's impossible to tell."

They did not notice Sonata standing in the middle of the room until they heard her gasp. For a moment she appeared to be groping for words but when found, she released them in a torrent of anger: "God damn it! What are you doing? What are you doing with my drawings? How dare you take them out of my room!" She ran to the table and scooped up the papers. "And Dad's book! My God! You have the NERVE!"

"Oh Sonny!" Ruth began, her face flushed, "I was interested in what you were doing. I wanted to show Aunt Ethel—"

"Do you see me barging into your room, grabbing things and showing it around like I had every right? How do you have the nerve to take my belongings and spread them around the kitchen like this! Look what you've done. You've got margarine on the cover of Dad's book!" She pushed the book under Ethel's nose. Then: "Here, give me that!" Ethel had dampened a napkin with her tongue and was trying to remove the offensive grease spot.

"For God's sake, what's going on down here? All of you charging around like a bunch of wild animals!"

Bert stood in the doorway in shorts and bare feet. His legs and chest were bare, his hair still disheveled from sleep. "You still here?" he said to Ethel as he came into the room. "I thought you went home last night."

"I urged her to stay overnight," Ruth interjected. "It was seven before she got home from shopping and I get nervous when I see her driving out so late."

"I can understand that," he said, looking Ethel directly in the eye. "I get nervous when I see her driving *in*. Don't take it personally, Ethel." He brought a coffee cup to the table.

"Ethel smiled. "No dear, I won't." She shifted to the innermost seat and made room for him.

"So what's all the commotion about . . . and what in hell is *this* doing here? Ruth? Will somebody tell me what my drawings are doing on the kitchen table? Where did you find this?"

"I found it," Sonata announced.

"Sonny has been admiring your sketches, Bert. She's been trying to copy them." Ruth spoke as kindly as she could manage so he would hear the worship of him and the seeds of ambition embedded in that simple revelation.

"You? Since when?" He laughed with more scorn than mirth. "How long has this been going on?"

"A couple of weeks," Sonata mumbled. Her mouth was set in a thin, tight line and she narrowed her eyes at Ruth, as if wondering what other horrors her mother would divulge.

"And where did you get them from?"

"I found them in your studio."

"My studio, eh? You're not too old to get your hand slapped for taking things from my studio. Didn't I tell you to stay out of that room? Is this something you're hearing for the first time?" Sonata looked at her mother with ice in her eyes.

"Bert, it's my fault," Ruth began. "I was excited about Sonny's pictures and I wanted Ethel to—"

Sonata swept up the papers and turned to leave the room but Bert caught her arm. "Put the sketch books back in my studio, Sonny, and don't even think about taking them out again."

Ruth swallowed and spoke quickly. "Sonny's worked hard on those drawings, Bert. I think at the very least you should see what she's done."

He released her arm and looked at Ruth. The fire in her eyes flared, a command to do the right thing. He caught Ethel's vinegar eyes, expecting the opposite. He stood and poured himself a cup of coffee. "All right, sit down," he said. "Well, sit down!" He laid out the papers as Sonata sat beside him and once again Ethel made room on the table for the display. Bert separated several pages and regarded them, "So, I think we might have a cartoonist in the family. A real flair. Hmmn."

Grimly, Sonata kept her eyes on the drawings in front of her, staring at each page as it became exposed.

"Bert, I liked the reclining figure," Ruth ventured, "The one on the page under that. It's sensitive, isn't it?"

"Oh Mother, can't you stay out of this! It's enough everybody is sitting here gaping, do I have to listen to your ridiculous comments too?" She threw an acid glance at Ethel.

Bert regarded his daughter's face and something there made him decide to change tack. "Come on, Sonny, let's see the next page."

"Well, I'm going up to get dressed," said Ethel, shoving Bert lightly and making him get up to let her out. "I'm sure my opinion won't impress Sonny. Nevertheless, I'll give it as usual. I think they're lovely drawings." She squeezed her niece's shoulder and pretended not to notice the cringing under her hand. "They show a good deal of promise."

Ruth prepared breakfast as the two settled into a study of the drawings page by page. Sonata said nothing and Bert said little, only words here and there like balance, proportion, composition, shading, and occasionally drawing to demonstrate. No mention was made of the work itself, of success or failure. Somewhere, Ruth thought, there should be visible the mark of a father with his child: in his words, his expression. He was a teacher with a student, and not an interesting one; a student he was eager to be done with.

But it was not the same with Sonata. The expression of closeness, of wanting the contact to go on forever was unmistakable on her face as she watched the slight quiver of his mouth when he drew and made his infrequent comments, and as she followed his hand making its swift, sure patterns on the page, darkening, blending, coordinating the lines and shadows.

"Excuse me. Sonny, would you like eggs and some toast?"

Sonata looked up. The sour mouth reserved now for Ruth, she set into position. "I ate already."

"I thought you were going shopping today."

"I know. It's pretty obvious you thought I was gone for the day." She turned back to the drawings. "I forgot my charge-plate is all."

"Oh."

Sonata moved her chair closer to the drawings and to her father, serving notice that she was not to be disturbed again and for the next twenty minutes her attention was not diverted: by the clatter as Ruth scrambled eggs, by Ethel's entrance in search of safety pins, by her mother's fussing about as she served Bert his breakfast. Bert and Sonata were allies and Ruth the outsider.

Finally, with nothing more to do Ruth sat opposite them and when Bert's pencil paused, she dared a comment:

"Maybe we ought to send her to art school."

They both looked at her in unison and she felt like a waiter joining the conversation of the guests. Without replying, they returned to the lesson which continued until Bert closed his sketchbook and stacked her papers.

"Keep it up." he said at last.

Sonata nodded. "Can I hold on to your books for a while?" she asked.

"Sure."

"Thanks." She left without a backwards glance at Ruth. They heard the door close in her room, then seconds later it opened and she left out the front door.

"She's serious, Bert," Ruth said, watching through the window as she started the Ford. She had left it on the road; no wonder they hadn't heard her come in before. "Do you think there's any talent there?"

"No."

"Well." Ruth laughed, turning around, "That's an answer." She waited. "We should encourage her to go to art school, I think."

"Forget it. Waste of money, waste of time.' He drank his coffee. "She's making stick figures, that's the whole bit. You were doing better than that the first time you picked up a pencil."

"Maybe I'll go back to painting some day." She sat beside him. "I've been busy with the house, with Sonny, with you. I've never had the time to pursue—"

"Busy with Sonny, me, are you kidding? Listen, if you haven't done anything with it up to now you never will. No drive, that was always your problem, but talent you had."

"So talent's not worth much if you don't do anything with it?"

"Right." At the sink he poured himself a glass of water. "When is Ethel leaving?"

"In about an hour, I guess. Bert, is drive essential?"

"Yes, essential. Drive and energy."

"Do you really need talent then?"

"You're bargaining with me. It's not a car you're buying. You need talent and you need drive because talent doesn't move itself. And drive without talent is a neurosis."

"Well, in terms of Sonny, if a person has a lot of drive, like she seems to have now, couldn't talent be acquired as she goes along?"

"You don't mean talent, you mean technique. Yes, technique could be acquired, talent no."

"Why not?"

"Look, can't you light a fire under your sister's fat ass? Go tell her there's a sale at Bonwit's or something? I've got a painting started in the studio and just having her around here changes the colors in the tubes."

Ruth plugged in the coffeemaker to reheat. "Why couldn't Sonny's talent improve with effort and diligence, I mean, nose to the grindstone and all, the way she's working now?"

"That's still technique you're talking about, not talent." He carried his dishes to the sink. "Talent isn't so much a thing, Ruth. It's a person—mind and soul fused to make a way of seeing that nobody else has. Technique she might pick up, sure. Technique produces and she can learn to produce, but talent sees and nobody can give her that eye. She has to have it on her own. The rest is what I said, energy, drive, sweat. You need the whole works and Sonny doesn't have any of it."

"You're sure?"

"She has an interest in art. You know how many people in this world have an interest in art? Don't think about it. Listen, when Ethel gets her ass out of here, maybe you and I can get together. I'll hold off on the painting. What do you say?"

Ruth hesitated. There seemed so much to put right that wasn't. In the immediate, Sonata had left, taking with her for the day the problem of her future, and Ethel would soon also be gone with her baggage of judgments.

"The bedroom or the studio?" he asked. "Your choice."

But it was Bert's choices that caused chronic hesitation, the ones she knew about and the ones she never wanted to, putting aside the unseen. Bert's passion produced the exquisite work that emerged from his studio. She was a resource for that emergence, the necessary one. Was that her talent or technique . . . or drive? She laughed to herself.

"The studio," she answered finally. "It's been a long time since we've been in the studio."

"It's been a long time altogether."

"Two weeks, not so long." Ruth stopped short, recognizing she'd kept track.

"Yoo hoo, Ruth…I'm leaving."

"Ethel?" At the doorway, Ruth called out. "So fast! You're dressed and packed already?"

"I forgot. The Wiedermans are coming to play cards tonight. I have to pick up a cake and straighten the house. I'm rushing."

"Wait, Ethel, I'll go out to the car with you." She smiled at Bert. "The Wiedermans. What nice people."

PART TWO
VINCENT

1

The sound of the subway train roared on in its labored fatigue, so steadily Vincent ceased to hear it as noise. His thoughts, in contrast, clamored for attention like unruly urchins. He did a lot of serious contemplation in subways, the progression of the train's movement setting thoughts in motion. Outside, the shadowy darkness alternated with sequences of bright light as the express train sped past local stops without stopping. His thinking was itself a kind of subterranean travel, motoring on through the pitch dark, anticipating spotty arrivals of illumination and clarity.

He was vaguely irritated with himself for going to the League today because this morning a persistent idea had come to him that he needed to get away—from models, students, humanity in general. He thought about a train trip to the Laurentian Mountains, figuring on a Thoreau-type closeness to nature—crisp orange, red and bronze-colored October trees to spark his soul. By afternoon though, having gotten busy on painting the alley seen through the lone window of his apartment, he'd forgotten about it. He had to smile at the traffic of his mind of an ordinary day—dreaming of distant mountains and delighting in a dismal alley.

The subway slowed to a stop at the express station and three teenagers burst in like a gust of air. Their tumult subsided as they stood and sprawled on the benches opposite him. He didn't know why he had killed the plan this morning. Inertia, he supposed, but it told him something: He wanted change. Maybe not change of place but approach. Yeah, summoning courage to make *art* out of the self-portrait he was working on at the League. Always so damn cautious.

He was aware of bursts of shrill, half-stifled laughter. Deep into his thoughts, he'd not been conscious of it but now saw the laughter directed at him. Two giggling girls seated across the aisle with books balanced on their laps leaned into each other, a stocky, dark-haired boy beside them. One of the girl's books dropped to the floor and the boy bent to retrieve it, peering as he did at Vincent with a leer that defied his fifteen years.

Vincent realized the kids were seeing upside-down drawings of nude figures. He turned the pad to afford them a better look and added a friendly smirk as the little voyeurs retreated into their books. He stood as the train approached Fifty-Ninth Street, lurching when the train charged into the station without sufficient slowing, pulling to a stop like a startled horse. A cowboy conductor.

On the platform he remembered Kossoff's daughter was coming to talk to him tonight, meeting him up in the cafeteria at his dinner break. Leaving the station, he walked with long-legged strides the cross town blocks to the Art Students League. Catching his profile in a store window, he observed the concave sweep his body made from the tip of his short beard to the point of his loafer. He was aware of the line his body made deciding that as an artist he should have a say in designing what he could of his face, an aesthetic exercise of sorts. The beard made the face longer, the brow stronger with a more pronounced chin. The finished product wasn't anything he'd call handsome but satisfied him.

Entering the lobby of the League he glanced at the wall clock which posted 3:00 and planned his time: Secure a spot for the free early evening life drawing session down the hall, grab a few supplies from the lobby art shop, have his early dinner upstairs and afterwards get in most of the drawing session before he was due to work Kossoff's painting class. He walked through the swinging doors into the first of the two life drawing rooms along the corridor. Selecting a spot with good lighting, he set his stuff on a chair to reserve the place. Returning to the lobby he passed Freddie on break from the afternoon painting class he monitored.

"How ya doin' Vince?" Freddie greeted in his thin vibrating voice, "Coming in my room later?"

"No, my stuff's in the front room already."

Vincent headed toward the art supply store and Freddie fell in beside him, the top of his head coming barely to his shoulder. A dwarf with cavernous, intelligent eyes, Freddie's face had long angular features framed by a neatly cut square beard. With his stern, handsome face compelling your attention and his in-charge demeanor as a monitor, his disfigurement figured as one fact among many.

"Who's posing today?" Vince asked him, "Do you know?"

"Yeah, Juanita is in the back room with me and Irene is up front."

Waiting together at the art supply counter, Vincent thought for a moment. "Ah, Irene, great model. An ex-dancer."

"She hears you say that, she won't like it," said Freddie reproachfully.

"Why not?" Vincent picked up a few fine charcoal sticks and conte crayons to draw with upstairs; he kept materials on hand and one sketch book in case he spotted some interesting face in the crowd to draw. He gave his money to a long-haired youth behind the counter.

"She's not ex, still auditioning," Freddie answered, preceding him out of the shop. "You eating upstairs tonight?"

"Sure."

"Save a place. I'll be up after the painting class."

Pressing the button on the elevator, Vincent felt a tap on his shoulder and twisted around, startled to see his brother. "Howard, what the hell are you doing here?"

"Hey, the door's unlocked, they're open for business," his brother said jauntily. He turned to watch Juanita, wearing a bright flowered shift and silver heels, strut past them. Bracelets cascading down both arms jangled as she passed.

"Don't tell me you came to look at the girls?" Vincent said derisively, following Howard's gaze. "You get enough of that on your own, or don't you?"

"Nothing the matter with looking at the girls. Especially where they run around half naked."

"Why'd you come down here, Howard?"

"Listen, can we have a drink some place?"

"I haven't got the time."

"Why not? Where you heading now?"

"I'm going upstairs to grab a bite, then I come down to draw somebody like that woman you're leering at, then I set up the painting class. Same damn thing for two years, you should know the routine."

"I don't keep track of you. Hell, do you know what I do? And I'm at it longer." His eyes were on Juanita bending over the water fountain. "You have more fun though, looks like."

His brother, tall, good-looking and solidly sure of his capabilities, displayed an authority so melded with charisma he looked like a Senator, someone you'd choose to lead you. Their stepfather exuded pride in him and why not? His right hand in business and everything a man should be. A son in his own image.

The elevator came. "You can come up to the cafeteria and we can talk," Vince said reflexively.

"Good, I'll do that," he responded quickly, riding with Vince to the third floor."

Howard was only two years older but from childhood, Vincent felt him looming over him invading his thoughts and actions. With their stepfather's approval of what he did and society's praise for what he was—a handsome face, a commendable size and a business success— his brother was a well-rounded pain in the ass.

2

In the cafeteria, the sandwich, hamburger and omelet dinners were in full swing with all tables taken. Vincent and Howard got on line as Freddie came through the door, sketch pad and a stack of pen and ink drawings under his arm.

"Freddie is monitor of a painting class here and one of the early evening sketch classes," Vincent said, introducing them. "Important person and a damn fine artist."

"A schnook," Freddie elaborated, "like your brother Vince here, who is also a schnook. Monitors take crap in exchange for studio space to work. I've got all next week to go with this Juanita and I'm already medicating migraines. Jesus!"

"You'll have a few cups of coffee and feel better. Relax. Round one is over."

"Vince, I'm telling you, she's the greatest model and the biggest bitch to work with!"

Standing next to Howard, Freddie looked even smaller, yet Howard appeared awed by the guy and attentive to every word. The little man had put his imposing brother off his course.

"I'll get on line," said Freddie, "You and what's-his-name keep your eyes open for a table. Here, take my stuff."

Throughout the cluttered room, students crowded the tables, sitting, standing and sprawling about them, tipping chairs at oblique angles while their voices from all corners set a chaotic din.

"Informal dining at its finest, isn't it?" Howard observed.

Near a section marked *For Models Only* a girl holding a thick comb groomed a man's sternum-length graying beard as he leaned against a table talking to someone else.

"Hey, grab that table!" Freddie yelled from the end of the line as the man dispatched his groomer and got up to leave.

Vincent laughed. Freddie had a strong set of pipes.

"What'll you have?" Vince asked his brother when they were seated.

"Just coffee." Howard reached in his pocket for change but Vincent waved him off.

"Stay and hold the table and don't let anybody steal the chairs." Howard put a Johnston & Murphy foot on each chair base as Vincent left to join Freddie. The line moved quickly since half the cash-strapped crowd took only coffee or soup.

"The same, Freddie, eh?" Chico, the efficient all-in-one chef, food dispenser and cashier sang in a shrill clipped voice, already buttering bread and laying on the sliced cheese.

"Sure. You got something cheaper let me know."

Chico smiled showing empty spaces in a row of teeth that looked too big for his face.

"I'll have tuna on a roll, Chico," Vincent said, "and three coffees."

They carried the trays to the table and sat down. Juanita had arrived while they were on line and seated herself at the model's table with some others. When she saw Freddie she called across the table.

"Well hi, Frederick. Come over here, honey. I've got something to tell you."

"I got nothin' to say to you, doll." He winked at Vincent.

"Oh, come on, darlin'. Bring your cheese thing and sit down with us. I've got news for you, man."

"Juanita, baby, I get indigestion very easy. I'm a sick man."

"Go on," Vincent prodded, "you've got all next week with her. You better start building some interpersonal relations."

"Five days, my God, I'll be an old man." He took a long sip of coffee and turned stiffly in his seat, giving Juanita an indulgent smile, "You beast," he mumbled under his breath, getting up. He sighed. "Vince, I'm tellin' you the truth, I have made full canvases of that broad that were the greatest things I ever did. It's the color. The goddamn tones are terrific! And the body? A-1 perfect, but Christ!" He sighed again and took another fortifying sip of coffee.

Juanita sat smiling with legs crossed, arms folded, smoking in preference to eating.

"Thinks she's the Queen of Sheba around here," Freddie moaned. "Gives me the rear view all afternoon in the painting studio and now she wants me to wrestle the front room away from the ballet dancer there for the life class comin' up. That's what she's gonna nudge me about."

"Well, go over and explain—"

"Yeah, explain, you got a case there. What, you think she knows how to listen with those hangers for the earrings? A one-way English she picked up in Cuba."

When Freddie had transferred himself to the adjacent table Howard moved in closer to Vince. "Say, Vinnie," he began in a serious, confidential tone, "Tell me, what it's like, drawing a naked girl?" His eyes took in the model's table where two young women in robes and slippers sat sipping coffee next to Juanita.

"What?"

"Well, I mean, do you get kicks from it—you know?"

Vincent bit into his sandwich. He had no intention of adding to Howard's entertainment.

"You remember that doctor? You know, the guy who did an autopsy on his cousin? He used to live near us in the Bronx. Everybody thought he was a weirdo when he did that autopsy, you remember? The kids played tricks on him, threw stones at his house, treated him like regular Bluebeard. I did too. Then Mom told us his total approach was scientific, that he never thought of the cousin as a relative. Just a body, you know what I mean? No feeling in it. A body."

"Yeah." Vincent nodded, remembering all too well how he'd thought about it later. How a man could separate things that efficiently—taking a knife to a body so well recognized in life. Living, the cousin was a relative; dead, she was a medical question. But how strong-willed, even arrogant not to entrust the deed to others. "I remember, what about it?"

"Well, when you look at a woman, do you separate your art and your libido? I mean, do you feel like grabbing a piece or is drawing it all you want?"

Vincent knew his brother was not stupid. He had a sharp mind, alert in business as in everything, but he liked setting up intellectual distance between them, Vincent the brainy one and Howard, the all-around kid.

"Yeah, drawing it is all I want," he answered flatly. He bit into his sandwich and turned his attention away from Howard to his coffee. The truth was he *wanted* to explain. With his blunt invasions, Howard was like an overgrown bull ramming into his thoughts, upturning the well-ordered arrangements in his mind and leaving him to stack them up again. It wasn't bad to give the place an airing out, but the clutter that built up between them made it hard to get through to each other.

"Sorry, forget it," Howard said. "Not being in the business—" He waved an arm to encompass the room, the students—"I know nothing about this stuff."

"Well, I don't mind you asking, it's just the question's not easy to answer." Vincent was treading his way with his brother, as usual, like walking barefoot on a pebbled road. "I react as an artist to a woman's body when I'm drawing or painting—what I want from her at that moment. Does that make me less a man, I mean by not getting horny? I don't know."

Howard nodded. For several moments he said nothing. "To tell the truth, I envy you," he said after a while, "To be an artist, work for yourself, make your own bargains, do what the hell you want."

"You're your own boss, Howard."

"But the business is what I'm boss of. That's what makes the ground rules, sets the pace, tallies the score. You *are* the business. Spend your day working from the inside and pushing out. Me, I gotta get pushed from outside to react. Then I'm mad at myself for screwing up or jock-happy with some stupid success. It should be the other way around like with you."

"No, you don't want what I struggle with." Vincent said pensively. "You get more satisfactions from the outside world than I'll get in a lifetime. Little victories—sales, promotions, new ventures coming down the pike. The world has prizes for you in every pocket, even with the setbacks.

"What's on my side? Recognition is rare, money's hard to come by, and even if—praise God—you become successful, you can still feel a failure. Your vision is light years ahead of your ability to produce the damn images, so you never can conclude you've done what you set out to do. It's like Sisyphus with the stone rolling downhill every time he hauls it up."

"Who's Sissy Foot?"

"Forget it. What I mean is your motivation to keep going has to come from within you. So what's in there to keep it generating? Okay, I'll tell you." Were they communicating or was it only himself he was talking to? It didn't matter; he couldn't stop now. "It's your hang-ups, that's the generator—it's your neurosis, your groaning soul." He laughed without mirth, glanced at Howard extracting a cigarette, and motored on. "It's like the irritation inside the oyster that makes it produce a pearl, only there's no guarantee you'll produce a pearl. Only the irritation is guaranteed." He laughed again. "The irritation makes you move though, that's the thing."

Howard held out a cigarette. Vincent rarely smoked but he took the cigarette. Howard lit them both. "A groaning soul, huh? I like that."

Vincent shrugged. "Well, or like a jockey with a whip and steel spurs driving his horse to the finish line. But the finish line is moving too in art, all the time. It's damned hard to win."

The last time they had talked this way had been back in high school after Howard had gotten beaten up for taking out another guy's girl. Vincent had sat on the side of the bed then listening to Howard, his eyes purple and swollen, a blood-stained bandage around his head, while he told him how Tony D'Angelo vowed he'd wait outside the hotel where the dance was going on and if Howard came through the door with his girl, he'd give it to him. Sure enough, Tony stood there breathing fire and Howard almost lost an eye. Vincent had loved him in those moments. Admired him for his bravery but loved him for treating his kid brother as a friend.

"So that's what keeps you going?" Howard said. "The art life looked better downstairs with that model pitching her boobs over the drinking fountain. I'm kidding."

Vincent noticed that Howard had tilted his chair back, looking for all the world like he belonged here. He tried to put that impression aside to focus on the fact of the conversation, meeting his brother under the canopy of an idea. "Look at it another way," Vincent began, fearing he might already have lost him. "You're a golfer and you see guys out there slugging away at the ball every chance they get to better their score. They're competing against themselves and it's like that with an artist too but there's a big difference."

Howard nodded, alternately looking at him and eye-shopping the room.

"That guy like the golfer needs to see what he's got," Vincent continued, "but there is no par. He has to keep experimenting to find out what's in him that compels him to create his art. And when he's in doubt, which is pretty much always, there isn't a soul in the world who can help him."

Oh, for god's sake, so much more to tell about this hypothetical artist who is his miserable, pathetic self. He wanted to explain to Howard that when a canvas that took months to make is shit, that artist is nothing, said nothing. But when he produces something that comes even close to the images spinning in that artist's head he can look himself in the mirror because he exists. Then it's like underscoring a phrase in a book that makes you understand the whole damn thing, except you made that phrase yourself and it's for the world to underscore.

"You know I like this place," Howard said, rocking on the back legs of his chair. "The noise settles in after a while. Coffee's lousy but the atmosphere's cool." He surveyed the far corners of the room. "Say, I think somebody's looking at you over there—by the door."

Sonata had entered the cafeteria searching the tables. When she caught Vincent's eye she brightened and made her way towards his table. She wore jeans and a man-tailored shirt with a CPO jacket slung over her shoulders.

"Hi," she said, a little breathlessly, looking between Vincent and Howard and then glancing around the loud, lively room filled to capacity. She smiled awkwardly. "Well, I'm here."

"So I see. Here, sit down." Vincent pulled the chair Freddie had vacated closer to the table. He took a deep breath and exhaled it, releasing with it a sense of shame from having talked too much. "Sonata, this is my brother, Howard."

Howard nodded, appraising her, then standing, he asked, "You want some coffee?"

"No, no thanks," she said, sitting down. "Please call me Sonny."

"Sonny, okay. That goes down easy. Sure you don't want something? Tea, milk? What else they have here, Vinnie?"

"Nothing at all, thank you," she repeated and turned to Vincent. "I couldn't get those studio numbers and I wasn't able to contact anybody at all on your list. You remember," she added when he looked bewildered, "about my Dad's tribute?"

"Oh, sure, the tribute," he said, nodding. "Okay. Hang around, we'll make a quick tour and I'll show you where to go."

"I was hoping you'd say that," she said, heaving her shoulders and folding her hands. "I really appreciate what you're doing for me. You're so busy—he's monitor of the class," she explained to Howard, "My father's life painting class."

"Yeah, Vincent's an important fellow around here," Howard acknowledged.

"My father is Bert Kossoff," she explained. "the painter?"

"He won't be in till late," he said. "Anyway, I'll meet you in the art store downstairs, he never goes in there."

"I'm so happy you're helping me, Vince. Honestly, I wouldn't know how to begin without you. My father is lucky to have you as the assistant in his class." She addressed herself again to Howard. "Are you also an artist?"

"He's in men's clothing," Vincent contributed.

"But she can see that for herself, isn't that so, what's your name again?"

"Sonata Kossoff. Sonny."

"Ah! Bert Kossoff's daughter!"

Sonata smiled warily and settled back in her chair. For several seconds no one spoke. Then: "What do you do, manufacture or sell? Do you have a store or something?"

"I have a store, yes, and that reminds me why I came here today, Vinnie. Never got around to telling you."

"No, you never did."

"I tried calling you today, but you had blown and Mom gave me orders to touch base with you before I leave tonight."

"Where you going?"

"Boston. We're setting up a new branch. I'll be based there for a while, well, as long as it takes. You know Pop's been negotiating for an outlet up there and finally got it. The place needs renovation, but he got a good price and he's sending me to get it rolling."

"I never even heard about it."

"Well, you heard but weren't listening. Business, finance, goods, it's another language. Hey, I understand."

"But I spoke to Pete and Mom too on the phone yesterday and neither one said anything. Strange, they didn't mention a big move like this."

"Not strange. Pop talks with me because I'm in the business and Mom talks *art* with you. She's not interested either except the business pays the rent and keeps you painting."

He turned to Sonata: "Our mother would take a brush and help this guy paint if he'd let her."

Sonata stared at him blankly, avoiding Vincent's eyes.

"Pete's our stepfather," Howard explained. "He and I make what you'd call green while Vince and Mom make rainbows. That right, Vinnie?"

Vincent focused his attention on some crumbs on the tabletop. He brushed them to the floor. Howard leaned back again, tipping the chair so far Vincent almost willed it to slide out from under him sending Pete's protégé sprawling.

"Speaking of clothes, how do you like what they wear around this place? You could wallpaper a circus tent with these colors."

"I like color," Sonata said cheerfully, sounding relieved for the change of subject. "I think clothes should be colorful—and fun, don't you?"

"Sure, why not?"

The crowd had thinned but a few dozen people remained to talk and smoke at the tables. Freddie waved to them and left some time ago with Juanita and the other models.

"Do you think clothes make the man, Sonny?" Howard asked, pursing his lips and touching a finger to them pensively.

"I don't know what you mean?"

"Well, does a man buy clothes to fit his personality or for contrast, to—say hide behind?" He tilted his body towards her and waited for an answer, as if her response would decide the next direction of his marketing strategy.

"It depends if he likes himself, I suppose. What do you think? You're in the business."

"Well, I don't know."

Sonata shrugged. "I think it's probably a little of both."

"How so?"

Howard kept his eyes on her, a moon-struck quality to the smile and the tilt of his head. Vincent had seen that look before when they double-dated in high school; it was sophomoric now as then, but Sonny Kossoff seemed to take it as custom-made for her. Big moon-struck eyes and small talk were Howard's specialty. Still, Vincent admired the ease with which his brother could steer a casual friendship and guide its run on patter, something unattainable for him.

"A man has a vague image of what he looks like," Sonata volunteered, "I mean, eye-sharp in the mirror but vague in his mind and he compares that with what he wants to look like—well, from ads and movies I guess—and one image gets superimposed on the other and there you have it: Taste. With that squiggly picture in his head he trots off to your store and buys himself a suit. I think that's essentially what happens when a man picks his clothes."

Vincent studied her, determining if she had anything substantial upstairs. She had seemed too shy to be such a talker, but Howard brought her out with his tell-it-to-me cue lines. Still, her face had a quiet look with smooth skin and calm dark eyes. Those eyes hooded by her dark eyebrows kind of gave weight to her words. Her mouth was small; big talkers usually had bigger mouths. Once or twice they each looked at him for assent or some other contribution to afford him functional presence.

"Clothes are a parade, really," Sonata said, elaborating. "Everybody marching around, winking at the judges to get the prize for individuality."

"Attention from the grandstands," Howard added. "Sure, you got it."

Suddenly, Vincent had enough and simply being at the table grated on his nerves. He glanced at the wall clock. The black and white clock was mounted above a large rear view nude draped in Titianesque reds. If he left now, he could make the mid-point of the daily sketch session and save something of this lost hour. He opened his sketch pad, ripped out a blank page, and leaning on the table, began writing.

"I have to go," he said, interrupting Sonata in the middle of a sentence, "I haven't got time to take you around like I said—well, it was a bad idea—but I'm drawing you a map of the instructors' rooms, the ones we talked about. You shouldn't have any trouble. You need me again, I'm usually up in that same studio you found me last time, same schedule."

Sonata nodded uncertainly, but before she could ask questions, Howard tapped her shoulder.

"Did you see his drawings? Look at these, Sonny. Hey, you're good, Vinnie!" He flipped pages of the sketchbook, holding it on his lap so that Vincent had to reach across the table to take it from him. A page tore and a fragment of paper fell on the floor. "You never showed me your sketches before—"

"I didn't show you now," he scowled, dropping the directions for Sonata he'd been preparing.

"Because you think it's over my head?" Howard sneered.

Vincent picked up the scrap of paper. There was more his brother wanted to say, Vincent knew, but it was too late, years too late.

"That's okay, never mind," Howard stated. "Go ahead and give her your map. We don't want to keep you from your class. You're a monitor!"

Vincent winced, swallowing the asshole retort his mouth urged him to make. Instead, he pushed into Sonata's hand the paper which she took without looking at it, her eyes fixed on him.

"That's all I need, Vince," Sonata mumbled. "I mean, the instructors' names and where to find them when I have the printed invitations. Thank you," she added.

Vincent nodded, producing what he hoped passed for a smile while collecting his dinner trash. "When is this shindig again?"

"December 12th, it's on a Friday. I thought people could come right from the League."

Vincent was about to question the logistics—the whole senseless thing—when he spotted Howard removing a little black book from his pocket.

"Look, I'd like to continue our discussion some other time," Howard said, standing and turning his broad shoulders toward Sonata. "Could I take your phone number and buzz you next time I'm in town?" He smiled. "I'd like to do that."

Flustered, Sonata looked at Vincent like a deer in the clearing hearing danger and choosing to leap into the woods or stay where the grass was fresh and green.

But Vincent left without waiting for that decision.

•   •   •

Vince heard the familiar scuffing of Irene's slippers before she returned to the model's stand. Helen's voice was thrown into the room like a referee's ball calling for a new game.

"The twenty-five minute pose," she announced. "Pose, please, honey."

Damn, he'd missed an hour of the session already. His drawing materials remained at the spot he'd left them. Students were courteous about it, grateful to have the daily life drawing sessions at all—free access for anyone enrolled in a regular class. Well, he'd accomplished something with Kossoff's daughter, or at least she seemed satisfied.

Irene had assumed a seated pose presenting him with an interesting foreshortening of her legs. He liked the challenge and for the next twenty minutes got into it. Looking up to grab more detail on the face—he loved drawing Irene's features, girlish with freckles, though she had to be late thirties—when he felt someone's eyes on him. Goddamnit! There was Howard standing in the doorway.

Howard nodded, a solicitous, head-waiter kind of nod, then ceremoniously removed a small black pad from his pocket, the one in which he'd inscribed Sonata's phone number. Gazing at Irene with squinted eyes, he proceeded to wave a pen over the thing. Enraged, Vincent could predict Howard telling his guys at the store: *What an eyeful! All you need is a pad and pen!* Vincent closed his sketchbook and put down his pencils. He watched his brother as he leaned against the door frame. The monitor was engrossed in her own picture or she'd have sent him packing. Helen could spot that look a mile away.

Howard began making pensive, cow-like movements with his mouth and stretching his thumb out towards Irene and back against his nose as if to measure some relationship. It was a cartoon, but Vincent wasn't laughing. Leaving his drawing supplies, he tiptoed out of the hushed room.

In the hall Howard avoided looking at his brother, instead lighting a cigarette and searching about for a place to drop the match. Furious, Vincent followed him into the lobby.

"You know it's totally crappy to do what you did. Horrible to the models at the very least, let alone making a mockery of—"

"Thanks for the lecture. Oh, and thanks for introducing me to the Kossoff girl. I'll probably be seeing her again."

He smiled over his shoulder, as with a flourish, he dropped the match into an ashtray. "See, I always know how to do the right thing."

Vincent opened his mouth to speak, but Howard had already advanced to the vestibule. There he pushed through the wide doors and was gone.

3

Vincent was late and the painting class underway when he stepped inside. He was never late. Why he had let Howard get to him, foolishly starting to traipse after him to admonish some more, was no surprise but allowing that girl to change his schedule and be late for the drawing session was another matter.

Paul Dobrin nodded to him that everything was under control.

"Thanks...Sorry." Paul was better than he at helping students, far more patient. Vincent rolled his sleeves, moved an easel into place and brought his painting and materials from the back room. Everyone around him seemed busy working, not needing anything from him, so he assembled his palette and brushes and stood comparing the model and his work.

Today was the mid-point of Bruce Polachek's pose on the stand. A youth of eighteen or so with a bushy head of dusty blond hair and a hairy chest, he stood about 5 foot 7 and compensated for his modest height by developing an impressive network of muscles. He had taken a pose in front of a T-pole with his muscular arms draped over the top like a crucified Christ, a jock strap covering his groin. Paul warned him the pose would be difficult to maintain for the two- week project; however, Bruce seemed reluctant to hide any portion of his grandeur from the students. Quite possibly a chance to show his capacity for suffering was also not to be missed, though that alone played havoc with the students' paintings because his body shifted. Thus, the pose changed from one moment to the next.

Vincent began to paint in small careful strokes, increasingly disappointed with his colors which were too fresh, too cold. They lacked subtlety and the shadows were too much one hue. He had used no imagination to treat the shadows in Bruce's playful muscles. Bruce would love it, but it wasn't art. *The artist has left the room.*

At the break, Bruce stepped down from the stand and fastened his robe like a winning prizefighter leaving the ring. He bounced gingerly around the room looking eagerly from canvas to canvas, grateful for everything he saw and afire with the spirit of generosity that comes from giving what you want to be taken. "Gee, do I really look like that?" and "Christ, you're good!" His remarks were followed by an apathy thick as fog, but Bruce stepped right through it.

As Vincent walked out into the hall for a stretch, joining some others, Bert Kossoff walked past him into the room and whatever conversation had been going on quickly shifted.

"He's here early today," Paul Dobrin observed, "The class is only half over."

"It's a sacrifice he's making already," said Dave Sudak, "leaving his studio for a couple hours to give us the benefit of his wisdom." Dave was a thirty-year-old graphics convert married to the League's bookkeeper, who supported him.

"Considering he gets paid for three hours of wisdom twice a week, I think he's crap," offered Ted Riley. Ted was the heartthrob of the class, a tall, good looking, fast-moving artist whose abstract paintings had already been accepted in some national shows.

"You're just sore because the real juice he's not sharing, like how he collects his snatch," said Dave. "Listen, he's a busy man and first things first."

"Busy painting don't forget" said Paul Dobrin. "And the more I see the more I like. It gets to you after a while. You can close your eyes and still see the colors."

"Who wants to see the colors?" said Ted Riley, shielding his face with the back of his hand as if Dobrin's remark could scar him. "When I close my eyes, it's Riley I want to see and if Kossoff ever gets under my skin, I'll throw in the towel."

"Yeah but his style can get under your skin—it's why I chose him," Paul remarked. "You don't get that with anyone else teaching here."

"Except sharing is not part of that style. The guy's not much of a teacher." Ted grinned. "Which is why I love him. Leaves me alone and doesn't get in my way."

Dave sighed. "T G I F," he moaned. "I don't know if I could take Spruced Bruce for another week. You need an easel on wheels to keep sights on him."

"Who's booked next?" Paul asked. "You know, Vince?"

Vincent shook his head. Bruce was on the stand again and the men moved inside. Vincent was not particularly friendly with the members of the class. The only persons with whom he had exchanged words of any import were Kossoff and Paul Dobrin. Paul had been in the class for three years, a serious painter just beginning to develop his own style.

Paul had just been awarded a year-long merit scholarship that gave him access to this class, which he used as a studio. He rarely even looked at the models. Paul's wife had left him for a lover, taking the kid he was crazy about to live half a continent away. He was always showing around pictures of that kid, six or seven, not so much cute as elf-like with mischief in his eyes. But Paul hadn't the money to fly out to see him.

Vincent wanted to get to know Paul better but the opportunity never seemed there. He was a man at ease with himself. He had dark sensitive eyes that looked at you without judgment. A listener, always suspecting there was more to learn from any person, any time or place. Paul was optimistic about the kid. They were writing back and forth and sending painted pictures, not photographs.

Vincent spent the rest of the evening working at his painting, annoyed that he hadn't the conviction to destroy it. He wondered if he would have fared any better monitoring another class but he sensed it would be the same. He knew the score with Kossoff and so did Paul and Dave and Ted and most of the other serious students. They knew what their problems were and wanted an affordable space to be left alone to work them out with a model on hand, which made Kossoff's class a good choice. Except for them, the class had frequent turnover.

Beginners stayed for about a year. Attracted to the instructor's unique style of painting in choosing the class, it took them that long to realize they weren't getting his instruction.

Vincent watched Kossoff circulate around the room. He was tall and built well with a face that seemed to belong on another body. From the rear he looked like an Adonis—slim hips, broad shoulders and a full head of dark hair any man would envy—but when he turned, the face was too long, the features too broad.

His painting was a different matter; that had a consistent effect no matter which way you looked at it. The colors were blazing and the textures thick: paints mixed and applied with palette knives in projectile peaks, fabric and any other stuff that caught his eye, all layered on with a stellar intuition for placement.

Poor Bruce. His biceps twitched helplessly while he still tried to keep his chest out and look great. He'd learn eventually that nobody gave a crap for his bulges. Bruce knew so little of what artists needed from him. If he wanted to keep his job he'd have to stop equating his fine nude body with being the best dressed man in town. At least while he was on the stand.

Kossoff approached the new girl who was hard at work next to Vincent. She stopped painting and waited expectantly. He looked from her painting to the model and back again several times. "Any problems?" he asked finally, smiling cordially. It seemed more a greeting than a query, but she merely shrugged and shook her head.

"You have no bones in that hand," he volunteered after a moment. "Look." He sketched the position of the hand quickly and expertly on a piece of scrap paper, indicating with swift bold strokes the phalanges, the metacarpal heads, the wrist and a fragment of forearm. Then he smiled again and sauntered off to another student.

Nothing about application of paint, control of space, color, depth, nothing about any of the problems of picture making. No bones in the hand, Christ! Okay for a class in anatomy, but for a new student, it's like ninety-eighth on the list.

Vincent suspected dimly that his anger at Kossoff was fueled by his own frustration. He continued to paint, persevering rather than creating. He abstracted the genitals as he did other forms ignoring

Bruce's jock strap. Bruce's muscular anatomy lent itself to abstraction. Ted, working across from him, had a field day, making pure geometric patterns of the muscular formations.

"I'm finished," Vincent mumbled to himself toward the end of the session. He set about cleaning his palette and brushes and placed the materials in his locker. He nodded to Paul on his way out.

·   ·   ·

The following Thursday was the final session of Bruce on the stand. Vincent labored at finishing his painting. He was annoyed that he lacked the courage to destroy it and more angry than sympathetic for Bruce.

At the end of the session, Bruce jauntily stepped off the platform and stopped by each students' picture on his way to the changing room.

"I like it," he pronounced, eyeing Vincent's abstraction.

"Thanks, Bruce. Take care now." Vincent thought about dispensing a word of advice, a little modeling 101 but figured it wouldn't make a difference.

The studio had emptied and he was tidying up when Sonata Kossoff poked her head through the door.

"Hi," she called. She appeared hesitant about coming in.

Vincent smiled. She looked different, her curly hair pulled back in a tie.

"I hope I'm not bothering you. I just wanted to give you the printed invitations, you know, to give out to the students. My father's students," she added following Vincent's blank stare.

"Oh sure. Come on in," he muttered, though she had already crossed the threshold, taking his smile as welcome. He hadn't been welcoming, his focus on the dour prospect of taking his painting home and having to look at Bruce forever until he got around to chucking him. Only the thought of having wasted so much time stopped him from doing it now.

"I have a bundle of invitations right here. But most people might not want to travel out to Forest Hills." She handed him the stack.

"I don't know about that. "Everyone enjoys a party—free food and drink—they probably will come." He laughed. He recognized the odd sensation, like his face cracking. The thought made him laugh again and this time she joined him.

"Well, there will be food and drink, lots of it. And you were so helpful with the names of instructors. I left a printed invitation with each one and told them to invite spouses if they wanted. They seemed receptive. I don't know, we'll see."

Vincent nodded. "Yeah, we'll find out." He doubted Kossoff had much currency with other instructors at the league. He went his own way like they did, coming in to teach their courses and back to their easels, hardly ever meeting. But the food and drink thing was appealing and mixing it up with colleagues was good for getting their names out there. Artists were always searching out exhibition venues. Still— "You're sure you want to do this? I mean, it's a lot of effort."

"You sound like my Mom. But yes, I do. My father deserves to be recognized. He's a wonderful painter…and teacher."

Vincent's snide laugh slid out again though he tried to catch it. He quickly added, "Anything else you want me to do?" Talking about Kossoff put him in the mindset to head home. "I'll hand out these invites next class."

"I found gallery notices of my dad's exhibitions—my mom saved these—and I'm going around to personally hand the directors an invitation."

"That works. Okay, you're off to a good start." He picked up the wrapping paper he'd left next to Bruce. Fortunately, the miserable picture was facing the wall.

"Only one more thing. Will you agree to make that painting?" she asked, "you know, for the top of his cake?"

"We have to talk about that," he demurred. "Not exactly in my job description."

She smiled. "You're funny," she said as she turned to leave, smiling again at the door.

•   •   •

Taking the subway downtown, Vincent got off at Sheridan Square and walked the six blocks to his apartment on East Eighth street. Setting Bruce in his wrapping on the cracked linoleum floor of the landing he found his key among grocery receipts in his back pocket collected for Alexandra though his mother never asked to see them.

The apartment on the top floor of a four-story walk-up wasn't much: a single room furnished with a cot, bookcase and assorted tables and chairs. There was a bathroom with a stall shower just wide enough if he gained no weight and a Pullman kitchen that appeared and disappeared via a Masonite partition that slid reluctantly in its track. Paintings covered almost every inch of wall space and leaning against the walls were others without screw eyes or wire waiting for space to inhabit. The apartment had only one window which faced the inner courtyard of the building. Natural light was inadequate for painting but Vincent invested heavily in artificial light when he took the apartment eleven months ago. Brushes stood like blooming flowers in coffee tins by the window and the apartment smelled of linseed oil and turpentine.

He unwrapped Bruce and with a narrow brush and a scowl signed his name in the lower right-hand corner, remembering times he'd found pleasure in the ritual. Taking a beer from the refrigerator he crossed to the cot and dropped down on it to study the damn painting. The wet acrylic signature caught the light from the lamp and glistened, the only sense of life in the picture.

The phone rang. Howard, in from Boston wanting to get together.

"I'm here for a couple days. Take you out for some drinks? How about it?"

"No, I've got too much to take care of, Howard, but thanks."

"My treat, Bro, you sure?"

"I'm sure. How long are you in for?"

"Only through the weekend. I have meetings with some buyers. Should I give you a call before I leave?"

"Do that. We'll try to hook up."

"Okay, kid, I'll see you."

The word "kid" was as offensive as ever. He was two years younger than Howard, hardly grounds for kid brotherhood at this stage, particularly since there were times when he felt more like his father.

He poured another beer, careless about the thickness of the head and it spilled over his wrist. Howard wanted to hit a few bars with him, 'his treat.' What Howard liked was waving his happy-go-lucky at him like a home-team banner, showing his misguided brother how to live and enjoy. Well, he couldn't argue with the premise: Vincent living in solitude and introspection, guarding his only possession—his so called talent. What more perfect subject for a missionary of fun?

Howard often tried to convert him from heavy and hard-on-himself to light and easy. He remembered the summer during high school when they worked on a farm outside Albany. Howard's friends Matt and Buff Janis arranged for it with their uncle. It was a miserable summer. The work was dogged and he hadn't the stamina for it let alone interest. They planted stuff, picked stuff and fixed things. Everything broke at one time or another: the silo, animal pens, barn, tools and nothing stayed intact even after they'd fixed it. But Howard and the Janis boys took it in stride. They had a vigorous camaraderie whether working or horsing around and Vincent never learned the language. His relationship with all three of them was as labored as the exertion expended to get through the day. Why it was important for him to do whatever Howard did, he didn't know. He should have outgrown that attitude in grammar school. He'd painted a pretty nice picture of the farmhouse and grazing field to show his accomplishments, which only served to established him as a goof-off.

Returning to the cot with a bag of pistachio nuts, he sat back, enjoying the crunch and the mindless repetition as he worked the salty nuts loose and tossed their shells into an ashtray. His eyes traveled the walls—nudes, cityscapes, semi-abstracts, and the one unfinished seascape that Alexandra liked so much. He should finish it and present it as a birthday present. Or maybe the new painting of Bruce. His ornery step father deserved to have Bruce on his wall. Crunching his nuts, he looked at the walls as they looked back and wondered if his name was already signed forever in some lower right-hand corner. Finito. That's all folks. Toast.

Howard called him late in the day on Sunday.

"Hey, little brother, calling to touch base. It worked out fine, you not going with me."

"Oh,?"

"Right. I called that lady with the cute name, Sonata. I took her out to dinner. We had a fine time," he added.

Vincent questioned why this news upset him, the information oddly like a painting he couldn't fix, crowded with things that didn't belong in one picture, shapes colliding.

"What do you mean 'fine time'"? he asked.

"No, nothing like that. Enjoyed her company. She's a nice girl."

"Yeah, she is," he agreed. "By the way, if you're seeing her again, tell her I can't make that thing for the cake she wanted."

"Tell her what?"

"The cake thing. She'll know."

"Well, whatever that means, you'll have to tell her yourself. I'm on my way."

"Okay, Howard. Call when you come in next time."

"Will do. I'll see you, kid. Take care."

4

Sonata had butterflies as she stopped work to visualize for the hundredth time the party for her father in progress. She imagined the guests looking up as Bert Kossoff opened the door and stood on the threshold. She wondered what his first thoughts would be when he saw them here in his home to honor him: a sea of smiling faces, people whom he liked and respected, as they liked and respected him.

Wheeling her cart along the library stacks, she had trouble focusing on the book bindings to read and stack the right numbers. All she had thought about these past weeks was the tribute. Notes to herself, reminders about what to do and what to get and whom to call were all over the bedroom and even in her cubby here at the library.

Ruth was as unconvinced as ever about having the party, but at least she agreed to go along with it. Vince, she could sense, dismissed any reason for a Kossoff tribute. Several times he'd asked one way or another why she wanted to do it. He also expressed surprise about the number of people coming. But he did admit that instructors like a chance to get together, though probably didn't know students were invited. Vince was so serious, but he could be funny. She liked him both ways.

She bit her lip and leaned against the stacks causing a couple of books to tumble to the floor. Poor Howard Denfield must have been bored to death hearing her talking about the tribute the night they dated. But there were not many people she could talk to and still keep it a surprise. Retrieving the books and squeezing them back in, she recalled how interested he seemed. He had no trouble understanding why she wanted to make the party. He didn't need to ask the kind of questions Vince did. So interested, she almost asked him to come. It was on the tip of her tongue—*if you you're in town why not stop in?*—but something stopped her. A loyalty to his brother? No, not that. He just didn't belong in a tribute for Dad. Vince would come, of course.

They talked about Vincent that night. Howard complained about not having his brother's artistic talent. They were sitting indoors under an arbor at Enrico and Paglieri's waiting for antipasto, pretending, she supposed, that it was spring and not mid-November. They occupied a table in a garden setting with live foliage and flowers and a fountain in the center, charming but chilly, and Sonata joked that this was carrying the atmosphere too far. Howard laughed and gave her his jacket to put on.

"Drawing the figure is fun, you should try it some time. I sketch in my room some evenings, but I have my father's drawings to learn from."

"I could have Vincent's drawings," he said and they laughed over that, the poor relations getting the leftovers.

The brothers did not get along too well, she could see that, and were very different. Vincent was quieter, almost morose, and Howard was the opposite, too glib. She didn't really like either of them when they were with each other.

"I always wanted to draw or paint or do something with my hands, something constructive," Howard said mistily. "That's a confession."

"Not me. I never wanted to until recently, but if you feel that way you should do something about it."

"No, it's too late, the die is cast. I'll be in men's clothes when they bury me."

She laughed. After that they fell into talk about the progress of the Boston store. The antipasto came and then the veal Marsala and finally the rum cake. And after Enrico's they taxied to The Upstairs at the Downstairs or The Downstairs at the Upstairs, she forgot which, and after some drinks and listening to the music, he took her home.

At the door she let him kiss her, but when he asked to be invited in, she said no. He urged a little but accepted it. They parted with a pleasant glow because it had been a nice evening all around.

And yes, she said. "I would see you again."

PART THREE
IRENE

1

Irene ascended the marble stairs outside the Art Students League and hurried through the large double doors into the lobby, glad to get in from a chilly October wind.

In the office she found Helen and Freddie, monitors for one of the two sketch classes she was booked for. "Hi there, honey, you in my room this week?" Helen greeted her. "Freddie and I just waiting for Bess to come back from dinner."

"I hope it's your room," Irene said, setting down the satchel carrying her robe and slippers. Helen, coal-skinned, soft spoken and so thin bony ridges poked through cheeks and clavicles, was about the calmest woman Irene had ever known. She'd monitored the daily sketch classes and the testy models posing in them for upwards of twenty years. Irene had never seen her in anything but the battered gray smock she wore now, her hair tightly drawn into a thin bun.

"Oh, no offense, Freddie. I mean about wanting the front room," Irene added.

Freddie shrugged. "No offense taken. I'm gonna install a sign by Helen's with an arrow pointing my way—'*Longer poses, better lighting, bigger breasts—come on down!*'"

Helen laughed, a cheery sound like a wild bird call. "Now, Freddie, what do you care? Gives you more time for yourself." She turned to Irene and spoke in a confidential tone. "Truth is the man grumbles every time somebody walks into that back studio. Hates to be interrupted while he's drawing. Thinks that place is his own private atelier, right, honey?"

"Wrong. In my own private atelier I'd have less grime. Also longer poses, better lighting, bigger…"

"Oh, you!" Helen made a motion to jab him in the ribs with her elbow but didn't follow through. Irene noticed. You don't jostle a man that size.

Bess walked into the room, a plump, efficient woman with glasses strung on a cord resting on her bosom. The air stirred with the rustle of paper as she seated herself at the desk. Nodding to the group she opened a thick brown folder.

"Irene, I've got you with Helen this week in the front room," she began. "You can go get changed and—"

"No ma'am, darlin', you are not sending me down the hall!" The husky voice emanated from the doorway where Juanita stood perched on hairpin heels. The honey color of her skin toned blush at the cheeks and her lips were full and painted crimson. She leaned against the wall, dark, sultry eyes from deep sockets stared at Bess as if the two of them were alone in the room. "No ma'am," she repeated. "I been around this place too long relegated to the back room."

Bess wrote a pay slip authorization and held it out, but Juanita did not move. "Oh come on now, I've had you in the front room most times you've worked the sketch class, now what difference does it make if once in a while you're in the back?"

"You want me to pose, you put me in the front, that's all, darlin'." Her nostrils flared as she crossed her arms, prepared to wait it out.

"I'm sorry, Juanita, but I have it scheduled already, it's in the book."

"Look, sweetness', I been haulin' my ass around this building since before you heard of the place so don't tell me about the book!"

"C'mon, Juanita," Freddie urged. "What the hell difference does it make which room? It's quiet back there, you can relax."

"Too quiet, it's dead, time drags. Hey, Frederick, stay out of it like a good boy, will ya?"

"All yours, Bess," said Freddie, spreading his palms. "I'm gonna set up."

"Juanita, simmer down, girl," Helen put in gently, as if talking to a child. "Next time you'll be in the front room, now Irene here has got it this week."

"Sure, baby, Irene and me gonna talk it all over with Bess."

"Nothing to talk over," Bess said, adjusting her glasses and beginning to type out a report. "Your seniority and priority don't impress me one bit. This is the way it is. Take it or leave it."

"What you gonna do if I leave it, honey?"

"Oh, call up Stella over on Ninth Avenue, I guess." Bess consulted her watch. "She can be here in twenty minutes, time to set that fancy hat on her head and trot on over. When class is late today, we'll recall that some models are more dependable than others." She let her glasses flop onto her chest and regarded Juanita with raised brows. "Come on, Juanita," She brushed the scheduling book with the back of her hand. "You've got more bookings this month in the painting classes alone than any other model in the League. They love you! So you don't get your way this time, don't make a Federal case. Go on now, time's running out."

Juanita unfolded her arms and sidled over to the desk. She picked up her pay slip without another glance at Bess but throwing an acid smile to Irene on her way out.

Bess and Helen exchanged a sigh, then Irene took her own pay slip and left the room. "That girl doesn't walk, she glides," Helen said to Beth as they watched her cross the lobby. "A dancer all the way."

Heading for the swinging doors leading to the studios Irene took passing note at the busts of famous past instructors mounted on pedestals along the wall. Fleetingly, she imagined Bert Kossoff's long bony face among them, a familiar but silly thought, as these were giants of the art world which the long history of the League took credit for.

Bert hadn't been teaching here long but he was a fine painter and would make his name known, she was sure of it.

She pushed through the doors marked *Students Only Beyond This Point* and entered the first studio along the corridor. She noticed several chairs occupied already by students waiting for the daily session to begin. Entering the closet that served as dressing room, she drew the curtain, removed her jacket and skirt and unbuttoned her blouse. The separate area, containing little more than a stool, was as much for her privacy as for the transition it provided. The line between her nudity and the students waiting for her beyond was as thin as the curtain. A model undressing in front of them would be as indecent as one roaming nude in the halls.

She unhooked her pastel bra and pulled off her half-slip. "Damn!" she uttered, snagging her panty hose on the stool's edge and hoping no one heard. She peered through the slits in the curtains. Many were familiar faces. Drawing seemed not the main thing for a few, like a woman she noticed in a French beret and silk scarf looking idly around the room, perhaps hoping for adventure. To meet an artist, a sensitive man, their husbands failing to notice them, body or soul. Souls needed attention. Maybe some would like to be up on the platform themselves to feel a man's eyes on them, a man's concentration with no distractions. Imaginations glistened like silver in silences like those out there.

Well, most came only to draw, she knew, but others didn't know what they wanted and were searching. Art seemed so free and wild and yet solid. A perfect raft for the floating.

Men and women, more than a score now, were entering the studio. Helen had set up in her usual seat by the door to collect admit slips as people around her found chairs and laid out their supplies. "Waiting for the curtain to go up," she mumbled and laughed. "There should be an overture."

She stepped out of her nylon panties and folded them on top of the small pile of clothing, then rubbed her waist where the elastic had left a faint mark. She fluffed her pubic hair, glad it showed her a natural blond. The chill in the room was making the nipples on her small breasts rise and she hastily tied her robe around her, a pastel peach rayon that descended to mid-calf. Wedging her feet into cotton mules, she emerged from the curtains and scuffed over to the platform. It was good posing in this room where artists surrounded the raised platform. Where Juanita modeled, the platform stood at one end with people facing it, the arrangement more academic. Posing here was like being the sun in the center of a solar system, planets spinning all around on their separate paths.

"Pose please," Helen chirped from her command post, her pencil poised to begin. The rustle of papers whistled through the room like a soft breeze, as the artists flipped open pages of their sketch pads.

Irene loosened her robe, her own silent overture, and let it fall carelessly in a heap behind her. She twisted her long hair up in a tie. The artists needed to see the neck in most poses but Helen usually asked her to leave it loose for the last pose, the long one.

"We'll have ten one-minute poses and three fives," Helen announced. "You warm enough, honey?" she called, as Irene dropped her slippers from the platform.

Irene nodded. She clasped her hands overhead and twisted her torso. Her waist was narrow but her hips flared broadly, tapering in a long sweep down the thighs. Her calves were muscular from dancing, but her feet had a high instep and graceful arch. She had her father's feet, the best she could say for him.

The artists were quiet now as they began to work. The silence was pure crystal as each one of them settled into orbit a million miles away. *The center of the universe.* She closed her eyes against the white glare of the overhead light. *Not a bad place to be.*

2

At the break Irene sat down on a bench in the lobby next to Helen.

"How's business?" Irene asked, glancing at the admit slips she was counting.

"Pretty good, we got a 'specially fine model today." She gave Irene a friendly poke without looking up. They sat next to the doors which swung open like fans as people ambled into the lobby or returned to the studios. "How about you, honey? You workin' much these days?"

Irene bent over to massage a cramp in the calf of her leg. "Just modeling. Two bookings this month—a one-week stand and a three-day—but I have to travel out to Long Island for one and Jersey for the other. Pays not bad though."

"So long you workin' honey, that's what matters." Helen wrapped an elastic band around the admission slips. "They pay you the travel?"

"No." Irene straightened. "What I really want is a steady dance job." She leaned back against the paneled wall. "Pounding the pavements for years and nothing to show for it but worn out soles, two down there and one up here. Some fill-in spots now and then in that new club uptown. The Bistro, near Columbia, you know it?"

"Uh uh. You have a dance partner works with you?" Helen asked, her dark gentle eyes now on Irene's face.

"Just me."

"You ought to get one, change your luck, maybe. I've seen dance acts like that. The guy lifts the lady in the air, totes her around, swings her—looks so easy. I always wondered what it would feel like, spinning in the air like that."

Irene laughed. "No thanks, I don't need a partner spinning me around. I have enough trouble keeping my feet on the ground."

"I know what you mean, girl," Helen said with a chuckle. "That man of mine got me spinning sometimes, like to fall on my head!" She stood. "Don't worry, honey, you gonna make it on your own. Excuse me now, gotta bring these slips to Bess."

Irene watched her walk towards the office, greeting a few people on her way. Bending over, she resumed work on the persistent leg cramp garnered from the last pose.

Bert Kossoff entered the lobby. He looked around, found her and came over. She straightened as he approached.

"Don't get up on my account," he said, sitting down closely beside her. He studied her with cool gray eyes, then smiled.

Even smiling, his expression had a firmness to it like the bones of his brow and jaw, designed perhaps to keep people at a distance so he could go about his work undisturbed. His eyes, softening now, brought her into that private space.

"You're here early tonight for your class," she said, beginning to inspect her nails.

"Well I just stopped in now to find you. I heard you were modeling this week."

"Good news travels fast, I guess. Why did you want to find me?"

"I'd like the pleasure of your company for a drink later on. How about it?"

She consulted her hands, rubbing them where they were chafed. "No, I don't think it'll work out tonight. I'm through at six-thirty, not booked for any night classes, and you're teaching till ten. Our timing's off." Actually, she'd been looking to break it off with Bert Kossoff; she had done so off and on during the many years they had been seeing each other.

"Our timing's never off, you know it."

The comment bothered her. "No, I'm sorry, Bert, it won't work." She bent forward, rubbing again at her leg cramp. Kossoff's attraction to women was not a secret at the League, perhaps also not to his wife. Irene had seen them together occasionally at League gallery openings, Ruth Kossoff smiling, making a good show of it.

Juanita coming through the swinging doors sauntered by them. Her robe, crimson and magenta silk, dropped just above her knees. She avoided Irene but smiled at Bert as she sidled past. Bert's eyes followed her for a moment then returned to watch Irene manipulate her calf.

"Look, I can help you with that little problem. I used to get cramps like that all the time."

"Thanks, I'll manage."

"Come on, have a drink with me tonight, Irene. No tryouts tomorrow are there?"

"No." Irene wondered if Bert has ever slept with Juanita.

"Say, how'd you make out with the tryout last week?" Irene pointed thumbs down. He shook his head and touched her arm. "Their loss. They don't know a good thing when they see it!"

"Do you know?" Juanita was too hot tempered; he wouldn't have risked it.

His eyes dropped from her face to the loose-fitting robe, open slightly above the waist from working on her calves. His hand traveled up her arm, "I do know it. Come on, Renie," he urged, whispering close to her ear. "I need you, let me come tonight? Okay?"

His voice was a little hoarse. He wasn't good at small things like whisperings and pleadings, but the name 'Renie' spoken so close to her cheek stirred her.

Still, she said again, "The timing's not good, Bert, really."

"Everything's good with us." He waited, glancing at his own hand along her arm. "Look, go home after you finish here and wait for me and I'll come up to your place. I'll breeze in and out of my class tonight and make it soon as I can. Okay, Renie?"

"No, Bert, that's late and I'll be bushed after I leave here."

Helen spotted Juanita in the hall and they talked. The two women walking toward the swinging doors on their way back to the studios were a study in contrast—Juanita, a blaze of loose color, towering in silver high-heeled slippers, Helen, dark and purposeful in her gray smock and sneakers.

Irene rose and Bert stood too. "Don't wait for me," she called to him at the swinging door. "Back to work now."

Over her shoulder, she spotted him looking after her as the door swung to a close.

. . .

Irene spread her robe and lay back on it, her head falling below the edge of the platform. This was a ten-minute followed by a fifteen. The pose made a good foreshortening opportunity for the artists.

After several minutes looking up at the fluorescents with her head so low, she felt dizzy. Why make it so hard on herself, she wondered for probably the umpteenth time? Do the artists give her credit for it? If the head dropped off and fell to the floor would they stand with hats pressed to their chests and call her the best model the League ever had? No, they would just draw feet till the session was over.

Ouch, my neck hurts…Helen, save me.

"Change, please."

Thank you! She sat up and rolled her head in a slow circle several times before assuming a simple seated pose, which she kept until the break.

Bert waited for her on a bench just outside the swinging doors. He had drawn her from imagination. She sat beside him and looked at it over his shoulder. He had drawn her nude in conte crayon, seated and looking out into the distance as if something enchanting had caught her eye.

"It's beautiful, Bert."

"Because you're beautiful," he said. He removed the page from his pad and rolled it up. "Would you like to have it?"

"I would. Thank you, Bert." Irene grasped the edges of the roll, careful not to bend it. "Bert, you understand about tonight, don't you? I need to go home and rest."

"Sure, we'll catch up another time."

They were interrupted by Freddie who unceremoniously hoisted himself on the bench beside her. He looked terrible. Taking a handkerchief from a pocket of his jeans he daubed his beard and forehead.

"What a mumser, I'm dying in there! This Juanita is a pip you wouldn't believe!"

"I believe." Bert laughed. "What's she doing to you?"

"What isn't she doing? Like not posing. The best I can say is she's got the clothes off and the body's there. That, at least, and the color. She's got great color—well, you know that. How many times you book her in painting? Except it's a drawing class, so we got no action." He exhaled loudly. "One more pose left, thank God. Hey, some crowd in room one."

Irene grinned and nodded.

"Well, back to the salt mines," he exclaimed, jumping down.

"I've gotta go too," Irene said. "Thanks so much for the picture, Bert. I love it."

For the next pose, Irene took a seated position, one knee forward, one back, a hand behind her, supporting her weight. Pencils, craypas, pens and brushes moved like musical instruments as if she'd brought down the baton.

Bert's drawing lay in the dressing room on top of her pile of clothes. She wondered if he viewed her as the woman in that drawing, pensive, serene…beautiful. Or if he simply produced the drawing to please her. The rendering was exquisite.

Standing room only, she observed, looking out at the crowded room. The space and her place in it felt comfortable after almost a decade of modeling here, though from the start she'd considered it temporary. The building's high gray walls and floor to ceiling windows, so covered with grime no shades were needed, was now like a second home.

Latecomers and transfers from the other drawing studio still drifted in, drawing wherever they could find a spot to balance their pads. Irene cast her eyes about, not moving her head to spoil the pose, only her eyes, idly, like a fisherman's line in the water. She recognized Vincent, the monitor from Bert's painting class, usually here but arriving late today.

Her gaze rested on someone standing in the doorway, not drawing like the others, just watching her. He was looking at her in that intimate but distant way a man regards a prostitute when he's dressed and ready to leave and she remains still naked on the bed. Irene felt an immediate dislike for the man. He should be drawing like the others or leave, but he was simply standing there looking, as if she were there for him personally. His eyes left her face and descended to her breasts and drifted lower. Suddenly, she regretted that her knees were spread, that she faced in his direction. Then seeing her eyes on him, the man pulled something from his pocket and pretended to draw. Helen, busy drawing herself, didn't see him or he would be gone.

She remembered another time when a man looked at her that way. She was sixteen at a party on a blind date. The guy was older by about four years, good looking and a smooth talker. He had taken her out into the hall and tried to unbutton her blouse. When she tried to stop him, he called her a tease and pulled her hand away and when his fingers dipped inside the blouse a button tore off. He grinned then but when she shoved him away, his eyes turned nasty and he looked at her the way that man in the doorway regarded her now, accusing her with his eyes of every indecency he expected her to provide. She had made her own way home from the party confused and ashamed. That familiar flash of shame, now there again.

She looked back at this man. He was handsome and well dressed. It was always the very sure of themselves who hurt her most. She stared at him now, unblinking. Her gaze would be on him when he looked up from the dark creases and pink flesh his eyes explored like maggots feeding. And he would know by the fury in her eyes, that she wasn't there for him, or for anyone not of her choosing.

A surge of power rose in her, as familiar as her shame, to go out into that world on 57th Street and beyond and make good, brilliantly good, a name for herself. To show them all, this man and the tryout directors and the others waiting in Xenia Ohio to hear she'd been arrested or murdered or killed in a wild car crash . . . to show them all that she is on top of her life. Then maybe the shame that stalked her and leaped out upon her like this, will give up defeated. She is the woman in Bert's drawing. That woman of serenity.

"Rest, please," Helen's cheerful voice called.

She heard it like a thundering finale and hurriedly tied her robe. The man was gone.

When she emerged from the dressing room in her street clothes a few students still remained applying finishing touches to their drawings. A pretty young woman, eighteen or so, tilted up her drawing to show Irene as she passed on her way to the door. The lines were timid, faint, and Irene had to bend to see them. It was a rather stilted drawing of the last pose. If the seated figure in the picture were to bend, its parts would break into pieces like a China teacup.

"It's very nice," Irene lied. The girl, encouraged, turned the pages of her sketch book to show other drawings equally clumsy. Irene was compelled to comment on each one though both of them were aware she knew nothing about drawing technique. Perhaps this was the amount of feedback the girl risked asking for.

Irene left the studio, glad she had said no to Bert tonight. She wanted to go home, take a hot bath, eat dinner and search out the best setting to hang his picture. To see herself through his eyes.

3

After fixing herself a dinner of Muenster cheese and tomato sauce on pita bread, lettuce and tomato salad and a hot dog because she was still hungry, Irene slipped into pajamas and propped herself up in bed facing Bert's picture. She'd pasted the top edge on cardboard and leaned it against the mirror on her dresser. The woman sitting there gazing out and beyond seemed to make the bedroom expand into that space.

Bert had a quiet side to him, a side she loved, which probably kept her from permanently breaking off their relationship. She remembered the first time they made love, how it began and the stunning, impossible ending.

He was one of the first men she had gone out with after moving to New York. After several assignments to his painting class and casual coffees together and drinks at the Topside across from the league, they began to date. She didn't know at first that he was married. He neither hid it from her nor told her and he behaved so much like a bachelor she didn't think to ask. She found out during the terrible events of that night that he was.

The evening began uneventfully. From the League they drove to Syd Allen's in New Jersey for drinks and a late supper. A couple at the next table latched onto them talking about modern art and movies and some hours passed. Then without telling her where they were headed, he drove back across the George Washington Bridge into Manhattan and down the East Side Drive to 34th Street and the Queens Midtown

Tunnel. When they emerged onto the Grand Central Parkway, she suspected his plan.

"You're going to show me your etchings, I don't believe it."

"I don't etch," he said. Steering with one arm, he put the other around her hips and slid her over to him along the vinyl seat.

The Parkway was only lightly trafficked at this late hour. She murmured something and closed her eyes. She had heard that he was something of a womanizer, but also that he was a fabulous artist, and on the stand he had treated her professionally and with respect. He knew she was a dancer and in their conversations often asked how things were going.

They traveled without very much speaking. He complained about all the lights along Queens Boulevard and she could see he was eager to arrive at his studio. He also seemed captivated by the outrageous notion of bringing her home with him to Forest Hills. Finally he came to the turnoff into the side streets leading to his home.

She opened her eyes with the contrast of bright lights to shadowy darkness. "We're almost there?" she asked.

"Not too far now." He kissed her cheek. The car jolted, and caught off balance, she slid from the seat onto the floor. "Ow, my head!" she cried, struggling to raise herself back onto the seat. "What happened?"

"We hit something. A cat, I think. Are you okay?"

"Yeah, I'm okay, I guess. We didn't hit it very hard. Do you think we killed it?" She crawled back on the seat and twisted to look out the rear of the car. Her head ached slightly. "I don't see the cat."

"It must have crawled off."

"To die, that's what they do when they can." She remembered once as a teen being in a boy's car back home. He was driving but he let her handle the wheel. It was a Saturday night and they had been on the town and all of a sudden they spotted a cat sitting there on the road, paralyzed by the headlights. She turned the wheel to avoid the animal but he grabbed the wheel away from her and headed straight for it. They struck the beast with the tiniest thud and when Irene looked back, she could see it under the street lamp sitting stiffly upright, its paws frozen to its chest.

"You're sure you're okay?" he said again. She nodded and they drove on. "You can't see those animals. They're so damn fast."

A few minutes later he pointed out his house. "That's it. Oh," he said, surprised.

"What?"

"I thought nobody'd be home. She was going off to a spa with her sister, taking our daughter, and my son's out on a sleep-over. But I see her car."

"Bert! You're married? You never told me."

"Oh, Irene, I'm sorry. I thought you knew."

"You're married? And she's here?" Irene was astounded. "Bert, I don't like this. Turn around and take me home! I don't like this at all!" It was against all rules, even the dishonest rules of an affair since that's what it turned out they were having.

"Irene," he said softly, it's too late. We're both tired. I'm sorry you didn't know I had a family, I thought everyone at the League knew. We'll just go inside and rest a bit in my studio. No one ever goes in there, it's kind of a rule. Then I'll take you home."

Irene sat motionless in the parked car, not wanting to move out of the car let alone approach the darkened house. "It's so dark, not even a night light. Doesn't she leave a light for you if she's there and you're not?" She couldn't believe she was asking the mundane, married-life question, but it went unanswered. The idea that she doesn't want to know ran through Irene's mind. To pretend that everything is tucked away until morning when the sun will come out and fill all the corners with natural light.

"Come, Irene, please. I'm so sorry." She followed his gaze set again on the house. The upstairs windows were as dark as the ones below. "I wondered why she was going off with her sister in the first place, she hates those things." Please, let's just rest for an hour inside. It's so late now, not even safe to drive all the way back without a rest."

Irene still hesitated. What he said was true. He was tired enough to hit the cat, who knew what other trouble they'd run into. It was after midnight, plus everyone up there was probably asleep. Bert had come around to her side of the car and reluctantly, she let him help her out of the seat.

"Shhh, we'll go in. I've got my key here somewhere."

The house was a compact, brick, two-story dwelling with only a driveway separating it from the next houses on either side. A lone tree bordered by a low hedge graced the small square front yard. The Kossoff's house differed from the ones flanking it because it had a separate entrance like a doctor's office might have. They entered the private door and Irene made a shuddering sound deep in her throat. Bert motioned her to be quiet, then he lifted her in his arms and carried her to the daybed. It was quick thinking for she surely would have stumbled on something. It was so unfair, being here. *Unfair to her. Where was she? Which room upstairs?*

He set her down and stripped back the cover. "Here," he whispered, "we'll rest for bit and leave."

Soundlessly, he removed his shoes, then hers and lay down beside her. After a few moments, he put his arm around her. Then he drew her to him. She turned away from him, staring at a dark wall which could have been a door or a shaded window. It was all unreal. She didn't belong here. Then she felt him stroking her, slowly, through her clothes. A kiss followed and more kisses and a gentle hand placed on her neck and through her hair. If nature was taking its course, it wasn't surprising.

She was aware of a dizzying euphoric feeling as he began undressing her because of where and how they were. She wanted to talk, to explain why they could not make love in this room, not now, but even whispers seemed prohibited. They lay in an open-ended darkness to which her eyes had not yet adjusted. Unseen canvases surrounded them, only the smell of paint and turpentine familiar, the room itself a black unknown. An almost mystical silence surrounded them by their circumstance. Even Bert had to be imagined for she could not see him and could barely hear him, only his breathing as he gripped her, the passion confined in the car now coursing through his limbs and his mouth as he kissed her body, bending it to him. She resisted at first, her mind on the woman upstairs, until his strong movements pulled her in like an undertow displacing everything.

The daybed was low to the floor and in his arms as he moved her, she could not discern the head of the bed from the foot. The disorientation was peculiar. Her head and shoulders tilted down. The gentle incline produced a heady, sensual feeling, and in the last thrusting moments he kept her that way until at last they both slipped to the floor and lay exhausted there. Bert's cheek, rough with morning beard, came to rest beside her.

Her eyes slowly adjusted to the dark, a glimpse of white pillows fallen to the floor. Bert was falling asleep. She whispered to him that they should leave but when he mumbled something incoherent, she thought it probably best to let him sleep for an hour before the drive. What now was the harm? How long she lay beside him she wasn't sure; perhaps she too dozed off.

A phone rang in another part of the house. Irene's head lifted with a start. The phone was picked up on the fourth ring. *My God, she is there.* The vagueness of knowing this before took on crystal clarity when the ringing stopped. And who could be calling at this hour? Bert sat up and sprang to his feet. Irene and Bert said nothing but the thought coursed through them both. Now Irene could see the outline of his body. He was waiting. They listened, trying to discern her voice but heard nothing more. Then they heard the slap of the receiver replaced. Light appeared through the cracks of the door.

Irene rose, startled, and sat on the edge of the daybed.

A tentative knock on the door. "Bert. Bert. Are you in there? Bert…?" The woman waited, called again—a choked and croaking voice—"Bert! Are you there?" Waiting. And then her steps receded.

"Something is terribly wrong," Bert whispered. Blindly he searched with his hands the floor and the bed, delivering her clothes as he found them. It was like a dream, a ballet.

They heard a car stop in front of the house. Two doors slammed. Footsteps were quick and the doorbell rang, chimed. Idyllic bells, half church, half castle, other-world bells transported to homes like this. The woman answered it.

Bert tried to listen at the door then spun around. "Something's happened, I don't know what. Irene, we have to get you out of here."

The voices in the next room grew more compelling, the voices of two men, both restrained, one husky in tone, the other more mellow, urging. Ruth's voice was dominant, insistent, verging on hysteria. Then, words broke through the muted tones: "I want to see him. I want to see him! Let me see him!"

Bert noiselessly unlatched the door to the outside and led Irene down the path. Once out in the street they could speak for the first time.

"Don't you think you should stay, Bert...if something did happen?"

"How would you get home?" he demanded, more to himself than her. "No, it's too dangerous. We can't get a taxi now and you will not use the subways at this hour. I'd have to be crazy."

No, she couldn't. Her friend was mugged just one week ago and in broad daylight. In retrospect, once trapped in the studio there was no other way out. Bert drove her home and Ruth went it alone. She took that awful route, the end of the line for a mother, with no one but two strangers there to help.

Bert phoned Irene the next day with the horrifying news. His son Billy had died that night.

PART FOUR
PAINTING LESSONS

I

Bert had begun a new study in his abstract series on cloud configurations. But the cumulous clouds were emerging on his canvas too real in their voluminous shapes and departing from other colors in the series. Not concentrating, he had curiously reverted to his more classic style of years ago. Resolutely, he extracted stronger hues from his paint box to enclose the shapes, the vivid colors of his current style: vermillion, cadmium yellow, malachite green, a receding Prussian blue for a sense of sky.

He glanced at Sonata bent over her sketchpad with an oil pastel clutched in her fingers, diligent in attending to the exercise he had given her. Her presence in the room had begun affecting his work. Even so he had to smile at her tongue peeking out between her lips and the fierce frown curling her brow. She was trying.

And he was as well because Ruth had gotten her way with him. Women had subtle power after sex and he, a satisfied swain, was of no mind to argue. He'd agreed to share a bit of the artists' way with their daughter who now occupied his studio playing havoc with his mindset.

He decided to let her work on an easel after this exercise. That would make her feel good and would also return his table to him with more space to mix his palette. "It's magical," she said when she observed him mixing colors this morning. He liked her enthusiasm because it could indeed feel magical to see colors transforming.

She stood up, her back to him, leaning the sketchbook against the wall and stepping away to observe what she had done. There was something boyish about her—a small waist and a kind of gangly gait—although she had hips that were womanly. The right clothes would help. Ruth should go with her to shop; she had an eye.

"I think I'm finished," Sonata said, still studying her work.

"Let's see. Bring it here."

She turned and with a critical pout trying to hide her satisfaction, propped the pad on an easel beside him. She arched her neck to study his face as together they studied her work.

"Better, much better," he said. He could give her that. It couldn't get much worse.

She beamed. "I tried to control the space the way you told me to. See, look here. I used the side of the oil pastel to fill up this whole area of negative space with big strokes of color."

He tapped his lips with a forefinger and regarded her "space." How quickly they pick up the words, these neophytes, the jargon so much easier than the concepts. Words are learned in the head, sight perceived by the senses; that was the difference and not very teachable. Still, she was putting in genuine effort.

"Ok," he said, "I'm going to let you work on the easel now. Let's stretch a canvas, you know how to do that?"

She shook her head, a stroke of panic crossing her face.

"Here, watch me." He selected four wood strips, each end already mitered and grooved, of a size to make a small canvas and pressed them together, checking all the right angles with a T-Square. Then he cut a piece of canvas from a roll. She watched him set the frame over it leaving a border all around. He folded the canvas over the stretcher bar on the long side, stapling it in the middle and then stretched the other side, stapling that in the middle. She watched him maneuver around the frame, pulling and stapling along all sides until the canvas was taut. She tried to help by holding the frame as he tucked and stapled the corners but he waved her off, moving fast.

"Okay, got that?"

She nodded hesitantly.

"Don't worry, I'll help you next time," he said, grinning as he saw her straining to remember each step. "So, okay, this is for you, lady," he said, placing the framed canvas on an easel. "Go to it."

"Go to it?" she repeated.

"Right. Use your oil pastel study as a guide but just as a start. Leave it if the paint directs you elsewhere."

"What do you mean, elsewhere?"

"I mean the picture may not work in paint the way it does in oil pastel, so be ready to change course."

"Oh. Oh?"

"You're exploring the paint medium now," he explained, recognizing the glint of terror, that dry fear of inadequacy blanketing her face. "The only reason you made a study first is to give you confidence in approaching the blank canvas."

She nodded, staring at the blank canvas like a mirror on which she would produce her image and reveal her ugliness. "I need confidence," she said.

"Of course you do. You have nothing to go on but what's in you, and you don't know yet what that is. Look, you're creating, not copying; you're making things up. Most people only know how to copy and doing it well or poorly is their measure of success. Nothing wrong with that, it's an accomplishment, but what you're attempting is more an adventure than an accomplishment. Confidence will come with your track record." He enjoyed giving her a pep talk. Never gave such talks to his League students; must be her pathetic eyes, so scared, or maybe Ruth's power still hexing him.

"I don't know how to keep score yet, Dad," she said. "I won't know what's good and what isn't."

"Eventually you will." He handed her a palette and directed her towards the tubes of acrylic paint laid out on an old oak dresser he used for both storage and counter top. He indicated the two dozen brushes of varying sizes that stood brush side up, ready for use.

He pulled over his table, glad to have it again. She had made a mess with peelings from the oil pastels. Would she know if it was no good, he mused as he filled water in a jar and stacked some loose studies in his series to set them out of the way. And if it wasn't would she quit or persist like nine-tenths of the doomed artists in the world who wouldn't or couldn't quit. He had forced himself to believe early on that he was not one of them, and so did the nine-tenths.

He turned and saw her staring at the canvas, her open sketchbook study beside her.

"Dad, I don't know what to do," she said, turning to him. He thought he saw moisture building in her eyes.

With effort Bert subdued his urgency to get back to his work and his impatience with this obstacle that had attached itself to him like gum on a shoe. Even his beginning students, older and more vulnerable to failure, had more courage. How could she make art without courage? But there she stood, her eyes filling, blinding her to sight, let alone perception. He recognized that to abandon her now would send her floundering creative spirit sprawling.

He crossed the room and standing behind her, took her arm, grasping it at the wrist. He made broad sweeping movements in the air. "Look at the movement you created in your study? Well, this is the sweep of it. Now, acrylics bleed and blend while they're wet but they can be covered over when they're dry. So try to work with some freedom and abandon until you see how the paint flows, how it makes edges, how thin, how thick you can make it. See how the colors mix with water to make them as transparent as you want."

He took her hand, closed it over a brush, squeezed out some pigments with his other hand and daubed her brush into them, adding a splash of water and mixing the colors on the palette. The guided hand stroked a piece of scrap paper on the counter where soft pastel colors reassuringly appeared. "Do that. Do that with all your colors and later you can build them up. And look, mix the colors; don't use them right from the tube."

"Why not?"

"They blare at you, they're awful."

He dipped her hand toward the palette, not touching, then waved her hand in front of her canvas, making sweeps and dots and slashes in the air; then dipping down again to the palette, swept the hand up to form imaginary arcs. Releasing the brush into the jar of water, he closed her fingers over a rag which made as if to daub the canvas here and there. He dropped the rag and closed the fingers over a thin brush, then a thicker one, beckoning each to make its invisible strokes.

Sonata laughed. "It's like dancing on your shoes when I was little." She giggled. "I felt like I was actually dancing."

"And now you feel like you're actually painting."

"Yeah," she breathed, hiding another giggle.

"Try it all. The more you explore, the bigger the adventure and that's what art is: charting new territory, opening it up so everybody can have a look. Go to it." He released her hand and patted her on the shoulder. "I think I'll leave you alone now. It'll be easier for you without me prowling around. Use any of the brushes but give them a good wash afterwards with soap and water and don't wait too long or you'll have to use turps; the acrylics are only water soluble while they're wet."

Sonata regarded the display and nodded, more emphatically this time. "Dad, how long can I stay here?"

"An hour. That's enough for a start. I'll come back then and have a look. Now I'll bother your mother for a while—or maybe I'll work on this in the kitchen."

She watched him gather his sketch pad and colored pencils. He turned at the door. "You'll leave after that and let me get back to work?"

She smiled. "Oh, sure. Thanks, Dad. Hey, I really appreciate this."

"Remember, don't try so hard to control things in the beginning, not until you get a sense of how the pictures is moving and what's working?" For some reason, he had an urge to give her a bonus. Maybe it was her gleeful grin as she tried waving the *magic wand* in front of her canvas. "Let the paint show you what it's got. Keep looking, that's the key."

• • •

Bert found Ruth in the laundry room.

"You've been helping Sonny." She said it as a matter of fact, her eyes on the collection of socks she was pairing. Glancing over her shoulder at him, she barely concealed her pleasure.

"What have you been feeding that person? She's an Amazon."

"She's not. Just a little big in the hips. She has a tiny waist."

"Compared to what? And tall. What is she, five-ten or something? How did a wee one like you spawn such a giant? Takes up the whole damn studio, floor to ceiling, wall to wall."

"She's five-seven and nicely proportioned. You're just not used to having anyone else in the studio, so it's crowded. How's she doing anyway?"

"She's doing."

"Is she getting anywhere?"

"She's getting in my way, that's where."

"It's nice, I mean, your helping her."

He started to make a flip comment but stopped himself with a fleeting image of his daughter's face, so frightened by the mighty canvas, and Ruth, so foolishly hopeful. They both had expectations, but only he knew that nothing would come of it. A fling, that was the long and short of it. Well, so what? He'd had plenty of flings, why shouldn't they? Leaving the laundry room, he spread his materials on the kitchen table. He checked his watch: only forty-five minutes more.

2

Forty minutes were left. Sonata faced the canvas hopelessly. It was white, so white. Any mark she made would make a mess.

"Agghh, I can't stand it." She clenched her fist as the guttural cry escaped. *It's a piece of canvas, for God's sake! What's the matter with me?* But the material seemed so sure of itself so undefiled. Sighing and shaking her head, she swung her arm in the air the way her father had led her and laughed. Not the intended outcome of the exercise, but the chuckle relieved her a little. Maybe music would help. She turned on the radio, changing stations until she settled on jazz improvisations, then went back to face the unfriendly canvas. The music was distracting; she crossed the room to switch it off, glad for the excursion. She looked at her study and the canvas, back and forth several times, then at her watch. *Only thirty minutes left...oh God.*

She tentatively squeezed white paint from a tube onto her palette. She brushed this on the alien battlefield and watched it appear only barely whiter than the background. Encouraged by its invisibility, she squeezed out a mere speck of blue, mixed it with the white on her palette, bathed the mixture in a small puddle of water and applied it tentatively above the white. It dripped and ran in small vertical streamers.

"Damn! I've spoiled it already," she cried, alarmed that he would walk in early before she could fix it. As if she could fix it.

Furtively she daubed the streaks with her rag. The mess reminded her of tears. Her own tears, dripping with no hanky on hand, and wiping them away but everyone seeing the streaks and knowing she'd been crying like a baby. But none of her classmates asked why. Tears are a kind of display, an outside display of feelings inside so someone can ask what's the matter if they're interested. Tears are supposed to be useful that way, like a cat arching its back to look twice its size and ferocious when inside it's scared to death. A display, so it can defend itself. Her tears were useless.

Chinese red caught her misty eye and a drop of it in the light blue paint turned it lavender. She touched it to the canvas near the first marks but it was horrible so she daubed it away. And there were the rubbed-out tears appearing again.

In eighth grade she was as fat as she had ever been and trying to climb the rope ladder her gym suit ripped and she saw the girls laughing. Already midway up she didn't know whether to climb further or slither down. She tried to sop up her tears on the coarse rope and then with no more strength, came down and managed a croaked laugh when they called her piggy.

She wasn't thinking anymore about the tears as she squeezed some burnt sienna and raw umber into the white on her palette and blended them and added a few drops of water. Brushing this across the midsection of the canvas she saw distant mountains form. She felt something coming to life on the canvas and inside her too. A feeling good slowly happening like when Novocain wears off.

A little bolder now, she let a thicker stroke show itself near the distant mountains. Jumping down from the rope ladder and facing the kids' laugh was the hardest thing she'd ever done. Texture appeared as she picked up the palette knife and swirled burnt umber and yellow ochre in a half moon across the lower part of the picture. But that was the year Billy died. She could cry on a dime.

She returned to the pale blue now and with a wide brush washed it across the upper third of the picture. The painting began to look like a place in outer space, an inviting space that she had never seen, but the dark, craggy orb emerging at the bottom held hiding places, nooks and crannies that seemed familiar. Behind the slats under the house had been a fun place to hide with Billy. They had a clubhouse there with some other kids from down the block who were admitted, although others like the McElroy's were excluded. The floor was dirt and the slats were too low for standing, so they had to crouch and crawl around. She was president, the one in charge who made the rules. Billy brought a kitten into the clubhouse—he had found it on the street—and they gave it milk in a bowl and she made a rule that kittens could be members but the McElroy's could not.

She stopped painting and regarded her oil pastel study. The painting looked altogether different than the study. She put down her brush, exhausted. Then, staring at the canvas, she had the odd sensation that part of her had jumped out of her skin like the cartoon rabbit who could be in two places at once. God, how tired she was.

She was not aware that her father had returned until he tapped her on the shoulder. "Good girl," he said. "You got something going, didn't you?"

She wanted to reach up and hug him but stopped herself because they had never actually hugged and he might shrug her off. So she smiled and shrugged her shoulders and looked with him at the picture of her orb, her private place, and wondered was it good, bad, did it *work*, was it painterly, why didn't that matter? What was happening? Why did she feel like she was bobbing in an ocean, not even able to swim but laughing?

As her father began mixing his colors, she gathered her brushes and brought them to the sink, washing each one thoroughly the way he'd taught her.

·   ·   ·

In the week that followed Bert allowed Sonata into his studio when he was not using it and a few times when he was. On those occasions, so excited about being in that legendary space alongside him, she had to stop herself from blurting out "Dad, I'm throwing a party for you—a tribute to *you*. An all-out bash!"

They didn't talk much about her art endeavors though he gave her hints now and then, tricks of the trade, but every so often he would say something about his own work. Not so much conversation as letting things escape. Once, he spoke about a quest he had, not for the sunset but his perceptual use of sunset; not landscape but his intimate bond to landscape: absorbing the confidence in its hills and valleys, the creativity of the sky and the earth's and the river's patterns. They were close then in those moments, closer than they had ever been.

One of their longest talks or one of his longest musings was about his faults. Defects, he called them, that helped him produce his work. "Cracks in the concrete that allow dirt to collect and seeds to sprout. A fetish about not wasting is one of them, impatience is another."

"Not wasting isn't a fault," Sonata argued.

"It is when it's compulsive. If I see an item discarded in the street, I think how to use it and the wheels start turning. If I can't use it, the physical detritus on a canvas, I store it—the attributes: shape, color, texture—remembering, is what I mean."

Sonata wasn't sure exactly what he meant and didn't dare ask, too thrilled that he was talking to her like a person, an actual person.

"Take heat," he said abruptly. "I hate wasting heat." He laughed. "I don't do this now when I can raise up a thermostat, but when I was younger and poorer, I worked in a loft in the village and heated the place with a kerosene space heater. Well, I was lazy and I had other things I wanted to do besides paint so starting in was always hard. You have to psyche yourself up to put yourself through all the decision making that goes into making art, so—"

"So?"

"So, I'd climb to the loft and light the heater, that part was easy. Then, I'd go down and have a beer and talk to some guys, but all the time I'd be worrying about the kerosene being wasted and sooner or later that would pull me up there like a magnet."

Sonata laughed. She tried to think about kerosene, the meaning of the story and this being funny but could think only of his talking to her, confiding. *Had he told anyone else this story or just her?*

He laughed too. "I'd have about twenty minutes of grace without guilt while the place was warming up. Then the compulsion to use the damn heat would work on me. But my impatience—well, that's something else."

"Impatience? What do you mean?" A silly smile remained plastered on her face.

"I can't stand a blank canvas, that's it."

"That's it?"

"I can't stand it looking at me in the face, challenging me if I'm up to it. So I've got to cover it quickly and start going. I pay a price re-working it sometimes but the impatience gets me started. What propels the energy is what we're talking about. For me, it's my fetishes and faults."

"But your talent—"

"My talent *is* what it is, but what moves that to create something might come from the worst aspects of my personality."

Sonata could say nothing in response to this confidence. She watched him go back to his picture. Reluctantly she returned to her troubled canvas, the dumb smile from the treasured conversation still on her face. Her father was special, so different from ordinary men. She remembered watching him carve the turkey like a master chef at Ethel's house when they used to go there on Thanksgiving and comparing him to her uncle Lou, mopping tears while he sliced onions for gravy. Everything about her father was manly and in control.

Applying herself again to mixing colors for her picture, she thought about her father working in his studio from which through the years she and Billy and even Ruth had been barred—alone in there with his fetishes and faults. It struck her suddenly that her father, all those many years, had been a lonely man.

But all she could think about now was the tribute.

PART FIVE
THE TRIBUTE

I

"Mother! I can't find the extension cord, where is it?" Sonata shouted up from the downstairs hall. "Mo-ther?"

"She can't hear you, she's in the shower," Ethel called to her, "What do you need it for?" She was knitting a sweater by the dining-room window, feeding her needles from a continuous stream of dark green wool which flowed from a wicker basket beside her.

"I need it for the hot tray. There are so damn few outlets in this ancient house! God, she's been in that shower for an hour already. When is she coming out?"

"She just went in. For heaven's sake, take it easy." Ethel clucked her tongue and shook her head and through the doorway watched Sonata hurl open cabinets and drawers. "My goodness, the party hasn't even started and you're already bursting at the seams. What's going to happen when thirty or forty people get here?"

"Look, I want everything ready ahead of time, you can't blame me for that, and the hot tray has got to be where people can get to it easily. I made a ton of those pigs in blankets and I'll be passing them all night unless people can help themselves."

Ethel sighed. "My dear, I have a feeling this crowd will ferret out your little frankfurters if you hide them in a closet."

"Do you think I made enough punch? You saw the bowl in the kitchen, what do you think?"

"I think you made plenty, dear, because nobody's going to drink it. Do you have enough whiskey and beer?"

"Tons."

"Good.

"And tons of cold turkey for sandwiches later, and salads and bread . . . everything." She slammed a drawer shut. "Except that damn extension cord!" Hands on her hips with two clenched fists, she attacked the room with scavenging eyes, figuring out her next move. "What time is it?"

Ethel looked at her watch, a slight flick of the wrist without missing a stitch. "Seven-thirty. When are they coming?"

"Right after the classes. It should be about ten, I think."

"Look dear, why don't you lie down or something until your mother gets out of the shower? Just stretch out and relax for a few minutes, it'll do you good."

Another drawer crashed to a shuddering close. "I am relaxed!"

"Good heavens! All right, go downstairs in the basement, why don't you. Maybe the extension cord is with the tools. I'd help you look but I've got my hands tangled up in this wool."

"Don't you think you better quit that now?" Sonata suggested through the doorway with no small hint of sarcasm. "There's a lot you could do around here if you wanted to make yourself useful."

"I intend to be useful, that's why I'm here. When I finish these few rows, I'll be useful."

Later, crossing the upstairs hall in bra and panties on her way to take a bath, Sonata collided with Ethel, half buried under a pile of coats. "What are you doing with that stuff?"

"I'm clearing the front hall closet, what does it look like? It's my contribution to your Thing. Who was on the phone just now?"

"Oh, that was Willie. He called to tell us he spoke to Dad last night and reminded him, so it's all set for tonight." She grinned conspiratorially. "See, Dad expects to meet Willie after his class to help him choose slides for a show. We wanted to make sure he got here at the right time. Oh Ethel, I'm so excited, I don't know how I'll live till this party starts!"

"You'll live. Look, I'm putting these things in my room so don't go searching all over the house if you need something."

"Ethel, I never even thought about the front closet!" Impulsively she kissed her aunt and the two top coats fell off the pile into her arms.

"Do me a favor and take a few more off, while you're at it. Ah, that's better." They dumped the clothing on the bed. "Well, now that I've done the head work, you can do the leg work and bring up the rest."

"I'm in my underwear. I have one foot in the tub."

"Oh, go ahead, you run around like that all the time."

"Some contribution," Sonata grumbled going down the steps. The front closet was still full of coats. Taking a bundle in her arms, she stopped to look over the living room. Once again as so many times these last two weeks, she imagined the party in full swing. Now that she knew her father a little better from spending actual quality time with him in his studio, she could visualize him looking at her like they had a pact between them. He'd be so honored that she'd make a tribute. To him.

Sonata stumbled up the steps to Ethel's room. It was the guest room officially, but since Ethel was the only one who ever used it, it was hers by squatter's rights. Ethel was reading a magazine on an uncluttered parcel of the bed and nodded her approval.

"There's more but it's your turn next," Sonata said, "I'm taking my bath."

In the bathroom Ruth was in a crisp yellow housecoat, drying her hair near the sink. Sonata sat on the edge of the tub and opened the taps. The pressure was poor and the water came in slowly.

She watched Ruth pat her hair between the ends of a towel. Her head was tipped to the side and thick strands of hair with their deep brown-auburn tones glistened as they tumbled in and out of the material. "Why don't you ever wear it that way?" she asked.

"What way?" Ruth asked her.

"Loose."

"Loose like this?" She let the hair fall in front of her face. "You think it's becoming, do you?"

Sonata laughed. "Is that your front or your back, I can't tell?"

Ruth threw her head back and smiled. She picked up her comb, a wide-toothed tool for long hair and pulled the comb through where it sprang into easy waves. "It's too untidy. Anyway I'm too old to go around like that. If I were your age, maybe."

"When did you start growing it long?"

A knot fought the comb and she worked at it. "When I married your father. He never wanted me to cut it."

"No kidding, because of him, really?" Sonata smiled, amused. "I never knew that."

"Well I liked it myself. I wouldn't have done it if I didn't want to."

Sonata tilted her head, letting her own hair dip sideways as she tested the temperature of the water. "Maybe I'll grow mine long," she said, dreamily. "It's the natural way when you think about it." She brought her hair forward and measured it against her shoulder. "It's just too darn curly." Then as if suddenly chilly, she crossed her arms. "Just two hours till the party starts. I'm so excited, aren't you?"

Ruth smiled but said nothing.

Sonata wished she could see some enthusiasm on her mother's face, more cooperation, at least. It wasn't as if the party was a strain on her. She had done all of the preparations herself—the invitations, shopping, cooking—and cleaned the house today and set everything up with no assistance whatever from her.

The bartender did promise to come early to help with the last-minute details and she was glad of that. It was a professional touch, the bartender, something she'd thought of on her own, an extravagance not absolutely necessary but the tribute had more stature with a bartender.

She hadn't minded doing everything herself up to now; she'd agreed to this. Still, it was Ruth's husband they were honoring and Ruth should show some enthusiasm for that. Oh, she paid the bills—not the bartender, she wouldn't pay that, which would come from her graduation stash—but she offered no suggestions, no anything. Actually, they talked less about the party these past weeks than about the weather. And Sonata deliberately avoided discussion for fear of having anything seem difficult and Ruth calling the whole thing off. This possibility was always in the back of her mind but with the party only a few hours away she could allow herself a little righteous indignation. It had been difficult, making all those plans and decisions alone.

"What are you going to wear?"

"I hadn't thought about it." Ruth smiled in a girl-to-girl way. "Don't worry, I won't embarrass you. I'll try not to, anyway."

"But what *are* you going to wear?" Sonata persisted.

Ruth looked at Sonata in mild surprise. "You are worried, aren't you?"

"No, I'd just like to know, that's all. I've picked out my dress and I thought you'd have too." Her jaw was hurting and she knew she'd been grinding her teeth. "You didn't have so much to do with this tribute that you couldn't find a minute to pick out your dress." *Oh, take your bath and forget it, don't ruin everything now.* But her resentment had picked up speed with the party upon them and was barreling down the runway on a course of its own.

"Sonny," Ruth said, her tone patient, "you wanted this party and you are getting it. I agreed and I'm paying for it and that is the extent of my responsibility. I've cooperated with this tribute of yours not because I'm in favor of it but because I know how much it means to you." She stopped combing her hair which seemed to curl up wildly, no longer sleek. "To be honest, I think you'd have been better putting this enthusiasm and effort to work on something else. Something closer to your own—"

"Closer to what? What is closer to me than my own father?" She shut off the tap. "My god! Something must be the matter with you! Anybody would think you'd be knocking yourself out to make this party unforgettable. An occasion to remember. To make it successful, at least. He's your husband, he's a great artist! Haven't you been telling me that for years…how dedicated he is to his work—above everything else? He gives life where there wasn't any, he creates life. What could be more worthy than that?" She pushed herself upright and glared at her mother. "We know this and it's for *us* to tell the world."

Ruth turned to face the mirror and looked at Sonata through it. Her mouth opened to say something, then closed tightly.

"Look, I stopped from saying anything before, but the truth is you have done absolutely nothing, Mother, not one blasted thing for this tribute, except simply agree to it!" She clenched her fists almost as if she would strike her mother if she were to let them go.

This anger, where was it coming from? Why couldn't she shut up, walk out of the room? She was getting her tribute. But it wasn't her tribute, it was Bert Kossoff's. Why did Ruth keep talking about her?

"Sonny," Ruth began, speaking softly, like she had when Sonata's social studies project fell apart in third grade, "you've been very concerned about this party and working hard on it—too hard, maybe—and you're upset. Let's not talk about this now. Ethel is right across the hall with her door open. We'll talk later. I don't think this discussion is anything you want her to hear."

"I don't give a damn about Ethel! Whether she hears or doesn't hear." Then as she stared harshly at Ruth, her mouth twisted in what might have been a smile though her bottom lip wavered. "You're jealous," she pronounced. "That's what it is. You're jealous that he's the genius, the great artist, and not you."

"Sonny! What are you saying?"

"You don't want him to have this tribute. It's killing you, isn't it? You know he deserves it, but it's killing you. His friends know, his students, gallery people—that's why they're coming. They're all coming."

"I won't listen, Sonny. You're upset from all the arrangements and the excitement." She started to leave but Sonata got to the door first. Leaning against it, she faced her mother squarely. Her breast heaved in the skimpy cotton bra and for a moment her words would not come. Then she set her lips. "He's devoted his life to *making* life while you do nothing. What have you done, Mother? What have you ever done that was worth anything?" She stared into her mother's startled eyes, blue sky eyes shrouded by a ledge of furrowed brow, as she waited for an answer. Then Sonata opened the door and stood back, freeing her captive, the bright canary that had never been outside its cage.

Ethel was standing motionless in the hallway, but Sonata ignored her as she made her final thrust. "You don't deserve him, Mother. You never did."

Ruth went hastily into her room and closed the door without turning. Sonata returned Ethel's stare from the doorway. When she spoke, her belligerent tone was unchanged. "Hadn't you better begin dressing? This party starts in one hour."

"I am dressed," Ethel said with unblinking eyes, spitting out the words. "For this party."

Disgusted, Sonata spun around and locked the door. She turned on the hot water tap with all its meager force. The bath had gotten cold.

2

Irene lay uncovered in the loose pants and top she slept in, staring at the door. There was a creaking sound, as if someone were standing just outside.

She began to feel a familiar tightness in her throat, lying very still, half expecting the door to open. In the dim light coming through the window from the street lamp, she could see the faint highlights of the brass bolt. The lock was as old as the rooming house itself. An intruder could easily force it. An intruder was always imagined—a man, heavyset and determined and incapable of reason. An animal.

She summoned explanations: the tenant in the room down the corridor having a friend in to spend the night searching about for the right door, the landlord checking for something amiss in the hall. But sounds persisted intermittently. Fear lessened when she moved, took some action; panic seemed to be born on the wings of imagination. Irene opted for courage and rose from the bed. She turned on the lamp and crossed the small room. She would open the door and prove that the hallway was empty or there would be no sleep that night. She'd planned on a full eight hours tonight, every lost minute showing up on her face tomorrow at the dance tryout.

She slid the bolt slowly, her other hand on the handle, ready to crack open the door a fraction and slam it shut if necessary. She heard the door to the bathroom down the hall open then close with a dull thud. There was silence, then a coarse flush of water and finally, heavy footsteps fading at the end of the corridor.

Irene opened her door wide and peered down the windowless hall which was dimly lit by a forty-watt bulb that burned both day and night. No one there. She sighed and re-locked the door.

Taking a bottle of Gallo wine from a makeshift cabinet she'd made of orange crates she filled half a tumbler and took a long sip. The phone rang, startling her, so focused had she been on sounds beyond the room. Bert Kossoff. Seconds passed in a confused transition. "It's after nine, Bert. I'm going to bed early to be at my best for the tryout tomorrow." She maneuvered a cigarette from a pack lying on the orange crate beginning actually to feel drowsy for the first time tonight.

"It's not the sort of greeting I was hoping for." Bert spoke softly, as if he were in a crowded room with secret information to share though she knew he must be alone in a phone booth somewhere near the Art Students League. He wanted to come up and see her. Yes, he knew it was late and he appreciated the fact that she had a tryout in the morning, but he wanted to come up. He wanted to talk.

"Bert, if I look like a rag tomorrow, I won't stand a chance of making it." It was hard enough when you looked your best. There'd be forty girls knocking themselves out for six openings in a club chorus, memorizing routines on the spot and still hoping to do them with more style than anyone else. Most of the girls were younger which made it even harder for her to shine. At twenty-nine, she had a shapely body and legs but the others were closer to nineteen, fresh and dewy.

There were footsteps in the corridor. They passed along the hall then stopped outside her door. Bert had been saying something, but she didn't hear for the sounds of silence her ears were straining towards. She held the receiver away from her and listened for the footsteps to proceed down the hall, but there were no discernible sounds. *Oh, come on, every footfall doesn't announce itself and every step isn't pointed at her.* But the steps seemed not exactly to go into the bathroom, just stopped making noises.

Maybe it wasn't a bad idea for Bert to come over—she waited and strained to hear a flush—and it came, a satisfying splash and gurgle. She agreed, replaced the receiver and then remembered she should have told Bert to bring something to eat. But maybe he would anyway. He was thoughtful that way.

3

Ethel stood for a while outside Ruth's bedroom wondering whether or not to go in, finally deciding against it. Later, when Ruth was ready for it, they would talk.

She sat on a chair in her room reviewing what Sonata had shouted at her sister. They were malicious words. What new seed was growing to spawn such an outpouring of animosity? Ruth had done everything conceivable for her. She lived for the child—for her daughter, not her husband, the honored man of the hour. How well Ethel knew. So what caused this sudden rejection, for that's what it was; not a difference of opinion or misunderstanding or any of the other makings of a normal argument but an attempt to put Ruth out of the picture? A picture featuring solely the celebrant father.

Ethel approached Ruth's door again, not wanting to wait any longer when she heard Sonata singing in the tub. Her blood rose at the insidious contrast of those cheerful notes and the invectives hurled at her sister and decided she was too angry herself to be of any help to Ruth. Instead, she headed downstairs, needing something soothing. Tea perhaps.

At the foot of the stairs the door to the closet was open revealing many coats still hanging. Well, it was Sonata's problem. In the kitchen, waiting for water to boil, she heard Ruth coming down the steps.

"I'm going for a walk, Ethel...some fresh air." She looked beyond her sister, avoiding her eyes. "I'll be back soon." She had grabbed her coat from a hall hook and was gone without hearing or acknowledging Ethel call out "I'll go with you."

From the window, Ethel watched her cross the street and start down the block, continuing until she was out of sight. There were not many streetlights, but Sonata had switched on the outside house lights for the guests. In the distance, the lights blazed along Queens Boulevard and the noise of the traffic was a drone, mounting and receding like the irregular breathing of a leathery old drunk. A man stopped in front of the house, checked a slip of paper in his hand, then walked up the path. When the bell rang Ethel opened the door.

"This the Kossoff place? I'm Joe Papadopoulos, bartender." He lifted his hat.

He was a small, stocky fellow in his forties or maybe fifties with a ruddy complexion that included a short scar on the left cheek and a broad smile that he seemed to rely on.

Ethel nodded and tried to return a smile of her own. "Yes, they're expecting you. Come in."

"You the lady of the house?" he asked, following her inside.

"No, just a relative. Here, put your jacket in the closet."

He hung it up carefully, way in the back, then brought several hangers forward and placed them in the front. "For the company," he said efficiently. "You gotta think this stuff when you run a party. Lotta details to keep in mind, believe me."

"Yes, well I believe you. Mrs. Kossoff and her daughter will be here to help you in a few minutes." The phone rang. "Would you like to get started meanwhile?" It rang again.

"Ethel, get the phone!" Sonata commanded, a dim voice from the bathroom.

"The table you're supposed to use is this one here—I'm getting it!" Ethel yelled back. "—The glasses and bottles and things are over there in the cabinet and there's a bowl of punch in the fridge."

"Ethel!"

"—I have it, I have it!— The towels are in the kitchen. Hello."

"Yes ma'am, don't you worry about a thing. I'm doing this twenty-five years and I know my business." He removed his jacket and folded it over a chair, then rolled his sleeves to the elbows. He studied the table Ethel pointed to and the room and moved the table to a place closer to the wall. "Make room here for thirsty customers, ha, ha. We wanna make it nice 'n easy for 'em. Yes ma'am, what's a party for?" He spread a towel and smoothed it.

"Ruth can't come to the phone just now, can I give her a message?"

"You tell the lady of the house she can relax and enjoy herself tonight. Joe Papadopoulos will take care of everything, pass the food, clean up the place, everything. You treat me right, I treat you right, that's the way I operate, twenty-five years I'm doin' this."

Listening to the voice on the other end of the phone, Ethel watched Joe Papadopoulos arrange the glasses in neat rows according to their size. "I understand. I'll give her that message, yes. Yes. Goodbye." She watched him as he read the label on each bottle and lined them like sentinels along the border of the table. "They treat me right, I treat them right, it's my policy. You tell the lady to enjoy herself tonight. Joe Papadopoulos is here."

"Yes, Joe, I'll tell her that."

4

Irene finished her wine and lay back on the bed, watching the quiver of the thin muslin curtain over the window as it played with the breeze, whipping it into gentle folds and then riding high on the back of the breeze. The window was the one place worthy of attention in the dismal room. Beyond it were all the unknown experiences and adventures she had been anticipating since moving to New York from Xenia Ohio five years ago; in front of it were all the known, predictable things she wanted to leave behind.

Five years ago, was it that long? And yet, she still felt it was coming, whatever *it* was. She thought often about what she really wanted to find out there beyond those busy curtains but she could never phrase it clearly in her mind or make an organized procedure to go about getting it. Other people seemed to be clear about reaching their goals with concrete objectives and a plan of attack. What did she want when it came right down to it?

Well, she supposed she wanted a measure of success, some recognition that she was a pretty fine dancer. And after that, she wanted a man of her own and home of her own and a career and happiness. All of this was pure mental masturbation not a plan, but at least something to try to envision when there was no glimmer of an end in sight.

Anything else? Sure, how about money and fame and beauty and love? Yes, all that. Put it up in lights. And a kid. Yes, that more than anything.

The breeze was getting too wild, too pushy. She got up and closed the window and then began putting things in order before Bert's arrival. The room was decorated in early cheap with painted wood crates serving as end tables. Some were draped with experimental woven fabrics given to her by Ray who lived downstairs. He used to be a dancer but gave up on it and turned instead to weaving. He had made himself a loom and was turning out dozens of pieces in a frenzy of discovery. Samples, he called them, like the chocolates. There was a dancer's touch to the weaving, a choreography to the warp, the way the colors danced in and out and mingled with one another, a kind of tempo to the woven lines. A mattress lying on the floor and draped with a spread was used as a couch and more of Ray's handiwork covered the scatter pillows.

Irene suddenly felt good. The gripping fear of an intruder, so intense a little while ago, had charged her energies. She felt revived. Sitting down on the floor mattress among Ray's dancing pillows, she smiled at the thought that Bert was on his way.

5

People arrived for the most part in groups, most students coming right from the League, others meeting up to take the subway together.

Her mother stood under a large canvas called *Study in Blues*, Bert's painting which won first prize in oils at the Venice International. She wore a white blouse, ruffled at the collar, and a dark brown full cut skirt, looking feminine and attractive as usual. Talking to Jacob Miller, an instructor of life painting at the League, she smiled at something he said, then took a sip from the vodka and tonic Joe had made her. Her hair was piled high in the usual bun on top but a portion hung loose in the back. Sonata decided she wore it the new way because of their conversation, pleased she'd influenced her.

Kossoff's students congregated around the sofa—on the seats and arm rests—and on chairs pulled up close. It was odd that they sat while the older people stood; it should have been the other way around. They wore the same spotted jeans and old shirts she had seen them wearing in class and found herself worrying about the furniture. Why hadn't she thought about that before? Of course, coming right from class they'd be in those same messy clothes. It was stupid not to have remembered and prepared for it. How prepare? Plastics on the upholstery? Horrible! Establishment! Well, but if she had remembered she would at least have worn something plainer herself, not this silk jersey, taffeta-trimmed dress. She would have worn a skirt and blouse, something casual and simple, like Ruth.

.   .   .

Willie came alone since he lived close by. In the kitchen, he set down a carton of beer he'd brought and found Sonata in the living room.

"You got it all set up. It's perfect!" Willie said, putting his chubby arm around Sonata's shoulder and giving it a squeeze. "The food is looking scrumptious—cold cuts, salads, breads, cakes…and so much drinks! How could you do it without me?"

"We have Joe…see?" Joe was busy at the concession he had arranged for himself, pouring, mixing and talking. He saw Sonata watching him and became busier. The food table did look good, she was proud of it, though disappointed that Vince had begged off making a birthday cake top to look like a Kossoff painting. Just too busy, he'd said.

"But where's my father?" she blurted, remembering that Willie had arranged to meet him ahead of time with the ruse of helping him select work for a show.

"Yes he was coming to me 9:30 direct from the class. I take to my bed early, he knows, so is a good arrangement. I wait at home until 10:30. He is not coming. He forgets, so I come myself here and he will come soon." Seeing her open-mouthed chagrinned expression over the failure of his mission, he produced from the pocket of his jacket a large envelope. "Look, I have with me slides. I think if he is here, before even the people, I push him in his studio and show the slides."

.   .   .

Ruth observed Joe Papadopoulos, bartender for twenty-five years, from a vantage point behind him and to one side. From what she overhead and from what she saw for herself, he seemed to be making more than a respectable amount of errors. There were two full glasses on the table in front of him and suspicious signs pointed to the possibility that he was drinking his mistakes. It also appeared he was pouring liquor at an alarming rate. He was acting more the generous host than the bartender, freshening drinks that did not need freshening and spilling out what he considered flat drinks, or at least bringing them into the kitchen. What he spilled them into was a matter of speculation. She decided to watch him closely for a while to be sure, then speak to him; they needed him sober tonight or not at all. And where was Ethel? Her car was not in the drive. Probably Sonny had sent her to pick up something. Joe would run out of quite a few things at the rate he was going.

Ruth was amazed at how few of the guests she knew. Some of them, the more pre-eminent, she had met at gallery receptions where they chatted about the show on view and the artists and little more. She felt there was more to speak about with them, philosophical subjects having to do with the nature of creativity and discipline, and where fulfillment lay, maybe to learn why she herself had stopped making art, yet such talk had always seemed impossible. Artists were such alone creatures. Others in the room she had heard Bert speak about but never met, like Emory Williams, anatomy lecturer at the League, a burly man with blunt features and a quiet voice. Williams was reputed to be one of the foremost authorities in the nation on anatomy for artists and his lecture series gave prestige to the school. It was rumored he was being considered for a senior post at the Met Museum.

He was holding court as he had been for some time, gesturing with his hands as he pondered the technical questions posed to him, then waiting long minutes to answer. The admirers gathered around him seemed to accept the delays as his style. Jacob Miller, a painting instructor, stood beside him. Board member, Oscar Fenton, was on his other side, looking down and rocking on his feet, hands clasped behind his back. He threw out questions like fish to a seal—good questions, he smiled after each one—and Emory Williams devoured the questions in his quiet ponderous way and the others waited and drank their freshened drinks until he produced his answer.

Ruth glanced at her watch. Eleven o'clock. Looking about the room, she thought it safe to say that all the invited guests had arrived. Also the uninvited in prodigious numbers for she was certain that students brought friends along for the ride. Sonny should have limited the guest list to his contemporaries, no earthly reason to invite his class. What did any of them mean to Bert? She glanced from one animated group to another. A few people sitting on the stairway burst into loud laughter. It was all so pointless, so unnecessary. These people, this mixed kettle of fish, meant nothing to Bert and nothing to each other either. They lived in their own worlds in their own way. How little Sonny understood. *He loves you, child, because you are his own, only because of that and in that way. None of this matters, not even you…what you do, what you become, what you are. That matters to you and to me but it doesn't to him. You're his own, that's all. Understand and you might get away unscathed.*

•   •   •

A student of her father's, Ted Riley, had brought a guitar and asked Sonata if he could play it. The others encouraged him. "Yes, later, certainly later," Sonata said, "after Dad gets here." There was such a let-down after that that she was glad Joe signaled to her and she could move on. "Excuse me," she said with the same exuberance that nixed the guitar.

Well, what did they expect, after all? Wouldn't it be great to have a jamboree going when Dad walked in the door? That was not what she had in mind at all and Ted Riley should have understood. He was an arrogant guy, so sure of himself, so smooth. She had already observed how attracted women in the room were to him. A girl standing beside him fingered his guitar seductively.

Joe was out of rocks glasses. "Already, Joe? The party's just begun." Had he opened his collar or was it that way when he started? "I been mixen 'em for over an hour, Miss." "Is it *that* late?" "Yes Ma'am, it is." Was he accusing her? "Well, collect some glasses from around the room and wash them, Joe. They can mix their own while you wash glasses, it won't kill them." They'll live, as Ethel would say.

Where was Ethel? She hadn't seen her since the party began. "Whatever you say, Miss, you're the boss." *Yes, the boss.*

She moved to the window and looked out. He always came from the right, from the subway stop on Queens Boulevard. She could see almost a block and a half in the distance under the dim street lights but no one was coming.

Vincent was talking to Paul Dobrin, another guy in her father's class and she joined them. They stopped talking as she approached and smiled at her. "I'm not interrupting anything?"

"Not a thing, just the usual—"

"Vince, how did it go after class, I'm sort of curious? Did my father notice anything, do you think? I mean, did he see you all getting together? Did he overhear the students talking?"

Vincent shook his head. "No. No," he repeated, "I don't think he noticed anything. Paul mentioned that he saw him leave before class ended, so he wasn't even there when we all got together."

"Oh." Joe was motioning to her again. She liked that he called for her instead of Ruth. "Excuse me, I'll be right back."

He couldn't find the towels. "Oh God, Joe, just look in the drawers. Where do you think towels are?" She should not have spoken so sharply. Still, he should know where towels are kept if he's been in the business for twenty-five years! She steered him to the drawer and returned to the living room. There, Vincent and Paul had moved over to join the students inspecting Ted Riley's guitar. She felt like their house-mother, passing so near and yet so far. They hated her. She was *Establishment* personified. Plastic covers would have fit right in.

She took her post once again by the window and scanned the street. A full block was visible before the turn toward the subway. She felt Willie's heavy hand on her arm. "Oh, hi, Willie. Having fun?"

Willie nodded. "I am having fun," he droned, bending as if he might ask her to dance or something. "You don't see him coming?" He strained to look for himself out the window. "Maybe soon." He looked tired. His face was fleshy and drooped with his changing expressions.

"Willie, there's no question that he expected to meet you tonight, is there?"

He shook his head and the jowls trembled. "I spoke to him again, it was last night...Yes, I called you after, but we arranged it more than a week ago. Yesterday was to remind him only, so should be no slip-up. Tonight I go out to buy beer to bring to the party then wait for him." He produced again an envelope from his sagging pocket. "You see here? If for a reason he's coming straight home instead, I take him in the studio and show him the slides. See...look, the slides."

Sonata nodded at the slides. His accent was so thick, it was possible her father had not even understood him. The more she listened to him, the more she thought this idea credible. One would think after twenty-two years in this country, he would speak better English.

6

"We don't want any," Irene called out about an hour later hearing Bert's familiar knock on the door.

"I'll bet you do. I stopped at the Stage Delicatessen."

"Ah well, I didn't know it was a catered affair," she said, letting him in.

Bert put the paper bag on the floor after looking about for a clear surface. He took her face between his hands and kissed her.

"So what's in the package?" Irene asked, smiling up at him. "No, don't tell me, let me guess. Corned beef? No, pastrami, right?"

"Wrong, try again." Bert reached in the bag and pulled out a six-pack of beer and two sandwiches wrapped in waxed paper. "Last chance," he said, unwrapping them.

"Roast beef. Good, I'm starving." She cleared a surface on the vinyl-topped table that served as her *kitchen* and pulled up two matching chairs. "What did I have for supper? I can't even remember." She produced glasses for the beer and they toasted to art and life as they usually did. She ate with relish and he laughed, watching her. "So how did your class go tonight?" she asked.

"The usual. When's your next session with us, we miss you? By the way, Helen thinks you're the best model the sketch class ever had. She's been there fifteen years, so that's a compliment." He unwrapped his sandwich then leaned across and kissed her.

"Darling?"

"Yes?"

"You're spilling my beer."

"Sorry." He blot the spot with his napkin and sat back to address his food.

"A trained dancer like me has no business modeling."

"It's a great service you're doing. A noble effort for the advancement of art. They'll remember you for it."

"Who will?"

"Me."

She laughed.

"No, I like to think of you modeling. A lot, matter of fact, at odd hours. Thought about it tonight before I called."

"You did."

"I like the one minute poses best. You have style, my lady." He leaned over and took her empty beer bottle. "When are you coming back?"

She laughed. "Next week if I don't get that chorus job at the tryouts." She picked up the wrappings of her meal. "You finished?"

"Just about. You know your hair needs brushing. You need to spiff it up for the tryouts. I'll brush it for you." He let her take his napkin and sandwich wrap and leaning toward her, wrapped his hands around her head, kissing her long and deeply. Then he filled his hand with the long brown hair hanging below a barrette and brought the ends forward for her to see. "The first thing they'll notice at your tryouts tomorrow. Healthy hair, I'm serious."

She laughed.

"Go get your hairbrush. Go on, be a good girl."

Irene rose stiffly and got her brush from a cubby-hole near the window. Returning, she found him sitting on the floor mattress in the dark, leaning against the wall. She curled up in front of him and felt the clip unfasten and the satisfying sensation of the bristles against her scalp. Bert did it strongly, stroking the hair back and with his other hand smoothed the hair from her face.

"Your wife has long hair too, doesn't she?"

"Ummn, how did you know that?"

"You told me. Is it longer than mine?"

"Yes, much longer. Shhhh."

"Do you brush her hair?"

"No."

"You told me you did brush her hair."

"I did a long time ago, not anymore. Keep still, please. You have an artist at work here." He kissed her neck as he stroked the hair away. "You like it?"

She nodded and folded her legs under her and said nothing more for several minutes. Then: "How long is her hair, would you say?"

Bert slid his hand slowly down her back. "Down to there."

"Bert, it is not. Stop."

"Stop what, you mean this?"

"Yes, that."

"Actually, I'm not sure anymore. It might go all the way down to there . . . maybe it ends somewhere around here, I just can't remember, but it'll come to me." He kissed her gently at first then pressed her lips open. He slipped his hand under the shirt to find her breast as he eased her back on the mattress.

"I'm going to be a poor hopeless mess at the tryouts tomorrow. I hope you know that."

"You'll be beautiful." He slipped the sweat bottoms down as she lifted her hips to help him. "This is the best way to get in shape. I'm surprised they didn't tell you that in dancing school."

7

"Put the slides away," Sonata said. A long deep exhale seemed to propel her to the window once again. Willie waited behind her. What was he waiting for? She heard his breath, labored and heavy, clumsy like everything else he did. No, that wasn't fair, for she had seen his work, the graceful limbs and lyrical contours of the figures he created, radiant in their Kodachrome reproductions.

"Will you have a drink, my dear? I see you are not drinking. So, I bring you something, yes?"

"No thanks, Willie, I don't care for anything right now. Maybe later, maybe when…Later. Thank you."

"Then excuse me, I take myself something."

They were playing the guitar. They didn't ask her this time but she was glad. It made noise. It was not Ted Riley, though, someone else. One of the students started to dance by himself. It was a rock beat and he was good. There was applause. After a while, others got up to dance. "Ok if we pull the rug back?" Ted Riley asked, sprinting over to her. But without waiting, he set about doing it with two others helping.

She peered through the window. It had started to snow very lightly. The windowpane misted over from her breath and she wiped it with a napkin from the table beside her. The napkin had lipstick on it and she threw it in an ashtray. She felt a tide running out inside of her, happening quickly and no soaring wave on its way. Nothing. All things leaving and nothing on the way.

Willie, to blame you! To despise you because a father needs an arrangement to bring him home. The dark night, cool and smooth against the glass, mercifully did not watch her cry.

.   .   .

Vincent sat at the desk in Kossoff's studio with Paul Dobrin standing behind him. The noise of the party swelled into the room as Dave Sudak opened the door and thrust his head inside. "Anything?"

Paul lifted his hand. "Vince is still on the phone. We tried the Sea Island Bar and the Meadows, no dice."

Freddie slipped under Dave Sudak's arm and came into the room. "What's with the Topside? He's not there?"

Paul shrugged. "They're paging him now. The line's been busy."

"If he's not there, where next?" asked Sudak.

"You got any ideas?" asked Paul. "Hey, close the door, for Christ's sake."

Dave closed the door and moved inside, sliding onto the desk. He lit a cigarette and threw the match belligerently on Kossoff's floor, "You know damn well where." He paused. "We'll start at the top of the list and work our way down."

"They won't all be listed in the phone book, I hope you realize," said Freddie.

"We realize, we realize. What the hell," Paul said, "we can try."

"Geez, this is terrible."

"I feel sorry for what's-her-name, his daughter," Dave said. "It's a shitty deal."

"Sonata," Vincent answered. "Sonny." He held the receiver still pressed against his cheek waiting for Topside to page Bert Kossoff on the slim chance he'd be there. He leaned with his elbow on the desk. Kossoff's doodles meandered over the surface on scraps of paper, elaborate contrivances with swirls and loops.

"What?"

"Nothing. I said her name was Sonny."

"She went to all that trouble," Dave moaned, "with a bartender yet!"

"What about the food and the booze? Christ," sighed Freddie, "it cost, don't kid yourself."

"Emory Williams is here…and Fenton and old Jake Miller, for Christ's sake. It's unbelievable!"

"Freddie shook his head and looked down at his feet. "Tell you the truth, I don't even want to look at her, at either of 'em. Embarrassed, you know what I mean? The girl, Sonny?—she was all so . . . spunky when we came in, like a kid before Christmas."

"The hell," Dave said, "Come on, stop cryin', will ya! Get off the phone with Topside, Vince, that's a dead end. We'll give the models a try. Look, we'll do the best we can. Anyway, like Freddie said, it's better than sitting out there and having to look at them."

"She's pretty, his wife is," Vincent said, still not giving up his connection with the Topside. "First time I ever saw her."

"I like her hair. You see how long it is in back?" said Paul. "It's down to her whatsis!" Dave said, demonstrating.

"Can you imagine how she feels now? Nah, you can't," Freddie said. "I can't."

"All right don't start in again. Who's number one?" asked Dave jumping off the desk.

"I don't know," said Paul, "I think it's Irene."

"No, it isn't, it's Celeste, the new one."

"Ok, go ahead, try it," said Dave, "What's her number?"

"Christ, I don't know," said Paul, "How do you think I should know that? Look it up in the book. Do you know her last name at least?"

"Wait a minute," said Dave, "I'll get Betsy, she knows everybody. She does payroll."

"I thought she was at the front desk—reception."

"No, she used to be. They switched her to payroll because she's smart. I got a smart wife."

"Dave, you need a smart wife."

"Wait right here, I'll get her." At the door, he turned. "She doesn't know about Kossoff. She's gonna wonder why we're calling these gals."

Freddie pursed his lips and nodded. "Whatever she didn't know before, I guarantee she'll know before this night is out, no assistance from us."

"And she's not the only one," added Vincent. He replaced the receiver and stared at it. "Kossoff is not at the Topside, that's official."

He looked up at Dave still standing at the door. "Go get your wife, Dave, we'll start at the top and work down."

"That's Irene."

"The hell," said Freddie, "It's Celeste. Could be Juanita now I think of it."

8

Later, Bert stood over Irene in the darkness as she lay on the mattress among the colorful pillows.

"Close your eyes, Irene, I have to turn on the light."

The whisper sounded as if he were a distance away. She smiled, remembering how her father had carried her from the car after a trip. Inside, he would set her down on the couch—the only gentle act of his she could remember—and tell her to close her eyes and she would wait there obediently, keeping her eyes shut against the light while he took care of things. Mother whispered orders as he carried in the luggage and opened the windows. All the responsibilities were theirs. He carried her upstairs to bed and her mother would tuck her in fully clothed so she could hold on to the illusion of sleep, that thin bubble of time between sleep and wakefulness which might break if jostled.

Now, again, she did as she was told, keeping her eyes tightly shut against the light. But her body, a woman's body, lay naked and exposed in the brightness and she felt strangely deceptive. The responsibilities were her own and keeping the light away made no sense at all. Then gratefully, it was dark again and Bert picked her up and carried her to the bed.

"Goodnight, love," he said, snugly covering her. "Lots of luck tomorrow, but don't give 'em too much. They don't deserve it. I'll call you."

He kissed her and then he was gone. She fell asleep, trying vaguely to remember what she had been so frightened of before he came.

9

It was well after midnight and some older guests had left, Williams and Fenton and a few others, but most others remained. Vincent sat next to Sonata on the couch, but they said little to each other. There was enough noise without them. The radio was tuned to WABC and people sat on the floor, smoking, talking, some dancing to The Righteous Brothers, *You've Lost That Lovin Feeling.* Freddie sat on the other side of Vincent, drinking punch.

"It's not bad," he said to Sonata, "You make it?"

Sonata nodded and smiled. "Would you like some, Vince?"

"Thanks, no. I'm on beer." She smiled again. "Would you like a refill? I'll call Joe."

Her tone was awful, Vincent thought, her smile too. Edgy, helpless.

"I'll have a drink now, I think." She raised her voice, "Joe! Oh, Joe—"

Joe Papadopoulos was still with it, collecting glasses, emptying ashtrays. Vincent watched him round the corner into the kitchen, not hearing Sonata call him. Freddie was watching too.

"He's bashed," Freddie said, speaking low. "What in hell is holding him up is what I'd like to know?"

"Stamina," someone said, overhearing. "Same thing that holds Kossoff up!" Some others laughed at that. Vincent looked at Sonata, but her eyes were on the kitchen doorway, waiting for Joe. There were other remarks, less subtle.

"I'd like to dance with you," Vincent said, touching her to force her eyes on him.

She looked at him and smiled, the performance smile offered before. "I'm waiting for Joe…for my drink."

"Never mind that now. Will you dance with me, Sonny?"

She shrugged, the smile skidding off her face. "It's a silly place to dance, this room. Funny, I never pictured people dancing here. I've lived in this house all my life and no one has ever danced in this room." She looked out over the room, at the couples dancing. "It's so out of place."

He gripped her hand; it was damp and trembled. He led her to a corner of the room and put his arms around her waist. Dutifully she lifted hers to his shoulders.

Vincent pressed her body against his and they moved, rocking with the tempo. Sonata tried to feel the music or at least register what was playing. Vincent felt the tension in her body and eased her head against his cheek. They both could see Joe leaning against the doorway laughing with someone and gesturing with his hands, but Sonata had lost interest in the drink.

When the music ended and a disk jockey began talking about a movie, Vincent led her into the studio and closed the door. The sounds from the other room grew distant as he kissed her and the wild confusion in her mind steadied enough for her to feel her body soften as he held her very close. Then after a few minutes, sitting side by side on the narrow cot with her hand clasped in his, she asked him questions and he answered and told her what she wanted to know.

•   •   •

Willie, his thick hands listless on his thighs, sat by himself and watched Ruth make a fool of herself. Once or twice he had suggested to her that they take a walk, have a quiet talk, take coffee together in the kitchen. He even urged her to terminate the party.

"Send them away. They stay, they wait. For what? To see him walk in the door? What will they say when he walks in the door at 2 A.M.?" But all that had been earlier when she was with them. Now she was alone, alone with more talking and touching and nonsense than he had ever seen from her.

Ruth sat on the floor between Eli Tanninger and Phillip Orenson, instructors whom Willie had known for many years. She was looking up at Tanninger and smiling. There is a way that a young girl looks at a boy and this was her way now, a coyness and innocence together. How easy it would be to destroy her now. Her shoes were off and her legs were curled under her. Her hair hung loosely, some forward of her shoulders, some behind. She was a beautiful woman, Willie thought, remembering her quietness, the way she moved, graceful and swift with simple efficiency.

A student approached their little enclave and was invited to join them. When he bent to sit with them on the floor, the three moved closer to one another and Willie saw the casual rubbing against Ruth's arms and thighs. As Ted Riley began playing quiet love songs on his guitar, she leaned back, listening, her eyes closed. The men stole glances at her, separately. It was only when she left them like that, closed all of them off, that she was with them. When she rejoined them with her desperate eyes and her eagerness to listen, it was then she was no longer there.

10

With the powder room downstairs in use, Sonata decided to use the upstairs bathroom but found it locked.

She tried not to be annoyed that guests had taken the liberty of using the family bathroom but was, and embarrassed because she had not straightened it for company. The curlers were out and make-up and who knows what else and there was probably a rim around the tub from her bath. It was one of those things you just took for granted: company waited for the powder room to be free. She stood for a disgruntled moment outside the door wanting to kick it in, then turned away.

In her bedroom she propped a pillow on the bed and kicked off her shoes to wait. The sounds coming from downstairs were boisterous. People were having fun with or without him. WABC was cooperative: The Beatles, The Supremes, The Temptations.

And what about him? Well, she knew more now; why he was not here and why not altogether here when he was. He just didn't care—about her or Ruth. And what about Ruth? Sitting back all these years to take whatever he gave her, any way he gave it. A dustpan to scoop up the crumbs he left in the sheets.

She lowered the pillow and turned on her side. My God, she thought now, how could he have any respect for a wife who lets him handle anybody he can get his hot hands on? And did *they* know—all those people downstairs? Sure they knew. It was obvious the way they looked at her mother. They had no respect for her, how could they? Tonight was a tribute, all right, to a dustpan. Hats off!

She turned off the lamp by her bed and closed her eyes feeling dizzy. Joe's drinks were taking their toll. She may have dozed off when a door opened in the hall and she sprang out of bed, remembering she was waiting for the bathroom. But it was her mother's door that opened. To her astonishment she saw Ted Riley step out into the hall, closing the door softly behind him. He wiped his mouth with a handkerchief, checked his fly, then removed a small pocket comb and ran it through his hair. He looked up to see Sonata staring. His mouth twitched, but it was a second's discomfort, for the smile was back again as self-assured as earlier in the living room playing his guitar. He tucked the comb into his pocket and sprinted down the stairs, humming a spirited tune.

Sonata stepped back into the darkness of her room and waited. Several minutes passed before her mother emerged from her bedroom. She hesitated for a moment outside her door as if preparing to descend into the hell awaiting her.

For a long while, Sonata stood there in the dark. Her body was shaking but her mind felt clear—almost as if she expected—but still her body trembled. And she felt ill. Everything was unraveling at once, everything she knew or thought she knew. She closed the door and turned on the lamp. Her stuffed teddy bear, fallen to the floor, gazed at her with his one eye. She kicked him hard. Only then as he lay flat against the wall, did she stumble across the floor to grab him in her arms and sob.

Noises sounded in the hall. She daubed at her eyes and opened the door. Betsy, white and grim, came out of the bathroom and crossed the carpeted floor passing Sonata s room like an ashen ghost. She proceeded to the end of the hall and then continued stiffly down the stairs.

Poor Betsy. No wonder she was in the bathroom for so long and it didn't matter about the curlers and rim around the tub because Betsy would never have noticed. Sonata entered the bathroom locking the door. She straightened the counter, putting all the rollers, pins, jars and tubes in their places and then she scoured the sink, and on her hands and knees washed the tub. After she had done that and replaced the mat, she raised herself and turned to the bowl and was ill, just like poor Betsy.

II

Willie slumped into a chair which had been pushed back from the improvised dance floor. His customary bedtime was before this party even began. He was content now to merely sit and watch the goings-on. When Joe Papadopoulos started to dance there were already eight or ten couples out there, the floor vibrating with the pounding of feet.

They were all doing some kind of Greek dance. A handkerchief dangled from Ted Riley's mouth. Betsy was weaving under and around it, Dave yelling at her from the other end of the room to sit down before she fell on her face.

Joe apparently knew the dance. "Goddamn it, I'm a Greek!" It was true that despite his legs which buckled now and then, he danced fairly well. He threw out his chest and held in his stomach as he bent his knees and rocked his head with the rhythm. Most of the people were not watching the exhibition. Now and then some did and laughed and turned away.

"Look here," he said, interrupting his own dance. "You never saw this before, damn it." He took a glass and filled it halfway with Sonata's punch and showed it around the room. "Look. You see it?"

If anyone had known what he intended to do, it would have been different. Later, Willie blamed himself that he hadn't realized what was happening. Somewhere years ago in a West Side bar he had seen a guy do the same thing with a glass of water.

Ceremoniously, Joe took a place in the middle of the room and leaned far back, his head almost parallel to the floor. The music was playing, but the dancers stopped and moved away from him when he put the glass on his forehead. It was by their moving back, pressing closer to the walls to give him room that the accident happened.

It was Betsy who veered suddenly when Joe Papadopoulos swerved towards her. But it was Paul Dobrin, veering away from Betsy crying "The crazy fool's got his knees leading him around—can't see where he's going!"—who actually knocked *Study in Blues* off the wall.

Everything happened so quickly after that, it was hard to say who did what. The glass fell off Joe's forehead—he claimed it was absolute perfect balance—"Somebody knocked it off! I done that professionally for Christ's sake!" It fell against the frame and broke and the purple punch spilled over the canvas and then Paul, or perhaps it was Betsy since they both lunged simultaneously in an effort to catch the glass, lost balance and stepped into the canvas, ripping it in the middle and destroying the four-foot painting that had won first prize for oils at the Venice International Biennial.

Willie scrambled to his feet, his hands pressed to his head, not knowing how or what or whom to rescue.

It was when Ruth knelt on her knees beside the mutilated picture, shoveling glass into her shoe and cheerfully telling everybody that everything—absolutely everything—was perfectly all right, that Bert Kossoff opened the door and entered his home.

The guests stared at Bert. His jacket was snow dusted, his hair wind ravaged. His mouth gaped open and slack as he stared back.

·　　·　　·

Dazed, Bert looked out at the crowded room. For a moment there was confusion, broken images that his mind strived to reconstruct: people, a face and another face, recognizable, familiar. He began to understand that they were here in his own living room and it was a drunken whoring hour in the morning and he was coming home. But they were waiting for him to come home. And when he fully comprehended that the strained and awful smiles of Willie and Orenson and Tanninger and Dobrin and all the rest were on him and for him, he felt a rage that was like a beast trapped inside him, beating against the inner wall of his chest.

How dare they wait for him? What have they done here in his own home? He saw Ruth on the floor by the shambles of his painting, slashed and ruined. *How dare she open his life to them!*

He had no idea how long he stood there or what he did or what he said, if he said anything. For the first time in his life, he felt a total collapse of his control over it.

Blindly, he stormed up the stairs.

．　　．　　．

And Willie thought: *What would happen to them now? What happens when you can no longer make believe that everything is all right, when all the pictures you have created shatter before your eyes? Ah, then make believe matures. It grows into a full grown lie.*

He saw Bert throw his jacket on the floor and stride upstairs. Then he looked at Ruth with the fragments of destruction beneath her and watched her struggle to her feet. *What happens when make-believe matures and the lie emerges? It becomes truth.* Yes. It can become truth.

．　　．　　．

Sonata had disappeared when Kossoff came in and Vincent was worried. He sent Betsy upstairs to look for her while he checked the downstairs but she wasn't anywhere there. He grabbed his jacket and searched outside in the front and back of the house and peered up the street in both directions, all without success. Returning, he heard Betsy and Dave and Freddie and old Willie at the door saying goodbye to Ruth. Separately, they spoke their thank-you's and told her how sorry they were…about the picture. They were sorry about the picture.

Ted Riley and Paul Dobrin stopped in the doorway. They had unrolled the rug and put the furniture back in place.

"Thank you," Ruth said, her voice rising with difficulty. "I'm sorry you had to go to all that trouble."

"It's nothing, the least we could do. Hey. so sorry about how things—"

"Goodnight, Ted . . . Paul. Thank you both."

Outside, they wanted to wait with Vincent for Sonata but he sent them on. He watched as they passed under the streetlamp, the sidewalk wet from snow flurries earlier. Their voices and others blended into the endless, distant drone of night city traffic.

Vincent stood there for a little while wondering what to do, wondering if she would come home now, ever. And then he heard Kossoff's voice, resonant over his wife's soft questions.

"But I called and canceled out on Willie! Tonight! He didn't answer so I called here. I told your goddamn sister, that's who."

Vincent turned and walked to the subway station at Queens Boulevard.

Inside, in front of the deserted newsstand, shivering in silk jersey and taffeta, Sonata waited for him.

PART SIX
NAKED UNDER THE LIGHTS

I

It was a little past 4:00 AM according to the brass wall clock over the coat rack. Waffles were the specialty in this coffee shop open twenty-four hours a day and they both had ordered and devoured them with sliced, warm apples.

Sonata sat next to Vincent in a booth as they waited for their third or fourth cup of coffee. She rested her cheek in one hand and drummed the table with the other and when the sleepy-eyed waiter, neither expecting nor offering a smile, brought her coffee she pulled it toward her without moving. "Please let me, Vincent. It's not something I'll be sorry for. I'm not going back there."

Vincent picked up the fingers again tapping beside the cup. They were slender and long with neat oval edges, fingers not used to working, good for table tapping and waiting. "What would you do, Sonata? I mean, if you came with me, and if your father didn't call the police?" She had gotten into the subway train with him at the Queens station, mainly to get out of the cold and talk, and ridden with him to the near bottom of Manhattan where he lived. She'd refused to let him put her on a ride back home and here they were.

"Oh, Vincent."

"Well, what would you do? I go to the League and I paint and that's the whole story for me. For you it would be dull and lonely and—" He tried to make her meet his eyes. "—Sonny, my life is not the kind that shares well."

170

"I know that. God, don't I know all about that?" she exclaimed, glancing at him, then down again to her fingers. "One thing I am used to is people who don't share their lives. Dad sure can't and Mom just gives it away." Her fingers stopped tapping to rest in his hand. "I think it's right that you don't share your life and I'm not asking for that."

She smoothed the hairs on the surface of his hand and wrist. "That party for my father was a disaster for sure, but the failure wasn't my fault. I think I was happier than I'd ever been, planning and pulling it off—the party itself, I mean—it showed me what I can do." She straightened and twisted toward him, knocking over a knife which clattered noisily to the floor in the quiet, empty restaurant. "Oh Vincent, I could help you. I mean, I understand what it's like to live with an artist. Your needs are special, I know it. And I would go to the League myself and learn to draw—the right way, with a model. It's ridiculous the way I've been doing it, first copying my father's old faded drawings and then depending on him to teach me everything—drawing, painting, stretching a canvas—and he hates doing it, I'd be blind not to see it. I'm like a lump of furniture dumped in his studio he can't wait to get rid of. Oh, Vincent, I could go to the afternoon sketch class like Willie does and you and those others I met tonight. And maybe you could help me, you know, show me what I'm doing wrong. And I'd take a class in the afternoon...maybe with Jacob Minter, he seems like he'd be a great teacher."

Vincent picked the knife up off the floor and sipped his coffee, letting her plans for the future settle about them. He had nothing to add.

"Vincent, there's something else. I've...well, we've all known situations where a woman becomes an inspiration for a man. You're still young, but I believe you're going to be a great man one day."

Vincent smiled, then laughed out loud. It was so simple, the way she said it: A great man. He used to say it to himself all the time.

"I'd model for you," she declared, folding her hands primly on the table.

He grinned. "What do you mean, you'd model for me?"

"Just that," she said, tilting her head coyly, "I'd model for you."

"You mean you would model for me without clothes on."

"Yes, I mean that." She drank her coffee, and then looked him in the eye, having made her offer.

"Ah well, now." He laughed. His eyes were merry, hers were mischievous. Vincent unfolded her hands and stroked the smooth white fingers. He pursed his lips. "It's a tempting proposal. Very tempting."

"Oh Vincent, stop joking. I've never been more serious about anything in my life. I want to help you and be part of the wonderful things you do and *will* do. You'll see I can. Please let me, Vincent. If you don't, I...I don't know what—"

She turned away and buried her face in her hands and a half smothered voice mumbled, "I won't go back there. I never will."

"Shhhh, come on, Sonny, stop it now." She continued to whimper as he pat her head and stroked her hair. "We have to give this more thought. I can't just whisk you away like this."

"I'll never go back to them," she cried again. "I'll sleep in the street tonight or whatever." She struggled away from him and half rose in her seat as if to leave.

"Okay, okay. Sit down. We'll work something out."

The bleary-eyed waiter approached. "You folks gonna order anything else?" he asked, already laying their check on the table.

•   •   •

They walked along Sixth Avenue, past half-deserted streets where buildings loomed ponderous like pre-historic animals while city dwellers slept in their cat-nap kind of peace, a sleep not to dream, but to brace for another day. What was he letting himself in for by agreeing to let her come home with him? What would he do with her and how in God's name would he fit her into the cramped confines of his apartment and his life?

Was it foolish to worry about comfort? He thought about his cot which was too narrow to begin with and caved in the middle; however he slept he slid into that rut and it was not a rut big enough for two. Was this an opportunity or a drag and could he afford not to know the difference? He glanced at Sonata walking with her arm in his, shivering in no coat and refusing his jacket, with her bosom trembling seductively and her lips moist and eager to part for him.

Okay, he would get a new bed. Maybe he could think up something clever to get Pete to pay for it. The last thought delighted him and impulsively, he put his arm around Sonata and squeezed her shoulder. She smiled and tucked her arm around his waist and Vincent thought oddly: it's the first time anyone has done that. It was an awkward way to walk, their own four-legged amble. They rounded the corners into Sheridan Square and the mixed up streets of Greenwich Village as the sun came up.

In the apartment, Vincent handed her a phone to call her parents. "You have to call them, they've gotta be worried you're not in your bed."

"My mother, maybe, not him."

"No, your father too. Go ahead."

Vincent barely made out what she said into the phone extension in his kitchenette, she spoke so softly, but he heard his name mentioned several times. Sonata said nothing coming back into the room and he let it go, satisfied that at least they knew where she was. He lay propped on his cot, hands behind his head, and watched Sonata walk around the room inspecting his work. She glanced back at him now and then smiling her approval.

It was morning and the whole day stretched before them. What would he do with her all this day and the next and after that? There'd been a stray kitten when he was a kid, grayish-white and fluffy, that he had found trapped in a tree, too frightened to come down and he rescued it and brought it home. And the kitten, cute and playful, tore up everything it could get its paws on; so they clipped its nails and then it could not protect itself so they had to keep it inside and it grew to a dismal, bad-tempered cat-hood. The cat drew blood when it bit him, yet still Vincent felt an unexplainable pain when the SPCA van came and took the animal away. He'd had no choice as a compassionate human to take the kitten in and no choice as an intelligent human but to put it out.

If this arrangement was going to work, it would have to be productive for both of them and that meant through work. Sonata's idea of modeling for him might be right after all. Rising to sit on the end of his cot, he lit a cigarette and continued to watch her stroll from canvas to canvas, taking in everything as if his room was a gallery. She praised his technique in one picture and choice of colors in another but just liking it was her judgment on most. She sat down at last in the one easy chair in the room with her legs stretched out, hands folded on her lap and smiled up at him.

"Thanks for the comments," he said. Then, as if confirming a decision, he slapped his thighs and stood. "Well, I guess we should get started." He began busily moving around the room, pushing a table to one side to make space for a chair near the window, carrying it there, setting up a light.

He turned and saw her watching him. "You can change in there," he said, waving her towards the bathroom.

"Change?"

"Get undressed, I mean."

"Undressed?"

"Yes. We can work now, the light's not too terrible."

"Oh. Oh sure."

Vincent saw through the corner of his eye that she hadn't moved. Nevertheless, he began arranging his brushes and paints on the table. He pulled the slim muslin curtain open all the way and when he turned back to the room saw she had disappeared into the bathroom.

Now he began to anticipate this new experience with quiet excitement. He'd never had a model sit for him personally. Sonata was not professional but she wanted to please and would be willing to let him pose her. Leaving space for his easel, he moved the chair to catch whatever light came through the window. Studying the scene for a moment he grabbed a gray cotton blanket from his bed and draped it over the chair.

He whistled as he selected his colors, thinking of her skin tones and shadow values and also that maybe the arrangement would work out after all. A live-in model. He chuckled softly.

She stood just outside the bathroom door wrapped in a towel and waiting, as if she might have forgotten something inside. Vincent watched her approach the chair. He was glad she had thought of the towel but he would wait and let her take it off when she felt comfortable.

2

At first, Sonata had not understood what "get started" meant. She watched him pull a kitchen chair to the far end of the room near the window, then drape a grayish blanket on it from his bed. In the restaurant she hadn't projected this far; how the modeling would be accomplished. She had only a vague idea that it would be more natural than this; that they would lead into it, after they made love or something; after they lived together awhile and knew each other better. Was she supposed to trot over there and sit on that chair or what?

The scene felt wrong. She wasn't just a model, and she wasn't just a friend; they hadn't established anything yet, just two ideas getting together. And he was so professional all of a sudden, so formal.

She'd looked for the lock on the bathroom door but there was none. It disturbed her. This was a peculiar feeling too because why should she need a lock to undress when she was about to walk out without any clothes on? Should she take off her underwear? When she had sex, those couple of times with the only boyfriend she'd ever had sex with, she'd kept her bra and panties on and let him take them off. But this wasn't sex.

Why couldn't he have waited? Until tomorrow, yes? Tomorrow after breakfast would have been fine: sunny-side eggs over lightly, she was good cooking that. Also, fatigue was washing over her. She wanted to go to sleep. Sleep in her own bed. No, no, his bed. Any bed.

Sonata kept one hand on the towel and contemplated Vincent's white canvas propped on an easel. She tried to imagine her image somewhere on it, hoping this would help her. Still, she suspected the longer she waited, the harder it would be. *Just drop the thing, like the models shed their robes. One, two, three, drop it. What do you have there that's spectacular? He's seen a thousand bodies.*

"I thought I'd pose you sitting down to start, how's that?"

"Oh fine! I'd like to sit down."

"Good."

She smiled hesitantly.

"So, how about sitting down?"

"Yes." She turned toward the chair. "I suppose you'd prefer me without the towel, unless you want this blue color in the picture. It's a pretty shade."

"No, I don't need the towel."

"Sure." She nodded, and her hand on the chairback, watched him work on his preparations. She remembered once on a camp trip trying to jump off the top of a large ship into the water like her friends were doing; she'd curled her toes over the edge of the deck and wanted to let go and jump, but she couldn't. Others were diving, she had only to let go, jump, and fall into the water.

If only he would help her. If only he would kiss her and caress her and then take off the towel himself and set it aside and gaze at her, pleased with what he saw, well then it would make sense.

3

Vincent knew that it would take another minute or so and she would feel comfortable enough to take off the towel. He would keep busy for a few minutes more and stay out of her way. Then he'd say something, something that would ease the initial shock.

"Pose, please."

"What?"

"Would you take a seat on the chair?"

Sonata drew a long breath. She settled herself on the chair. The drape of the towel covering her fell in folds on her lap.

"Sonata, would you mind if I loosened the towel?" Vincent asked. He wasn't used to this new voice of his, the voice that cooed to the cat and told it everything would be fine while he waited for the SPCA.

Sonata nodded, still staring at the folds in her lap.

Vincent gently parted the towel. He let the loose end of it drape over her pubic area then placed her hand on her thigh, close to the towel, as if to guard it from being removed.

He stepped back. There was an instant sense of importance in the air. Yes, nudity did that. It was the same at the League now that he pictured it. He was pleased with her body. Her breasts were small and pale and her belly had a perfect roundness. He was glad about her belly because she looked so flat in clothes. Her pubic hair was a soft brown fuzz, lighter than the hair on her head and that pleased him too.

"Well, here I am," she said with a little laugh, sitting stiffly.

"Are you cold, Sonny?" he asked catching her shudder.

"No, I'm fine."

"Can you turn a little, just a little? Keep going, there, that's it. Now, bring your head back like it was. Too much…okay, good. Now, can you hold this pose? Is it comfortable? That's it, lean on your hand a bit if it's helpful."

She nodded without answering. She could hold her body, the problem was that her voice had gone. Funny, she thought, how easy it was to pretend with your body, to pose it, and how hard to make your voice behave like that. Glancing around at her unfamiliar surroundings and situation, she half expected someone to come through the door and demand an explanation: a stranger or neighbor from another apartment. Ruth? A sudden vision of her father seeing her was too painful and she threw it off. Still, she fought the urge to grab the towel and pull it over her breasts.

Vincent covered the edges of the canvas with a pale gray wash then added more pigment to block in the overall pose. Sonata sat so stiffly he was afraid she would fall over from lack of breath. Still, he mused, she had a lovely body, a curving pyramid above the draped chair. How much lovelier her body was nude than in clothes, like in the long loose tops she wore, probably to hide those sweeping hips. And how poetic her long bare legs, in contrast to her covered legs striding in their awkward gait— even in the party shoes she wore last night. Was it only last night? How far they had come!

"Sonny," he said, after a while, "You have a nice body…beautiful in fact." He smiled as he saw her shoulders relax and breath return under the ribs.

Gradually, he began to concentrate less on her and more on the figure emerging on his canvas. He kept her there a long time in his absorption, longer than he had intended and when he realized it, he put his brush down and said, "You'd better rest. I'm sorry. I forgot you're not used to this." He crossed the room and took his bathrobe from the closet.

"It's all right," she said cheerfully, "I'm not tired. I was before. Keep working, I can hold it."

"No. Here, take this. You have to rest now or you'll be stiff for next time. I don't want you to wear out."

She laughed." I don't wear out so easily, Vince." But she put the robe on anyway and stepped off the chair.

"Walk around a little, stretch your muscles," he said, once again picking up his brush.

She ambled to a spot behind him watching him work. He squeezed titanium white from a tube and a drop of mars black for the drape covering the chair and daubed chromium oxide green into the shadows. With a palette knife he blended a small mound of yellow ochre into that and applied it to the canvas and the drape began to have some texture.

"Okay, Sonny, could you pose again please? The exact same way. How do you feel?"

"I'm fine." She climbed on the chair with ease and settled into the pose. "Oh, I forgot to take this thing off," she said, laughing and untying the robe. When she lifted herself to throw it on a chair, she caught a glimpse of Vincent's face, slightly impatient. His expression surprised and dismayed her and she thought about it all the while she held her pose. He seemed so inconsistent, stern and demanding one minute and considerate and anxious for her the next. He was not going to be an easy person to understand, but she had felt this the first day they met in his painting class, weighing her words, seeming to judge her. But then, the friendliness of his smile and inviting her to come back later when he'd have more time. And it wasn't only with her, this inconsistency; she had observed him with his friends last night, Dave Sudak and his wife and Ted Riley. He seemed unsure of them, and how he should behave around them. He seemed always to be settling people in his mind.

She realized she had been eager to see Vincent and her father together. She'd imagined the two of them conversing, seeing in Vincent's eyes his respect and admiration for him. Well, now that she knew better it didn't matter. Vincent could think what he wanted about Bert Kossoff and vice versa, she couldn't care less.

Time passed; a gentle purring of a clock sounded somewhere near. She couldn't turn her head to see, though she wondered what time it was. Behind a partition, the refrigerator motor turned on and hummed, drowning out the clock.

Across the room a portrait of a semi-nude seated woman, not so unlike herself, peered at her from its wood-strip frame. As she regarded its rosy flesh, she began to see herself as if through a viewer's eyes: posed on the stool, a man looking at her body with a paint brush clasped in his fingers. Seeing herself this way at first simply felt weird as she became aware of her thighs and calves and each of her toes as never before. Then slowly a bristling sensation overtook her that she was in a place she didn't belong. This apartment, Vincent . . . but where did she belong? Nowhere.

Coming home late one night from the library, stopping to stand outside she had seen her parents facing each other in the brightly lit living room. There was nothing unusual happening, yet standing on the dark street, the scene looked eerily unnatural, like a pantomime where the audience, denied words, had to search out the essential meaning. The scene then as now seemed to have no answers, only questions.

For a fleeting moment she had the urge to jump down from the stool, gather her clothes and leave, but that would be ridiculous. She had begged to be doing exactly this. It felt wrong only because it was new. She would get used to it in time.

4

In the weeks that followed, Vincent evolved a schedule. He found that he was successful painting her from memory; therefore, he would pose her in the morning and make sketches from different angles and then in the afternoon put the sketches away and paint from memory, abstracting the forms as he pleased. She was free then to wander around the Village, looking in the shop windows and at people, whom she found far more interesting than those on the streets of Forest Hills.

He was imbued with a new spirit of freedom which he discovered in all of his work that included her. Her body encouraged his style like an intent listener encourages wit. She was not so much posing when she sat for him as waiting, expecting him to do something important, and he did.

It was not the same in bed. Her body was not waiting and expectant in bed and this surprised him because she'd said there was only one guy before him, so he thought she'd be more timid and reticent. In the beginning she was, serving her apprenticeship, so to speak, but when she got the hang of it, and it didn't take her long, she became a director. She took the lead, manipulating him like something that belonged to her. Her thighs had a strong grip. At first he'd been excited to feel her respond to him with such energy, thrusting against him and pulling him to her, but soon it was she who set the rhythm of their movements. Her whispers were like commands and his pace was slackened and quickened by the intensity of those cries. Her hips, those gently curving valleys and hills on canvas, were great mother's hips in bed and there were times when he felt more like a boy than a man.

But the freedom in his painting was undeniable. His method of working had always been first, the conception—a mix of the visuals in his mind and his sensual responses—then, disciplined compositional design and last, laborious execution in the selection of his colors, rendering his contours and shading the forms. Now he found he had all the results he wanted achieved not with agony but ease. He enjoyed working and this, he realized with some astonishment, was new.

He had stopped going to the daily sketch classes at the League and to Kossoff's painting class as well. Paul Dobrin was substituting for him as monitor. He would go back to it, but for now he wanted to make certain he did not confuse the images of Sonata, which were growing ever sharper, with any other model. It was seeing her purely from his personal vision that gave him the deepest satisfaction. All things extraneous to that vision were sifted out and discarded. What she was to her father, her mother or even herself had no meaning for him. Never before had he felt his perception to be so uniquely his own, so influenced by nothing other than his reaction to this woman and taking nothing more from her each time than what he saw there.

The more he succeeded in expressing what he saw, the more confidence he had that his personal vision was secure and could be trusted. This was the primary tool, the basic necessity of his craft, and he had doubted that vision for too long.

One morning watching Sonata asleep in their narrow bed, huddled in his robe to keep warm, he wondered if it was possible for him to have the same clear vision of himself as he had of her. He wondered if he could get rid of the useless baggage he carried around and arrive unencumbered at the clear image of Vincent Denfield—not the whole man, which was impossible—but that part of the man he had interest in, the creative force inhabiting him.

He moved his easel by the full-length mirror in the hall and then studied the reflected face. The short squat beard was in the way and Vincent Denfield was not clearly seen. On an impulse he went into the bathroom and shaved it off. When he looked again in the mirror, he was momentarily staggered by the absence of premeditation in his action. He did not make impromptu decisions. Never, until he made the one allowing Sonata to live with him.

He laughed in the mirror and watched the face become happy. He would need to expose that pale chin to some sunlight before it looked like it belonged on the front of his face; now it was as naked and white as his backside in summer.

He laughed again and stroked the chin affectionately like the return of a long-lost friend.

He began to paint, making several bad starts, washing each one out with thinned paint and beginning again. He thought about Sonata and wondered if the coarse wool of his bathrobe irritated her skin as it did his when he wore it. She would be nude underneath though the apartment was cold today. The whole building was cold. Only one radiator heated each corridor, hardly enough in this weather, and the draft under the door was brutal. "It's cold as a witch's tit in here," Pete had said when he saw the place for the first and last time a year ago. Was it a year ago? Yes, because now it was February again.

"One year of living like a bum and that's it!" Pete had roared, granting Alexandra's appeals for his sustenance. "After that he goes to work for a living like the rest of us. You hear, Alex? And you, Mr. Bum, you hear?"

They didn't know about Sonata. He had kept on with occasional Sunday dinner visits and collected his monthly checks and everything looked exactly the same except that it was different as it could be.

The face on the canvas was beginning to resemble Howard's. Funny, there he was shooting straight from the inner eye and out came Howard. Well, there was a resemblance between them people said, though he couldn't see it. Sonata said there was.

He was eager for her to wake up so they could begin work together and becoming impatient with the self-portrait. Approaching the bed he found her just as she was before, on her side, knees almost touching her chest.

He pulled the covers off and she stirred. The robe did irritate her; he could tell by the way she rolled over and grimaced as it rubbed against her back. He untied and opened it. He kissed her and brought his hand down to soothe the abused sensitive skin. For a moment when he saw her smile in her half sleep, he felt like crawling into the irritating bathrobe with her. He held back, anxious to use that energy on canvas, not lose it in bed.

He left the robe open and watched the cold force her eyes open. Hastily, she pulled the covers back up to her chin and groaned. "Jesus, it's freezing!"

"Come on, get up! I've hung around for hours waiting. I've got a sensational idea for a pose."

With her eyes closed, she was feeling under the covers for the ends of the robe, trying to close it around her. "Oh God, Vince, you don't expect me to stand out there in my altogether today? I'll be a mummy in ten minutes."

"It's not so bad once you get used to it. I'm not kidding, Sonny, I have a great idea. I'm posing us both together—you and me in the same picture."

"Vincent, what are you talking about? You're not making sense."

"Listen, I have compositions in mind and ways to use the color contrasts—your whiteness against my ruddiness—to play around with."

"Play around with, you mean naked? Both of us naked?"

"Sure, why not?"

"It sounds pornographic."

"Oh, come on," he urged, jostling her shoulder, "You've been lying in bed too long. See that, you're thinking sex instead of art." He bent down and kissed her and whispered, "Think art." His hand slipped under the covers and traveled over her body and wedged between her thighs pressed tightly together for warmth. He whispered again, "Think art. Think color. Get rid of those nasty thoughts, you sinful child."

She opened her eyes finally and looked at him. "Vincent! You've shaved your beard."

"Sure, I've been busy. What do you think? I lie around all day like you?"

She pulled him down and kissed him, caressing the new chin. Then she opened the covers and wriggled back, smiling. "Come, lie around all day like me."

He sighed and shook his head, then removed his clothes. When he climbed into the bed beside her she took him protectively in her arms bringing the covers up around his shoulders. She leaned over him as she touched his body and whispered, "Think sex, that's a good boy. Think sex."

She wanted to go back to sleep afterwards, but he wouldn't allow it. "Come on! Up and at 'em!" He pulled the covers off, tossing them on the floor and rolled her out of the robe. "Let's go."

She sat up and huddled on the side of the bed looking at the defeated covers. "Vincent, it's hard making the bed from scratch." She shivered, then yawned, then shivered again.

"Let's go!" Look, I've got everything set up by the mirror."

She searched for the robe. "Well let me wash my face first, for God's sake."

"Do it later," he said, squeezing fresh colors onto his palette. "Come on, I mean it! Before I run out of steam."

Getting up she started to stretch but huddled instead from the cold. "I'm going to the bathroom, hold your steam." From the bathroom she called out, "News! Your landlord ran out of steam. This radiator is ice cold!"

"Well hurry over to this one. It's working and warm as toast."

When she emerged, he posed her sitting and put himself behind her and a little to one side. He set his easel and paints up in front of him, everything in line with the mirror.

Sonata laughed, staring at the images in the mirror. "This is real silly. It's so funny seeing you paint with your thing bouncing around every time you lean over to fill your brush."

He didn't respond to that.

"Don't get paint on it," she advised.

The canvas began to materialize, the Vincent forms elongated and angular, the Sonata contours curved and delicate. Vincent was delighted with the contrasts and played with the color contrasts as well, painting Sonata pale and painting himself ruddy and darkly somber.

It was a romantic picture. He put it aside and changed his materials from the acrylics to pen and ink and watercolors. He did several quick loose sketches on white paper, designs suggested by the interrelationship of their bodies. Since he had to draw, paint and model too in these changing poses, he made himself a fulcrum around which he had Sonata move.

"Stretch your arms out like this," he told her. "I'm trying for a long extended diagonal line against this straight one."

"Which straight one?"

"Me," he said impatiently."

"Oh." She laughed and arranged herself as "diagonally" as she could.

He worked fast, sketching first in pen and ink and then applying a wash in warm amber tones.

"Okay, enough of that," he said, stepping back to view what he had done. "Now, just sort of twist around. I want curved arching lines around the straight this time."

"Around that straight one?" she touched his phallus. "You can make your own curved arching line, how about it?"

"Jesus, Sonny!" He blocked in the new pose, tilting himself slightly to achieve the design he was after.

"Hey, when do I get to eat around here?" Sonata demanded. "I mean it, Vincent, no food, no clothes…how long do you think I'm gonna work at this job? It's sure not for the money."

"Okay, we'll quit in a minute. It's going great, I hate to. But all right…just let me finish this."

5

Since Vincent no longer needed her in the afternoon for modeling, Sonata enrolled in a daily afternoon painting class at the League. Taking Vincent's advice after a discussion one night over pizza and beer, she decided a life painting class was the best choice and Miller was probably the best teacher for her to begin with.

"Ordinarily I'd suggest a life drawing class for a start if you had no preference yourself," Vincent said, filling her glass. "But you want to paint, so that has priority because interest can carry you a long way, especially in the beginning. Anyway, you'll get drawing technique as you go. Miller believes in drawing as the surest expression of an idea. He even blocks in his figures in pencil before he paints and he'll probably have you doing that too. He's conscientious, takes his teaching seriously."

He let linger in the air, as Sonata sipped her beer, that some teachers were not so conscientious.

"I'm not surprised about the painting class over the drawing, but I thought you were going to steer me towards still-life in the beginning," she said, replacing a strand of cheese that escaped from her wedge. She was on her second piece and ate it slowly, making it last. They had a standard way of dividing the pizza, four slices for him, two for her, and two to bring home for whoever wanted it later.

"Why did you think I'd choose still-life?" Vincent wanted to know.

"Well, because the figure is difficult, I guess."

"And still-life? You think apples and oranges are easy?"

"Easi-er, I would imagine."

"In my opinion you have to want to do what you're doing, and if you're not interested in painting fruit but love the figure, you should go for it."

"But anyone would agree the figure is way more interesting, so why do people want to spend time painting fruit?" The beer was ice cold from the tap.

"They paint apples and oranges because the forms are interesting," Vincent explained. "And the change in color and shadows that light makes and the spatial juxtaposition of the objects, things like that."

This was becoming a lecture, Sonata thought. But no, it was important if she expected to get anything out of her studies. "So, isn't it the same with the figure?" she volunteered. "I mean the body is lines and shadows and colors—forms—like apples are. Anatomy is kind of an assortment of apples and oranges when you get down to it—and bananas?" She grinned. "Sorry, it just slipped out. Hey, since I'm sitting around naked all morning I think about sex more than I used to. This new career of mine could be trouble."

"Lot of artists these days see the body only as a combination of lines and colors and forms," Vincent went on, prowling deeper into his thoughts. "Like fruit, you could say. Not me. Drawing the human body is different from anything you could feel drawing still-life or nature or animals." He sat forward and drained his glass. "Wait until Monday," he said, wiping his lips. "Wait till you walk into that class and set up your easel and your paints and stand face to face with a body that holds a living person inside. Sonny, you won't think apples then. That's a promise."

•   •   •

Jacob Miller was a patient, long suffering man with an ample threshold in his heart for beginners, Sunday painters, and men and woman who came to his class directly from lunch with friends. He had a therapist's approach in his individual critiques to students. He was unhurried and encouraging.

Today Sonata hoped to finish the painting she'd been working on for several weeks and to bring it home for Vincent to see. It was her first picture and she prayed he wouldn't be too critical. The model was resting and Sonata used the time to tone down the lusty shade of pink she had ended up with for flesh color. If only Miller was in today to give her the final word, although there was no way she could complain about any lack of his attention all these weeks.

He'd helped her probably more than any other student in the class. Because she was Kossoff's daughter perhaps, but it could be that he recognized some talent of her father's emerging in her. By the time the class ended she remained unsatisfied, the awful pink subdued but not obliterated. "It is what it is," she muttered and pronounced it finished.

Staying at the League after class to draw during the open life sketch session had become routine. She arrived and looked around the room for a spot to sit, propping her painting to face the wall so it couldn't be seen. She noticed Willie Brockstein and took the empty seat beside him.

For a while she felt uncomfortable seeing Willie or one of the teachers or students who had come to the tribute, but they were all so kind towards her and so ready to make up for it, as if the disaster was through some fault of their own, that she felt at ease with them. A few, like Willie and Freddie, took time to work with her during the sketch class to show her what she was doing wrong.

Agnes, a model of about twenty-five, long, lean and cold-eyed, was seated on a stool and Sonata had a side view of her. In two minutes of drawing she had lost all possibility of having room for a head on her figure. Her drawings always seemed to overflow the paper and one extremity or another would disappear in the sharp guillotine of the paper's edge. She had changed the size of her pad but it only helped to make everything bigger and still the head and feet fell off the page.

When the model rested, Sonata looked over at Willie's drawing. It was a simple rendering of a figure, neatly spaced in the middle of a small piece of paper and beautiful. Willie worked with pen and India ink. To Sonata this was on par with walking a high wire without a net. Next to him, Sergio, his friend for twenty years, was working with watercolor, adding touches of ink as the paper dried.

"This Japanese brush works well," he told Willie, "I'm using it all week. I like it."

Willie inspected the brush while Sonata studied Sergio. His age was hard to guess. His face was weathered but his body was like a boy's, small and lithe. He had come to the States from Santo Domingo twenty-five years ago and worked at his trade, cabinet making. He did this during the day and then came to the sketch class afterwards, every weekday late afternoon without fail. Willie told her about Sergio: At home on West 93rd Street he would have dinner with his wife and daughters and then work all evening on the drawings he had made that day in the sketch class. He would clothe the model in the drape of biblical times and surround her with cherubs or angels. Sometimes a crucifix appeared in the background and often a legend would be inscribed at the bottom of the picture in his careful scroll. Then he would frame the pictures in standard black plastic from Woolworth's and bring them to a shop for religious articles where they would sell for about fifty dollars apiece.

At the next break Willie asked to see Sonata's drawings. He studied them wordlessly while she issued a variety of excuses for each. Showing her work to Willie was like displaying a glass ring to a jeweler, but he nodded pleasantly as he looked, tapping his cheek and making little dents that sprang back like finger marks in warm cake. He talked about creating a sensitive line by pressing the pencil lightly and with feeling for the contour it evokes, which Sonata had tried but failed to achieve. "Takes time, takes patience," Willie explained, "You have always to work, always to see," and Willie went on about how the eye becomes trained, how you must simplify what you see and sometimes put what you don't see. Willie loved to talk. He relished words as if they had nourishment and taste. In Europe he had only his faculties and his fat and in the hard times he suffered, he lived off both. His enthusiasm was contagious, but although she understood everything he was trying to tell her, it was frustrating not to be able to do it.

Agnes again stepped onto the platform. With one sweeping gesture she bent forward, grasped the hem of her shift and pulled it over and away from her head. She peered at the students from the summit where she stood, as if deciding how much pose the group was entitled to, then lay down and settled into a reclining position for the last and longest pose of the day.

As usual, after the blocking in Sonata was left with a torso and feetless legs. As she continued to work with what she had, she became more and more annoyed at the ponderous and dull quality of her drawing. Her figure was wearing its nudity, hanging like a badly fitted slipcover over a sleek couch. As she kept trying to improve it, the picture became worse instead of better and she slammed her pad shut when the break was announced before Willie could see how little she had gotten from his lesson.

Glancing at his sketch she saw that it was finished and perfect, suitable for matting and framing, and selling too. Sergio remained working. There was something more than Agnes in the picture but Sonata could not make out what it was. Willie pointed to it over his shoulder.

"You see what happened to the gentle Agnes," Willie whispered to her, "Agnes, whose breast overflows with the milk of human kindness?"

"May I see your drawing?" she asked Sergio, leaning over.

"It is just blocked in now," Sergio said, tipping the paper towards her, "Tonight I make it good." Agnes was drawn exquisitely, her long back curving sensuously, her head resting on her arm facing her feet. Behind her feet, slumped against the stump of a tree, was the semi-draped figure of a bearded man. Standing over the man were the outlines of two robed female figures. "It's going to be very lovely," Sonata acknowledged.

"It will sell," said Willie. He collected his supplies. "How about coffee together? Sergio? Sonny?"

"No, I cannot today," Sergio said, "I must take the children to the catechism study." He picked up his things. "I will see you tomorrow. Goodbye, Miss."

"I'll take a rain-check too, Willie," Sonata said when Sergio had gone. "I have to get home in a hurry now and make some dinner.'"

"Dinner," Willie repeated, as if pondering the word. He paused. Then, trying to be cheerful: "You are quite the little domestic now, aren't you, my dear? You make dinner, you keep house." Again he paused, as if he had run out of cheer and was waiting for it to return. "Are you happy, Sonny?" he asked.

Sonata smiled, but she was annoyed at the question. "Why yes, Willie, I'm very happy."

"My dear," Willie began," Will you delay your dinner for a little while, a few minutes? I would like to talk to you. I have wanted to but there was no opportunity." He waited for her reply without saying more but still an air of urgency prevailed in the way he stood, not moving, just looking at her.

"All right, Willie," she said at last, "We can go upstairs to the cafeteria."

She found a seat, setting her painting against the table legs while Willie went on line. He returned in a few minutes with muffins and coffee.

For a few minutes they drank their coffee in silence but Sonata felt a lecture coming. Up to now he had said nothing about the fact that she was living with Vincent. How many people knew, she had no idea but no one said anything and in this place she assumed things like that were taken for granted. Willie was *old school* though and besides, he was close to her mother and father. Maybe he was representing them now. If so, she didn't care to hear what he had to say.

"Sergio is an interesting fellow, isn't he?" Sonata commented.

"Not really. He is nice, pleasant and good-natured, but no, not very interesting."

"He's very religious."

"Yes, that is what he is, very religious and uninteresting."

"They say that religious people are happier, do you think that's so, Willie?"

"I think they are contented." He shrugged. "Like day laborers on a tobacco farm can be contented. A roof over their heads, no important decisions to make; satisfied, resigned, perhaps. Happy? No, I don't think they are so happy."

"But the security, I mean, being able to think that it's God's will when something terrible happens."

"In a prison there is security too, yes?" Willie divided his muffin into sections and ate them one at a time, shaking the crumbs from his fingers. "I think, Sonny, that if people were forced against their will to live in the state of infirmity that their own religions ask of them, they would make immediately a violent revolution." He opened his heavy hand on the table and then squeezed the fingers closed. "Humility, meekness, self-belittlement…this eats at a man's vitality like tent caterpillars at a tree."

"But what about love? Religion is love too. Love of God, love of man."

"My dear, to love you must understand the loved one, and to understand you must be your first pupil. And how can you understand yourself without being free to think and feel and to judge for yourself? If you are always a guest in God's house you are careful not to disturb the belongings, And you must never be in the way."

Sonata frowned. She didn't like what he was saying and the way he was eating either. She noticed a spot of muffin next to his lips. "I'm surprised to hear you talk like this, Willie. I always thought you had a strong feeling for being Jewish. I know you lost your father and your brother over there and I thought that—"

"A strong feeling? Where does such sentiment come from? From experiences. We did not have such fine experiences. Oh, my brother Moshe and my Papa accepted who they were and being Jewish was one thing, not all, though to others in Heidelberg it was all. I think my Papa always felt like an immigrant with a visitor's visa in a gentile world and I think he knew somewhere in his heart, someday the visa would expire. For him it was the hardest." He paused and then he shook his head. "If they would listen to Willie, they would turn all of these tired old places—these fancy synagogues and churches and mosques and temples—into simple meeting places where people could share experiences to solve the problems of people and not think so much about God. They should mind their *own* business." He smiled then and reached across the table and took Sonata's hand. "So, do you worry about people, Sonny?"

"I suppose I do," she said cautiously.

"How long is it since you are away from your mother?"

Sonata was angered by the question. It was a school principal's question, but she answered him. "About three months, I guess. The night of the party, that's when I left." She withdrew her hand.

"Have you asked about her? Do you know how she is?"

"Well no, but I haven't heard anything, so I assume she's fine. I stopped over there a few days after I left to get some clothes. I had to let myself in because nobody was home, but everything looked pretty much the same."

"Things can look the same for a long time."

"Willie, are you trying to tell me something? If you are, I wish you would say it right out. Is my mother all right or is something the matter with her?"

Willie sighed. "She is all right. She is not dying of consumption."

"What's the matter, Willie? You look so gloomy and…mad at me all of a sudden! Is it so terrible that I got away from that house? I mean if you're concerned about people then be concerned about me! How should I have behaved, do you think? Should I have stayed there acting as if nothing had happened, stayed to congratulate her for being a doormat to him and a liar to me? I wouldn't have liked saying those things to her and I didn't have to. I left."

Again Willie sighed. It was depressing, his sighing and his dark suffering eyes that bore such a burden.

"I think it would be right that you go back," Willie said. "Not forever but a visit. You should talk with your mother and listen to what she has to say. You are not so wise, my dear Sonata, that you know all the answers but not asking the questions. Things are never so easy. People close to us cannot be dismissed so nicely in a phrase that has a pleasant ring. If they must go, they go slowly, with much that lingers behind. You will have to concern yourself with that too, you know…the things they leave behind."

"I'm sorry, Willie, I'm not going back there to talk to her. I have nothing to say, and there's nothing more she can tell me that I don't already know. "

"Do you know that they are getting a divorce?"

Sonata was startled to hear him say that but only for a moment. She thought, why not? Of all people, why not them? What did they have together anyway? "I didn't know it," she said, "I guess I'm sorry to hear that." Judging from what she had seen at the tribute many people might have wondered what kept them together all these years. No, it would not come as a surprise to anyone.

"So, is she making any plans?" Sonata asked. "Will she keep the house?" What did she care and why was she asking these questions—next-door neighbor questions?

"Why don't you go to her and ask her yourself?" Willie suggested.

For a moment they looked at each other without speaking.

"She will not come to you."

Sonata pushed back her chair. "I have to leave, Willie," she said, too abruptly but fearing if she stayed she would say something regrettable. "Are you staying?"

"Yes, for a bit," he said, wiping his lips and folding his napkin.

"Well then," she said, and for want of anything else: "Have a nice weekend." How were his weekends? Lonely? Sad? She thought neither. Willie had a capacity for joyous moods, for all the mystery behind his brooding eyes.

"Think about what I have suggested," Willie said, "You owe this visit to your mother."

"Willie, I don't think you understand everything that has happened. I see things differently than you do and I have my own conscience to satisfy."

"To satisfy your conscience is the same as to satisfy your appetite," he said lumbering to his feet, "when there are others near you who are hungry."

She put on her coat and buttoned it, "You love people and try to help, I know that Willie, but you don't understand me. Look, when you lose people you love and thought loved you it takes time to get over it. You have to give me time." She smiled. "Goodbye, Willie, thanks for the coffee." She picked up her art supplies and the cumbersome painting and left, choosing to traipse down the three flights of stairs instead of waiting for the elevator.

6

When Sonata stepped into the lobby someone called her by name and she turned toward the benches by the door. "Howard! What are you doing here?"

"Waiting for you, what do you think?" He stood and greeted her with a kiss on the cheek. She felt his wet coat and surmised it must have started to rain. "Which way you heading? I'll walk with you."

"To the subway, but—Howard, how long have you been here? How did you know I was even enrolled?" He looked so handsome in his dark belted raincoat. She hadn't remembered him so tall.

"A little private eye work, simple stuff," he said, as they continued out the door and down the outside steps. He opened his umbrella and took her arm. "What happened is after calling your home and leaving messages—you never there—and the library where they said you weren't working anymore, I came down here to find your Dad and ask him where the hell you were. So when I asked for Kossoff in the office and told them the problem, voila! They told me you were enrolled in one of the afternoon classes and could be right then in the open sketch class."

"Yes, I was, earlier. Wow, you really—"

"—I saw you drawing inside." He grinned. "Do you know you stick your tongue out when you draw? Never mind, it's appealing, not too professional though. Anyway, while I was waiting for the class to end, I took a walk down the corridor to look around, came back, and you were gone. I asked for you and somebody said you were still in the building, so I've been waiting. What took you so long? I was thinking you knew I was here and slipped out a basement window or something."

She laughed at his comment, at his adventure to find her. "How come you're in town? I thought you were in Boston."

"Yep, that's where I've been. Spring break time now and the folks wanted to get down to Florida. But I don't want to talk about work." They crossed Seventh Avenue and turned on Broadway toward the subway. "Rain's stopped," he said, looking up and closing his umbrella. "A fancy one-of-a-kind Ball is coming up sponsored by your art school. I read about it in the paper."

"Oh, you're talking about The Art Students League Costume ball."

"That's it—supposed to be a wild affair like the Beaux arts thing in Paris. I'd like to go."

"Well, I don't know. They'll be selling tickets in the office to students. I suppose I could get you one if I lied a little."

"Great. Do that then. Pick up two and I'll reimburse you. I thought we could go as Lady Godiva and her horse. All you'll have to do is take stuff off and I'll make myself horsier than I already am. I read that anything goes and people line the street for hours just to see the costumes walk in!"

Sonata stopped walking and looked at him quizzically. "You want to go with me?"

"Sure, unless you're booked already." When she didn't answer he took her arm to continue walking. "I was going to ask Vinnie to get me a ticket and then keep trying to find you, but this is easier all around."

"Did you mention this yet to Vincent?"

"No, I just read about it a couple days ago."

"I can't, Howard," she said, stopping again. "I mean, I can't go with you."

"Why not?"

"You haven't spoken to Vincent recently at all, have you?"

"A few times on the phone, why?"

"And didn't he tell you? Look, didn't he say anything about me?"

He frowned and shook his head, not understanding. "What should he have said?"

"I, well, I'm staying with him, Howard. I…we're living together."

His mouth opened and he stared at her. "I don't believe it," he said. "You cannot be serious!" As effusive as he had just been, his voice now breathed into a whisper. "Vincent?" His eyes narrowed and suddenly, he lifted his hand, whether to strike her or just stop her from talking, she didn't know. Then he shoved the hand into his pocket and clenching his lips as if to seal them from a word escaping, he turned on his heels and tore away.

She stood for a moment feeling the sting of the undelivered blow across her face. Deserving it, somehow. As if she had been waiting for a blow from someone since that first morning when she sat naked on a chair in front of Vincent's easel, feeling that something was wrong, wrong beyond all righting.

Then, watching Howard's figure fade into the distance, she wondered if the heat of Howard's anger had been toward Vincent not her. It mattered, though it made no difference to her now. Both brothers, it flashed through her mind, had the power to hurt her.

The painting was heavy under her arm. All at once she felt nervous about walking into the apartment with it. Vincent might laugh at it or he might be silent and that would be worse. She couldn't predict his reactions. Her depressing conversation with Willie now weighted upon her as well. She felt the satisfaction of having completed her first painting, lousy as it was, dissipating inside the cloud of these encounters.

Reluctantly, she headed toward the subway and home. The image of Howard in his dark raincoat, his eyes piercing, his hand ready to strike, did not fade.

7

Undecided whether to use her key or not, Sonata stood at her mother's door. She rang the bell instead. Ruth might not even be living there anymore. It was late March and a lot had happened in the last few months. Waiting, she fought a desire to walk away and forget the whole thing. What would it accomplish, coming here like this? She had no intention of staying.

It was Ethel who opened the door. She stood for a moment in the doorway, a look of skeptical surprise on her face and an expression not friendly.

A spider web of lines Sonata had never observed before made her Aunt look older and somewhat weary.

"Oh," Sonata said, "I didn't expect to see you here."

"I could say the same thing. Well, come on in," she added. Her voice appeared as tired as her appearance. She held the door open to let her pass.

Stepping inside, Sonata looked around the familiar foyer and living room feeling like the uninvited guest she was, at least to Ethel who was watching her warily. Why? As a carrier of some future disaster for her sister?

"Ruth's not here," Ethel said. "She's in town meeting with her lawyer." She paused. "I suppose you've heard."

"Yes, I've heard."

"Come into the living room. You want something, a cold drink, coffee?"

"No thank you, nothing," she said, seating herself on the sofa, but feeling more welcome for the hospitality. "I just thought I should stop by to see how she was." The last time she had sat on this couch it was next to Vincent; how different now from that naïve, good little daughter. The house seemed quiet, stagnant, like the sense of the house when Billy died and family and friends came to pay their respects. Now she was sitting with Ethel as the bereaved, Ruth no longer with them. No, her mother would return, it would be for the loss of Bert, or herself, or all of them. The family was dead.

"How did you expect she would be?" Ethel said with critical detachment.

Sonata watched her pick up a pack of cigarettes without much interest in it. She had never looked at her aunt very closely. The woman was not attractive—hard and coarse, very different from her mother who was supple in features, her way of moving in a room.

"I don't know. I hadn't thought about her state of mind. Well, divorce isn't pleasant, so I imagine she's depressed about it, or maybe happy—relieved?"

Ethel shrugged in response.

Her aunt was untypically cool, not her usual bull-in-the-china-shop self. "So, how is she, you must know? You're her confidant, aren't you?"

"Come off it, Sonny."

"What? I came back to see her because I thought I owed her that. If you don't want me here I'll just leave," she said, standing.

"Oh, sit down for God's sake and stop acting like Bette Davis." Ethel sat down herself in the chair opposite and lit the cigarette.

"Something new," Sonata said, tilting her head. "Since when? I thought your husband objected to that. Refuses to put ashtrays in his office or some such defiant thing?"

"Lou isn't smoking this," she said acridly. "I don't smoke much, I eat to keep normal. Your mother smokes—too much."

"I know."

"No, you don't," Ethel said, still cool, still on top, "You don't know anything."

"And what is that supposed to mean?"

"Do you know that she cries? She's an unhappy woman, did you know that?"

"Oh, shit, here comes the melodrama! I can hardly wait."

Ethel didn't answer. She exhaled a thin mist of smoke and watched it dissipate.

Sonata pursed her lips and sat back. Not wanting to give her aunt the benefit of her attention, she looked around the room. A different picture of Bert's hung near the bookcase, a more recent one. She stood and walked over to it. It had been in his studio before she left: reds and golds and dark browns, a thick projectile abstract. "So," she said, "were they ever able to do anything with *Study in Blues*? It was awful what happened to that wonderful picture."

"Yes, Ruth did something. She collected the insurance."

Sonata nodded, not sure what her response wanted to be. "I always loved that painting."

"He'll make more."

For a while they were silent. Sonata could think of nothing to say and Ethel was not even trying, just waiting.

"Where is my father now? I mean, where is he living, do you know?"

"I haven't any idea where he's living or with whom. He's not my concern, your mother is."

Sonata smiled scornfully, "You're such a faithful soul, always there when she needs you, always ready to come and help and give advice. You've been giving my mother your opinions right along, haven't you? Where would she be now without her big sister Ethel?"

"I try to help. She needs someone who is interested in her, who gives a damn. It's not enough, you know, having a husband and having a daughter or maybe you think it is. That's the kind of egos you both have, deciding just belonging to her is enough."

"Yes," Sonata said. "Having us gave her pride and that's something. She was always proud of Dad's painting and proud of me, no matter what I did, except since graduating high school when I've been—well, unsettled. I think it is enough, having that pride. She had nothing to be proud of on her own, you know."

Ethel sneered audibly. "How little you know."

"And you know more? You don't even have any children so what makes you an authority on what a mother wants from her kid?"

"It's Ruth we're discussing, Sonny, not motherhood. I know my sister."

"And you had a lot to say to her, I can see that. You must have talked your head off all these years because you've always had it in for my father. You were jealous, that's really the reason, isn't it? Jealous because Lou is so ordinary and Bert is a man? Oh what a revolutionary figure Lou is: no ashtrays in the waiting room! Sure, I'll bet you talked, and whined your jealous brains out and I'll bet my mother listened. She never could make up her own mind about anything because she's just about the weakest person that ever walked this earth."

"Your mother did listen to me and she talked to me because she needed to."

"My mother was happy, I never heard her complain."

"You didn't know."

"Well, that may be so, but you did know, of course. To you she complained. That's what you bring out in people, their complaints. You have a flair for it. My father complained every time he had to look at you."

"Your mother was an unhappy woman, Sonny, a brave but miserable woman."

"Oh cut the melodrama, she was no miserable woman! I lived with her, I should know that much."

"She adored you, Sonny, she would have done anything for you. She suffered him because of you."

"Because of me? What kind of nonsense! He was a man, my father, and she was crazy about him. She just couldn't keep him that's all. She was too weak for him. He's strong in his mind and his emotions and in his body—yes, that—and she didn't know how to hold on to a man like that. She deserved somebody like Lou, with holes all over to grab onto." *My God, where was this defense of her father coming from? Lou? What did he have to do with it?*

Ethel stood angrily. She dashed her cigarette into the ashtray, mindless of the ashes that spilled over onto the table. "A strong man, oh yes! Shall I tell you what kind of man he really is?"

"You tell me? That's a laugh. There is nothing you could tell me about Bert Kossoff. Tell me about Lou, that's your speed!" *Again, Lou!*

"You close-minded, egotistical child! There is a lot I can tell you and I will because you're going his way now, I see it. Lustful, selfish, walking in his very footsteps. Planning a tribute for him! Imagine! For him of all people!"

"Ethel, where were you at the tribute?" Sonata asked, suddenly remembering that she had not seen her after the party started.

"I went home," she said, turning her head and focusing on the painting over the bookcase, and seeing instead, perhaps, the lost painting that had been there.

"Home?"

"Yes, I went back to Connecticut."

"You must have left right after people started coming. I didn't see you after that. Why did you leave?"

"Because I didn't want to see it."

"What do you mean, you didn't want to see it?"

She turned and looked at Sonata. "I don't like suffering. Maybe that's why I chose to be a nurse, to help where I'm needed, but still I hate to witness it. Ruth suffered with your father—you don't want to know how much—but it reached a climax with the horrid things you said to her upstairs, and that awful tribute." She rubbed her eye, which was red and swollen when she took her hand away. "It had to end and I helped it along because she never would have had the strength to do it on her own. But I didn't want to see it, so I left." Her expression softened, whether induced by nicotine or nostalgia, but her voice was soft when she walked towards her. "Ruth will forget Bert if you come back. Sonny, she needs you."

Sonata turned away, glad Ruth wasn't here, glad too that she hadn't accepted anything to drink, hadn't hung up her coat, had no commitments. On her way to the door, she smiled derisively. "She doesn't need me," Sonata said, "She has you."

"All right, only me. Is that the way you want to leave it?" Her hand pressed against her lips. Her usual fastidious makeup was worn away and a reddish smear appeared on her fingers. "Sit down, Sonny. I'm going to tell you something about your precious father. I'll shatter that rose colored glass you insist on seeing him through with a little story. It begins and ends on the night Billy died. Well . . . sit down, damn it, and let me get it over with quickly."

"What does Billy have to do with this? And what's the matter with you anyway, you look so freaked out all of a sudden?"

"Billy died of a ruptured spleen," Ethel announced, neither responding nor looking at Sonata. She began a slow, methodical pacing, toward the wall and returning, pacing. "That's what the autopsy showed, but I refused to accept that report as a complete explanation."

"Why not? The doctor was satisfied." Sonata returned to the sofa and sat on the arm rest.

"I wasn't. Perhaps because I loved that little boy so much, I couldn't accept such a sudden incongruous end. I had to know more, but without upsetting Ruth. And without upsetting Anne Calnon, Mike's mother, because it happened in her house and the poor woman was almost as destroyed as we were. I went there."

"To the Calnon's?"

"Yes, and I talked to Anne. It wasn't easy. We talked until the early hours of the morning. Every time we were getting somewhere she tried to stop our discussion. Still, I forced myself upon her and I wouldn't leave. I guess you know I'm not too easy to get rid of." She stopped pacing and parked herself again in the chair. "Anyway, don't ask me how I knew something was wrong, I just knew it."

Sonata began to feel apprehensive. Ethel's face had become pale. She talked without looking at her, her eyes instead drifting to the walls, the ceiling and her hands as the words spilled out.

"Finally," she continued, "I forced the story from her. It's possible I saved Anne from a breakdown, living with what she knew, not even telling her husband."

"Go on! Living with what, for God's sake!" Sonata's eyes were now riveted on Ethel, trying to direct her focus.

"She had done her own questioning, you see, from little Mike, and I can imagine that her sessions with him were no easier than mine with her."

"Billy didn't die of a ruptured spleen, is that what you're going to say?"

"No, he did."

"Well, what is it then…why are you so goddamned spooky about all this?"

Ethel faced her squarely now, "I'm going to tell you, so that for once in your life you can see the truth, what exists and not the myths and the guessing and the rationales. For once, you can see your mother as the gentle, loving and beautiful soul she is and your father—and I curse him openly now as I tell this—for what he is."

Sonata was torn between grabbing her handbag and crashing out the door before another word was spoken or sitting on the edge of her seat as Ethel started pouring out her story, but once Ethel began, there was no turning back.

"Putting the pieces together from Anne Calnon's account, I have a pretty thorough picture of what happened to Billy that night."

Ethel related the events of that deadly October sleepover and Sonata listened, sitting frozen on the arm of the sofa. Afterwards, she crossed the floor and slapped Ethel roughly across her cheek, then overturned the ashtray so that the contents covered her lap.

"You are a jealous, conniving liar. If you ever tell that freaky fabrication to anyone…anyone, I'll have you locked in an institution!"

•   •   •

Days went by and nights and weeks, trying to paint, trying to hear what the instructor was saying to her, what Willie and Sergio were chatting about with her between classes. The ordinary seemed impossible. Only the extraordinary words in her head seemed real. Her tears came even while Vincent made love to her. She buried the wetness in the pillows. There was no one she could tell. Her throat at times welled up with such a choking sensation, she couldn't speak. The words became disjointed and jumbled, tumbling around tenaciously in her mind—Ethel's words that had become a never ending rumble of thunder in a ceaseless storm.

Your brother died at the hands of your father in the car, his arms around a woman…on his way—oh, I'll say it—to fucking her, his hands I can imagine where…late at night, dark, his mind elsewhere, he strikes something…a stray animal, barely hears the bump…little Billy on a sleepover at his friend Mike's house…eleven-year-old kids and Mike mad at his mom not letting them sleep out in a tent…they steal out in the night, teach her a lesson all right, not finding them home…said they could pitch the tent then couldn't, teach her a lesson…and out on the street with their sleeping bags Billy sees the car, his father's car…going slow, close to his own house…woman in the car, woman not his mom, and the car passes close, nicks his side in the dark…hurt a little but he's okay…then lying with Mike under a tree, a belly ache, bad one starting to hurt, hurt really bad, trying not to cry…cry like a girl…tells Mike about the car, his father's car…makes Mike swear not to tell…and then both of them scared of the dark, never mind camping out…and back at Mike's house worse, horribly worse…the pain, and Billy ashamed, crying like a baby…until he didn't cry anymore. Mike vowed he'd never tell…and didn't.

PART SEVEN
THE BEAUX ARTS BALL

I

Vincent did not want to go to the Beaux arts Masquerade Ball. They were having supper and Sonata tried serving the idea again between the salad and the canned peaches but he wasn't buying.

"It's a waste of time and you shouldn't have bought the tickets without asking me if I wanted to go."

"But it's a famous affair," Sonata insisted, quoting Howard, "It was written up in the Times as something truly worth seeing."

"I have seen it and I can tell you it's nothing, just a bunch of perverted exhibitionists. They get their kicks from that but I don't, so forget it. Find somebody to buy the tickets."

They finished dinner and Sonata did not mention it again until much later after she had cleaned up and they had sat around listening to records, drinking beer, and finally lying side by side on the new Beauty Rest mattress. "Vince, I really want to go. You've seen the Beaux arts Ball but I never have and I'd like to see for myself what it's all about, you can't blame me for that. Why not go just to please me?"

"Look, it's wasting an evening of my life for something totally pointless. I have work to do, well you know that."

When the light was out she said, "I saw Howard, did I ever tell you? I bumped into him on the street three or four weeks ago."

"Yeah, I saw him too, last Sunday, at home."

"Oh, you didn't tell me."

"What's to tell?" She felt him roll over. "Let me sleep now Sonny, please, I'm bushed."

"When I saw him, he talked about going to this affair. He said he heard about it."

"I know," Vincent mumbled from under the covers. "I told him it's a waste of time, same thing I'm telling you."

"Well, if he still wants to go, I mean, if he wants to and can't get a ticket—they're hard to get now that it's only a week away, and the thing is really popular, no matter what you think—should I give him yours?"

"Yeah, give him mine, but make sure he pays for it. Goodnight, Sonny."

"Listen, if he still wants to go, would you mind if I went too with the other ticket?"

Vincent rolled back towards her to get comfortable.

"Vince?"

"Mmmn?"

"Can I?"

"Can I what?"

"Can I use the other ticket if he decides to go?"

"Of course, use the ticket—what do I care? Leave me alone now, would you, Sonny?" He reached out and touched her shoulder and then in a little while his breathing was heavy and regular and he was asleep.

Howard was glad to get the ticket but he wanted to bring someone else, a date with the other ticket. Sonata told him she was using it and he could have the one she'd bought for Vince. Sonata was relieved that he'd accepted though she wasn't sure why. Was it a chance to punish him or herself she wanted? The way they parted had caught her off guard with no defenses, just confusion without resolution.

But it wasn't only that. What did she want then, his approval? But how idiotic! How could he approve her being mistress and model for his kid brother Vinnie? Yet that was it. She laughed. What a damn strange thought! It struck her then she'd take anyone's approval for what she was doing, not able to count on her own.

. . .

On the day of the masquerade ball, Sonata was surprised that Vincent remembered she was going and remembered she was going with Howard. He paid no attention to her costume preparation all the while she dressed, working on a new canvas. It appeared to be the largest canvas he had ever made and Sonata had no small problem keeping her frilly bouffant gown out of the paint.

He did take the time to assist her down the steps and into a taxi. Her dress had a wide hoop under the gown which made it stand out "four people's worth" he said. She had rented the costume in New Jersey at an out-of-the-way place on Route 17 because she thought it would be cheaper than in New York. But adding a wide-brimmed hat that tied in a bow under the chin and gloves and a basket handbag she spent thirty dollars, not including the bus fare to Jersey.

"You're all wrong for this affair," Vincent said, watching her adjust herself in the taxi, taking up the whole seat.

"Overdressed, you mean?" she said, laughing. "I know."

"Just all wrong," he repeated without humor.

"Well, I'm going to see, not be seen. Anyway, if I'm so wrong it's your fault. You could have helped me a little. You're an artist with the imagination."

"It's because I'm an artist I'm staying out of this and up there where I belong." He closed the cab door and blew a kiss.

She rolled down the window, "Aren't you going to tell me to be home by midnight, Fairy Godmother?" The taxi lurched forward and she was unable to turn in the stiff costume to wave goodbye.

When she arrived at the Plaza Hotel, she saw an eager crowd jostling each other to get a better view as people descended from cars and taxis. It was just as Howard said it would be. All eyes followed the bizarrely costumed and half-nude skin-painted attendees as they walked the short distance from the curb to the canopy and through the revolving doors into the lobby.

No eyes followed her as she walked hastily into the lobby. Howard was waiting on a lounge chair dressed as a butler with an eye-patch. All wrong too, like her.

"Hi. Isn't it funny that we go together," she said gaily, "A southern belle and her butler, without even planning it!"

Howard merely nodded. He looked tired, but Sonata sensed it was not fatigue that darkened his expression but a signal of avoidance, closing her off like installing dark blinds to prevent light coming through. Still, he was strikingly handsome; his stern demeanor added an air of distinction to his face and she noticed people glancing at him as they passed and women's eyes lingering.

"I own a tuxedo," he said, glancing down at his apparel. "I didn't know what to wear, so I put it on."

"Well, the eye-patch is something. That's unique. I mean, a butler with an eye patch. You don't see that every day."

"No, I guess not," he said, glancing about at the clusters of costumed people entering the lobby. "Well, I had to do something. You have the tickets? Want to give them to me?"

"Yes, right here." She reached into the silly beribboned basket and produced the tickets. Taking the elevator to the first floor, they approached the closed entrance to the Grand Ballroom where a deathly pale man with dark under lids, menacing brow, sharp white teeth and horns took their tickets. It took until the old devil welcomed them to go in that Sonata recognized a cheerful young woman under all the paint.

Inside, the orchestra was blaring. Two male singers and one female undulated to the beat, their voices breaking like waves over the billowing music. The dance floor was crowded with throbbing bodies and for a few moments Sonata and Howard just stood there, gazing in fascinated stupor at the vibrant color and movement.

"We should find a table," Howard said finally, taking her arm but then dropping it like something he shouldn't be handling. He walked ahead of her with the efficiency of a head-waiter, skirting people and furnishings as if he knew the room. He removed his eye patch to see better and Sonata thought someone might stop him to ask where the restroom was or something. All the tables were large ones for eight to twelve people or more and when he found some empty seats at a table for eight, miles from the orchestra, he settled for it. Set-ups, ice and glasses were on the table.

"Oh Christ, it's one of these," he said, clenching his teeth. "I didn't bring a bottle."

"Hey, don't worry about it, man, plenty to go 'round, plenty for everybody! Got another stashed away." A lean Black fellow, gleaming from face to waist in red and yellow iridescent paint, pushed a bottle of Packard's Scotch in front of him.

"Thanks, thanks very much. I'll chip in," Howard said, reaching into his pocket and taking out some bills.

"You don't have to, man," he said waving Howard's money away, but Howard pressed the money into his hand and he grinned and gave it to his girlfriend. "I got no place for money, got no place for money tonight."

His girlfriend, a petite girl about Sonata's age with long stringy blond hair, took the bills. Sonata wondered where she was going to put it. Her costume was a sort of bikini but the top consisted of two white gloves, one curving over each breast with thin transparent nylon strings holding them in place over her shoulders and around her back. As Sonata followed the threads from back to front to see how they were staying on, she was stunned to see little pink nipples poking through the thumb and forefinger of each glove.

She looked quickly at Howard who had discovered it about the same time she did but wasn't taking his eyes off her, watching the movement of the nipples and the fingers of the gloves as she twisted around for her purse on the chair back.

"Hey, my name is Cyrus and this here is Nomi. Hey, if you're gonna be here for a while, will ya keep an eye on her bag? We gonna dance now, eh doll? Come on babe."

"Sure," Howard said, taking the purse. Cyrus led the "hands" away and Sonata and Howard watched her hips swinging toward the dance floor, laughing when they saw that her rump was semi-covered by another glove, a big, black, man-sized glove that creased and puckered as she moved.

Two girls sat opposite them at the other end of the table. Their costumes were similar to each other and rather ordinary: leotards and net stockings with multi-colored felt shapes sewn on in various places and they wore long thick hairpieces, one platinum, the other jet black.

"What are you supposed to be?" Howard asked them jovially.

One looked at the other and giggled and Sonata realized again how appealing Howard was and she was aware, too, of how unattached he was to her. Well, she was Vince's girl so it made no difference.

She thought about Vincent hard at work now on his enormous canvas. He was constantly working. She admired him for that though it was lonely, his being so deeply into his work. Even in bed it was she who had to begin things and that too had tapered off. They were like old married folks. Maybe it was better before they got the Beauty Rest mattress. They had been sort of thrown together in the concave cot and the friction helped, like two sticks starting a fire.

"We're discotheque girls, cantcha see?" the platinum one said.

"He can't see," said the other, "He's blind to the finer things."

"What are you supposed to be?" Platinum wanted to know.

"I think you got directed to the wrong affair," Jet Black said, giggling again. "Downstairs they're having a businessmen's convention, are you sure you didn't make a mistake?"

Howard grinned and put on his eye-patch, "Is that better?"

"Go on!" They both laughed. "It's worse, you're still a businessman—half blind is all!"

Another couple joined them, returning to their seats from the dance floor.

"Hi," said the girl. Her date squeezed a rubber bulb in his hand and white lights shone from the region of her breasts and pubis over a skin-tight jersey.

"I get a charge out of that," her date said, probably for the fortieth time tonight. "Hey you dig that? Cool, huh?" He lit her up again.

"Ok, enough! Down boy," she demanded. "Just pour me a drink and let go the current for a while, Charlie, okay?"

Charlie was wearing tight black pants with a fuse box painted on his chest and wires sprouting out of a band across his head, He sat down and reached for the ice. "I really turn her on tonight, don't you think?" He chuckled and poured gin in both glasses from a pint bottle that he removed from his back pocket and replaced, "Say, you're not drinking, want some of this mother's milk?" He patted his pocket.

"No, no thanks. Yes, we're drinking," Howard explained, "Just got carried away here for a while. Scotch and soda, Sonata?"

She nodded, aware he'd not called her Sonny.

"You two study at the League?" Howard asked, pouring the drinks.

"Peggy does, I don't," said Charlie.

"Charlie's an electrician, can't you tell?" Peggy volunteered.

"Behind-the-scenes artist," he added, squeezing the bulb again.

"All right cut it out now," she said with some annoyance, touching her breast to shield the light. "I would like to enjoy this gin in total absolute darkness please."

"Whose class are you in?" Sonata asked the girl. Her drink was strong. She wasn't used to hard liquor but the mixers were now at the other end of the table.

"Seidman's sculpture class. How about you guys?"

"I'm in Jacob Minter's painting class but Howard is not at the League, he's in men's clothes."

"Waiter's clothes. Haw!"

"Oh, for Christ sake, Charlie!" To Sonata: "Pity him, he's in pain. Do you like Minter? I hear he's a bland sort of instructor."

"He's good for me. Patient, easy-going, doesn't expect too much."

"She's a beginner," Howard explained, "but her father's an artist. Bert Kossoff. You must know him if you're at the League. He teaches there."

"Oh sure," said Platinum, "He's my instructor. I just started in his class a few months ago. Say, he's here tonight, did you see him?"

Startled, Sonata looked at Howard, but then remembered that he knew nothing about the divorce or what happened at the party or any of it.

"He's in a fun sort of get-up," offered Jet Black. "I think it's sweet, the teachers getting in the spirit of things."

"What's his costume?" Howard asked.

"I don't know what you'd call it," Platinum reflected, glancing around for help. "Kind of animal, I guess? Not anything queer or outlandish, just funny, that's all. He's really with it."

"I'd like to see him," Sonata said, glancing at Howard, and then deciding with conviction that she should see him. It was time. He was still her father. And certainly if he was here in the room she had no business sitting at this table with strangers.

Howard nodded. "Finish your drink first," he said to her. "When we find him we may want to stay over there."

And suddenly she remembered how keenly Howard had understood her feelings about the tribute. He hadn't thought it foolish, like so many others—her mother, Vince, Ethel, and a lot of the guests, as it turned out.

"Thank you, Howard."

2

Still, they stayed at the table for an hour or so while the white gloves returned led by a different man who wore only a painted jockstrap with matching colors spread over his naked body. He left her to return to the dance floor. Drinks were poured and then Cyrus came back but didn't seem upset about his girlfriend dancing with the jockstrap. A gargoyle and a zombie approached the discotheque girls who went off to dance, and then somebody poured Sonata another drink which she drank because Howard was dancing with the white gloves, who had asked him, and she was getting used to the taste of Scotch which wasn't so bad. She was glad Howard was having fun; he was a tourist here, so to speak, and dancing with an artist gave him the flavor of the affair, like meeting a picturesque native in a foreign country.

He returned with the girl on his arm, settling her in with her partner. Then he surprised her saying, "Come on, let's see if we can find your father." Later, she was to remember that single phrase with affection. He had taken the initiative for her sake.

She had difficulty getting up. The wide skirt caught under the seat. "I feel so ridiculous in this horrible costume," she whispered to him as she struggled. "I should have splattered some paint on a pair of jeans and come like those girls over there, something simple. Howard looked, then they both laughed, observing when the girls turned that their backsides were bared.

"Am I clear of the table?"

"Okay in front but you look like you're about to take off in back. Oh, now you're out. Stay close," he said, adjusting his eye patch as they walked. "I'll never find you with one eye in this crowd. Maybe if you had a couple of neon lights on your boobs."

It was the first "Howard" thing he had said all night. Sonata felt her spirits rise. Also, he had taken her hand, relieving her from having to direct their pathway. His hand was warm and firm as he led her through the tangle of animated bodies standing and chattering in groups between the tables.

They passed a towering chandelier headdress on a tawny-skinned model, the pattern continued on down with glass crystals hanging from her shoulders and her breasts and her hips, all clinking as she walked and making a pleasant ringing sound. One crystal, the largest, hung from the cleft of her bosom down to her groin and dangled there, agitating and spinning as she moved.

There were many painted nudes in the ballroom, genitals covered and breasts partially with areolas uniquely shielded. Bodies were decorated with flamboyant designs and almost all the revelers wore elaborate headdresses or wigs or both. In addition to these, there were "flower children," done up in paint and collage with odds and ends pasted onto their bodies.

"Can I jump in your hoop, baby?" someone whispered to Sonata then chuckled and went on.

Howard laughed. She liked hearing him laugh; he was coming around again to his natural good humor. "It's fantastic!" he exclaimed, "Look over there. How do they get away with that without getting arrested?" He pointed to a young woman, completely nude except for a man's toupee covering her private parts. Two strands of her wig—a long black fall—partially covered her breasts and as they watched a man approached, lifted the hair, kissed each side and replaced the hair as he'd found it.

"Hey, Howard said. "If I haven't thanked you yet, thanks. And how much do I owe for the tickets?"

"It's printed on the ticket but give it to me later, I don't want to carry it around here. Anyway, I'm the one who should thank you because I never would have thought of coming if you hadn't talked about it. Vince considers it a complete waste of . . . "She let her voice fade off as he turned away from her, pretending not to hear. "I wonder if we'll ever find my Dad in this crowd…it's impossible!"

"Sonata, is that you?"

She turned and after a moment's hesitation recognized Paul Dobrin. He had a moustache and beard and wore a beret. A Frenchman; also no imagination.

"Hi," he said seeming surprised but pleased to see her. "Oh, this is my girlfriend, Tanis," he said, presenting a small dark-haired girl who was dressed as his female counterpart but who did look French. He explained to Tanis that Sonata was Kossoff's daughter.

"He's here, you've seen him?" Tanis asked.

"No, not yet, we're looking for him. I'm sorry, this is Howard Denfield. Howard, meet Paul Dobrin, substitute monitor of that fabulous Kossoff class."

"No relation to Vincent, I suppose," Paul asked, putting the question to Sonata.

"Brother," Howard acknowledged.

"Oh really? Well, how is Vince getting along, everything all right? I haven't seen him in ages."

"He's . . . everything is fine, Paul. He's painting at home. Well, I guess we'll just keep looking till we find him."

"Who, Kossoff? He's right over there. One - two - three tables down," Paul counted. "With a bunch of celebrities." He looked at Sonata and smiled. "I guess you're proud of him these days but he deserves what he's getting."

"What do you mean? What is he getting that I should be proud of?" Her eyes searched the tables further down trying to spot him.

"Well, his show up in Connecticut being such a success. The two columns they gave him in the Times last Sunday got things rolling—you saw it of course—" She hadn't seen it and realized with a sudden shock how few people there were now who might have told her about it. A year ago, a few months ago, a review in the Times would have produced an avalanche of phone calls to their home; now, she hadn't even known. "—Yeah, he's becoming known. Not that it will faze him much. He'll see what he wants to see, paint what he wants to paint and do what he's always done, well, you know him."

"Yes." No, she didn't know him. Did Paul? Did anybody?

"There he is, in that group over there," Tanis said, pointing.

"Oh, I see him now," Sonata called out. "Thanks Paul, Tanis. Have a good time, we'll catch you later."

Howard followed her towards Kossoff's table. The table was crowded but Kossoff seemed the focal point, others addressing themselves to him. She tapped him lightly on the shoulder.

"Hi, Dad, fancy meeting you in a joint like this."

He turned in his chair and when he saw her was noticeably stunned and made no attempt to hide it. "Sonny?" He got up. "Hey," he said, recovering. "It's good to see you." He embraced her and then extended his arms to take her in. "You look wonderful!"

"You don't. You look pretty silly." She laughed, feeling wonderful. "What are you supposed to be? I see some funky ears, but can't figure it out"

"Oh, a Seuss thing, just spare parts put together, nothing special. Here, sit down. Say, everybody, this is my daughter. Let's make some room here."

"Dad, this is Howard Denfield, you remember. You met him at the house?"

"No, to be honest I don't, but that's all right. Sit down, Howard." The others squeezed together and someone brought over chairs. The other men and women at the table were older than she and Howard, closer to her father's age and older. A few wore costumes but the rest were in tuxedos and gowns.

While the others talked and got up to dance, Bert put his arm on the back of her chair, his eyes merrier than she had ever seen them. "Sonny, it's *so* good to see you, I've missed you. We both have, your mother very much."

She was surprised to hear the "we" in his concern, but then she thought, why not? Ruth was still her mother and her mother had missed her. She would have to get used to being his daughter and hers separately.

He said, "Sonny, I've been meaning to let you know where I am. I'm living in Riverdale now. Here, I'll write down the address, you should have it."

She took the paper. "Dad, do you know where I've been?" she asked softly.

"I suppose I do, if you're still cohabitating with my previous monitor." He handled his glass, turning it this way and that. Then: "I was pretty upset with you running off that night." He scowled as he looked at her.

"It didn't seem to matter, I mean, what I did." She turned away.

Howard was deep in conversation with the woman next to him. She seemed almost a generation older than Howard but beautiful, with high cheekbones and smooth, glowing skin. She wore the scanty bra and silk pants of a Greek belly dancer and wore it well. Leaning over the table nudging Howard with a naughty shoulder she was giving him her rapt attention, breasts in their sequined bowls rising and falling.

"It matters. Your mother was frantic with worry, so I was out there on the streets the whole night trying to track you down."

Sonata couldn't help it, she smiled: the thought of him chasing after her like a father, like a worried father whose daughter had run away. But that's what happened.

"Don't be wise, Sonny, it was no joke. I was dead tired, wanted to be home in my bed. Home? That was no home—a disaster area. It wasn't only the picture that was destroyed, my studio was invaded, at least it felt that way to me with people—students, no less—all over the place. You know how private I keep my space!" He took a long swallow of his drink. "Anyway, I found out where you were. It wasn't too hard. You were waiting in the subway station for half an hour with no coat and Ruth said you spent a lot of time with Vincent at the party and the subway attendant said the guy you were with had a chin beard and that was that." He paused. "But I didn't do anything about it."

"Why, Dad?" His answer seemed important, though she hadn't ever thought of his coming after her.

"Well, your mother wanted you out of there instantly, no matter what time it was, but I didn't think it was such a crisis. The worst was done already. You had run off and were spending the night with him.

I thought about going up there—I know where he lives—bursting in and bringing you home, using force if necessary. I went through it all in my mind, and then I didn't do anything." He studied her, gauging her response, and then he said, "I know Vincent."

She waited, anxious for what he would say about Vincent, but he followed the remark saying, "Early in the morning you called to tell us and that was that."

"You drinking Scotch? Hey, Kossoff's daughter, you drinking Scotch? I'm Pat."

She turned and smiled, for the "Hey, Kossoff's daughter" not for the Scotch, but he poured a drink and set it in front of her. She didn't see any water or soda poured with it. The man looked familiar. She had seen him on TV but couldn't remember the show, an interview program.

Howard was not at the table. She looked out on the dance floor.

"He's dancing with Sophia," Pat told her. "You don't mind, well, considering there's nothing you can do about it."

"No, of course not," she replied quickly and laughed. The group was playing *Nowhere to Run*. It ended and they went into the music from *Goldfinger*. She tried to see Howard and Sophia on the dance floor but couldn't. She took a swallow of her drink and it burned going down but felt good at the same time like a scalding shower.

"Sophia's a great lady," Pat said with assurance, "You don't have to worry."

"Oh, I'm not," Sonata gamely responded.

Bert asked, "Who is he, that fellow you're with? Where's Vince?"

"That's Vince's brother, Howard." Then seeing her father's scowl, she said, "Oh gosh, Dad, don't look shocked."

But he was visibly disturbed. She observed a cold mistrust of her in his cool steady gaze but his next comment astounded her. "So you're keeping it in the family."

"Dad! I don't go out with Howard. This was a convenience tonight for both of us."

He studied her and his eyes darkened with a new estrangement, something she had never seen there before. She was stung that he could reach reproachful conclusions about her with his own shameful love life apparent to everyone.

"Sonny, wasn't this the man I met at the house back before you left home? I do remember him. He took you to dinner."

"Yes, but tonight is something different—"

"Sonata, I want you to know one thing…never mind, just keep quiet and listen to me. I don't know what's going on and I don't think I want to know but let me tell you, it's one thing to go with a man for…say romance, or some other personal need, but taking a man—men for sport—well, that changes the whole picture. That's a slut, honey." He stopped, letting it sink in.

Her mouth went dry. She tried to summon words in her own defense but couldn't. She feared he might hurl another incrimination at her with yet more ominous darkening of his eyes than those leveled on her now. Deserving more? For in those accusing eyes was the same condemnation she had seen on Howard's face that rainy March night walking from the League when he discovered she was living with his brother.

No. She became suddenly furious. How dare her father chastise her? He who whores with any woman he can get his hands on? Did he think she was sleeping with Howard, sleeping with both of them? Did he think she was like him? The thought struck her she was conceived by his lust, for that was all he had for her mother, the same as for all his women.

Sonata gasped at the vileness of this thought and what it said about her mother and choking, she took a step away from the table. She heard her father join the bustle and gaiety of the table, as if the sordid lesson he had just delivered to his daughter had never occurred. How quickly he packed her up into the back of his mind. Just like the night she left home. Why had he not pursued her to Vincent's apartment, as he said he thought about doing—concerned about her safety? Her morals, whatever? He "knew Vincent." Vincent could handle things, just as he handled his class for him, so he could get back to more important things.

She returned to the table and sipped her drink wishing Howard would return. She felt alone and stranded at this table, with her father but without him, with an escort but without him. Again she thought of her mother. *Frantic with worry, he'd said.* But still she hadn't come by herself to Vincent's place and begged her to come home. A sense of aloneness suddenly overwhelmed her, surrounded by people here and everywhere who had no interest in her. Vincent as well, whose appreciation of her skimmed across the surface of her being and no deeper.

She shook herself to dispel the agonizing thoughts before they went any further. She managed then for whomever might be looking, to produce a party smile.

Eventually, after what seemed like hours though it was probably no more than twenty minutes, Sophia returned with Howard behind her. Her hands patted her bosom as she sat down and Howard pushed in her chair.

"Oh, I am exhausted!" she panted. "I haven't danced with someone as swift on his feet as you in ages." She smiled up at him, playing with the bangles and spangles on both arms, then turned her attention to the table and asked Pat to pour her another drink.

"Hi," Sonata said, as Howard sat down beside her. "Long time no see."

"Talk softly. I'm in shock."

"She's old enough to be your mother, Howard, you should be ashamed."

"Mamma Mia." He laughed. "I'm more tired than I am ashamed. She's some dancer! I had to keep up. My manhood was at stake."

"With beautiful women like her I guess men have to defend everything they have."

Howard smiled. "She's nice. No, I mean it. I dig her and you would too, like if you met her at a bridge party with clothes on." Then on impulse or apology, he stood. "It's a slow one. Would you like to dance?"

"I would but you wouldn't. No, you're tired, it's okay."

"Come on, let's dance." Helping her up, he faced again the problem of her hoop. "I hope they don't laugh you off the floor or anything gross like that."

"Listen, if you keep insulting me, I'm going to have to fire you. Who needs a butler anyway?"

On the dance floor, Howard said, "It feels peculiar, your hoop bumping up against me."

"It's not like what Sophia bumped against you."

"No." He smiled. "Somehow I can't get through to you tonight."

Sonata laughed. Then a long sigh escaped. "To be honest, Howard, I feel sort of woozy. While you were whooping it up out here with Sophia, they were whooping it down back there at the table. That heavy fellow—what's his name?"

"Fat Pat."

"Who?"

"That's what they call him, Fat Pat. He has a daily TV show. Hey, your father's going to be on next week—Sophia told me—so what about him?"

"Well, he kept filling my glass and like a merry old boozer, I kept guzzling." She closed her eyes. "It's hitting me now like a ton of bricks. I didn't feel it so much sitting down or standing still, but now...wow! I hope I don't do anything silly like die right here on the dance floor."

"There's no chance of that. You can't even fall down in that outfit, it's like a parachute. Anyway, this is not music to die by, pick something with more class."

The music had a strong beat but it was heavy and nostalgic, folk rock she thought, and the singer's voice heaved as if it was the last song he ever wanted to sing in his life. She felt as if the beat was holding her up, supporting her; sure of itself, sure to go on without her and without this roomful of people—too naked, too dressed, too exposed, too concealed, too anxious. The steady beat expelled anxiety even blaring as it did through the electronic amplifiers and the speakers turned up wild. The room was glittering and trembling and tinkling like the crystals on that dark girl's costume.

Howard held her firmly and she closed her eyes and leaned against him, light-headed but happy. When she opened her eyes, she saw her father. He was dancing with someone from the table, a young woman dressed as a ballerina, but he was looking at her and his gaze was level and then he moved on.

When the music ended, she panicked for one brief moment, afraid to go back to the table, to go back to him. Howard felt her hesitate and his arms went around her waist again and they stayed there, swaying with the new music.

Fat Pat brushed past them dancing with Sophia and Sophia laughed, like bells ringing. Howard moved and she felt his duty to the music. He began dancing like the others, apart from her. She tried to share the obligation and moved bravely and apart as well, but something between her ears betrayed her. She felt a wave of heat, then cold, then heat again and suddenly she was dizzy and would have fallen in spite of the dress that was a parachute but Howard caught her. She remembered smiling and thinking, there, I've got you holding on to me again…and then he was leading her back to the table, that awful table, but Sophia was beside them and talking to Howard.

"What's the matter with her? She's not feeling well?"

"Just a little too much to drink," Howard said.

"It's the tight waist and bodice on that ridiculous costume. She should get it off right away and lie down."

"I better get her home—"

"Nonsense. The dance is not even half over and there's still the parade to come, the best part. Listen, her father took a room in the hotel for the night. Why don't we take her up there and let her stretch out for a little while? You'll see, in fifteen or twenty minutes she'll be fine. Then she can come back down in something sensible. A hotel bath towel!"

Howard laughed. "Shall we do that, Sonny," he whispered, steadying her with his arm firmly around her. "You'll be a lot less conspicuous here in a bath towel than you are in this…or how about a wash rag? Anyway you should lie down."

Sonata nodded and mumbled something about causing trouble but Sophia had already taken over, sending Fat Pat back to the table to get the room key from Bert.

Sonata hoped they would not have to explain it to him, that he would just hand over the key and she would be able to go up there and unfasten her dress which was unbearable—and ridiculous, Sophia right on both counts—and she would stretch out and relax and not think about what her father was going to do in the room later which was more unbearable.

3

In the room, Sophia undid the plethora of hooks securing Sonata's costume and put a cover over her as she lay on the bed in her slip. Sonata thought she heard Sophia whisper something to Howard about coming down as soon as he could get away. When she left, he went into the bathroom and came out with a glass of water which he placed by the bed, after which Sonata thought he would fly out of the room at once. With her stashed away he had ample opportunity to get Mamma Mia's phone number inscribed in his ubiquitous little black book for future reference.

But he didn't go. Instead, he removed his jacket and shoes and sat down on an easy chair with his feet propped up on the bed. He folded his arms and looked at her, smiling and patient. Then he put his eye-patch on and looked at her some more.

"I'm sorry," she said. "I really am ruining your night."

"You should be sorry…lying there with a red nose. You look like the town drunk."

"I'm not used to it. I should never have done it, I mean drink like that."

"Why did you then?"

"Well, Fat Pat, he kept—"

"Come on, Sonny, you can lead a horse to water and a young lady to booze, but you know the rest." He gazed at her, not smiling now. "Was it something your father said?"

She turned on her side, facing the window.

"I thought so. I had an idea there was something going on between you."

"I...I haven't seen him for a long while. He and my mother, they're getting divorced. I haven't seen either of them. Not since that glorious tribute I told you I was planning—to which everybody came, but he didn't."

"Oh! I didn't know. You'd sounded so excited about it."

She groaned, remembering it all again. And then suddenly, tears came and kept coming, foolishly falling like the folds of her silly dress lying in defeat across the chair. "I'm sorry, I shouldn't—"

Howard sprang up and sat on the edge of the bed. He gave her his handkerchief.

"He doesn't see me, not me, and I...I'm afraid who he sees." She wiped her eyes, holding the handkerchief tightly in her hands, "Sometimes he really is my father and I love him and I want him to love me—a father kind of thing, whether he's much interested in me or not—but it's like we can't get to each other at all. I can't find him, and I know by the way he looks at me, he doesn't even see who I am." *He never saw Billy either. My God never saw him, his car nicking Billy, and never knowing, just driving on. His son, as wounded and invisible as me.*

"Maybe it's not your fault, Sonny. Maybe you've done your best and he's just not reachable." He removed the wet crumpled handkerchief and set a box of tissues on her lap. "Some people are like that, just unreachable."

Sonata thought he wanted to say more about unreachable people and was going to, but instead he leaned over and wiped some tears from the edge of her cheek. And then he kissed her, her forehead and her cheek and then her lips. Maybe he meant it, or thought he meant it as a kiss of understanding but she kissed him back. She brought her arms around his shoulders. The covers fell as she twisted towards him and his hands began moving over the smooth silk of her slip and the dry warmth under the slip. He whispered in her ear, even as he caressed her. "Sonny, it's not Pat with the drink. You can't...just make an excuse and let this happen. Your father...he can't have anything to do with this."

"But he does. He has everything to do with it. How can he not?"

"You know what I mean. It can't be because you're angry or hurt. I can't make up for him. Nobody can." His hand was stroking her under the slip. "Go on, please, Sonata, tell me to stop." His lips parted against her ear. "Push me away!"

But she was pressing him closer, not sending him away. She understood that it was up to her, that her breasts when he removed her bra, were a stolen softness that did not belong to him but to his brother, that her thighs that had thrust against Vincent's body were yielding now to his hands. But she could not make the choice for him. It demanded too much of her. She could not even make the choice for herself. He could not make up for her father, she knew that. Neither could Vincent, especially not Vincent; he looked at her too closely and saw too much. She could not hide from him or make believe she was someone else as she could with Howard.

Who was she now? A seductress—like Sophia—yes because for Howard she could change as she changed out of her chaste costume to a wanton trollop. He didn't care about her. In that way, he was just like her father. She wanted him to suffer as she was suffering. Why shouldn't he?

Almost as if he could read her thoughts, Howard searched her face. "Sonny, do you know what you're doing?"

She felt his breath and his body and pressed her hips against him. There was nothing she could answer, all of this too confusing. Still, she reached for him. Then she felt him draw away, the air suddenly cold around her. His hands were no longer touching her. He sat up. She saw him looking at the slip raised up from her legs, her belly rising and falling, and she pulled it down. She knew he was thinking of Vincent now and painfully, though all evening long Vincent had been with them.

He clenched his hands and his lips tightened over his mouth. Was it a wave of lust or hate he felt for her submission to him? He drew the cover lightly over her and got up from the bed.

"I stopped for both of us," he said.

Sonata stared up at the ceiling, at the faint cracks and patched plaster and the dull brass fixture faintly reflecting light from the lamp. She grasped the cover tightly against her body as if someone might try to take it away from her and watched him lace his shoes and fix his shirt and smooth his pants. When he put on his jacket she said, "I feel all right now if you want to help get me home."

"Sonny—" he began.

"Are you afraid we'll make love again? We won't."

"Look, I don't think you're recovered yet. The whiskey doesn't wear off that fast. I think you should stay here for a while longer. Then when you feel up to it, get dressed and the doorman outside will put you in a cab. I'm going home myself now."

He looked at her once more in a probing way, as Vincent would sometimes look at her, and he bit his lower lip. Had she bruised it? She hoped so. She turned away and closed her eyes. After what seemed like a long stretch of time feeling his eyes on her, she heard the door quietly close.

She lay on the bed, too warm but still not willing to release the cover; no longer dizzy but still she lay there, not able to think clearly about anything but willing to dream about many things. She wanted to fall asleep and dream and wake up in her own bedroom a long time ago.

She tried to sleep but she was far from oblivion. Why had she clung to Howard? Was it so that he wouldn't leave, wouldn't leave her alone in this room? The faint odor of the after-shave he wore lingered in the room and she breathed it in. Or was it her own physical desire? If that, it was for the strength of his body that she needed to take from him.

After about an hour, she roused herself from the bed and began to dress. She fastened with so much difficulty the awful colonial gown, she feared it couldn't be done but at last succeeded with enough hooks to keep it closed, then went to the dresser to comb her hair.

There were two twenty-dollar bills on the dresser and over it a note torn from the black book in which he had written her phone number in front of Vincent at the League so many months ago.

"For the ticket and cab fare. Thanks for a really good time."

Money and this note, as if...*don't think about it.*

Her hand quivered as she put the money in her silly basket handbag and threw the paper in the waste basket. Then mindful her father would be using the room, she retrieved the paper and tore it into unrecognizable fragments. She made the bed and tightly smoothed the bedspread. A quick search of the room produced her hat which had been flung on a chair when she came in, the silly bonnet accompanying her silly dress. At the door then, the final check. Everything was in order. It was ready for him.

PART EIGHT
TRANSITIONS

I

Vincent lay in bed listening to Sonata's breathing. He couldn't sleep. Maybe the excitement of working at fever pitch all day, rising at six and going strong until just three hours ago, had pushed too much adrenalin into his veins, simple as that.

He got up and turned on the overhead light. It wouldn't bother her; nothing bothered her when she slept. Then he lit a cigarette which tasted terrible this early in the morning. In the kitchenette he looked at the clock which read 2:00 AM. He made coffee.

The apartment was stuffy and he opened a window, letting in a waft of cool spring air that rustled some papers on the table. The view outside was the best it could be, pitch black. He stood at the window looking out until his eyes got adjusted and the ugly cement walls and soot-darkened windows and garbage cans in the courtyard below came into view.

His mother had been here about a month ago, complaining as usual about the dismal view from his only window: a patch of sky and then walls and more walls and finally those garbage cans. She said there was a moral lesson in the view: the descent of man, or the ascent, depending on one's outlook. His outlook, she concluded, must be upbeat since he'd actually painted the view.

But Alex didn't talk about that when she was here a week ago. There were more important things. Sonata, for one.

It was a shock to ring the bell and find *the girl*, as she put it, open the door at 9:30 in the morning. Vincent was in the room painting and his first thought was *it could have been worse, she could have been modeling.*

"How long has this been going on, Vinny? Speak frankly to me. I deserve an honest answer after all I've done for you, all my support, all my standing up for you with your father. How long you have been abusing our gifts in this way?"

Her hands were folded over her purse, her back straight and her legs stiff as she sat on the upright wooden chair by the kitchen table where he ate his meals, looking as if she were in a dentist's office waiting for a tooth to be drilled.

"About four months," Vincent said.

And Sonata said, "I'm here close to five months."

How hard Alexandra was hit by this and what she considered her son's deliberate deception, he only found out much later when, in a more peaceful exchange, she relayed to him her feelings. She had been played the fool. Shattered was the conviction that had sustained her that Vincent considered her his closest ally in the pursuit of his career. For there he was, supporting a mistress in the apartment for five months—women remembered such dates better than men—with money she had practically begged from Pete, and worst of all, not confiding in her about it. All the Sunday dinners they had shared, their conversations about his work, and all that time *the girl* living here in the apartment, eating and sleeping and filing her nails and washing her hair and doing the things mistresses do. Yet, had he told her: *Mother there's a woman. I know you'll understand,* she would have tried to consider his need for that. No, not tried. She would have understood. That kind of thing was not uncommon among artists. Artists always had mistresses. She would have told Vincent that it was all right and it would change nothing. She might even have been able to extract a few more dollars from Pete for the extra living expenses, without telling him of course; Pete was too narrow-minded to understand a thing like that.

At any rate, it was done. Vincent had not confided in her and therefore it was not as difficult as she had distressed about to deliver the message she had been preparing all the way down in the subway.

"I suppose you're wondering why I've come, Vinny, it's so rare for me to visit you," she'd began. "I never want to interrupt the important work that you do"—casting a significant glance at the girl—"But of necessity now, I've come with a message."

"Yes, Alex, I know."

"You know? You mean you remembered Pete's condition about the arrangement? That it terminates after one year?" When he merely shrugged, she went on. "You never brought the matter up or asked for an extension, so I assumed you forgot about it in the heat of your creative involvement. Vinny dear, I don't know if you realize it," she said, and it seemed to Vincent she was fighting back tears, "But I have been having nearly daily battles with your father about your support. I managed to extend the termination agreement two months. After that, I sent you money from other resources. I think Pete was aware of what I was doing but he turned the other cheek and permitted me my hand in the till. But yesterday, he clamped the lid on. Out of the blue, he said, 'No more handouts for a bum who stays home all day and squeezes tubes! Let him find out what it's like to squeeze a living for a change.'"

And so the subway ride and so the message. She wanted to deliver it in person to explain Pete's side of it and to help Vincent decide what he must do. And she wanted to do it, she told him, here in his studio surrounded by his work, so he would not lose heart and give it all up. And, finally, she wanted to come alone, without Pete, so that his father would not call him a bum to his face.

But now *the girl* and the picture changed.

Vincent said, "I understand, Mom, please don't feel bad about it." He called her Mom, always when he felt close to her. "You did your best to look out for me, I know that, and I'm grateful to you. I'll always be grateful. I mean that."

He had looked at her sitting stiffly on the chair, like a social worker ill at ease in the neighborhood coming to take something dear away. Then he walked over to her and kissed her.

She began to cry. Her purse opened and he saw a white Swiss handkerchief with roses on it struggling in her hand. He put his arm around her shoulder.

"Make some coffee, Sonny," he said. "Mom, would you like a crescent roll? Sonata just bought some yesterday at the bakery."

Alexandra nodded, her head still cradled in her hand.

"I bet you haven't even had breakfast yet. Come on, we'll have breakfast together."

And so they had breakfast—Vincent, Alexandra and *the girl*—and they talked about what he would do.

Should he work? He had given up being monitor of Kossoff's class to Paul Dobrin, having no desire any longer to work at the League and so he was free in terms of his schedule, but working was a waste of precious time they all agreed. It would be a pity for him to be out doing some ridiculous job that anyone could do when he could be here at his easel creating a product which was of far greater value. Convincing Pete of this was out of the question so there was no use thinking in that direction. Still, he had to eat. It was Sonata who came up with the idea that would solve the problem. She would go out and get a job.

The idea was logical and practical and agreeable to everyone. The discussion at the breakfast table was one of straight-forward, clear-headed domestic planning. Sonata, like a dutiful daughter-in-law, was taking over the tasks that formerly belonged to Vincent's mother. Alexandra later confessed to Vincent that this last bit of line holding him to her shore was especially hard to relinquish, for she foresaw that now he would drift completely out of her reach. She had left the apartment that morning with a heavy heart.

Sonata got a job at Macy's department store. It was like seeing the world, she told him: Toledo ware from Spain on the tenth floor and an Indian tourist from New Delhi at her counter buying a slip for his aunt back home; the Russian diplomatic entourage passing ponderously down the aisle; and camel saddles from Morocco in the basement annex. She came home to Vincent brimming with news.

Every encounter was an adventure and so it went for several weeks, but after a while, just as with seeing the world, her feet got tired and that was what she talked about.

.   .   .

Vincent unplugged the coffee maker and sleepy at last, trudged barefoot across the cold floor to his bed. Curled in her nightly fetal position there lay his mistress, model, muse and salaried Macy's benefactor. Lowering himself as softly as he could, he settled in beside her. Her body heat warmed him, head to toe and within minutes, he was asleep.

2

Feeling free as never before, Vincent stretched his canvases and painted with vigor and excitement His style and method had followed a certain progression in the months that Sonata had been living with him and serving as his model. He had gradually moved from figurative representation of her to semi-abstract studies, trying to develop a perception that was uniquely his own. He had to see her as she was to him, the artist, and not as she was to anyone else. The freedom, but at the same time the drastic limitations that this imposed excited him and fired his energy so that he worked each day literally until his hands could no longer hold the brush. If he could see her clearly with an inner vision of his own, then he could see anything, abstract anything, and that essential tool of creation, his vision, could be trusted. Only with that could he ever be secure in his craft, secure as Paul Dobrin was, as Freddie often was, and as Kossoff always was. For Bert Kossoff had it, even with his damnable self-centeredness that cared so little about the outside world, he had that vision: Knowing with crystal clarity what he wanted to see on that canvas and producing a truthful image. He envied him.

In search of that inner vision, he had begun in the last few weeks to work in total abstraction, drawing upon Sonata for ideas about color, form and shape, but taking from within himself the integrity of the picture. Sometimes pure emotion displayed itself on the canvas—anger, joy, childish delight. Other times, his pictures revealed elements of poems and stories he had read, mythology, or songs he liked, always so abstracted the source was solely for himself to understand. And then, in one exhausting but exhilarating session he made a breakthrough. He produced an explosive cacophony of color, a symphony of discordant tones; it was the largest canvas he had ever attempted. Encouraged beyond his wildest expectations, he went further in his exploration of abstraction, each canvas building on the one before it. The "Sonata" series was developing.

He decided one morning that it was time to declare himself. The series, unique as it was, deserved a solo exhibition. He bought a camera and spent a day shooting slides of what he considered the most evocative examples of the series. When he got the slides back, he studied them and was satisfied the work was good. He sat at his desk with the latest monthly Gallery Guides and prepared a list of galleries he thought would respond to his style.

Later, walking along Madison Avenue with the list in his pocket and his portfolio under his arm, he debated which gallery to enter first. He suspected he was doing it wrong. Writing or phoning for an appointment would have been more sensible, but he was motivated and if he put it off, he might not be soon again. The Dan Gallery was not on his list but had prints and paintings in the window that he liked. Peering through the glass, he recognized Albers, Johns, a Rauschenberg and other trail blazers, "old friends" who had influenced him at various times. Perhaps Dan would be friendly too.

The gallery was empty of visitors but the distinguished looking man at the desk, dressed in a finely tailored European suit with narrow lapels whose name Vincent never learned, was busy and impatient. Nothing but a telephone and a pad and pencil was visible on the clear shiny surface of the desk behind which he sat.

"We handle mainly well-known artists—with international reputations?" The end of the phrase stood up with the lilt of his brow like a question which required no answer.

Vincent may have been expected to fold his tent and disappear into the dusty macadam from which he had come, but this being his first effort, he stood rooted to the spot.

"All right then," sigh, "let's have a look."

Vincent took from his portfolio the plastic slide carriers holding views and close-up images of his paintings. "These are representative of the series I am now doing."

"Yes, well...indeed...uhmm." The owner of the Dan Gallery held the first page and then the second to the light as Vincent looked over his shoulder adding a word of explanation to this one and that.

Vincent waited with as professional a smile as he could muster as the slide holders were handed back. The Dan man's own smile was dismissive and well worn.

"Thank you so much for stopping in."

The Diefenbach Gallery on 67th Street had a full stable and was not looking at any work. "We're so sorry."

At the Renouer Gallery, Vincent's greeting by a young, immaculately groomed young woman with a French accent was receptive. She looked at the slides and nodded thoughtfully, smiled and praised the technique. The verdict: Mr. Renouer was in Europe looking for paintings and would not be back for five or six months. "Why not stop back then?"

The Robert Elton Gallery was specific. Mr. Robert Elton was there, looked, did not care for what he saw and said "No, it's not for us."

In the Lembruch Gallery, Vincent found producing his slides uncomfortable as gallery visitors milled about, glancing at him as at a traveling salesman with a foot stuck in the door of a very fine house. The gallery was run by Mrs. Lembruch, Vincent discovered, after a pleasant and useless twenty minutes with Mr. Lembruch who talked about smog in the city, garbage collection, the scarcity of affordable apartments and the Mayor's job approval rating to which Vincent could contribute nothing but his willingness to listen. Mr. Lembruch would tell his wife about Vincent, and no, there was no point in leaving the slides.

The last gallery was encouraging. The assistant, an exotic Persian woman with sleek black hair and enormous almond-shaped eyes, introduced him cordially to the gallery owner. Mr. Salvador, a heavy-set ponderous man with rimless glasses asked him to sit down. They discussed Vincent's work, viewed carefully by the window where the light was best. They discussed his method, his stylistic direction. Vincent's pride returned. Mr. Salvador's voice and manner was charged with all the respect a young artist might hope to receive and he was giving his work the time it needed. Mr. Salvador stroked his chin and nodded his approval. He inquired the prices—Vincent hadn't thought about prices—asked how many canvases he had and then sat down and cleaned his glasses and tallied what it would cost Vincent to have a show.

"Well certainly, a new artist, unknown, and rents so high on Madison Avenue, galleries closing right and left, it will come to roughly fifteen hundred. This includes," he went on, as Vincent stared at the paper unseeing, "the printing, mailing, opening reception, insurance, the guaranty to the gallery...Of course there will be helpful reviews in one or two of the local East Side magazines—we can't predict a review in the Times, of course, or Art News, Art Forum and such—but the exposure is what you need now, dear friend." Turning pages of his desk calendar: "Well, now, I have three weeks free in July."

•   •   •

Vincent sat now in his room on the side of his bed, stranded between sleepless night and dawn. On the floor propped against the wall was his massive breakthrough painting. "On the easel was a painting in vivid polymer paint inspired by the early work of Fran Stella, not finished. On the walls there were others—finished, inspired paintings. Did he like them? Were they his vision?

Who was it?—Dostoevsky, maybe—who said that people fall into three categories: Those who haven't got much going for them and don't want much, contented souls; they're in one group. Then those who have a lot going but want more than they are capable of are a second group. These folks suffer, believing in their preeminence but never rise to the top. And lastly, the geniuses: the ones who have it and know it and the world knows too. But listen, D— or whoever—there are lots who are great on their own terms, even the contented ones in category-one. The standards change like everything else in life, the judges too, who might value greatness by what's lacking in themselves.

He could be a genius if his mother and Sonny were the curators. And why doubt them? What purpose would it serve? To be okay with your life and in accord with the times is what matters. On the easel was a painting in vivid polymer paint inspired by the early work of Frank Stella, not finished. He could hardly separate the two conditions. That's what his productivity boiled down to, what being alive did for that matter. For when something completed was on the wall or stored away, he would have made some compromise with his dissatisfaction.

Art and life, little difference. If people judged his art at all, they'd believe he intended it just that way, not understanding that work rarely turns out as intended. Attempts, all of it—a great idea one day, a stupid action the next that sets a life course. Nothing is ever finished and final. We breathe in the flux around us like air, small satisfactions appearing like apparitions.

He crossed the room to the window overlooking the courtyard to look at the stingy piece of sky that came with the cramped apartment. With a sense of foreboding that he could not explain, he approached the stack of paintings leaning against the wall. All the work he had done in the feverish months since Sonata had come to him was here, extending out into the room. He'd had no patience and no time to fasten screw eyes and wire and hang them; only to make them then make more.

He separated out a few and stood back and looked and judged. And now, there seemed to be plenty of time. Before he had felt rushed, a morning lost, an hour unforgivable. But a sleepless night is like the blackness in which it resides: too dark to discern a beginning or an end, time hovering like a close friend whom you'd rather didn't stick around, but who does.

He had made more than fifty studies of Sonata and fourteen of the two of them together, some more abstract than others but all discernible nudes. He pulled out more, propping them against the wall so that before long the entire room was lined with pictures. He lacked space to see them all together as he intended, but it would not be necessary, for a slow rage was beginning to burn inside him. He was being deceived, incredibly deceived all along. His vision had been playing tricks on him. He saw himself as a boy sitting up in bed in the dark of night fighting off a man, animal, monster—flailing his arms to feel it. But then, as now, he felt his vision playing those tricks. Why now? Was fear driving it still and if so what fear—of failure...of success?

Where was the beauty of the gently curving back, the movement and line that he had *captured* in those urgent morning poses? And the colors, those shades he mixed that he perceived to be so muted and subtle? He saw them now as raw, tediously the same in every picture. His vision had played havoc with his mind, his energies.

His mounting rage turned to embarrassment when he viewed the nude studies of Sonata and himself together. Vulgar, insidious. They were Beauty and the Beast in comic books. He forced himself to look at others and cringed as each jarred him with sharper insult. And then the later ones, the total abstractions which he anticipated would be the breakthrough to the Vincent Denfield style. In them he found a jungle of disorganized color, tangled vines of directionless line, an overgrown forest.

He walked past the pictures overlapping each other in the room and tiny hallway. Perhaps he was too severe, only the depressing night and sleeplessness. But no, it was useless and he knew it—knew with white light clarity, for his anger illuminated critical, analytical judgment. No apparition, this. It was a vision he could trust.

He dropped into the chair and closed his eyes and wondered what desperation had made him believe he was one of the gifted. What weakness had made him see Sonata as an inspiration for those gifts? What dependencies did he have upon these women, these idolizers, these mothers who praised him and offered themselves as sacrifices to his ego?

His eyes fell to the *breakthrough* painting. He saw his name carefully written in the lower right-hand corner and for the first time felt no joy in the familiar letters.

"Mediocrity," he cried aloud, raising his arms like a minister to a congregation, "Thou art mediocre, every inspired one of you! Thou art shit!" He dropped his arms with a sense of finality.

And then he looked at Sonata, breathing with her mouth open. Her faithful feet that stood all day behind a Macy's counter for the sake of him, dangled over the side of the bed and she was wearing his irritating plaid bathrobe. What did she think she was doing here? Was he a crusade to float a banner for? A cause, a means to renew herself? Well, he was through playing the Salvation Army.

He pulled back the covers and jostled her shoulder. "Let's go," he said, shaking her awake. "Come on, out of bed now. Let's wake up here!"

She squirmed, trying to avoid the persistent hand and then finally opened her eyes. When she saw him standing over her, she sat up, startled. "What's the matter! Why are you shaking me like that?"

"I said get out of bed. You're going home wherever the hell that is. Come on."

"What? What are you saying? Vincent, what's the matter?" Her lips were trembling and her shoulders began to shake.

"Get up and put your clothes on. You need to go."

"I don't understand…what have I done?" she wrapped her arms around the bathrobe huddling inside of it.

"There's nothing to understand, just go."

"But where? I'm not going home, where should I go? Why? My God, look, it's the middle of the night!" She was standing now, straining her eyes toward the darkness of the courtyard and shivering uncontrollably.

He gathered her clothes from the dresser, the bathroom, the chairs, the closet, a few things from under the bed. He threw over her jeans and a sweater and began stuffing the rest into her backpack.

"Vincent, what did I do? Why are you angry with me?" She was holding the clothes and sobbing and searching the pockets of the bathrobe for a tissue.

"I'm not angry with you, I just need you to go," he said, looking away. "It will be light out soon, so you don't have to worry about getting mugged, anything dramatic like that, and your paycheck should still be in your bag." He glanced at her, then quickly away again, unexpected emotion rising in his throat, misting his eyes in spite of himself, his clarity. He could not, would not allow himself to falter. A conviction deep within him, a sense of survival, was pushing to the surface even as he spoke.

"I'm sorry, Sonny," he said softly, then more strongly over the catch in his voice: "We needed each other for a while, we should leave it at that." She was staring at him blankly, her eyes red, a tissue scrunched between her fingers. He unlocked the door to the hall. "Please hurry and go."

Vincent crossed to the window and waited there while she dressed, forced to watch the dismal truth of the courtyard slowly come into focus—the concrete walls, the trash-bins, the narrow shaft of space that beckoned to a vaster sky. He remained standing there, hearing her soft whimpering, the creak of the floor as she went to the bathroom, then gathered her possessions and finally, her farewell.

"Goodbye, Vincent. You son of a bitch!"

He turned only when he heard the door close and knew that she was gone.

3

Alone in the room and stretched out in bed Vincent stared at the ceiling. He missed the old cot with its familiar dip in the middle, that nest he had made for himself with a year of turning and tossing. Pulling the covers up to his chin, he felt the place where the beard had been. He missed it. So much, just lost. He had no will to paint and that was lost, the power to conceive, like a fertile woman grown old. He would become used to it, didn't matter. There were lipstick stains on the pillow and that didn't matter.

He stared at the swirls and cracks in the ceiling, bright now with the full force of Saturday, and mumbled aloud: "There is more imagination in you than all the crap in this room. I lie at your feet in awe."

His head fell sideways on the pillow to observe again the long line of paintings against the wall. They seemed to be waiting for something after their death sentence as a group. Individual burials.

He swung his legs over the bed and sat up, looking with a cold and abject eye at the painting closest to him. Then he stood, got a pad and pencil and began to write a judgment of the picture with succinct purposeful phrases.

Unconvincing manipulation of media for effect alone; lacking in integral purpose. The complete disposal of it was satisfying. He went on to the next:

Cluttered and trivial. Mr. Denfield attempts grandly and fails in the same manner to make an original contribution.

And then the next: *Contrived and disorganized; absent entirely is any synergy of movement and space.*

And so on. In some, he had a word of kindness to offer: *Trenchant but overly calculated excursions into color mystique.*

And in another: *Competent if uninspired. The reclining nude appears as fatigued as the artist.*

He was beginning to enjoy himself. He put a kettle on for coffee and continued his tour around the room. It took only a minute or two to compose each synoptic epitaph. One sharp, clear, steady look and the phrases leaped onto the page.

A disturbing diversity of style in this painting, sometimes suggesting versatility but more often vacillation.

It took him most of the day, unnumbered cups of coffee and one of the best breakfasts he'd enjoyed in months, but when finished, he had upwards of thirty critiques, each one no more than four lines—sharp, smart and to the point. Some of them were witty, some satirical, all pithy and entertaining.

The next day, Sunday, he re-read them and sifted out the best, adding splashes of humor and references to this well-known artist or that. He invented Russian, Italian and French names to add some class and culture and tried throughout for a tone as droll and cryptic as he'd seen other writers employ to slaughter artists in the high art journals: *Miss Jessup demands more, I'm afraid, from her viewers than she does from her canvases.*

On Monday, he assembled them neatly in a portfolio with a brown, shiny cover—a glossy, shit color that he purchased in a stationery store. On Tuesday morning, he took the portfolio to Art Newsmakers Magazine. The following Friday, by phone, he was offered a starting position as staff critic of group gallery shows in the Manhattan area.

When Vincent Denfield appeared at his parents' home on Mother's Day, he was a wage earner. Pete was not entirely convinced this was a job, though he grudgingly admitted it was *something*, but Alex's joy was indescribable. Her son's talent had at last been recognized.

He was on his way.

PART NINE
RIVERDALE

1

It was a chilly day for May. A woman hurrying down the street towards home was anxious to escape the chill but boys playing with a football in an empty lot were invigorated by it, running to catch the ball on the run and hurl it back. For each, the cold air set the pace.

Sonata stopped in front of a dark Victorian house, glanced at the address scribbled on a scrap of paper and checked it against the number on the door. She was nervous and had an inclination to stuff the paper in her pocket and walk away. It was foolish not to have called first. Arriving at his doorstep would have been easier if he expected her, but what could she have said on the phone? She thought about it. No, it had to be done this way: arrive…talk. Then maybe he would let her stay.

She looked up at the building, three stories high with pigeons landing on the ledges. She wondered which room was her father's studio. Was he watching her now from his window, questioning what she was doing in front of his house? She didn't look her best, wearing a sweater, jeans and loose fitting wind breaker. In fact, she looked a mess. Her clothes being stuffed into a backpack didn't add to any haute couture, though she'd been trying to hang out their wrinkles in her small cubby at the Y.

In the vestibule she saw her father's name on a plaque. There were two other plaques: Mrs. Rose Lapidus and L'Ecole de Ballet.

She rang the bell under his name and after what seemed like a long time a thin responding buzz released the door lock. It surprised her, so she failed to turn the door handle before the buzzing stopped. She rang again, keeping her hand on the door knob. This time the buzzer, as if annoyed, rang long after she was inside.

Although the hall was brightly lit, she could not clearly see the face of the woman who waited at the top of the stairway peering down at her. "I'm looking for Mr. Kossoff."

"Yes…?" The woman hesitated. "What did you want?"

"Well, I want to see him." She hadn't expected this. Who was this woman? Sonata stepped to the bottom rung of the stairs.

"Is he expecting you?" Then: "Wait, you look familiar. I've seen you before."

"I'm his daughter. No, he's not expecting me."

"You're Sonata, of course. Well, why didn't you say so? Come up, come inside." She held out her hand as Sonata approached the landing. "Oh gosh! Will he be surprised to see you!"

"Oh, he's not here?" she asked inside, looking around. The room she entered was sparsely furnished, a few places to sit, some tables, a bookcase and that was pretty much all. Beyond, through wide open double doors, she saw what looked like a vast empty space.

The woman, Sonata now realized, was at the Masquerade Ball dressed as a dancer. Bert had not introduced them. Now she was in jeans and a man's shirt; her hair blondish brown was loose and she wore no make-up.

"Your father went out a while ago to get a few things, he'll be back soon. I'm Irene." She closed the door behind them. "I can't believe you're here, just like that on a Sunday morning. I've heard so much about you!"

"Have you? Really?"

"I understand you're going to the League now too."

"Yes, well, I was…I still am."

"Give me your jacket. There we go." She hung it in the closet, a welcoming gesture that moved Sonata almost to tears, she couldn't say why.

"I was just having breakfast, will you sit down with me?"

Sonata followed her into the kitchen, a cheerful room with a small round table in the middle and lavender curtains on the window and the smell of cinnamon toast and coffee.

"We eat at odd times. Actually, Bert's been up for hours. He'll be ready for lunch when he gets back," she said with a quick laugh. "Toast?"

"No thanks, I've eaten. I'll have coffee with you though."

"Where are you coming from now?" she asked, pouring coffee into white Melomac cups with daisies on them.

"Right now from the Y.W.C.A."

"Oh." She looked up surprised, then continued pouring and setting out milk. "I'm an expert on Y's," Irene went on, "New York, Chicago, Detroit, Washington—" She shared with Sonata her reflections on reception desks manned by impervious keepers of the keys, lobbies with rules and regulations posted on the walls along with notices of cultural events which somehow you were never in the market for, lounges with cigarette-stained carpets and tattered waste baskets and TV sets always on. "I remember the depressing cafeterias looking for a place to sit where you could be most invisible while you ate your tuna sandwich and tomato soup and wondered what you were going to do with your life."

They talked about Sonata's class at the League and about Jacob Miller as an instructor and Irene was telling her that Davidoff's life class was something she should try to get into if she had the opportunity. Modeling for different classes, she had a sense of the good instructors, listening and watching them circulate.

Sonata's disappointment at finding a woman living in her father's house was changing to a sense of kinship with this person. It seemed a long time since she had the company of another woman and she thought of her mother. But how different these two were and how odd that she should be here talking and smiling and enjoying her father's mistress. Yet sitting with her now in this cheerful kitchen, it was her father she was beginning to dread.

. . .

When she heard his key in the door, she tensed and felt the color drain from her face as Irene repeated her welcoming exclamation. "Will he be surprised to see you!"

But if so, it was only for a moment. Raising his brows he studied her, head to toe. "One quart of milk and a shaving cream later and look what I find in my kitchen!"

Sonata smiled hesitantly and stood. "See that, give your address to strangers when you've had some drinks and you never know when they'll turn up." Then bravely she walked over to where he stood in the kitchen doorway and touched his arm.

He smiled and his eyes softened. He set his package on the table. "Well, I'm glad you came."

"May I stay?" she blurted. Damn it! Where was the speech she'd drafted and practiced over and over again in that closet of a room? "Oh shoot!" she said aloud.

His lips tightened and he looked at her critically as he had on the dance floor when her head lay against Howard's shoulder. How did he know what she was going to do that night when she hadn't known herself? And wasn't it his insinuations that led to it? No, that wasn't fair. She was cut from the same cloth, that was all; they had the same paucity of character. They belonged together.

She pressed back the lump forming in her throat and forced herself not to see the narrowed eyes and the pause held too long. He had to want her to stay without tears, without begging.

"What happened to Vincent?" he asked finally.

"He asked me to leave."

He laughed a dull, short, unfunny laugh. "Good, maybe now I'll get my monitor back." He looked at Irene. "What do you think, Renie, should we ask her in? Should we go in the other room and talk about it while she waits and then come out and give her the verdict? What do you think?"

Irene stood and put an arm around Sonata's shoulder. "I'd like you to stay," she said, smiling. "I don't know about that son-of-a-bitch over there, but I'd like you to stay with us."

2

The house was owned by Mrs. Ellie Lapidus, a widow who had it converted to a two family dwelling, renting out the second floor and keeping for herself a small apartment on the ground floor, the third floor never renovated. An old Victorian structure on a residential street one block from the shopping center, the location in Riverdale was ideal for the small commercial enterprise that Irene embarked upon. Their space contained a huge room with wood floors that a previous owner had used for a billiard room. Bert had thought of using the room as a studio for himself but he agreed that Irene's dance studio was a better plan and rented a studio near the League.

Irene was still in the throes of excitement about her venture and described to Sonata the details of how it got started. She had put a small but impressive ad in the local paper and to her astonishment got immediate results. It was the line about her tour with the French Ballet Company that did it.

"Irene Lewis, the ad read, formerly on tour with a renowned French Ballet Company"—she couldn't remember the name but it was just as well since it was not so renowned and she'd been fired after two weeks of the tour and you could never tell if somebody knew of it— "announces the opening of her Ecole de Ballet. Registration is open to children ages four to fourteen." And she had given the phone number and address. Her opening coincided with the beginning of spring break in the grade schools which was helpful for families to stop by to see the set-up.

"Enrollment is important now that the divorce is costing Bert so much," she confided, "I'm determined to make a success of it. For him as well as me."

Irene seemed as delighted by the friendship with her lover's daughter as Sonata was with her, sometimes forgetting the girl was her mother's daughter too. She confided to Sonata her opinion that Bert had gotten a rotten deal. "He wasn't a great husband, but to rake him over the coals like Ruth's lawyer did…I mean the fundamental unfairness of it," she complained. "All of his creative output going to Ruth! Anyway, now that I have my own business underway I can manage the business end of his. I've been making the rounds of galleries, getting him booked for exhibitions, talking him up to dealers who have ins with the collectors. You know I'm the one who got the Connecticut show that did so well for him."

But as far as Sonata could see, Bert hardly concerned himself with any of it: not the divorce or the bleak finances or the surrender of his art work to Ruth. Nothing seemed to touch him, even positive things like the notoriety that fell to him from the Connecticut show. Irene said as much. "As long as he can still paint, none of it matters to him. That's the beautiful side of your father," she said. "Blind but beautiful."

Their schedules managed to miss each other like pendants on a mobile. Sonata left for Macy's shortly after Irene's morning dance students arrived. She always had the pre-school children first, and next the kindergartners who had a half-day of school in the afternoons; and after that, those who'd had their half-day of school in the mornings. Then after three o'clock, she took school children in two classes according to their ages. By the time Sonata returned from Macy's, Irene's final class was ending and they would usually prepare dinner together. Bert painted during the day at his rented studio and taught at Pratt and the League on scheduled evenings. He had dinner at the house irregularly and Sonata might not see him before she left for the night class she was now taking at the League.

Life between Irene and Bert seemed to Sonata to be completely harmonious, lacking in friction and full of discussion, mostly about Bert's career. Irene's efficiency and her knowledge of the art world was genuine. Her mother lacked this knowledge in spite of the fact that she had studied art. As far as Sonata could determine, Ruth never had the sort of relationship with Bert that Irene seemed to have. Still, there was something she didn't trust about Irene. She was a woman who had been around and it showed, like the way she sometimes flirted with Bert, little things she said. Irene had been around.

At least her father was honest. He didn't want her here and it showed, mostly by ignoring her presence. And despite the outward gestures of friendship, Irene probably thought the same, never mind all the girl talk in the kitchen about dinner choices and what the little ballerinas were saying in the classes. Sonata knew she was altering their life. If she weren't here they'd be screwing in the living-room or on the kitchen table while the potatoes were boiling.

But it was she who should stay, when it came down to it, not Irene. Irene came into her father's life as a stranger and would go out that way because they'd never get married. Irene was filling a gap, transient, but Sonata belonged whether he liked it or not. They were family. He had no one close to him now with Ruth gone, no living parents, no other kids. Only her. *And I have only him.*

She vowed to be more accepting of her father as a person. After all, he didn't beat her or anything; he wasn't a terrible father, just had his ways, was involved in his own world. She could get him to take interest in her if she really tried. The tribute was a fluke. He didn't *mean* to hurt her.

3

Sonata sat at the small desk situated in a corner of Irene's makeshift dance studio, the only furnishing in the large room other than a ballet barre, record player and wall-to-wall mirror. She was flipping through help wanted ads, hoping to find something more appealing than selling at Macy's. Irene had asked her to stay in the room as an adult presence while she sorted through music she intended using for the day. Sonata actually delighted in the task, enjoying the children's chatter.

In the center of the room little girls in black leotards, chubby legged and flat fronted, fidgeted and giggled but did as they had been told and did not run wildly around while they waited for their class to begin. Still, there were bold ones like Jennifer and Roberta who every so often ran across the floor and dared anyone to stop them.

"My mommy says we might go to a foreign country," said Jennifer flopping down next to Roberta on the floor.

"Why?" asked Roberta.

"Because my daddy has a sabotage."

"What's that?" Roberta asked, not looking up. She was sitting on her feet and falling back on her rump and repeating the process trying to balance.

"It's what you get in seven years."

"So, what's so great about that?"

"I wouldn't have to go to school for a whole year with stinky Miss Kaminsky. That's a hundred days…it's two hundred…it's a thousand fifty days!"

"I'm gonna go to a foreign country too," Roberta said, balancing this time for several seconds before falling sideways. "My mommy says this summer she's taking me and Michael."

"You're just saying that to copy me!"

"I am not!"

"Where are you going then?" Jennifer challenged. "We're going to Italy and that's a hundred miles away...it's a hundred thousand and fifty miles."

"So what, we're going even more away than that!"

"Where? Your father doesn't even have a sabotage."

"We're going to Florida! My mother says!"

Irene came into the room, her hair pulled backed in a French twist and wearing a black leotard and pink tights. She smiled as the children stood up and greeted her and began at once to arrange them into two straight lines.

"Spread out a little more, girls. Come on, there's plenty of space here, don't crowd yourselves." Looking up at Sonata, she called to her, "Thanks, honey, see you tonight."

Sonata took her papers and got up but waited by the door watching as Irene began her lesson.

"Plies in first position and let's keep those backs straight." She put a record on the phonograph and then counted with them as they slowly squatted in deep knee bends and straightened. "Smoothly with your arms out now, 1-2-3-4-5-6-7 and-a 1-2-3-4...control it, Jennifer, don't drop...that's better, and-a 1-2-3-4-5-6-7-8...once again. In second position now, pull up and pull in. Turn those knees out Linda, and-a 1-2-3-4—"

Sonata could hear Bert below coming into the building and treading up the stairs. Irene had confided to her how pleasant it felt to have a house, even if it wasn't your own, and a business that could grow. She loved teaching and it hadn't taken her long to brush up on the ballet barre and floor work. You don't forget those movements and combinations, doing them over and over for years. And of course she'd never stopped dancing while modeling, just a different kind.

Sonata watched Irene teaching the children a little routine: "*Glissade, arabesque, pas de bourree, changement.* Change your feet, Suzanne, it's the other one in front."

"Miss Irene," called Emily, "I just saw your Daddy."

"Yeah," giggled Jennifer, "He just sticked his head in."

4

Friday evening Sonata and Irene were preparing dinner together, shelling shrimp. Midway through, Irene declared it boring work and took out some ice and mixed them each a gin and tonic. "To celebrate half a bowl of clean shrimp, why not?"

Seated at the table they began discussing Bert's new alliance with the prestigious La Marca Gallery on Fifty-Seventh Street. Irene had made the contact. Sonata watched her light a cigarette and extinguish the match flame by shaking it. Blowing it out was so much smoother. "How long have you known my father?" she asked then.

"A long time. Let's see...I met him at the League when I first came out here, I guess it was five or six years ago."

"That long! I had no idea you were such old friends." She sipped her drink and discovered that Irene had made it too strong again as usual.

Has he changed much? I mean with you, or have you always been on, sort of an even keel?"

"We get along," she said. "We've fought a few times but basically we are what you might call very compatible." She smiled. "Oh, Bert's changed, I suppose. Well, I have too for that matter. I'm a lot more subdued than in the good old days."

"How would you say Bert changed?"

"I guess in the same way, more subdued. In those days he was more full of surprises than now."

Sonata laughed dryly. "Surprises? My father? He always seemed to me very serious."

"Well, with family a man acts differently than with...you know. One night he took me out to see his studio."

"What's so surprising about that?"

Irene smiled. "Only the fact that it was the wee hours of the morning and his family was home." She stopped for a moment then shrugged and continued. "I suppose it doesn't matter, my telling this now that they're divorced, or does it?" She asked.

"Oh no, go on! You mean, he sneaked you in?" Sonata was stunned at the thought of him creeping into the studio with a woman while they were all sleeping. What nerve! She remembered a night the girls in scout camp raided the kitchen boys' cabin. She had been scared to death and all they did was look at each other and eat potato chips. One girl got kissed, hardly worth staying awake for all night plus three days of planning. How detached she was, no longer the daughter inside the house with the deceived wife; now she was on the other side of the wall with them.

"Say, I remember one night a long time ago, my brother Billy woke us up crying that there was a robber in the house. It was in the studio, yes, that's where he heard the noises and Dad wasn't home (or was he?) because Mother was the one who herded us back to bed saying it's nothing, a little squirrel in the wall." She laughed. "Were you that little squirrel, Irene?"

Irene laughed too and then coughed from the cigarette. "I don't know, I think there might have been other little squirrels in that wall from time to time."

Then all at once, Irene's face clouded and the smile faded. "No." She shook her head slowly. "Billy wasn't home that night. It was...it was the night he died, I'd forgotten. How stupid of me to tell this story! I...I forgot the way it ended. Oh, gosh, forgive me, Sonny." She said nothing for a long while. She picked up her drink, looked at it, then put it down. "At the time we didn't know, of course, but Bert called me later and told me. I'm so sorry."

"It's all right." Sonata lowered her eyes, thinking of Billy. How worried he had been about robbers in the night, yet how brave. He had wanted to take a poker from the fireplace and go after them. Maybe he should have. Somebody should have. But Billy wasn't there to defend the family against this robber sitting here with her. Then suddenly, a warm flush of blood rushed to her head. Ethel's insane account of the night Billy died... *Bert in his car with a girl.* No, the story was a fabrication, the invention of a vengeful woman using poor Anne Calnon, Billy's friend's mother, as a pawn. *Sneaking her into his studio...* Yes, but certainly if there was an accident Irene would not have blithely brought the subject up and she would not have forgotten *the way it ended.* Of course. But now would be a good time to bury the slander because if Irene was with him that night then she must know.

Sonata went to the fridge and added tonic to her drink. "Irene, did anything unusual happen on your way out to the studio that night? In the car, I mean?"

"No." She smiled. "It was...you know, cozy, that's all."

"You didn't have an accident or anything?" How foolish to go on with it. This was Ethel's inquisition, not hers. How much like Ethel she felt now.

"No, of course not, Bert's an excellent driver, why do you ask? Oh—"

"What?"

"We did hit a cat just a little ways before we got there."

"A cat?"

"Yes. It gave us a jolt. But it ran off in the dark, we didn't see it. What are you getting at? Is something wrong?"

"Nothing, no. It ran off? Did you hear it or anything? Are you sure you hit it?"

"No, we didn't hear it and yes, it ran off because we didn't see a trace of it, and yes, I'm sure. Anything else?"

"I see. No, I—I just wondered." She sat down, steadying herself against the table.

Irene got up to continue work on the shrimp while Sonata sipped her drink, staring into it trying to crush the hard lump rising in her throat. *Oh, Billy, forgive him...forgive him...This evil woman, this seductress, this bitch who made him crazy wild, she did it.* Irene turned on the radio. Sonata sat at the table for several minutes. Her rage mounted though she could not utter a sound of it aloud. Then a gut wrenching premonition of loneliness rising like flood waters and with it a vow: *Irene alone must bear the guilt. Or there would be no one left for her.*

She stood finally, her glass in hand and watched the slope of Irene's strong dancer's back as she worked at the sink, her weight resting on one muscular leg. How she hated this woman! How she wanted to fling the reality of that night into her face, strike her with it like a hammer blow! But the blow would bring down her father as well.

But to do nothing? *Billy, to do nothing? Oh, Billy, I loved you so much! I cried so hard I thought the tears would never stop. Billy, do you want her to be punishment? Do you?*

Because there are ways to do it.

She brought her glass to the sink. "Irene, would you mind finishing up alone? I'm not feeling so well. Maybe the drink was too strong."

"Sure thing, you go in and lie down. Sorry, I keep thinking you take it straight and strong, the way he does."

5

Sonata had become friendly with the landlady Mrs. Lapidus, after being asked one day when the woman was having trouble with her legs to pick up a newspaper for her at the subway corner. Since then, Sonata had gotten into the habit of getting the paper every day for her when she passed the newsstand on her way home from work or from the League. Often she was invited inside for a cup of tea which Sonata customarily declined. A day after the devastating conversation with Irene, she surprised Mrs. Lapidus by accepting.

"It's terrible with these legs. I'm telling you, I think it's getting worse and I thought the spring air was all I needed."

Sonata sipped her tea and helped herself to a piece of pound cake that Mrs. Lapidus had cut into small pickup portions. "Well, but the wind is gusty. Maybe that's what's bothering you."

"Yes, the wind is bad here, well, it's so near the river, that's why."

"It must be awful for the children," Sonata said. "I see Irene's girls out there shivering in their skimpy tights after class, you know, waiting for their mothers?"

"They should wait inside. They *should* wait inside, not to catch cold. I'll have to tell them. I heard a child coughing yesterday—a hacking cough—I was thinking she should see a doctor."

"Wouldn't it bother you, though? All those kids waiting in the hall next to your door? They make a racket when they get together like that, you know, without supervision."

"Children never bother me. No, I say noise like that is healthy noise. I have grandchildren—six, God bless them. The two big ones visited over Easter vacation. Maybe you saw them?"

"You *must* love children. I guess if I was living downstairs under all that noise of jumping feet, I'd never stand for it."

Mrs. Lapidus shrugged. "They're learning dancing, it's all right. It's nice for a girl to learn dancing. My grandchild—the youngest—she's quite the little ballerina!" She laughed.

"How about the neighbors? They don't mind either?"

"Mind? Mind what?"

"The dancing classes."

Mrs. Lapidus looked at Sonata quizzically for a second or two before answering. "Well, nobody's said anything. I don't know."

"I'm surprised. Well, I'm even surprised there isn't an ordinance about it. Isn't it a residential neighborhood?"

"I never gave it too much thought," Mrs. Lapidus said. She sipped her coffee. "They asked me when they took the lease if it was going to be all right upstairs and I said I didn't see why not and we left it like that. I don't know about an ordinance or anything."

"She's preparing a new brochure for next term and planning on more students. I don't know how many actual classes she's figuring on having but things like this have a way of spreading. It might be wise to check on it. I mean, with more kids there'll be more noise, more parents pulling up outside, more everything."

•   •   •

Sonata was in the apartment alone a week later when the phone rang. She had prepared a banana cake that was rising in the oven. She picked up the phone.

"Where'd I get you from?"

"Nowhere special—who is this?"

"Howard. What took you so long to answer?"

"Howard. Oh…" She paused. "I was baking a cake, a banana cake."

"You?"

"Yes, me. A cake for my father's desert tonight." She was using up bananas that were getting rotten because Irene refused to put them in the refrigerator, singing the silly song about Chiquita to prove her point. They had spoken very little in the past week. Nothing had changed since her tea with Mrs. Lapidus, but the frown on the woman's face as Sonata thanked her for the tea and left could have meant anything.

"Yeah, I heard you moved in there," said Howard.

"How did you hear? Where did you get my number?"

"From the League where else? If anybody wants to keep a secret, they shouldn't say beans to that receptionist there. She tells all, you just ask. She knows also that one of the school's models is living up there with you. Sounds like one big happy family!"

"Irene is not modeling anymore." She flushed, just mentioning Irene's name.

"No? Well, I'll jot that down. Report the information right away to correct her records."

"Yeah, do that."

"Sonny?"

"Yes?"

"Can I see you?"

The request was so unexpected, she looked down at the receiver, as if to find something that hadn't come through. She answered hesitantly. "Do you *want* to?"

"Yes, I want to." His voice was softer now; the flip edge of it off. "I miss you. It's cold out here in the world."

She wasn't sure what to say. Then found herself shifting into the casual tone he'd set, following his lead. Is that what she excelled at—with both brothers? Vincent seemed so far away now, like he never happened. "You have lots of coats and suits to keep you warm," she said flippantly. "Still working in Boston?"

"No, that's set up already. It's running itself now with a local manager and I'm in New York again to stay. Here to pick up where we left off. Sonny, I'd like to see you."

"Howard, is this something between you and Vincent? I mean, am I caught in the middle of some private thing going on between you two?"

"Maybe you are, I don't know." He paused. "I suppose you were caught in the beginning. Now, I don't know."

"Well, you're honest at least." The phone cord passed between her fingers. "Have you spoken to Vincent?"

"Yes. He told me you had left."

"Is that all?"

"That's all. Vince is not much of a talker in case you don't already know."

"Howard, did you tell him?"

"Tell him what?"

"Well, about us, about me?"

"You mean the Plaza affair? Of course not...Sonny, I'm sorry about that, do you believe me? I should have understood. I just got all mixed up that night."

"It's all right, Howard. I was pretty mixed up too."

"Look, will you see me? Can I pick you up tomorrow after your still-life class? See that, I even know what class you're in. You changed from life painting to still-life, right? I'm gonna have to give that receptionist a Christmas present." He waited. "Come on, Sonata, meet me tomorrow? Look, I'll give you some valuable advice on your pictures."

She laughed. "You're one for that, a businessman like you!"

"Well, I know what a pear's supposed to look like, for Christ's sake! Come on, Sonny. I've missed you. You did something good for me just in the few times we've been together, I felt like an okay person with you. I did the right things, I even thought the right things." He paused, then blurted, "To hell with Vincent! If Vinnie is here somewhere mixing me up again, I'll dig him out and get rid of him. Look, he mixed you up too, didn't he? Damn right he did! He has the capacity to make everybody around him feel...inadequate or something, just by the tilt of his head or his crooked smile or his goddamn cold stares. He's where he belongs now, cutting people to ribbons with sharp little paragraphs in print. Christ, I've never seen him so happy. A critic!" He laughed. "Of course! That was his whole goddamned problem. Critic of Vincent Denfield first and foremost and carrying a grudge in his pocket on everyone close. I mean, he's my brother, but the guy has serious—"

Sonata screamed. "The cake is burning." She dropped the receiver and scrambled to the oven.

"Hey, save me a piece." Howard yelled, his voice loud and clear as it dangled from the end of the cord. "I'll get it tomorrow night. Okay? Sonny? Did you hear me?"

"I heard you!" she yelled back. The cake had oozed into the oven and was smoldering. The whole kitchen smelled of char.

"I'll meet you in the school lobby, in front of Mercury's big toe right after your class. Okay?"

"All right, Howard, I'll be there."

"Sonny?" he yelled again.

"What is it? For God's sake, Howard, the banana cake is all over the place!"

"I think I love you. To hell with the banana cake!"

6

Irene's dancing classes came to an end. It was not Mrs. Lapidus who called a halt to them but Mrs. Wyeth, a neighbor who lived across the street.

Sonata had begun baby-sitting for Mrs. Wyeth on weekends when she was not working at Macy's. The job was convenient and easy because there was no traveling and the two young children were usually napping when she got there. It also gave her an excuse to be out of the house for a few hours when Irene and Bert were home.

Sonata had only casually mentioned to Mrs. Wyeth some problems with having so many young dance students in the house at one time and Mrs. Wyeth sympathized. For her own part, she told Sonata, it was only out of the goodness of her heart that she tolerated the situation: cars parked constantly in front of her home and the hair-raising shrieks of those children when they waited to be picked up after class.

Sonata assured herself long afterwards as she sat by the window looking out, hearing only the hum of passing cars and no children's laughter or scurrying footsteps hastening through the doorway, that it was not, in fact, her doing that closed the school. There were zoning laws in existence and with the school's expansion into some early evening hours, Mrs. Wyeth was motivated to check these out.

•   •   •

Towards the beginning of summer, Sonata noticed that Irene's attitude, generally subdued, rose several notches. She smiled for no apparent reason and hummed to herself and sang outright as she worked around the house. Indeed, she became more interested in the house than ever before, washing the slats on the blinds, replacing the curtains in the bedroom, shampooing the rugs.

"Late spring cleaning," Bert offered, observing this sudden onslaught of activity. "Go on, Sonata, pitch in and give her a hand." But neither Sonata nor Irene responded to his suggestion.

Seeing her so cheerful and good humored, Sonata thought it possible that Bert had asked her to marry him. But if that was the case, neither of them said anything about it and Bert continued his pattern of skipping occasional nights away from home as he had before.

Sonata's attention to both Irene and her father diminished now that she was seeing so much of Howard. Many of her evenings were spent with him. He would meet her at the League after her evening class with some plan of what they would do together. Sometimes they would go the Russian Tea Room just to talk and listen to the violins, other times to the Balalaika, a night club where, because it was the middle of the week, there would often be only three or four other couples in attendance besides them. Yet still the flame-thrower did his act and so did the singer and the exotic dancer. Sonata felt sorry for the flame-thrower who had to swallow a roaring flame for the entertainment of so few people. Seated at a table directly in front of him she wanted to tell him to forget it.

Sometimes she left her class early and they would walk along Fifth Avenue and look at the shops and Howard would explain the inside story of menswear and Sonata would talk about the art displays and the window decor. They rarely talked about Vincent. Parts of that life had begun to seem like a fanciful daydream—an appealing image of herself as artist's mistress and model. She was wearing nude when she modeled for him, like she'd prance around in something of her mother's when she was small, putting on something she didn't belong in. Extra flesh around her hips bothered her less exposed for him than under wraps for the world because the whole trip was unreal. Both of them had unwrapped themselves, at least for a time—yet two souls could never have been so hidden from each other.

Howard's lifestyle had begun, in recent weeks, to adapt to hers. He seemed relaxed and without pressure. The clipped banter that often bothered her had softened so that their talks together were easy and unforced. He frequently spoke about his family. His relationship with his stepfather was on solid footing because of his role in the business, but he felt his interactions with Alexandra were superficial. Ironically, Sonata's appearance on the scene changed that.

His parents knew all summer long that he was seeing a lot of one particular girl but Alexandra had no idea this girl was Sonata. Having first come upon her in Vincent's apartment, she was mortified the first time Howard brought her home to dinner. Then as Howard continued to see her, she began to feel a challenge that appealed to her sense of intrigue. The challenge was to conceal the girl's past from poor innocent Pete who knew nothing of the evil ways of the world.

"He would never in a million years accept such a thing," his mother told Howard, "To Pete, a thing like that is…well, he doesn't read books, he doesn't see plays, he's disgusted by what he sees on television. I try to tell him it's not the turn of the Century, but what can you do?"

Alexandra advised Howard to pretend that Sonata had never met Vincent and the girl should do the same. "It's the simplest way. Otherwise, you don't know what people will think."

"I'm not worried what people think," Howard said.

But according to Howard Alexandra was worried, people meaning Pete, and planned ahead for difficult situations. Also, having lost the close contact she had with Vincent since he had stopped painting to become a professional critic and no longer needed her support, she lost interest in art altogether.

Thus began a brand new alliance with her older son.

"You've become her common project with me," Howard told Sonata, "So here I am number one, the favorite son.

•   •   •

Alexandra invited Sonata to bring her painting materials to the house and to use the apartment as a place to work after class.

"The League is no place for an inspiration," she told her. "All the years Vincent went there, he never got an inspiration!"

But Sonata did not yet feel comfortable in Howard's home, not because of Alexandra's attitude towards her but Pete's, which evidenced no connection to her prior relationship with Vincent. Howard's stepfather was somber faced and tight lipped and looked out at her from the dark sockets of his eyes with their puffed under lids with one question behind the hostile eyes: *How in God's name did The Boy pick you in a crowd?*

Sonata often stayed for dinner and spent the evening with the family and at these times tried subtly and often openly to win Pete over. Why this was important to her she didn't know; he was not a person of such great appeal to go out of one's way to impress— Howard didn't seem to care if she impressed him—but still she worked to win his approval.

Then one day she stumbled upon a road of access, the way to his heart. It was a Sunday after dinner. He had brought some bookkeeping home from the store and was working at the dining room table. She offered to help him. Not one to turn down a free offer, he showed her what needed to be done and she picked it up quickly. The following weekend he brought home a second adding machine and the accounts receivable and set her up.

After that, it became a familiar scene: Pete at one end of the dining room table and Sonata at the other, communicating through the rhythmic rattle of numbers totaling on the machines. Then it wasn't long before he offered her a part-time job at the store doing the same thing, plus a few other odd chores such as answering the phone and relieving Howard of some paperwork. Eventually, as she did her work efficiently, Pete came to trust her and was satisfied. Eventually too, Sonata realized this was the most she could hope for and was satisfied as well.

7

Life in Riverdale during this period had changed dramatically. The change began with the benign appearance of Irene's new attitude. Nothing upset her, no annoyance connected with Bert's career, no friction with Sonata in the kitchen, no remarks of the neighbors. Nothing seemed able to affect her remarkable state of wellbeing. Then on one balmy evening in late July, while Sonata was working with Pete and Bert was off somewhere, Irene left the house with her clothes and personal possessions and did not return. Bert had no idea where she had gone and neither did Sonata nor Mrs. Lapidus.

Her father was quieter than his usual quiet for a number of days. He had never been what Sonata could call "chatty" but after Irene's departure, he had little to contribute in the way of normal social behavior. His painting, however, involved him more fervently than ever. He began working at home in the abandoned dance studio instead of his rented place and in two weeks of work, more new paintings appeared for drying and storage than she had ever seen in so short a period. All the rooms began to reek of turpentine and although the smell was unpleasant to deal with on a daily basis, it was not nearly so insidious as what was to come.

And that was Josie. Josie was a wretched woman whose husband's business excursions to Europe and recently to the Far East had allowed her to be regularly available for Bert. Josie, unlike Irene, was easy to hate. In this woman there were no obstacles of warmth, good humor and gentleness to overcome. If there was any softness about her it would only have appeared to the touch for she was voluptuous in external contours.

From Sonata's point of view, a raccoon had invaded the household. Somehow, when the bedroom door was closed on Josie and Bert, her presence didn't matter so much. It was when she found her in the kitchen—her kitchen, preparing something to eat—that her appearance was most unwelcome. The raccoon then had its dripping purple mouth in her breadbox.

The worst situation was having Howard there when Josie was about. Then the small kitchen became like a cage with each of them stalking here and there, attempting to keep more physical distance than was possible. Kitchens were biologically constructed to economize on space with vital organs efficiently placed within a few step's reach. But that meant one set of steps. The Chinese symbol for trouble, she'd read, was two women under one roof, but two women in one small kitchen spelled disaster in Riverdale because there were often men there too.

Sonata observed that Josie tended to pretend the kitchen was more cramped than it was by sidling into Howard with a bumpy little rub. The action was accompanied by a slightly startled "Oh," and a polite "Excuse me please." Josie did not stay in the house for long periods, just a day or two, but the visits she made and the threat of their unannounced occurrence was unsettling.

For that reason Sonata tried to spend most of her time between Pete and Howard's place of business and their apartment. She'd given up her job at Macy's to work for Pete full time, and at the League, attended only her evening painting class. For a long while they did not see Vincent. He no longer came to Alexandra and Pete for Sunday dinners and his range of activities did not touch upon theirs.

Then one Tuesday evening Vincent arrived unexpectedly with a present for her, a painting wrapped in brown paper. "I thought there'd be a better chance of finding you here than up in Riverdale," he said.

She tried to read his face to see if the remark meant he approved or disapproved of Howard and her but, as usual, the task was impossible. His smile was so without pleasantness as he handed the package to her that she had the disquieting notion he was playing some malicious trick. It couldn't be that he was presenting her with an early picture of the two of them together in front of the mirror, or could it? It was too big, but still he might have enshrined the moment in a frame—her mighty hips, his limp, distracted penis.

"I'll open it later," she demurred, but he smiled and said, "No, open it now." And when she hesitated, he took it from her and removed the paper himself.

It was the large abstract that he finished the night she went with Howard to the Beaux arts Ball, the one he called his breakthrough. "I thought you should be the one to have it," he said with a peculiar turn of his brows and lips that was not familiar to her. New expressions seem to go with the job. Relieved that it was not their twin bodies in living color, she thanked him again and wondered where in the world she would put it.

8

Sonata tried to be helpful to her father by keeping the house and cooking and even to a degree helping with his selling arrangements, but it was a hardship, not so much because of the work but because he did not appreciate anything she did for him. The difference between what she had imagined their life together would be and the reality was too painfully obvious. Irene's presence, far from coming between them, she realized, was the only link they had. She tried to remember if in contrast to herself, he had been thoughtful towards Irene. But no, she did not recall him thanking her for making some special effort or noticing when she accomplished something particularly well. They shared topics surrounding his painting and day to day logistical concerns. With Sonata, there appeared no interest in anything with which she was involved. Nothing passed between them but bits and pieces of small talk. With a single exception, one Sunday morning at breakfast.

"Toast?" She asked.

"Ummn."

"Which one is that, yes or no?' Sonata asked, glancing at her father as he leaned over the table reading the New York Times, a strand of dark hair falling over his brow.

She decided to make the toast. "Eggs? It's Sunday." Irene had concluded Sunday breakfast must be a hangover from his childhood because he liked eggs on Sunday, never during the week. Sonata tried to remember Sunday breakfasts at home and Ruth did serve eggs, more often when Ethel was there.

"Ok, I'll have eggs. Do you have ham?" He looked up.

"No, bacon."

"Make it bacon." He chuckled and put down the paper. "Come, sit down here. I'll show you something."

Surprised by the sudden attention, Sonata quickly pulled up a chair as he wrote something on a napkin.

"Read it," he instructed.

"*A B F U N E X?*

S V F X.

A B F U N E M?

S V F M.

OKABMNX."

"Ok, I read it." She smiled tentatively. "Now what? Is it a code or something?" The toast popped and she started to get up.

"Sit still. Read it again." He was smiling.

He was in such a gay mood. It was contagious. She laughed and reread the letters. "Oh, Dad!" She sighed. "I don't get it at all. Wait a minute. A B F U N E X...S V F X. No, I don't get it. Maybe I'm dumb. Just a dumb broad."

"Ok, dumb broad, I'll read it for you. Ready?"

"Shoot."

"Abie, heff you eny eggs?"

"Yes ve heff eggs.

"Abie heff you eny hem?

"Yes ve heff hem.

"0 K Abie hem n eggs."

"Oh! Dad!" Sonata said, laughing. "You are too much!" She got up, still laughing."Ve heff eggs and bacon only today. Sorry."

"I'll take it. Can I have more coffee?"

She started the burners cooking and poured his coffee. Seeing him still smiling over the cup rim, she was encouraged to talk.

"Do you miss Irene doing all this for you?" she asked.

"Sure I do."

"I miss her too a little." She returned to the stove. "Not that we had that much to do with each other. Where do you think she went?"

"I don't know. Impossible to guess…she could have gone anywhere."

"Will she get in touch with you, do you suppose?"

"Maybe. Maybe not."

"Well, you don't seem to be suffering too much."

He looked up, appraising the comment, then shrugged. "Well, there's nothing I can do about it. She left of her own accord, that's all I can say. Women are hard for me to understand." He returned his attention to the paper. "No, I'm not suffering," he added.

Sonata dished out the eggs and handed the plate to him. When she brought the bacon to the table, she poured herself a cup of coffee and sat down. "Was it that way with Mom too when you separated?" They had never talked about Ruth in all this time. She was always afraid to bring up the subject while they were alone and with Irene around it seemed awkward. She was still afraid and the subject just as awkward. She hoped he would give her a straight answer. No codes like A B and X.

"No," he said, "It wasn't like that with Ruth."

Sonata nodded. "It must have been terrible for you. I mean losing your paintings—everything. It was really vicious. Irene told me about the settlement."

"No, it wasn't vicious. Ruth did what she was advised to do. Anyway, I don't care about it."

"Dad?"

"Pass the salt, would you?"

"Dad…did you…love Mother?" She asked the question but didn't think he would or could give her the answer she needed.

He looked up then and smiled. "Sure I loved her. Who wouldn't love Ruth?" He nodded slowly, as if agreeing with the virtues he then listed: "Sweet, beautiful, a good mother—didn't you think she was a good mother?"

Sonata nodded vigorously. "A good sister too!" She laughed.

Bert grinned. "Yes, she was a very good sister."

"Dad, was she…faithful to you, do you think?"

"Faithful?" He laughed. "You mean did she bring my slippers or did she screw around?" He paused when Sonata did not smile. "I wouldn't know." Then: "Ask her sister."

"Oh, I don't care that much. I guess I shouldn't have brought it up." She sipped her coffee. "Just something I saw…oh, never mind."

"What is it you saw?" he asked, half mockingly.

"Well, at your tribute. I suppose we can talk about this now since you and she are separated. It's just…I saw her with Ted Riley."

"Ted Riley, my student?"

She nodded.

"What do you mean, you saw her with Ted Riley?"

"He came out of the bedroom upstairs, your bedroom, and, oh, he was fixing himself—you know, how people do—before he went back downstairs to the party. And then after a bit, she came out. There was no mistaking…" Sonata flushed. *Why did she have to tell him this? Why expose her mother, 'sweet, beautiful Ruth' and why was he looking at her that way, his lips so tight? Ruth had left him. It was over.*

"No mistaking," he repeated, nodding.

"Right. I saw them from across the hall."

He set down his fork. "They could have been having a private chat—about me…you—how do you know what they were doing?"

"I know." *Stop, now. Say 'yes, they could have been chatting.' I love you, Dad. You need me. Say that. Say it!*

He shook his head, all traces of his good humor gone. "You don't know anything," he said crisply. Crumpling his napkin, he threw it on the table and stood. "And I hope you haven't been spreading such damn malicious gossip."

"No, no, I've only told it now, to you."

"Good." He turned to leave. "Just for the record—that's just in case there was a genuine question on the floor before—your mother did not screw around. There was one man in her life and that was me. That's for the record."

"Okay, Dad. I'm sorry I brought it up. Really, it was foolish of me."

"Thanks for breakfast."

9

The Sunday breakfast conversation was their biggest both in length and in weight. She didn't regret telling her father about the scene she observed in the upstairs hall, as she thought about it, though he was furious with her. The message put him down—*you're not the only man in Ruth's life*—but perhaps, in the role of messenger, it pulled her up. Returning home from uplifting interactions with Howard and even Pete, she sometimes felt insignificant in his presence, her spirits dampened. Conveying her news, she had some measure of power, and best of all, the power was shared with Ruth. *Good for her*, she couldn't help thinking.

There were conversations after that dealing with his shirts, the daily news, bills, but by and large they found it safer to avoid any personal references to each other's lives. Then, during a particularly humid stretch of weather, he did not return home for seven straight days without calling to let her know. When finally he came through the doorway late on a Sunday afternoon, sweaty, a jacket slung over his shoulder, she could not control her anger.

"Where have you been?" she demanded to know.

He smiled and walked past her into the kitchen.

"Answer me! Where have you been?" she shouted, following him. "I've waited for you every single evening! I prepared your supper every miserable hot night for seven days and you never showed up!" She snapped at him like a shrew, a fishwife, but she couldn't help herself.

He opened the refrigerator and took out a beer. He took out another and offered it but she ignored him and he put it back.

"Where were you?"

He drank from the can. "I took a holiday."

"A holiday?"

"Sure. It's too damned hot to work, don't you think so?"

"Yes it's hot but that didn't stop me from working on your house, from cooking your meals from washing your laundry."

He laughed the mocking way she'd almost gotten used to. "Cinderella, I'm sorry there's no ball for you. Too hot for a ball. You want me to get you a maid?"

"No. I don't want a maid. I just want you to have some consideration for me." Her lips quivered and she folded her arms. "Where did you go on your holiday?" She made no effort to keep the spite out of her inquiry.

He took another long swallow of beer and sat down. "New Jersey shore with Josie. We didn't plan it. Just a spur-of-the-moment thing. Got in the car and went."

"But why?"

"Why what?"

"Why did you go there?"

"Because it was nice and cool."

"Dad!"

"And because she was lonely. Her husband was having a business holiday in Europe and she thought she should have one too. So—"

"Oh, Dad. Seven days! And you never called me. You didn't think even to call."

"Yes." He paused. "I should have called."

"You don't give a damn about me, do you? You don't care what happens to me. All you care about is you. That's true isn't it?" She waited, searching his face.

"I care about you," he said. He pressed a finger against his bottom lip. "I was telling Josie all about you—"

"About me!" she shouted furiously. She wanted to strike him! Discussing her with that filthy piece of trash! "What could you tell a *whore* about me that it would enjoy hearing?" *I never talk like this…what am I doing? what do I want from him?*

Incredibly her outburst stopped him only for a moment.

"She was interested in you. I was entertaining her."

"Interested? Oh. Did she want to know if I slept around too…a slut just like her?" She flushed, so unintended had that word exploded, buried in her psyche since he threw it at her. But he did not move or walk away as she thought he must. He just stood there and looked at her, then when he spoke his eyes had that same bitter coolness as when they sat beside each other there at the Beaux arts Ball.

"Sonny, you have an unfortunate way of looking at life, a tendency to plow through green grass to get at the muck." He took the last swallow of beer and threw the can in the trash.

"You—you can talk about *my* way of looking at life! You pick up any woman you can find. Destroying Mom with your lust! Cutting me down and…and Billy…killing Billy. Murderer!" She screamed it now. "Murderer!"

"Calm yourself! For Christ's sake, take it easy." He had started to leave but her screaming alarmed him. "What the hell are you *saying?*"

"Oh sure, keep your cool. You didn't think I knew, did you?" Sonata sneered, her throat dry. "Years gone by, everything quiet…all forgotten. Scott free you slid out of it and nobody even slapped your hand. But I know what you did that night and you know. I just pray to God, Mother is spared—"

"What in hell? What are you talking about! Are you out of your mind?"

"You're terrific. To be so detached," she scoffed. "God, I wish I could stand outside my life the way you do, just coming in when it's pouring. You know damned well you hit Billy. In your car that night he died. You struck him down. Too busy making out with your Renie to watch the road—"

He stared at her, his mouth open. He started to speak, to ask something, but then he spun around and thundered out of the room.

Sonata sat down at the table, her knees weak. She buried her head in her arms. No tears, only a slow burning. She was alone, completely alone now.

No, she can't let him find her like this, hurt, ashamed, sorry for herself, sorry for everything. No! She stood on wobbly legs, feeling dazed. He was the one to be ashamed for he was guilty. Her crime was only that she knew about it.

·   ·   ·

Howard was coming for her soon. She went into the bathroom to shower.

Coming out, she passed her father's room and saw him lying on the bed his brow furrowed looking at the ceiling. He was wearing the same disheveled clothes including his shoes. She went into her room to dress and when the doorbell rang she passed his room again but the door was closed.

"I made a reservation at Enrico and Paglieri's," Howard said on their way to the car. "All right with you?"

"Fine," Sonata said. They hadn't been there since their first date. At the restaurant, Howard ordered a full dinner; he was ravenous but Sonata could scarcely eat and settled on only an appetizer. She wanted to tell him what happened but failed, trying to formulate the words. Shame, so much shame. But the shame could stay between her father and herself if she didn't speak. To Howard or anyone.

Howard was insensitive to her mood, and she was grateful. "Would you like some brandy?" he offered when the table had been cleared. She agreed. When the waiter returned and deposited two snifters of Courvoisier on the table, Howard lifted his glass. "How about a toast? Join me?"

She lifted her glass and tried to smile.

"How about a toast to you and me? To you and me together." He smiled.

She clinked her glass to his and sipped.

"How about it, Sonny?" he said without drinking. His eyes grew serious. "Marry me?"

His hand was on her arm. How had she not expected him to ask this? It was so natural, almost a suggestion, as ordinary as the clink of glasses, yet it seemed to come out of nowhere. Get married?

For the first time, the explosive words exchanged with her father fell away and a calm descended. She was not alone.

"Yes?" she said simply, a question and an answer, she wasn't sure which.

Howard leaped to his feet. "Yes!" he repeated, shouting the word. A startled waiter rushed over.

"Yes." She said, laughing. "Howard, sit down."

Smiling goofily at each other, they raised their glasses, clinked and drank. He kissed her with the sweet taste of brandy on his lips and then somehow it was official.

They went to the Top of the Sixes to celebrate with a bottle of French champagne and they talked about the date. Her spirits were rising. She began, in truth, to soar. It would be next year in early spring, she needed time to prepare. He wanted her to buy things, lots of things, and for the honeymoon they would go to Montego Bay because it was beautiful there; they would rent a cottage; he could take two weeks and they would live after that in Manhattan; he liked the village, would she be amenable to the village? She loved the village, had always wanted to live there; they would find a small apartment, maybe take an evening course together at New York University right there on the square; and they would get a dog and walk it around the park; a poodle, no, a dachshund, he had always wanted a dachshund; ooh, those creepy squirmy things, she hated dachshunds; all right, a poodle, but a girl poodle because the boy poodle looked so silly strutting around on its high heels with a penis; well, no, maybe some other kind, a compromise; how about a schnauzer? Yes, perfect, a schnauzer.

"Howard," she said, in the taxi, a little woozy and leaning against him, his arm around her as they headed for Riverdale, "Do you think I could stay over at your place tonight?"

"Sure," he said unquestioning. "You know, I sort of would like to keep this our secret for a little while, not long, but just to savor it ourselves before we share with the world, what do you think?"

"That's such a nice thought, romantic. You surprise me, Howard."

"I surprise myself when I'm with you, Sonny. I sort of like me a lot better." He squeezed her shoulder and kissed her as she looked up at him, then leaned forward toward the driver and gave him the change of destination.

PART TEN
HOMECOMING

I

On Friday evening of the Labor Day weekend, Willie arranged to visit Ruth with a prepared homemade German Jewish dinner. "I'm not even letting you into the kitchen," he announced, arriving with foil covered bowls containing beef brisket and onions, red cabbage, boiled potatoes, a challah bread and cole slaw, and for dessert an apple strudel. He confessed that he did not make any of it, all the genius of his woman friend with whom he was now living.

After dinner they drank coffee in the living room and smoked, Ruth her cigarettes and Willie, a cigar. Setting down his cup, Willie tapped his ash and then sat back. He folded his arms and looked at Ruth as she sat pensively gazing at the Oriental rug, recently purchased, her eyes following the patterns. Raising himself with difficulty from the couch, he brought more coffee and filled her cup. "Ruth," he said, settling himself again, "You know what I am thinking?"

"Uh oh, I hear a lecture on its way?" she said, peering over the brim of her cup.

Willie smiled and turned his face away to blow a stream of smoke. "I am thinking that you should do yourself a favor and go back to the Art Students League to draw and to paint again. You used to be good at it. The still lifes I think it was, yes?"

"The still lifes," she agreed. "No, it's pointless, I haven't got talent. Maybe I just painted to do something my sister can't do."

"So, that is a reason. Do it for something most people can't do."

She shrugged.

"Ah, Ruth, don't say a yes or a no. Just store the idea there in your clever mind and maybe a time will come when you will take it down. You are still a young woman, you know."

"Maybe, Willie," she said to forestall further discussion of the topic. But she was not 'a young woman.' Bert had made her feel young, and Sonata, too. But now there was just Ethel, and her mother Vera, both set in their ways as they had always been, and her agreeable father, now ailing, and Willie with his rallying pep talk. They were old, all of them. Well meaning, but old.

She smiled as Willie talked about his new life with his lady, glad for him to find love so late in life, especially after all he had been through. They talked about Ruth's job, elevated from window dresser to buyer, though still not very interesting to her, and the amazing show which they had both seen at the Imperial theater of Victor Borge at the piano. Then Willie cleared the dishes and over her objections, washed them.

"There are leftovers in the refrigerator. You will have tomorrow again a good meal."

"Thank you, Willie. The dinner was delicious."

He took her hand and kissed it in the German way.

"It was good of you to come," she said.

After Willie picked up his empty casserole dishes and left, Ruth turned out the living room lights and locked the front door, and although she was not tired, nothing seemed left to do but read for a while and go to sleep. She removed her shoes and stockings and the rest of the trappings endured for greeting a guest. Willie was a friend but she begrudged the effort of entertaining him. She had gotten used to slipping into a simple shift and sandals to scuff about the empty house and conversation also was a burden. Then, thinking of his dinner and the trouble he'd gone to and his encouragement for her to return to painting, she chastened herself for the unkind thoughts. She glanced at the wall where a painting hung that she'd done ages ago at the League of red and green apples in a bowl, inspired by Cezanne's works on the theme. Ethel had found the picture in a storage closet, framed it expensively and later presented it to them as an anniversary gift, so she'd had to hang it. It was a nice picture. Perhaps Willie was not simply being charitable encouraging her to pick up painting again and maybe she would.

Most of Bert's paintings acquired in the divorce settlement were stored in the Connecticut gallery now representing him. Some remained hanging in rooms throughout the house where they still seemed to belong. For a long time she had hoped her divorce might not become final, that there would be some snag, but of course it had to go through. Merle Chapin was the best divorce lawyer in town, according to her mother who selected him. And there was no reason to stop it from going through. The insults had reached a peak at the tribute and everyone knew it.

She put her clothes away and took out her nightgown. How simple Bert was, actually. He acted as he felt. There was no malice in it, although he hurt her. Others saw him as malicious. Ethel went so far as to involve him in Billy's death and called her a blind idiot when she laughed in her face. Billy always had stomach aches and often missed school because of it. "Faker!" Sonata used to call him and once claimed to see him sitting on the thermometer to make it go up. Anne Calnon came by commissioned by Ethel to verify her sister's ridiculous story but dropped it when Ruth explained the business of his stomach aches. Neither of them brought the subject up again.

With her nightgown held over her arm she regarded herself in the mirror. Her body had seemed quite special when she saw it through his eyes. He loved her breasts. Now her breasts seemed ordinary, not marble-smooth or even particularly shapely.

She slipped into her nightgown, washed up and removed the pins from her hair. She picked up her brush. When her hair cascaded down her back, her throat became tight with a fleeting memory of his touch and the brush slipped out of her hand. She would *not* think about him. It was over. Logic will rule, not quivering flesh.

Abandoning her thoughts, Ruth climbed into her welcoming bed. She read for a little while and then turned off the lamp. But it was a long time before she was able to sleep.

2

Ruth closed her sketch pad and put it on the chair to reserve her place when the model stepped down from the platform. She was enrolled in Rudolf Schneider's still life class, the instructor recommended by Willie, but she'd been going to the free early evening life drawing classes every day afterwards. There was no instructor in these sessions and she liked not having anyone look over her shoulder.

She stepped out into the hallway, joining other students who smoked and chatted with one another or strolled the corridor or sat together on the wooden benches lining the wall. Sonata had a class in the League today—Willie kept her informed—and Ruth was determined to see her. There were things that needed saying, that couldn't wait any longer because so much was happening to her daughter now. The destruction that had come with her leaving home didn't have to be forever. Bull-dozers plow down old broken buildings and skyscrapers go up in the spot. If a faulty chunk of her life with Sonny was leveled, there was still ground enough to build on. One of them had to want it badly enough and Ruth did.

Passing the glass case, she studied the announcement of Bert's forthcoming retrospective, *October 15–December 18.* Several reproductions were mounted in the case to promote the event. The show here was only a preview, afterwards traveling to the Boston Museum of Fine Art and then the Pennsylvania Museum. The photos could not convey the vibrancy of his canvases or in some of them, the impact of their size.

She thought back to Sonny's tribute for her father, not the disaster it ended up being, but her passion in wanting to recognize his achievements—how just at that juncture when she needed to prepare for her own achievements, her sights were set on his. Ruth was beginning to understand why. If Sonata could merge herself into her father's future, the daughter of an acclaimed artist, it would take her with him into a future without risk or vulnerability. Then too, his neglect of her through all these years could be minimized, even canceled out against the magnitude of his success. Sonata's devotion to Bert was rooted in survival for herself.

She needed to see her. Pushing through the swinging doors on her way back to the drawing session, Ruth had an idea: if she waited by the statue of Mercury after the class, Sonata would have to see her on her way in to the class that Willie mentioned she was taking. Then they might greet each other and go somewhere to talk. It would be difficult in the beginning, but then…yes, it might work. She had to make the move.

.   .   .

For a while, Ruth remained in her seat after the other students had packed their materials and left. She studied her last drawing, made a mark here and there, put the pencil down and studied it again. She knew she was stalling. The decision to wait for Sonata and to talk to her with honesty and intimacy seemed natural outside in a hallway resonant with other people's conversation. Here, in the stillness of this room it was difficult to summon the strength for such a confrontation. Suppose her daughter wanted nothing to do with her, reviled her for tolerating an unfaithful husband or despised her for not recognizing him as a genius?

No, this was no path to go down. Ending the rift between them would not happen with either of them agonizing over the past; these were buried resentments that served no purpose to uncover. A new set of reasons to be together were needed. Then suddenly, she knew what she would do and it had nothing to do with Sonata at all.

She would pursue the venture that had been in her head since the last of the divorce papers were signed when she explored the idea of using the settlement funds to open a gallery. She hadn't told anyone about it, though she was tempted to discuss it with Willie when he came to her with his home-made dinner. The idea was still tenuous and she was unsure she could make it work. But now she felt the surge of excitement she needed. Her gallery would focus on drawings, her first love, at least to start. The Krashauer Gallery on Madison Avenue was closing its doors. Renovations there would be modest and she had all but made an offer when she visited last week. Milt Krashauer knew of her, knew Bert, watched her walk around the space after they'd talked. They smiled at each other at the door, almost as if each of them knew what the future held.

Suddenly exhilarated and with a sense of purpose, she replaced her pencils in their case and bent to collect the wash drawings lying on the floor.

"Mother?"

She looked up stunned to see Sonata in the doorway. A tall, good looking man stood beside her.

"We were waiting for you out in the hall," Sonata said, hesitantly as if unsure about crossing the threshold. "Willie told us you'd be coming out that way."

*The irony, she coming to me. Oh, Willie…*For several moments Ruth could not speak, gazing up at her daughter as if seeing her in a dream, like so many dreams in which she'd appeared. Sonata looked lovely. She was thinner and her hair had grown long and she wore it straight, no longer its free flying curly bush.

"This is Howard," she said, as Ruth did not move, guiding him forward as if to deliver him. Howard walked toward her and put out his hand. "Well, he came to the house once, I don't know if you remember."

Ruth took his hand and smiled with a glance at her daughter, still feeling giddy but forcing herself to recover. "Yes, I think I do."

For a moment, the three of them stood together in an awkward circle as if preparing to play some game. Would it be another game?

Ruth wondered. She had not done very well at the ones they played before.

"Nice pictures," Howard said, tilting his head to see the drawings right side up on her sketchpad.

"Thank you," Ruth said, "I'm trying to be bolder, exploring what the materials can do."

"And what you can do. This is lovely," said Sonata, her eyes on the ink and wash drawing which Ruth had just completed.

Ruth nodded. "I don't suppose you were waiting all this time to offer a review of my work." She laughed uncomfortably. *A mother and a daughter so strained. Who had done this to them? How had she let it happen?*

Sonata sat down in the chair next to the one holding Ruth's drawing supplies. "Are you rushing away, Mother, or could we talk for a few minutes?"

"No, I have no place to go. There's a class in here in a half hour or so, that's all. Ruth moved to sit on the edge of the model's platform, facing them. "I'm glad to talk to you." *Try not to rush into it...not expect too much, not be thrilled...But she came to me.*

Howard settled himself rather stiffly next to Sonata, the chair too upright for a body that looked to be more comfortable in a slouch. He crossed his long legs with the edge of his foot resting on a knee. His other knee casually touched Sonata's thigh and Ruth could see that they were close friends.

"Mother, I wanted you to meet Howard to—"

"We already met," Howard said with a teasing smile that was small-boyish and pleasantly disarming. "Twice."

"Howard, don't make it harder for me." She turned to Ruth and spoke slowly and purposefully. "I wanted you to see him and get to know him a little."

Ruth smiled. "I think I am getting to know him and I'm glad you wanted me to."

"Mom, you might have heard about this already—we haven't made a formal announcement yet, but I wanted you to know—we're going to get married." She looked at Howard and then Ruth as if to unite them in some way. Almost simultaneously Ruth and Howard stood,

Ruth with a broad smile and her hands wide as if to take in them both. She turned to Sonata and the two locked eyes. Then with her arms outstretched, she met her daughter as they stepped toward each other and they embraced. Ruth felt the tension between them, an awkwardness, but it had been close to a year since they had spoken, much less touched.

"I'm not altogether surprised," Ruth said, turning to Howard and taking his hands in hers. "I heard rumors from Willie, but I am happy for both of you. If I could reach you up there, I'd give you a kiss."

Howard bent with a smile and they kissed cheeks lightly.

"I'll take good care of her, I promise," Howard said as they settled into seats again. "Just send me any instructions you have on maintenance and feeding so I don't make any mistakes."

"I think, judging from how things have been going between us, you'll do a better job without instructions from me."

"That's all going to change now, Mother."

"Is it?" Ruth was afraid to think ahead as to what she meant. This was all happening so fast.

"Yes it is. Well, I don't know if it'll all be in one shot," she continued, gaining a kind of momentum as the words rushed out, "but I've made a big jump. It's about this anger I've been carrying around—well, that's all about me, not anyone else. Look, I'm not sure of the what's and why's yet, but Mom…I know the *who's* now, and it isn't you."

Ruth looked at her daughter and tried to find a response to hold back the small watershed that was beginning to form behind her eyes.

A tall lanky student with a portfolio and papers under each arm poked her head in the doorway, looked around, walked inside to set her materials on a chair and then left. All three of them watched her progression in a kind of dazed intermission to the drama unfolding among them.

Ruth sighed. "So what will you do now? What are your plans?"

"Sonny's been helping my dad do the books at home and she's working down at his place. Becoming indispensable," he added with a grin. "You'll have to meet my folks. Say, why don't we set something up?" He pulled out a pocket calendar.

"I guess that's part of the deal, Mom," said Sonata. "I mean now that you and I are back with each other, you'll have to do the whole bit."

"I look forward to it." Ruth waited while they exchanged datebook information and tried to come to an agreement on time and place. She watched Howard accepting Sonata's lead, going along with her suggestions. Students had gradually been entering the studio, some leaving to grab a coffee before the class, some settling into chairs and preparing their materials. There still remained ten or so minutes until the session would start. Howard had a schedule of sales conference dates in front of him. Ruth perched again on the edge of the model's stand and took from her handbag her own datebook, so unmarked she hardly dared show it. She wrote down a date that Howard gave her and looked up to see Sonata staring at her. A penny for your thoughts, each of them had to be thinking.

. . .

Sonata, leaving the family dinner date for them to finalize, had a fleeting vision of her mother up there on the model's platform. She imagined that in a few minutes the students would take their pencils in hand and begin to study her. They would see her face first, despite contrary instruction in a life class. For in her face was to be found her mother's mystery, the secrets that lay behind the sky blue eyes. 'Sure I loved her. Who wouldn't love Ruth?' her father said. Banal and insulting, as if Ruth were a small child and all small children are lovable. Besides, Sonata had not loved her, she'd hated her for the doormat she had become, to her husband, to the witch sister…to her insufferable daughter. Howard was enchanted by Ruth, this was easy to see. He would like something of Ruth to be in her, she suspected, something of her softness. Is it softness? Or is it weakness?

Ruth is *not me*, she heard herself mutely declare in this phantom vision of her mother displayed on the model's stand for all to see. *She had a part in me, only a part, and we are not the same. I am not—I never have to be—as vulnerable as she.* And how constant and heavy that threat had been, she only now dared see.

"Come," Sonata said, standing. "We'd better go, they're gaining on us. If you sit there much longer, they'll make you take your clothes off."

"They'll be sorry," Ruth said.

Howard laughed.

"Look," she said, "we'll call Howard's folks tonight to set up a time."

"All right, Ruth replied. "I'm still at our house if you want to reach me."

"I know." She smiled. "Maybe I'll come by."

. . .

Ruth watched them as they left the studio, Sonata once again taking the lead. She would likely fill some gaps in his life, Ruth thought, as they both turned their heads and smiled to her before disappearing. What that consisted of she might know more about after she saw him with his family. But what would Howard give Sonata? He seemed gentle enough and responsible; he would take good care of her maintenance and feeding. Crude perhaps, no, not that, just close to the surface, and standing at a distance. Funny that she should view him in terms of space—surface and depth, distance and closeness. Had she ever viewed Bert that way or is this a new way of seeing, becoming natural from weeks of intimately staring at a nude when all the world beyond was covered and clothed?

Bert was not lacking in depth, as Howard seemed to be, but distant. Howard and Sonata, Bert and Ruth, each in their own space, meeting, sharing, crowding, displacing to make a life together. Ruth and Sonata, sharing primal space and still trying to form the right and good boundaries and be comfortable in each other's embrace.

She stacked the wash drawings and put them with her sketchpad in her carrying case. Her supplies packed, she put off leaving, not wanting the still warm proximity of her daughter to become altered as memory. Sonata was getting married. The two of them looked happy, clear about what they were doing. Howard seemed an *available* kind of man; he would be easier to reach than Bert ever was. Was there passion between them, a Bert force that would elude and mystify and sometimes thrust them into battle? Would there be silences and deep longing and moments of exhaustion—and in contrast, unbearable joy? Or would it be a tranquil space they would occupy together? A place she and Bert had never been.

3

One early afternoon in late November, Sonata saw Irene as both of them were leaving the League building having attended a memorial for Helen Allenton, a beloved monitor of the life drawing class. Irene was in the city for that and to view Bert's retrospective, flying back to Ohio tomorrow.

Sonata discovered that she was genuinely pleased to see her. Such a rush of good feeling escaped that she embraced her in an effusive hug. She was aware that Irene, though cordial, did not return her enthusiasm.

They sat down to coffee together at the corner luncheonette, and at Sonata's urging, Irene gave an account of herself since she left Riverdale and why.

"Well, I was pregnant. Going home to Xenia was a natural. Look, I had no illusions about Bert ready to change the direction of his life and become a parent and I wanted that baby more, I think, than I've ever wanted anything."

The news itself was less of a surprise to Sonata than her way of handling it—not to tell anyone. What would Bert have done with the news? Would he have cared, at least enough about Irene to alter his life?

"So he's two weeks old now," Irene said gayly, "He's named James after my grandfather—I loved that old fussy man—and I honestly believe he's the only one in all my days there that loved me."

"James," Sonata repeated, mulling pleasantly over the name. "Do the folks there know about the father? Wait…does my Dad know about James, I mean now?"

"No, I don't think so. I haven't spoken to him since I left."

"But he should know, Irene. I mean, he has a right to as the father, doesn't he?"

"Sonny, I don't want anything from your father. I'm not sure how much privy you are to his psyche—how much anyone is—but I know this is not something he can deal with even if he wanted to. And now, his star rising with all the attention he's getting, the last thing he needs is a commitment like this. As for him knowing, I agree with you, he should, as long as he understands I'm not looking for him to be involved."

"Then I'll tell him. That way, you won't need to have a big discussion, putting him on the spot or whatever you're thinking. He could even be angry at you for leaving and you don't want to deal with that now." To Sonata, this didn't seem likely, quick as he was to take up with Josie. Disappointed and maybe a little sad for a time, that's all.

"Thanks, Sonny. And about James, I sort of invented a story about the baby's dad being injured in an accident and people let it go at that. I don't have a whole lot of family or friends home in Ohio to care. I am back on good terms with my mom though. I guess she needs me with my Dad gone now and wants to make it work. She's helping me start a local dancing school and guess what? Classes are set to start in January and Mom's minding the baby."

"Oh, Irene, that's fantastic. I'm so happy for you," Somata said, meaning every word.

Irene's eyes were bright but had amber circles under them, probably from lack of sleep. She wore no makeup and had more freckles on her cheeks than Sonata remembered. Also, tiny dimples appeared when she smiled. Sonata had overlooked the dimples too during those many chats and meals they had shared. Her face was a curious combination of maturity and youth, of seriousness and animation. Sonata decided all at once that she liked Irene very much and felt a lump in the pit of her stomach recalling the means she devised to punish her.

"Tell me about you," Irene said. She summoned the waiter for more coffee. "Should we have something with it? A Danish?"

"Sure, let's. I'm supposed to head for work but this is more important. Anyway, I've never missed a day yet so I'm entitled to call in sick."

"Where do you work?" Irene asked.

"That's part of the story. For my future father-in-law in the men's clothing business."

"Sonny! All this time you've let me rattle on? Are you engaged? I'm so happy for you. Tell me everything. Who is he?"

Sonata sat forward, tilting her cup off its saucer and righting it. "Howard. You saw him with me at the Beaux arts Ball."

"Ah, yes. I did. Sonny, how exciting this is!"

The coffee came, followed by the Danish which they followed with hamburgers and fried onions. In between, Sonata phoned Pete to tell him she was not feeling well and not coming in. She then related to Irene how she met Howard and the events leading up to her engagement, his family and the business which Howard was an integral part of, the stepfather she was still trying to please. Howard, she described in glowing detail, contrasting him with Vincent from whom she was still smarting. As Irene seemed to understand everything about the ecstasies and agonies of her relationships with both of these men, it dawned on Sonata that the one thing missing in the excitement of her engagement was the ability to share it with anyone. Oh, there was Howard himself but discussing things with a man wasn't the same. You had to explain everything to a man; there didn't seem to be anything profound they just understood without a logical, sequential explanation. Anyway, she wanted to talk *about* Howard, not *to* him; that was the fun of it.

The waiter was giving them looks. The restaurant was getting crowded and they were breaking the unwritten first commandment of the midtown restaurant lunch hour noon to three: Thou shalt not sit without eating.

"Hey," Sonata said, standing. "I just remembered. Bert is up in Connecticut today. Bringing them some new paintings. Everybody wants his paintings these days. Anyway, I was wondering—"

"I connected him with that gallery in Connecticut. Oh, I saw in the League notice that the show is scheduled to travel afterwards. If there are reviews will you send them to me?"

"Sure, but about his work, how about coming back up to the house with me now? We'll have a drink and you can have a private preview of the new paintings he's made for the traveling shows."

Irene thought for a moment. "I better not," she said finally, "Bert may—"

"—Bert won't anything. He's in Connecticut all day and probably staying overnight. He told me not to look for him until tomorrow. Irene, you should see some of his newest work, it's very different. Hey, you're not paying for this. Close your purse."

"I would like to see the work," she said hesitantly. "He has them at home, you're sure?"

"I'm sure. You know him. With anything else, he doesn't give a damn but he's compulsive as hell about his work. He's doing all the matting and framing himself."

"Well, hey! I suppose I have a big investment of time and effort in that guy's career and I won't get in that soon again because I'm still nursing. I pumped for a couple of days ahead of this trip and left a veritable milk carton with my mom while I'm here." She paused again. "Okay then, let's go. But Sonny, I'll take that check. Come on, give it to me! Don't be a wiseacre, I'm your elder."

"Hey, James is my half-brother! That's so, isn't it?"

"I guess he is."

More excited than she thought she could be, Sonata grabbed the check, knowing it was nothing more than a pathetic stab at apology. "I'm a working woman about to marry into menswear and I can pay a hamburger check without an overdraft. It's done!" Together they took the subway uptown and walked the couple of blocks to the apartment. Sonata turned the key in the lock and entered with Irene behind her.

Irene stood for a moment looking at the familiar space. The blinds were down and it was rather dark but light filtered through the slats and cast shadows on the sofa and the easy chair and the second-hand Oriental rug that Bert chose for its colors. Beyond the living room straight ahead was the large room she had used for a dancing studio, before that, on the left, was the bedroom and opposite on the right, the bathroom. Directly to the left of the entrance was the kitchen and to the right, the small room where Sonata slept and Irene planned the music for her classes.

Sonata saw Irene cast her head in each of these directions and recalled that she too had stood in that spot, ill at ease, not belonging but wanting to belong when she first came to Riverdale to find her father and ask if she could stay. But Irene's thoughts must have centered on her past in these rooms, not the future as hers had been then. Strange how musing over what could have been and what might yet be held the same uneasiness. Together they formed the chronic tension of the present, vibrations which, if you had the nerve to listen, you could feel every moment you were alive.

"The new pictures are stacked in the bedroom. Come. He was nervous getting paint on them in the studio, he's working so large." Irene followed her across the colorful carpet. The bedroom door was closed. Sonata was momentarily surprised to see it closed since no one was home and Bert absentmindedly did not close anything when he left the house. The apartment had twice been left unlocked, though Bert was so upset about that he re-placed the door handle with an automatic locking device. Once, the refrigerator was left ajar overnight and she had to throw out everything but the pickles and mustard. Across the hall Sonata noticed the light on over the sink in the bathroom. That was where she made up and she had probably left it on this morning.

She opened the bedroom door and gasped. Her body jolted back so suddenly that she almost knocked Irene, standing behind her, to the floor. There were two figures in the bed. Their bodies were turned away from the door toward the wall and headboard. The woman was on her knees with her buttocks raised in the air, the man behind and over her, one hand supporting himself, the other under her breasts. He was plunging into her, heaving, with his own rear sailing up and down, all the while hoarsely groaning with each thrust of his body.

"My God," Sonata breathed almost inaudibly. "Irene…I'm so sorry. I thought—Oh, my God! I'm so sorry!"

They both stood in horror, transfixed by the sounds and the scene before them. The woman as well was groaning, her coarse, rasping sounds merging with his. With their attention cast downward they were oblivious to the intrusion. Irene was the first to move. She quickly closed the door and pulled Sonata to the kitchen where she sat her down at the table, nervously trying to steady herself at the same time. Then dragging a chair beside her, she said, "Well, what did we expect? Bert loves ass, he always did. Why are we so shocked?" She lit a cigarette, trying to laugh. "Why are we shocked?" she said again.

"Oh God, Irene, he was to be away in Connecticut all day…I am so sorry!"

Irene drew deeply on the cigarette, letting the smoke out in a slow even stream.

"I gave up, smoking," she said casually, as if that was the topic, "—and still carry the damn things, more dangerous now because they're stale." Then finally— "Who's the woman, do you know? Might be hard to tell from our angle of observation." Her head turned involuntarily to the bedroom. "That was some perspective! Even the master would have trouble getting *that* on paper!"

"Josie, of course! It has to be Josie. She's the woman in his life these days."

"Josie." She pondered the name. "Cute." She took another long drag, letting the smoke stay for a moment before exhaling. "I never liked it from behind. There isn't enough—closeness."

Sonata looked at Irene, seeing through her eyes the scene they had witnessed: the woman receiving, displacing her. She did not like it from behind. Was there really more contact the other way because arms reach out and lips touch? Those two in there, doing their own tribal dance—frontward or backward, I love you or I hate you—what did the words mean anyway in the heat of one's own fire? They were all so much alone, every damned one of them!

Startled from her reverie, Sonata turned and Irene pushed back her chair and jumped up as they heard the bedroom door open and someone's feet scuffling across the apartment floor. They had not expected the fires to burn out that fast, to end that soon. A man entered the bathroom, turned on the shower and began to sing.

Sonata leaped to her feet. With eyes bulging and lips shaking, she faced Irene and uttered, "Howard!" just as Josie scuffed naked into the room.

4

Dear Irene,

It's quiet in the League gallery, a good place to think and to write to you. You're a friend now, or I like to think so, and family too. Your baby and I share genes. I hope you don't mind that I'm writing you. I just sort of needed to finish stuff that we started talking about when we had lunch together.

Bert's retrospective is still on preview exhibit here before it ships out to Boston and then Pennsylvania. Thanks to the prep work you did at the outset, and the reviews from his show in Connecticut at that upscale gallery you connected him with, people are interested in him. If he gets reviewed in any of the national art magazines for the shows coming up, I'll send that to you like I promised.

Funny, he never craved recognition, or at least didn't go after it with both arms swinging. I wanted it for him and I think I know why. Success broadcasts your strengths and everyone hears it loud and clear, drowning out all that's weak, so even *you* don't hear the din. Success forgives. It's a gift—a Pope's laying hands on you—something *big* like that.

It helps me forgive him for not being the way a father is supposed to be. He's my successful, famous father. The handle fits snug inside *my* life, letting me taking credit just because I wanted it for him. Pretty tight inside there with nothing much else going on.

But I forgive him and that covers a lot. It covers Billy. If he did have anything to do with Billy's death, I'm certain now that he didn't know. And if he didn't, is it something I can go on hating him for? You didn't know either and one day I'll tell you the whole story. But he must have known that he hurt his wife—probably their whole marriage—and hurt me because of that same stupid blindness. No, not blindness, he was always seeing, perceiving things, but he never made connections, never thought about the causes and effects. He wasn't interested enough, I guess, caring more about moments than years. More about the life of his creativity than the lives of his family. I could use names for that—selfish, immature, irresponsible—and the names sure apply to him, but they don't help me. It's the effects of all that stuff that applies to me. So, I can decide not to be affected and I have, just like you did by getting on with your life and out of his.

Except I want to be in his life.

I want so much to tell him how I feel, to tell him the hurts are over. But we're not much talking these days. Truth is, we've hurt each other pretty bad.

There were hurts with Vincent and Howard that I think I'm getting over. Vincent was at a turning point and I happened to be right there in the middle of his life-swing-around. He could have dropped me off that loop easier, but I would have gotten dumped all the same. But Howard hurt me and there was no reason to. Maybe he'd been fooling around all the time, not just with Josie. We were engaged, but his thinking could be this was the chance to make all his single moments count. I should have suspected he wasn't all that sure about marriage when after I said *yes*, he suggested keeping the announcement quiet for a while "to savor between us."

But about his fooling around, I would have known when he made love to me if he had other women besides Josie. He was so solicitous of me, maybe too much. He let me take the reins; he wanted me to be totally satisfied. He used that word a lot. Like a child is after it gets what it wants or a guy in business closing on a good deal. Satisfied is not wanting more and I think the whole concept is crappy. Too temporal. Loving somebody should feel like a want that could go on forever.

Anyway, I'm pretty certain it was Josie, just as he said, who lured him into bed. I believe his story that he came up to see me after I called in sick and then found Josie there; that she offered him a cup of coffee and while they were sitting there, my father called to say he was staying over in Connecticut. She was probably furious at him, so she set her sights on poor defenseless Howard, and he was probably furious at me for lying about being sick and wondering what I was up to. I don't blame Howard so much. It's just that the sight of his ass bobbing up and down there is something I can't shake. It's a scene I can't reconcile with Howard waiting for me at the end of an aisle and everybody smiling and saying what a nice couple they make. What a nice coupling Howard and Josie made. And she was satisfied, I'm sure of that.

But Josie may have done me a favor. It made me think less about the two of them than the two of us. The problem is that there's so little to think about the two of us. I guess Howard was a fill-in, really. He played the acts between the acts for me, his audience of one. He filled in for the father act, the lost kid brother act, and the lover dumping me act. His personality adapts itself to filling in, of changing his personality to fit the relationship. You didn't see the way he was with Vincent—not a pretty picture—rough, tough, a know-it-all, and with his father, smart, smooth and on top of his game, while his way with me was whatever I wanted, all gentle and sweet. Then there's how he was or at least looked with Josie. She released a hurricane in the man. I've seen where that leads. The last thing I need is a mate who's that susceptible to women. I believe that Howard was a friend who came along when I needed a friend and he may still be one. I'm looking at it that way.

So now it's over and I'm on my own. I'm back at the Y but it's better now than that brief spell before I moved in with you and my dad in Riverdale. You know why? Because you told me you were a frequent resident of Y's all over the place and we laughed together about it. So I think of you sort of staying there with me and it's kind of comforting. I have money saved for an apartment from my job at Macy's and at Pete's place, so I won't be at the Y forever. But I gave my notice to Pete because it's Howard's business too. So I have to think about what's next. But first, if we're talking about forgiving people, I've got to forgive myself. I let myself feel like I was—I guess the word is—inconsequential. I'm stopping that, nipping it in the bud and not going that route anymore.

It's the end of November, too late to start at a college and I wouldn't even know what to study for. As far as getting a job goes, I'm not qualified for anything much. I shouldn't say that though because according to Pete, I was the fastest learner he ever employed, a math genius. (Alexandra told me, not Pete; he's not big on complements, worried it might cost him.) The thing is, I like both of them—sour-face Pete who told me he'd give me a good reference even though he didn't want me to leave. And Alexandra who's still inviting me to use her place to paint, taking me on like she did Vincent. She's sad about Howard and me breaking-up, though of course she doesn't know the reason. They're a family, the Denfields, each one of them different as day and night but they're linked. Not like my family. I saw some upright fence posts standing bare in a vacant lot today, the fencing that had been there shorn off. That's Mom, Dad and me. The Denfields still have the fencing hooked onto the posts, connecting one to another. And fencing off stuff that could do them harm. Even with all the ravages of wind and time, this is the way it should be.

Maybe I'll have a chat about the future with my Aunt Witch. For all her meddling, she has a pretty good grasp on what's real and maybe I need that.

But I have a plan for the immediate future. I'm going to surprise my mother later today and rake up her leaves. Last I saw there was a wild party of drunken leaves all over the place. She's probably waiting for her leaf service to come back, but it's my tree making the mess—the one they planted when I was planted—so I'm looking forward to getting reacquainted.

Well, so long for now. Give a kiss to James for me. I love you, Irene. And I'm sorry. You know.

Sonny

5

The painting was finished, he knew, yet he was reluctant to let go of it. Letting go would plunge him into an uncomfortable emptiness, a vacancy needing to be filled—like a motel sign lighting up inside him yelling bed made, towels ready, get in here.

His physical domain was vacant, that was a fact. Irene long gone and now Sonata checking out to live someplace else. He found himself looking forward to the resident mouse which sometimes scampered across the kitchen floor late at night when the two of them couldn't sleep and were looking for something to nibble on.

Bert stepped back from the painting and looked again. He contemplated a measured diagonal of black in the corner. Or perhaps a splash of deep violet to take the eye deeper into the canvas. No, not necessary. He sighed, giving it up. It was finished.

Washing his brushes, he glanced over his shoulder once more at the picture. Amazing how quiet and peaceful it looked after all they'd been through together, already missing the process of painting the picture, though in the midst of doing so, he had been eager for its completion. Like an engrossing book you were eager to finish but still sad to end the journey. Finishing and ending—the one, a task; the other, far more complex, containing all that you hoped to gain.

He covered his palette with plastic wrap, pretty certain he would not use the pigments again but keeping the option open. He'd sleep on it and tomorrow give it a pass, or not, before discarding the paints.

The thought of sleep made him think of night and then Irene. The long evenings were when he missed her most, but his thoughts had sharp edges since Sonata shocked him with the news of why she had left. "You've got a brand new son now," she announced, "though I doubt it will affect you in the least. But here's where they live." She slapped a paper in Irene's handwriting on his desk. "It'll make about as much difference to your life style as having that old daughter did years ago, remember her? And that other son?" He had not been able to say anything in response and Sonny knew she had plunged the knife in far enough this time to quit because she did quit. It was after that discussion, she took off to live somewhere else. He didn't know where, though he could track her down if he needed to. She came by to pick up some things she'd forgotten and was cordial if not warm. A decision, not an emotion.

Still, essentially, she was right. He had gone on doing what he did. He'd finished two very large paintings besides this one since she told him about Irene, damned good ones, totally immersed in each one.

The paper with Irene's address was pretty much where Sonny had left it. He would glance at it every so often. One breezy day when he opened the window, the paper rustled, and so it wouldn't blow away, he scotch taped it to the wall above the desk. Placing it in the desk drawer would have been smarter, but he didn't do that.

He got ready for bed, read for a while then went into the kitchen. He took a beer and sat at the table, moving quietly hoping the mouse would show up. He was tired but couldn't sleep; probably needed to take a few days off, go away. The whole traveling show thing had been exhausting, enduring the results, the interviews, the misrepresentations of who he was as an artist, what he intended in this work or that. In all, a series of polarized emotions persisted like a peristalsis of stomach cramps. He deserved to take some time.

Fully aware of where this was leading him, he walked to the desk and plucked from the wall the scrap of paper: Irene Lewis, 652 Whitewater Road, Xenia, Ohio. There was a phone number too but no, he wasn't going to call. A long distance conversation would be stiff, unpleasant. Too much time had passed. He folded the paper and placed it in his wallet.

. . .

The drive was horrendous. Miles from the airport at Dayton International in his rented car, the trip to Xenia along Route 35 took him through blistering winds onto roads not yet recovered from a snow storm. He didn't drive much, only once a week to and from Pratt in Brooklyn, commuting from Riverdale by subway—the number 1— to the League on West 57th Street and to the nearby studio he co-rented while Irene used the big room for her dance classes; he seldom went anywhere other than necessary trips to Connecticut and other art-related travels. The bedroom, kitchen, studio routine was the circular pattern his feet made most days.

Through the clouds of snow on the ground that billowed up on his windows he saw more churches than he imagined there was population to support; a couple of schools, possibly one of them where Irene would set up an after-school dancing class, and along the suburban streets, all manner of houses in a dizzying variety of styles and sizes. His focus, however, had not been as much on landscape as on snow-obscured road signs and stealing glances at the map he'd been given at the airport car rental office. When finally, his drive neared the neighborhood of his destination he noticed the houses lined up along the road were not very varied, row house types, similar to one another. Exceptions were in their colors, the addition of porches or garages and the different decorative front doors jazzing things up, mostly wrong for the architecture.

The house he was looking for found and his car parked beside the snow banks left by the plows, he allowed a few degrees of pleasure to rise up from his cold feet and the tension of the drive. It was mid-afternoon, the journey via standby on Continental Airlines successfully made, he began to feel a pleasant sense of adventure. He should take trips more often; with all the color poured into his canvases he owed it to nature to show a little gratitude.

Ringing the doorbell under the plastic letters "652" on the brick wall of the modest house and waiting for a response, he inspected the setting in which he had placed himself. A few cars passed by the tree-lined street, no pedestrians. A small park sprawled across the street in which a narrow footpath had been dutifully shoveled. The town looked well cared for. Farther down along the symmetric rows of dwellings and patches of lawn, a woman shoveled snow drifts from her porch. From his vantage point it seemed a thankless job though she appeared cheerful enough, not at all resigned to the repetitive task. The thought crossed his mind she might be the volunteer who'd cleared the footpath in the park across the street. Where he stood the shoveled snow had left an array of overturned brown leaves by the doorstep.

Trying the bell again, a tightening in his stomach took over the easily rolling senses of his observations as he wondered how Irene would receive him.

A tall, elderly lady came to the door, opened it a crack and peered out at him from above the chain lock. Xenia, like Manhattan, was apparently crime conscious, strangers guilty until proven innocent. "Hello," he said, perhaps too buoyantly, "I'm a friend of Irene Lewis. Is she here?"

The woman took ponderous moments laden with critical analysis of his face, clothes, satchel and face before answering. He thought her next move might ask to see a driver's license and major credit card.

"What's your name?"

Bert smiled a friendly greeting through the tension of the chain between them. "Bert Kossoff. You must be Irene's mother."

"I am." She did not return the smile. Her expression remained stern and unyielding. "Wait here, I'll see if she's in." She closed the door against the stranger's next move, an attempt to saw the chain with his pocket knife? *I'll see if she's in!* The house was a matchbox. Still, this door like others on the street seemed styled for a McMansion with its elaborate trim and frosted glass panels. The developer had the smarts to give buyers a first impression of what they craved but couldn't afford.

Irene's mother returned and unlocked the chain. The door swung open. "You can come in now," she offered with the same receptionist's formality.

"Thank you," he said. His smile was genuine but a small wave of anxiety followed. Ambivalence again. He was getting close to what he came for yet not sure what that was. The foyer was narrow and extending his hand to greet her his foot snagged on cracked floor covering.

"Oh. We need new linoleum. I'm sorry. How do you do—Mr. Kossoff, is it?" She took his hand limply and then helped him off with his coat. "I'm Mrs. Lewandowski." Her greeting was friendly, perhaps softened by the linoleum apology.

"Well, I'm very pleased to meet you." Irene hadn't told him that her name Lewis was an alteration, or she had and it didn't register. Bert watched his heavy jacket placed on a hanger and forcefully stuffed in the narrow hall closet, already packed with a few seasons of outerwear plus an upright vacuum cleaner and some folding chairs.

"Irene is nursing the baby—for another twenty minutes," she explained, facing him a little exhausted by her efforts with the coat. "She gives him twelve minutes on each side, evens it up, you see. I told her I'd have you wait in the living room but she says you're good friends so she doesn't mind if you come in. Please follow me. This way."

She led him down a short narrow hall. On the left were two bedrooms, one larger than the other, beds neatly made, cotton curtains decorated with rick-rack shielding the windows from the street. On the right, a bathroom.

"Could I freshen up here," he asked. "It's been a long trip."

"Oh, of course. Irene is in that room just next to us when you're done," she said with a wave of her hand.

Inside, he glanced in the mirror over the white enamel sink and whipped out a comb to go through the disheveled hair, nothing to do about the face needing a shave. He used the toilet, washed using soap in the shape of a rose sitting in a flowery dish, and dried with a dainty guest towel. Ladies only living here. He stood for a moment inside the small bathroom collecting his thoughts. *Standing here in Irene's house in Xenia Ohio where a baby that he was father to lay in the next room nursing.* He had come on impulse, almost as if directed by that alone, anxious to see Irene. But beyond that he had no direction, none at all, his mind a blank slate.

He stepped out into the quiet corridor, Ms. Lewandowski nowhere in sight, and moved to the next doorway on the right. There he saw Irene seated on a patchwork-quilted rocker, her legs raised upon an ottoman covered with an afghan.

"I can't get up to greet you." She smiled. "Well, this surely is a surprise."

Bert stood in the doorway looking at her. A hazy sun from the window fell on her shoulders and on the small mound of breast where a ball of rosy skin topped by a sparse nest of dark brown hair burrowed. A cradle covered with a blue and pink blanket, suggesting they hadn't known what the baby's sex would be, stood nearby along with a table supporting various baby task paraphernalia.

"I'll make some tea," said Mrs. Lewandowski appearing behind him. "You like tea, Mr. Kossoff?" He forced himself to turn to her and make something of a nod and she left them. His eyes returned to Irene's face smiling up at him and to the baby, his cheeks puckering as he suckled, his small hand clasping Irene's finger.

If sunlight had not been streaming in, if Irene had not had her dark hair loose, if she had on lipstick or rouge or eye shadow to startle him, if the baby had been less eager for the breast, if she had not smiled up at him as she held the treasure in her arms, if the room was more vast so that she and he and the baby could be more lost in it, then perhaps he would not have cried.

But he did cry. The choking in his throat came so unexpectedly that his tears emerged before he could manage to extricate anything to hide them. He found a chair, pulled out a handkerchief and tried to recover himself. Irene watched him without speaking. She waited until he looked up at her again. "Are you all right?" she asked tentatively.

"I'm sorry," he said, "that's no way to say hello." He tucked the handkerchief in his pocket. "I never cry," he added.

"I know. I've never seen you."

"I don't know what came over me." He stopped. "I really don't know."

"It's the shock of it, I suppose," Irene said, "seeing the baby."

He said nothing, but that wasn't it at all. It was her...or the baby with her...or something else, *oh never mind, it doesn't matter.* He

314

approached the rocker and looked down at the baby swathed in a thin yellow blanket that looked velvety to the touch. "What's his name?"

"James."

"James," he repeated, thinking about it. "Your father."

"Grandfather."

"Ah. You talked about him, I remember." His eyes were fastened on the baby. "What is James' last name?"

Irene stroked the stray wisps of hair and the baby's eyes opened and looked about at his pale, blue-veined environment. "It's James Lewis, my name."

He nodded slowly.

"I'm not asking anything of you, Bert. I wanted the baby and I have it. I'm grateful for that."

"I understand." He touched the baby's cheek with the side of his forefinger and the baby half smiled, then dislodged his lips from the nipple and turned to the finger.

"You've confused him," said Irene. "But it's okay. He's ready for side two anyway." She lifted him to rearrange his position.

"Can I hold him?"

Irene thought about it. "All right, but just for a minute. I don't want him to fall asleep before he gets the other side. Otherwise he'll be up in an hour. And so will I with a bursting bosom. Make sure you support his head."

He took the child as she gave it to him. The bundle in his arms made him feel at once intimidated, unprepared, incompetent, unsteady and a little inebriate. He rocked him slightly and then grinned as the baby looked at him. His lips were wet and his cheek damp where it had lain against the breast. "He looks better on you than on me," he quipped. But he feels good, you know? Solid."

"Careful you don't move him around too much. He might throw up."

"You had to say that."

"Here, put this cloth over your shoulder and hold him upright so he can burp. There. Just tap him gently but hold on to his head."

Bert followed the instructions carefully. He was getting used to the feel of the rump under his arm, the small knees pressing against him, the smell of Johnson's Baby Powder. When the burp came he laughed. "He's like me, no manners at all."

Irene held out her arms and he dipped James into them.

She had re-wrapped the one breast and exposed the other. He watched her nestle the baby against her body then adjust the nipple in his mouth and the baby's hand fluttering on the breast as he suckled. They looked like one body, one curve billowing into another. Irene laid her head back and looked up at him, unable to suppress the pride in her achievement. Bending over her then, he kissed her. The baby stirred, perhaps the kiss affecting the flow of milk. The kiss had a tenuous quality, whether in respect for her motherhood or of the retired passion between them. She kissed him back although her arms never left the baby. He smiled as her head rested against the back of the chair and he readjusted her feet on the ottoman. He pulled the chair up to sit near her. "Now tell me everything. Start with when you left. Was it June? Tell me everything that went on in your head."

"In my body."

"Yes, everything." The baby was suckling again and Bert felt as fastened to the sight of it as James was to his task. He shook his head and grinned. "How many times day and night do you two indulge in this revelry?"

"He'll go to sleep soon and nurse again in three hours or so. Whenever he wants it."

Irene turned her head from him to the baby, brushing his forehead with her lips. There was a rattle of cups and glasses in the dining room and Irene's mother called to them.

"Maybe after tea and crumpets, I can talk to you on the general topic of sorry and stupid," Bert said. "Do you think we can manage to have some time?"

"Are you going right back or…how long do you expect to stay?"

"Don't have a return ticket, I'm traveling standby."

She studied him for a moment before answering, meeting his gaze. "Well, I suppose then we'll have some time."

"I'll call for a room in a motel. I passed a decent prospect on the road coming down, in Beavercreek, I think—cute name, but I didn't want to check in, in case you didn't…well, I wasn't sure how you'd feel about me showing up. I didn't know myself why I was coming. It just felt so… unfinished, the way you left."

"Yes, but just beginning for me."

"You left so damn suddenly."

"I didn't know how to talk to you about it. You're angry with me."

"I was. I'm not angry now. God, how could I be? Look at you, you're so…beautiful, sitting there. And this little human wriggling its toes. They're stuck out of the blanket." He chuckled. "Look at his fingers, they're so goddamn perfect. Look at that pinky, the size of it with a fingernail and knuckles."

Irene laughed. "Yes, I've looked. I've seen it." She held the pinky then let it fall. The baby stopped nursing and raised his eyes. She volunteered herself to him again but he was finished. Lifting him, she threw the cloth over her shoulder and held him against her.

"Pat him gently and don't forget to hold his head," Bert advised.

"Here, you do it," she said, "while I wash up and put myself together. Then I'll put him to sleep and we'll have some tea."

"And then take a walk or something and talk?"

"I'm not walking in the snow. Look, it's started up again. But I'll call and make that motel reservation for you. I know which one you saw. It's the only halfway attractive one around here."

He took the baby and settled himself in the rocker. Soon he heard water running in the bathroom. Peering out of the window, he saw that snow had indeed started falling again and was picking up at a rapid pace. He heard the shrill shouts of children. He pictured them packing and throwing snowballs, ducking snowballs. He saw himself sitting in a colorful patchwork-quilt chair in Xenia with James Kossoff. No, James Lewis in his arms, patiently waiting for him to burp. Ah, there, but still he held him. The baby melded to his shoulder and his cheek was warm against his face. "James, you don't look right here in this place," he whispered. "Neither does your mother. Your Mom never belonged here." It was true. Irene was doing great with him in New York. They worked together. She helped him, and he helped her as well. He remembered installing the barre for her and the mirror across the whole span of the wall and helping with the layout of her ads. "You want to know the truth, James? Where you belong is New York City.

What do you have here? Little league? You're going to be one big tough guy and you need a big tough arena to move around in. James? Did you hear a word I said?" He'd fallen asleep. Bert eased him down from his shoulder and cradled him in his arms. His lips were parted and little half smiles flit across his face. "Dreams already? Or maybe gas. No, they're dreams, I know, I have 'em too."

He had another son…years ago. He must have held him like this and walked him but had no memory of it. Then again, probably not. Ruth took care of the children and he had little part in it. That was a mistake. So many mistakes. He wondered now if he could have felt like this. A roiling in his stomach made him adjust the baby in his arms. Had he played with Billy? Taken him anywhere, just the two of them? Tossed a football? He couldn't recall. Billy was slender, small for his age—puny, you could even say. He did remember asking Ruth if he ate enough. He tried to assemble Billy's features in his mind's eye. Big round brown eyes looking at him, and a little frown, the kind that didn't really belong on a little kid. Why the frown, that tiny furrow atop those dark brown balloons? Asking questions, always asking him something, saving the questions for when he'd emerge from the studio for dinner, those minutes between Ruth putting out his dinner and Billy being put to bed.

Did he provide the right answers? He couldn't remember—the questions or the answers. Again, he tried to assemble Billy in his mind. Cute. Yes, he was cute, and cuddly, that one time when he crawled onto his lap. He'd been flipping through Art News, getting more and more annoyed with the crap artist they were featuring as the crap celebrity of the month when little Billy—he guessed about four or five—crept up onto his lap, climbing like it was, well, not Mount Everest but something he wasn't used to doing. The kid with his scrambling arms crumpled the magazine that got there before him, so when Bert tossed the miserable rag to the floor, Billy took it like it was him who needed to be off that lap, swatted away. He scrambled down quicker than he'd made it up, like a cat that didn't belong on the furniture. Did he pick Billy up then and put him back on his lap or did Billy run off? He couldn't remember.

The image of a cat brought Sonny's story racing through his mind. Her heart-piercing accusation went through him again. Involuntarily, his stomach contracted and he eased James forward to rest in his lap lest he drop him. How could he accept that story and go on living? Yes, he remembered the drive to Forest Hills, and yes, Irene in the car; then stealing into his studio with her, and later the walls caving in on the horrific news. But that was all he remembered. Cat? There was no cat. It was a lie. Nothing happened! He drove and that was that. Yeah, you can say he was thoughtless, stupid, brutish even, bringing Irene to his house—into his studio, that sacrosanct place nobody in the family was allowed to invade—he can't deny that and won't.

The burning in his throat began again as it did standing in the doorway of this room and vehemently he pushed back against it. He lied to Irene about never crying. He had cried often since that putrid hot summer night when his daughter spat out her story. He cried for the loss of Billy, for the loss of Ruth, for the loss of Irene and Sonata too. He loved them all. But they hadn't known it.

He brought Sonny now to his mind's eye, trying to erase the venom he saw in her face as she spewed her accursed recounting of that fateful night. This was Edith's ranting—from her mouth, not Sonny's—brainwashed by her to hate him, no longer his adorable daughter of eighteen planning a tribute for her father. A tribute for *him*, never mind planning for college or career or a path to her dreams.

Something made her want to do this, something made her love him. She'd been quiet, even a bit morose in her teens. He hadn't seen many friends coming to the house, but then again, he probably wouldn't have if they did, being in the studio most of the time. Ruth kept things quiet in the house in deference to his work, so he wouldn't have heard commotion. He did remember taking the two of them out to dinner on occasion, somebody's birthday, and listening to meaningless talk around the table about school and after school and no school and other school kids that bothered her. That was their life, and it touched him somewhere about as close to his heart as his toenails. He remembered being eager to have it over so he could get back to work. But he loved them. Loved each of them.

He lifted James closer against his body, fondling the perfect fingers. He looked down at the sleeping baby's face, his cherubic cheeks round as plump nectarines, his lips, even in sleep, curved in a river-flowing smile, thinking of the next meal perhaps, *whenever he wants it*.

Why had they not known how he felt about them? Billy and Sonny and Ruth too. He enjoyed them, enjoyed listening to their sounds, relished looking at them aware that they were there. But that was it, wasn't it? He loved them through his eyes and ears; he didn't know them any other way. Was it necessary to know their days, their troubles, the meaning of the appointment scraps and clippings appearing on the refrigerator? What troubles did Ruth have—beyond those he gave her and was it necessary for him to know those scraps as well? There was no time for this—the paraphernalia of daily life.

James stirred in his arms and awkwardly, he rocked him.

Or was that jumbled language on the refrigerator door, these family reminders and lopsided pastings the trappings of love? If so, then he was, indeed, out of its range. He knew himself, at least that. He could not extend himself to reach out and grasp the trivial, to engage his time in matters that failed to spark his senses. He journeyed to fields more yielding of what he needed for his work. Selfish, lusting? Yes, he supposed you could call it such ugly names, though the words seemed meaningless to him. He sought out Irene and this was selfish and lusting, though it became other things—companionship, friendship, gratitude. Yes, gratitude, and isn't that a basis for love? Not the stuff of romance or song but taking what is offered and damn thankful to have it.

Irene knew him. She knew him well. He watched the baby's mouth quiver, a tentative smile like a breeze playing on his lips. He wondered, if he were to ask Irene, what reasons she would have to share her life with him again. James' fists floated above the blanket, playing the air like a musical instrument. Was he hearing sounds in his head or was it all bloat and gas and involuntary exercise?

What reasons? He was still a painter immersed in making art. He could decide not to pursue the ventures attached to the ugly words—and would—but still never know how to bring others into the world

of his perceptions, his lonely habitat. With James pressed to his chest
he began walking around the room to think more clearly, his large hand
encompassing the baby's fuzzy head. What reasons?

Well, for one, he argued as if to her, the responsibilities would be
shared. There were finances to be concerned with; for that he would
be a help, especially with his paintings doing so well. And Irene would
want to start her dancing classes again. He could help her do that;
create a dance studio again like before or simply rent one. He loved
hearing the kids giggling and the music rippling through the rooms and
Irene counting one, two, three and-a-one-two-three. The house was
alive. He realized how the vitality saw its way into his productions, even
working away from the house, in his choice of colors, the energy of his
lines on the canvas.

And James? Well, he'd need to be provided for. He needed to have
a father to take him places, to give him advice. He was beginning to
love this baby. But…he had loved before…Ruth, Sonny, Billy.

Billy.

Suddenly, like a rush of the sound of water in both ears, Bert was
flooded with an awareness of where he was, what he was thinking, how
he was pacing Hamlet-like around the room. And what he was
carrying.

The baby was awake now, making little grunting sounds. As Bert
brought him forward to cradle in his arms, the child stared up at him
without understanding, just as he himself now stared at little James
Lewis, like an apparition. The baby's lips quivered, not in a smile but
with instinctive awareness that this face was new and not quite right to
wake up to.

Another child to ignore, another life to…No, impossible, it did
not! It did not happen! His body shaking, his knees quivering, his legs
so unsteady he feared they would give way, he placed James in his
cradle. With shaking hands he slipped the blue and pink cover over
him. He looked furtively at the open doorway and then at the baby,
praying James would not cry, make a scene, create a reason for others
to dash in to remove the child. Before he could remove himself.

How had he dared intrude here—mother and daughter, Madonna
and child, Irene and her James? Vibrantly alive. None of them wanted

him, needed him even less. He made his way to the front hall and retrieved his coat from the cluttered closet. Hastily he opened the fussy, ornate front door and let himself out.

•   •   •

Outside, snow was falling heavily, the main performance, as if the snowfall he had arrived in was merely a teaser. The windshield, already partly frozen, made visibility difficult as he started the car and drove to the corner to make a U-turn. He lowered the driver side window to brush off the snow and side mirror, then managed to locate and run the rear windshield wiper. The defroster worked diligently if somewhat ineffectively but it managed to create a slowly widening patch of clarity as he drove, his speed about fifteen miles an hour. The wind threw snow clouds against the windshield, giving the wipers an exercise they seemed to resent, in turn frosting the windshield as much as clearing it.

After twenty minutes or so, the snow clouds blinding without let-up, Bert pulled over to the shoulder, keeping everything set to high: the heat, defroster, wipers. He sidled over the front seats to open and partially clear the passenger side window. He was grateful that he'd upgraded to a mid-sized at the suggestion of the rental agent who said she knew her way around these parts—though not enough to put a snow brush in it. In another twenty minutes he could probably reach the motel. Irene for sure had made the reservation. She always accomplished what she set out to do. Irene would understand the confusion of his thoughts, leaving suddenly as he did. She had always understood him: his distance—leaving and returning—his leaving now.

Go to the motel. Get off these miserable roads, the safe thing to do. And the right thing. Driving on to the airport and blundering into another car or a snow bank in the blinding snow to make a plane by standby tonight, if it could take off at all, was stupid, dangerously stupid.

He pictured himself driving on past the motel, careening along the yet to be plowed roads through the wicked blasts of snow, so ice-clad they clung to the car where they hit, as if their own short lives depended on the embrace. And with that image came the clutter behind his eyes—Billy climbing on his lap and then scrambling down, misunderstanding. What made him think to be discarded like a magazine?—his father's lap so unfamiliar and unwelcoming?—Irene's warm thigh under his hand, driving her to his studio, the sensation of her shiver going through his groin—Ruth's shrieks like a stricken nocturnal animal gored beyond saving—Billy not in his bed under the coverlet of Batman characters—his children's meaningless chatter about school and the nonsense growing louder in his ears, never discerning the words.

And still he was driving, moving on, urgently through the bridal whiteness, with brakes that should be screeching to a halt as tires without traction spun out of control and wipers surrendered unequal to the task. The windshield mercifully shielded his vision. And he felt a relief descend, even as a great burden lifted and raised him aloft within it, in there somewhere, safe, beyond his eyes. And he was happy, seeing nothing, only whiteness, a familiar wall of white he knew well and welcomed.

ABOUT THE AUTHOR

Judith Peck is Professor Emerita of Art, Ramapo College of New Jersey. She is author of several fiction and non-fiction works and a sculptor with work in eighty collections, including the Yale Gallery of Art, the Ghetto Fighters Museum in Israel, libraries, universities, and cultural and religious institutions here and abroad. Dr. Peck holds a doctoral degree from New York University and two master's degrees from Columbia University. She is recipient of the 2020 Albert Nelson Marquis Lifetime Achievement Award and has completed the first draft of a 4th novel about an art therapist who helps solve a school shooting. Judith grew up in Baltimore Maryland. She has four grown children and twelve grandchildren and resides in Mahwah, New Jersey.

Images and videos of her sculpture can be viewed at
www.jpecksculpture.com

Descriptions of her books can be seen at www.iapbooks.com

Visit Seeing in the Dark, Arielle's Story, another Peck novel at
www.SeeinginthedarkAriellesStory.com

NOTE FROM THE AUTHOR

Word-of-mouth is crucial for any author to succeed. If you enjoyed *Naked Under the Lights*, please leave a review online—anywhere you are able. Even if it's just a sentence or two. It would make all the difference and would be very much appreciated.

Thank you so much for reading one of
our New Adult Fiction novels.
If you enjoyed the experience, please check out
our recommended title for your next great read!

Sweet Jane by Joanne Kukanza Easley

2020 International Book Awards Finalist – Literary

2019 Faulkner/Wisdom Writing Award Finalist

Made in the USA
Middletown, DE
07 July 2023

34693090R00201